"I'm going to take a chance, Perry, and tip you off to some valuable information," said Lt. Tragg of homicide. "You are in a spot."

"From all the details you've given me," Mason said, "I presume you heard it from some witness. Who was it?"

"Perry Mason," Lt. Tragg answered.

"Talking in my sleep again?" Mason asked.

"No. A trap was laid for you. A tape recorder was installed to pick up sounds within the apartment and outside the door."

"I see," Mason said slowly. "My answer is 'no comment.'"

"I thought that would be your answer. Don't get your head in over your necktie."

But the warning came too late. Perry was already in —over his head!

THE CASE OF THE GREEN-EYED SISTER and
THE CASE OF THE TROUBLED TRUSTEE
were originally published by
William Morrow & Company, Inc.

Two Complete Novels by
ERLE STANLEY GARDNER

PERRY MASON

2 in 1

The Case of the Green-Eyed Sister

The Case of the Troubled Trustee

PUBLISHED BY POCKET BOOKS NEW YORK

PERRY MASON 2 IN 1

POCKET BOOK edition published September, 1975

The Case of the Green-Eyed Sister

William Morrow edition published 1953

POCKET BOOK edition published July, 1957
7th printing .... July, 1975

The Case of the Troubled Trustee

William Morrow edition published 1965

POCKET BOOK edition published October, 1966
4th printing .... July, 1975

L

The Case of the
Green-Eyed Sister

FOREWORD

Some twenty-eight years ago Ralph Turner, then a young lad of nine, started reading *The Adventures of Sherlock Holmes* and determined that he was going to become a detective.

Several million other young lads, inspired by the same literature, were reaching the same decision.

Ralph Turner's case was interesting for two reasons. First, he was handicapped by a very great speech impediment. He stuttered so badly it was difficult for him to carry on any kind of a conversation. The other interesting thing about Ralph Turner's ambition is that buried somewhere in his character was the quiet, dogged determination that held him steadfast in his decision.

In discussing his career with friends, Ralph Turner casually mentions that "in those days there was no such thing as Police Science as it is taught today." What he neglects to state is the fact that the reason Police Science is being taught today is in a very large measure due to his own quiet, unobtrusive, ceaseless efforts.

Ralph started out to study chemistry with the sole goal of learning how chemistry could aid in the detection of crime. These studies laid the foundation for his textbook, published by Charles C. Thomas in 1949, *Forensic Science and Laboratory Technics*.

This young man who stuttered decided that he had to get rid of his speech impediment in order to carry on his chosen career. His methodical approach to the problem was characteristic of everything he does. He investigated and found that the science of psychoanalysis might offer some hope. He submitted himself to psychiatric treatment, and not only cured his stuttering so that today he is in great demand as a lecturer, but learned enough about psychoanalysis to broaden his understanding of character and motivation—invaluable assets in his chosen field.

In the vanguard of every new movement there are two types. One is the inspired leader, who pioneers the ideas, whose visions would remain only dreams unless they could be implemented by practical, down-to-earth detail work. The other type is the quiet, self-effacing individual, who is usually appointed secretary and plunges into the terrific mass of detail, the extent of which is seldom realized even by close associates.

The pioneer visionary is long remembered. The detail man is referred to as "Good old So-and-So" and the general public never knows he exists.

Ralph Turner is a rare combination. He has inspirational ideas but he also has that ability to soak up detail, and, by some process of mental alchemy, transform those details into solid, substantial progress.

Slowly but surely progress in the field of Police Science is advancing the technique of investigative work, bringing about higher standards and greater efficiency.

Today the young man who wants to specialize in investigative work finds several colleges offering courses in Police Science.

This newly developed field of study is as important in the field of justice as is legal medicine.

The steady march of science has made tools available for the investigator if he but knows where to find those tools and how to use them. Too often jurors are called upon to rely on surmise or conjecture when, with proper investigative techniques, they could have been presented with solid, substantial proof.

Ralph Turner was made secretary of the American Academy of Forensic Sciences when that organization was brought into existence, and has held the job ever since. He is an associate editor of the *Journal of Criminal Law, Criminology and Police Science*. He is associate editor of the *American Lecture Series in Public Protection*. He is an associate professor in the Police Administration Department of Michigan State College; and for the past five years he and the well-known Dr. C. W. Muehlberger have directed a research project on the reliability of chemical tests for intoxication, the results of which were recently published by the National Safety Council Committee on Tests for Intoxication.

But Ralph Turner's progress in his life's work cannot be measured by any listing of academic degrees any more than by spectacular excursions into the field of the dramatic in forensic battles. Ralph Turner's value lies in his ability to create an enthusiasm which the other person feels was entirely self-inspired.

Where other men, temperamental leaders, insist upon recognition or they won't play, Ralph Turner is always willing to subordinate his own individuality, to take on the thankless job of wrestling with endless details in order to advance the cause.

Too frequently such men escape public recognition. The men who are in the limelight know and appreciate their indebtedness to these men, but the public never shares this knowledge. Because I want my readers to know something of this new field which is known as Police Science, and because I want to make a public acknowledgment of the outstanding work that has been so quietly, so faithfully performed by a man who has never been afraid of detail nor known what it is to shirk a responsibility, I dedicate this book to my friend:

RALPH F. TURNER

ERLE STANLEY GARDNER

CAST OF CHARACTERS

DELLA STREET, Perry Mason's confidential secretary, handed the lawyer a scented, engraved oblong of pasteboard.

"If you're going to do anything for this woman," she said, "you'd better get a retainer."

"In other words, you don't like her?" Mason asked.

"I didn't say that."

"But you don't?"

"I think she'd cut your heart out for thirty-seven cents, if that's what you mean."

Mason studied the card. "Sylvia Bain Atwood," he read aloud. "Miss or Mrs., Della?"

"She's Mrs. Atwood and her green eyes are as cold as a cash register," Della Street said. "Her manner, on the other hand, is a purely synthetic attempt to belie the expression of her eyes. I imagine her whole life has been like that."

"What does she want?"

"It's a business matter," Della Street said, her voice mimicking the mincing manner of the client. "A matter too complicated to be discussed except with a trained legal mind."

"Like that, eh?" Mason asked.

"Exactly like that," she said. "Very hoity-toity. Very snooty. Very superior. Very, very definitely moving in a different social stratum from that occupied by secretaries."

Mason laughed. "Well, send her in, Della."

"She'll turn those green eyes on you," Della warned, "and start twisting and squirming like a cat getting ready to rub against your leg."

Mason laughed. "Well, you've given me a pretty good description of a client whom I don't think I'm going to like. Let's have a look at her, Della."

Della Street returned to the outer office and escorted Sylvia Bain Atwood into Mason's presence.

The green eyes flickered upward in one swift appraisal, then the lids lowered demurely.

"Mr. Mason," she said, "I really feel diffident about approaching you with a problem as simple and as small as mine, but my father always said in dealing with professional men get the best. The best is *always* the cheapest."

"Thank you for the compliment," Mason said, taking her outstretched hand. "Please be seated. Tell me what I can do for you."

Once again the green eyes flashed in swift appraisal, then Mrs. Atwood settled in the client's comfortable chair. A coldly hostile glance at Della Street plainly showed her annoyance at the presence of a secretary. Then she twisted about in the chair in a peculiarly feline manner and adjusted herself into the most comfortable position.

"Go on," Mason said, "tell me what you want. I'll let you know if I'm in a position to be of help, and don't mind Miss Street. She stays and keeps notes on my interviews, puts them in a confidential locked file, and helps me remember things."

"My problem is very simple," Mrs. Atwood murmured deprecatingly.

Mason, catching Della Street's eye, let his own twinkle in amusement. "Then I dare say, Mrs. Atwood, you won't need me," he said. "I'm quite certain if it's such a simple problem you would do better to consult some attorney who is less busy than I am and who would consequently—"

"Oh no, no, no, no, no!" she interrupted quickly. "Please, Mr. Mason! It's—well, I mean it will be simple for *you,* but it might puzzle anyone else."

"Suppose you tell me what it is," Mason said.

"It concerns my family," she said.

2

"You're a widow?"

"Yes."

"Children?"

"No."

"Then your family?" Mason asked.

"Consists of my sister, Hattie Bain; my brother, Jarrett Bain; his wife, Phoebe; my father, Ned Bain, who is at present confined to his room in the house. He has heart trouble and is required to have absolute rest and quiet."

"Go on."

"*I* am naturally the adventurous type, Mr. Mason." She raised her eyes to his provocatively.

"Go on."

"Hattie is the stay-at-home type. I was always the venturesome one. Hattie stayed to take care of the family. I married. Then my husband died and left me with a not inconsiderable amount of property."

"And then you returned to live at home?"

"Good heavens no! I find the home atmosphere a little—well, a little confining. I like to live my own life. I have an apartment here in town, but I am very fond of my family and I do keep in close touch with them."

"Your mother?" Mason asked.

"She died about a year ago. She'd been sick for a long time."

Della Street glanced at Mason. Mason pursed his lips, thoughtfully regarded Sylvia Atwood.

"Who took care of your mother during her long illness?" he asked.

"Hattie. I don't see why she didn't hire a nurse, but Hattie wouldn't listen to it for a minute. Hattie had to do it all herself. She is the domestic one, the—well, I shouldn't say this, Mr. Mason, but she's the drudge type, the steady-going type."

"And probably a very good thing for your mother that she was."

"Oh, of course," Sylvia agreed readily enough. "She was wonderful to Mother. The point is that I loved Mother just as much as Hattie, but I couldn't have done all that detail work of taking care of her. I'd have stripped myself of all my possessions, if necessary, to have hired nurses, but I'd simply have died if I'd tried to stay home and do the nursing myself."

"I see," Mason observed dryly.

"I'm not certain that you do."

"Does it make any difference?"

"No."

"Then go on and tell me about the matter that's bothering you."

"I'm afraid, Mr. Mason, that I'm dealing with persons who may not be entirely honest."

"What do they want?"

"Money."

"Blackmail?"

"Well, if it is, it's so skillfully disguised that you could hardly call it that."

"Suppose you tell me about it."

"To start with, it goes back to a period several years ago. Texas oil was beginning to be a factor in the life of the state."

Mason nodded encouragement.

"My father had gone broke in the real-estate business. He at that time knew a very peculiar character by the name of Jeremiah Josiah Fritch."

"Quite a name," Mason said.

"They call him J.J., after his first initials."

Mason nodded.

"J.J. had some money. My father had an option on a huge tract of land that he thought might have oil on it, although it was pretty well out of what was then regarded as the oil belt.

"J.J. agreed to buy the land for my father and Dad would put in all of his money in a test well at a point to be designated by J.J."

"That was done?"

"Yes."

"What happened?"

"It was a dry hole. My father still had hope and faith.

4

No one else did. The property naturally declined in value. Dad mortgaged everything he had to J.J. for an option on the property. He secured a new loan from outsiders that were interested in adjoining property and were glad to have Dad exploring the formations. He put down a new well, this time at a spot where he felt there was oil, although J.J. just laughed at him and called the new drilling project 'Bain's Folly.' "

"What happened to that oil well ?"

"It opened up a whole new pool. People said it was just luck. They said Dad was trying to tie in on another anticline but stumbled on a new pool. Anyhow, Dad was able to pay off all his loans and buy the property from J.J. and more than recoup his losses."

Mason nodded.

"But the foundation of the whole thing," she said, "was this money J.J. gave Dad."

"Wasn't it a loan?"

"Not exactly. Dad and he were friends. J.J. had other interests. At the start it was a sort of partnership. The point is, Mr. Mason, that all of the money in the family grew out of this original arrangement with J.J. Fritch."

"That is important?" Mason asked.

She nodded.

"Why?"

"Because it now appears that J.J. was a bank robber. Did you ever hear of the spectacular bank robbery known as the Bank Inspector Robbery?"

Mason shook his head.

"A few years ago it was quite famous. A man with elaborately forged credentials as a bank examiner entered one of the big banks. He managed to get all the cash reserves in a readily accessible place. He also managed to disconnect the emergency alarm that would signal a holdup.

"Then two confederates entered the bank, held up the employees and calmly made off with half a million dollars in cash and traveler's checks."

"Are you trying to tell me that this holdup has some connection with your problem?" Mason asked.

"Exactly. The bank thinks J.J. was one of the gang and that the money he gave Dad was part of the loot."

"Your father wasn't one of the robbers?"

"No, of course not. But they might try to claim he was aware of the fact that the money had been stolen and thereby became a trustee, and in that way the bank could take over the oil lands."

"The bank is claiming that?"

"The bank *may* be *going* to claim that. Apparently— now I'm not able to verify this, Mr. Mason—but apparently as a result of a steady, conscientious search the authorities were able to check the thumbprint of J.J. Fritch on his driving license as being that of the spurious bank examiner."

"After all these years," Mason said.

She nodded.

"How do you know this?"

"From a man by the name of Brogan."

"Who is Brogan?"

"George Brogan, a private detective."

Mason's eyes narrowed. "This sounds like a racket, and I don't think I've ever heard of George Brogan."

"Well, he's an investigator, and I understand his reputation isn't *too* savory."

"It begins to look like an unusual type of blackmail," Mason said.

"So," she said, "if the bank could establish the identity of that money and prove that my father had knowledge, they would then be able to grab our property by claiming that my father had become an involuntary trustee or something of that sort. It's a legal matter, it's complicated and I don't know too much about it." ·

"The bank has made some effort to do this?"

"No, but I understand from Mr. Brogan that the bank will do it if it has certain information which it may get at any time."

"Tell me more about Brogan."

"Well, Mr. Brogan wants us to understand he definitely is *not* representing J.J. Fritch."

"Where is Fritch?"

"He's not available."

"You mean he's in hiding?"

"Not exactly. He's 'not available' is the way Mr. Brogan expresses it."

"And what does Fritch want?"

"He wants money."

"How much money?"

"A lot."

"That's a typical blackmail setup."

"I can understand that it certainly looks like blackmail."

"What," Mason asked, "specifically is the present situation?"

"George Brogan wants us to employ him to try and work out a solution."

"How much money does *he* want?"

"He says that he'll charge a nominal fee, but that J.J. is badly in need of money and that while he scorns J.J.'s morals, the only way we can be safe is to be certain J.J.'s testimony isn't unfavorable."

"And what do you propose doing?"

"I propose to pay whatever is necessary."

"Why?"

"Because it affects the entire family—not only the money involved but there's the question of the family reputation."

"You must have something more than this to go on," Mason said. "There's something that you haven't disclosed."

"George Brogan has a tape recording."

"Of what?"

"Of what is supposed to be a conversation between J.J. and Dad."

"When did this conversation take place?"

"About three years ago."

"How does it happen that Brogan has this tape recording?"

"Apparently Fritch trapped Dad into the conversation. It took place in Fritch's office and he had a tape recorder."

"Have you heard this tape recording?"

"I've heard part of it. He would only let me listen to just a few words."

"Is it a genuine recording?"

"It sounds like Dad's voice."

"Is it?"

"I don't know."

"Why?"

"Because I've been afraid to ask Dad. In his present condition I wouldn't want to do anything that would disturb him."

Mason nodded to Della Street. "Ring up the Drake Detective Agency," he said. "Get Paul on the phone."

"No, no, please!" Sylvia Atwood exclaimed. "Not another private detective. I detest them."

"Drake is an ethical detective," Mason said. "I have to contact him because I want to find out about Brogan."

Della Street's swift fingers dialed a number on the private unlisted trunk line which was on her desk and which detoured the switchboard in the outer office.

A moment later, when she had Paul Drake on the line, she nodded to Mason.

Mason picked up the extension phone on his desk, said, "Paul, this is Perry. I want to find out something about a George Brogan who seems to be a licensed private investigator. Do you know anything about him? . . . You do, eh? . . . All right, let me have it."

Mason listened for nearly a minute, then said, "Thanks, Paul. I may be calling you in connection with a case."

He hung up the telephone.

Sylvia Atwood's green eyes were intent with an unspoken question.

"Well," Mason said, "Brogan is quite a character. He drives an expensive automobile, maintains a membership in a country club and a yacht club, has a swank apartment, has been under fire three or four times over a question of losing his license, and no one seems to know just how he makes his money."

"Does he make professional contacts at his country club?" she asked.

Mason said, "According to my sources of information, the people who know him would be the last ones to give him business."

"In other words, your detective tells you that he's a high-class blackmailer."

Mason grinned. "If he'd told me that I wouldn't tell you."

"Well, *I'm* telling it to *you* then."

Mason said, "Of course, as between an attorney and client, it's a privileged, confidential communication, but I still wouldn't say it."

"And wouldn't admit that that was what your friend, Mr. Drake, had told you."

Mason grinned, shook his head.

"You mentioned a relationship of attorney and client," she said. "I hope that means that you are going to accept me as a client."

"And, to make it official," Mason said, "you're going to pay me a retainer of five hundred dollars, because when I take my next step I don't want to have any misunderstanding about whom I'm representing and what I'm trying to accomplish."

"What's going to be your next step?"

Mason merely held out his hand.

"Surely," she said, "I don't carry five hundred dollars in cash in my purse."

"Your check's good."

She hesitated a moment. Her green eyes were hard and appraising, then she opened her purse, took out a checkbook, and wrote Mason a check.

Mason studied the check carefully, then said, "Put on the back of it, 'As a retainer on account of legal services to be rendered.'"

9

She wrote as Mason suggested.

Mason blotted the check, handed it to Della Street, who placed a rubber stamp endorsement on it.

Mason pulled the telephone toward him, said, "You want me to handle this my own way?"

"I want results."

Mason said to Della Street, "Look up the number of George Brogan, Della. Get him on the line. We'll place that call through the switchboard."

"Do you think it's wise for you to talk with Mr. Brogan?" Sylvia Atwood asked.

"Somebody has to talk with him."

"*I've* already talked with him."

"I don't think it's wise for *you* to continue to talk with him."

"He assures me that he's just trying to be helpful, that every cent of money he receives will be accounted for, that he'll have to pay it over to Fritch in order to hold him in line."

"And in the meantime," Mason said sarcastically, "Fritch has given him possession of the spool of tape containing the recording of the conversation supposed to be between your father and Fritch?"

She nodded.

"Does that impress you as being a little unusual?"

"Well, of course, J.J. would have to do something in order to turn his information into money."

Della Street nodded to Perry Mason.

Mason picked up the telephone, said, "Hello. Brogan, this is Perry Mason. I want to see you. . . . It's about a matter in which I've been retained by Sylvia Bain Atwood. . . . That's right. . . . I want to hear the recording. . . . No, I want to hear it all, every bit of it. . . . Why not? . . . Well, you can't expect so much as a thin dime. . . . All right, tell Mr. Fritch that he can't expect even a thin dime unless I hear all of that recording and unless I'm satisfied it's an authentic recording. . . . To hell with that stuff. Tell your friend, Fritch, that he's dealing with a lawyer now. . . . All right, if he isn't your

10

friend, the message is still the same. . . . That's right, every bit of recording that's on that tape. . . . Every word. . . . Otherwise Fritch can go roll his hoop. . . . When I advise a client about buying a horse I want to see the horse, all of it. . . . That's right.

"When? . . . I can't. I'm going to be busy in court. . . . All right, then make it right away. I'll be over within ten minutes. . . . Why not? . . . All right, at your apartment then. I don't care. . . . An hour. . . . All right."

Mason hung up the telephone, said to Sylvia, "I'm going over to Brogan's apartment. I'm going to hear that recording. I'm going to hear all of it. You'll have to be there with me. I want you to listen carefully and tell me if you feel the voice you hear on the recording is that of your father. Now I'm going to tell you something else. I don't like blackmail."

"You think this is?"

"It's first cousin to it," Mason said. "It smells like blackmail, and it's an aroma I don't care for. Now I want you to do one other thing for me."

"What?"

Mason said, "When I go over there I'm going to wear a hearing aid. I'm going to pretend to be a little deaf. I want you to play up to me on that."

"Why the hearing aid?"

"Perhaps," Mason said, grinning, "because I want to hear better. Now we're to meet him at his apartment in an hour. I want you to meet me here in forty-five minutes. It'll take us about fifteen minutes to get to his apartment from here. In the meantime I don't want you to say anything to anyone about what we're doing."

She nodded.

"Now then," Mason went on, "suppose it turns out this is a genuine recording of a conversation that actually took place between your father and J. J. Fritch, and in that conversation your father admits in effect that he knew the money used by Fritch in the partnership deal was the proceeds of a bank robbery. What are you going to do?"

"We're going to pay off unless you can find some better way of handling it."

"How much are you going to pay?"

She hesitated. Her eyes avoided his.

"How much?" Mason asked.

"As much as he demands, if we have to."

"And then what?"

"And then I want to be very, very certain that there isn't any more proof, that all of the proof is in our hands."

"How do you propose to do that?"

"I don't know. That's why I came to you. I thought I'd leave that up to you."

Mason said, "You can take a spool of recorded tape and dub a dozen different duplications if you want to. If they're well made on good equipment those duplications will be just as faithful as the original."

"Mr. Brogan says he'll guarantee J.J.'s good faith in the matter, that there is only one recording, that no copies have been made."

"Just how does he propose to guarantee that?"

"I don't know. He said we could depend on his word."

"Do you think his word's any good?"

She said pointedly, "I gave you five hundred dollars, didn't I? That's the best answer I can make."

"I thought so," Mason said. "It's a mess. We'll try and handle it the best we can."

"And I'm to be back here in forty-five minutes?"

"Forty minutes now," Mason told her. "On the dot."

"Very well." She arose and left the office.

When the door had clicked shut behind her Della Street raised questioning eyes at Mason.

Mason said, "First, I'm going to find out whether that's her father's voice or not. I'm going to prove that much to my own satisfaction."

"How?"

"I'm going to listen to that recording and I'm going to keep on listening to it until I'm fully familiar with the voices, then I'm going to make it a point to see Ned Bain.

I'll talk with him about the weather or anything else. I'll study his voice and compare it with the voice on the recording, and I'll have a scientific comparison made. We'll slow the recording down and we'll slow down recordings of Bain's voice. We'll speed them up. We'll make every scientific comparison we can."

"But I don't see how you'll have any opportunity to make all those examinations of the voice on the record. Do you think Brogan will let you take the record to play with, or make a copy of it?"

Mason grinned. "You haven't heard about my affliction."

"What?"

"About being deaf."

Mason opened the drawer of his desk, took out a small, oblong metal container which he slipped into his side coat pocket, then he clipped a device which held a small microphone up against the bone of his head just over the right ear.

"All right," Della Street said, "that may help you to hear more distinctly, but how is it going to help you study what's on that tape recording?"

Mason said, "Of course, I'll conceal the wires, running them in through a hole in my coat pocket and up through the shoulder of the coat."

"But I still don't see," Della Street protested.

Mason reached in the drawer of his desk, took out a small compact extension speaker about four inches in diameter. He placed that on his desk, plugged it into the flat device in his pocket and flipped a switch.

Della Street heard her own voice, startlingly lifelike, say, "All right, that may help you to hear more distinctly, but how is it going to help you study what's on that tape recording?"

Mason grinned as he saw the expression of utter consternation on Della Street's face. He disconnected the loud-speaker and put it back in the drawer of his desk.

"Good heavens!" Della Street said. "How did you do that?"

"This little device," Mason said, "is of German manufacture. It makes a wire recording for two and a half
hours on wire that is so small it is all but invisible except
under a microscope. When there is no interference it gives
an astonishing fidelity of tone reception. While I am listening to that recording over in Brogan's apartment I'll
actually be making a copy of it that we can experiment
with."

"How do you get the power for that?" Della Street
asked.

"Batteries and tubes," Mason siad. "Just the same as
with a pocket radio set or with a hearing aid."

"Suppose Brogan finds out what you're doing?"

"He won't."

"But suppose he does."

"All right," Mason said, "what can he do?"

"He could—well, he could become very disagreeable."

"So can I," Mason told her, grinning.

2

MASON entered the office of the Drake Detective Agency.

"Paul in?" he asked the receptionist.

She nodded.

"Busy?"

"On the telephone is all. I'll tell him you're coming."

She plugged in a line, flashed a signal, then nodded to
Mason. "Go right on down."

Mason opened a latched gate in a waist-high partition,
walked down a long corridor which contained a veritable
rabbit warren of offices on each side, small cubbyholes for
the most part, where operatives could make their reports.

Paul Drake's office was at the far end of the corridor.
Drake was talking on the phone as Mason entered.

He motioned Mason to a seat, finished his telephone conversation, hung up and turned to grin at the lawyer.

Mason seated himself in an uncushioned wooden chair, regarded the detective across a desk which was decorated with half a dozen separate telephones.

"It's a wonder you wouldn't get a decently comfortable chair for clients," Mason said.

"Then they'd stay too long," Drake told him. "I can't charge whopping big fees the way a lawyer can. I have to carry on a volume of business. Right now I have a dozen cases going, with men out working on those cases, phoning in reports, asking for instructions. Why were you inquiring about Brogan? You aren't getting mixed up with him, are you?"

Mason took a cigarette case from his pocket, snapped it open, offered Drake a cigarette.

The detective, tall, languorous, his face carefully schooled to an expression of disinterest, stretched forth a lazy hand, extracted a cigarette, snapped a match into flame.

"You tangle up with Brogan," he went on, "and you'll learn something about the noble art of shakedown."

"I'm tangled with him," Mason said.

"In that case you'd better let Della keep all of your money for you until you get untangled."

"What's wrong with him, Paul?"

"Everything."

"You weren't too emphatic over the telephone."

"I try to be a little cautious over the telephone. I gave you the sketch, however."

"What about him?"

"Well," Drake said, "for one thing he's a blackmailer. They can't catch him at it, but he's a blackmailer."

"Why can't they catch him at it?"

"Because he's too damn clever. He never appears as a blackmailer. Apparently *he* never gets any part of the money that's paid over as blackmail, but you let Brogan get hold of a piece of confidential information and sometime within the next year or eighteen months, after no one would think of connecting it up with George Brogan, some blackmailer will approach Brogan and demand that Brogan's client pay a shakedown.

"Brogan, of course, will immediately get in touch with his client. Brogan will be completely dismayed. He'll accuse the client of having let the cat out of the bag. The client will assure him that the information Brogan had was completely confidential. Brogan will start cross-examining the client, asking him if he didn't tell someone, if he didn't tell his wife, if he didn't tell his sweetheart, if his secretary didn't know about it, if he didn't confide in his income-tax accountant or if he hadn't told someone at the club.

"Of course, the answer is always the same. During an eighteen-month period a man will have told *someone*. If he hasn't, Brogan will make him think he has. Then Brogan will be employed to settle the deal with the blackmailer.

"Brogan will look into the thing and advise the client that about the only thing he can do is to make a payoff; that Brogan, by reason of his reputation and his underworld connections, can manipulate things so that the payoff will only be about half what it would otherwise be, and he promises that he can fix things so there will only be one payoff; that he'll not only get the evidence but he'll put fear into the heart of the blackmailer so that there won't be any recurrence, any comeback, there won't be any question of a sucker being bled until he's white."

"And then what?" Mason asked.

"Then the sucker pays Brogan about half the amount of money that the blackmailer has first demanded, according to Brogan. That money disappears. Brogan turns the evidence back to the sucker and charges the sucker a fee, which is usually very nominal under the circumstances."

"And what becomes of the blackmail money?"

"Brogan gets the bulk of it," Drake said, "but you can't

prove it. They've tried to prove it half a dozen different times, but they've never been able to tag Brogan with anything. He's smart."

"How smart?"

"Plenty smart, in a slimy sort of way."

"And what happens when there's a comeback, when they start bleeding the sucker white?"

"That's the point," Drake said. "That's where Brogan gets by. They don't do it. When you're dealing with Brogan it's once on the line and that's all. He makes good on that. He claims that he puts fear into the heart of the blackmailer so that nothing happens. Actually, of course, he's in on the racket all the way through, but I couldn't tell you that over the telephone where you might repeat it to a client. I wouldn't dare to say it to anyone else."

Mason said, "It looks as though I'll have an interesting session with him."

"When?"

"In about twenty minutes. I'm to meet him at his apartment."

"Watch your step, Perry."

"I'm watching it," Mason said. "Now here's what I want you to do, Paul. You know Brogan."

"You mean personally?"

"Yes."

"Sure."

"You can describe him?"

Drake nodded.

"Do you have some operatives who know him personally?"

"I can probably get some. How much time do I have?"

"Not very much. Fifteen or twenty minutes."

Drake said, "You always want something in a rush."

Mason grinned. "You get paid for it, don't you?"

Drake nodded.

Mason said, "I have an appointment with Brogan at his apartment. Now I want a couple of operatives stationed at the door of that apartment house. I want men who know Brogan if possible. Otherwise I want you to give them a detailed description of Brogan. After I leave, Brogan is going to go some place, probably in a hurry. I want him shadowed. I want to know where he goes. I want to know with whom he talks. And if he talks with a man by the name of Fritch I want an operative to take over and shadow Fritch."

"Okay," Drake said, reaching for the telephone. "Can do."

Drake picked up the telephone, gave instructions to his secretary to have two operatives whom he named get in touch with him immediately. He dropped the telephone back into place, said to Mason, "What kind of a deal is it?"

"It's a deal involving a tape recording of a conversation," Mason said. "I think the tape recording is probably a phony, I don't know. But I'm going up there to listen to it. Brogan claims that he knows nothing whatever about that tape recording except that a man by the name of J. J. Fritch came to him and told him he had this tape recording, that it would completely ruin a family by the name of Bain, that it would wipe out extensive property holdings, that Fritch needed money, otherwise he'd use the tape recording in such a way that Bain would be ruined. Then Fritch, believe it or not, entrusted this tape recording to Brogan.

"Brogan apparently was very much shocked. He went to a representative of the family, a woman who has money, told her about it and asked her what she wanted to do. He said that she could count on him to do anything she wanted except that he couldn't destroy the tape recording because he had given Fritch his word that wouldn't happen.

"According to Brogan's story he is able to deal with these underworld characters because they respect him as being a man of his word. If he says he'll do something, he does it. They know that he's on the side of law and order and against blackmail, but they also know that if he gives them his word, his word is as good as his bond."

Drake grinned through cigarette smoke. "Ain't that a hell of a line, Perry?"

"Damned if it isn't," Mason admitted.

"So I suppose Brogan has promised that he can settle for just about half-price, and if the family deals through him they can rest assured there won't be any repetition of the blackmail."

"Something like that. I haven't heard all the line yet," Mason said. "I'm going over and talk with Brogan personally."

"He won't like the idea of you entering the case," Drake warned.

"I know it."

"He'll pretend that he welcomes you with open arms, but if he has a chance he'll stick a knife in your back when you aren't looking."

"I'll be looking," Mason said. "And, in the meantime, if I get a chance to sabotage his little game I'm going to do it."

Drake nodded, then, after a moment, said, "You won't have a chance."

"Why not?"

"Because Brogan is cautious, and Brogan knows your reputation. He respects your ability and he won't take any chances."

"If I can get my hands on that tape recording," Mason said, "I wouldn't have the slightest compunction about destroying it."

"Sure not," Drake agreed, "but you won't get the chance. You're underestimating Brogan."

"Perhaps I am," Mason admitted.

"I tell you the guy's clever. They haven't been able to pin anything on him. He still gets by. He does right well for himself. He has plenty of this world's goods."

"Okay," Mason said. "You get your men on the job. I want to know what happens after I have left Brogan."

"Why is he having the interview in his apartment instead of at his office?" Drake asked.

"I don't know," Mason said. "It may be he doesn't trust some of the help in his office."

"He doesn't trust anyone," Drake said, "but he has some reason—he's pulled plenty of deals in his office."

Mason shrugged. "Anyway, this one's to be at his apartment."

"How long will you be there?"

"Probably about an hour."

"Well," Drake said, "that will give me time to get my operatives spotted. Don't worry, Perry, I'll have the place covered."

"Okay," Mason said, "I'm leaving it up to you."

One of the telephones rang. Drake picked up the receiver, said, "Hello," then said into the instrument, "Just a minute. I have a rush job for you. You know George Brogan. I want him tailed."

He cupped his hand over the mouthpiece, said, "All right, Perry, I'm getting my men started."

Mason arose from the uncushioned chair. "Okay, Paul, I'm leaving it up to you."

Drake was talking in a low voice into the telephone as Mason left the office.

3

■

PROMPTLY ON TIME Perry Mason and his client emerged from the elevator at the floor on which Brogan had his apartment.

Mason's ring was answered almost immediately by a man whose figure had all the aesthetic grace of a spider. He was somewhere in his forties, with a short body, long arms and legs, a thick neck and a bald head on which had been placed a toupee, the hair of which was several shades darker than that on the sides of the head.

"Hello, Mr. Mason," Brogan said, grinning broadly, surveying Mason from large, protruding eyes that seemed to have been slightly bleached.

He grabbed Mason's hand, pumped it up and down in the warmth of an overly enthusiastic greeting.

"I'm certainly glad to meet you! I've heard a lot about you. I've followed your cases with great interest, Mr. Mason, in fact with the greatest admiration. I certainly am enjoying this meeting and hope I can be of some small service to you and to Mr. Bain. And how are you this morning, Mrs. Atwood? It's a real pleasure. Won't you step right in?"

Brogan ushered them into the living room of a sumptuously furnished apartment, closed the door, turned a knurled knob which slid a bolt into place, and then in addition snapped a chain into a socket, a chain that prevented the door from being opened more than an inch or two.

"Have to take precautions," he burbled. "You know how these things go, Mr. Mason. It's rather a tricky matter. I wouldn't want to have a lot of detectives break in on us. Now you understand my position in the matter, Mr. Mason."

"I'm not certain I do," Mason said. "In fact I'm quite certain I don't."

"Well, sit down. Make yourself comfortable. I wanted to have this little session in my apartment rather than in my office because a person never knows just what can happen in an office. One is always subject to interruptions and there's not really the privacy there that one has in his own apartment." He suddenly noted the lawyer's hearing aid and automatically raised his voice.

"Now I'm going to be perfectly frank with you, Mr. Mason. I'm keeping this roll of tape in a safe-deposit box. I have to take elaborate precautions in order to safeguard it. For instance, whenever I have it with me I'm always armed."

Brogan threw back his coat, displayed a shoulder holster in which a gun reposed under his armpit.

21

"You know how those things are, Mr. Mason."

Brogan chuckled.

"I see how they are now," Mason said.

"Ha ha ha," Brogan laughed. "You do have your little joke, don't you?—Well, Mr. Mason, I'm acting here somewhat in the nature of an intermediary. I happen to have the confidence of Mr. J. J. Fritch, that is, I have placed him in such a position that he has had to give me his confidence."

Brogan nodded and grinned.

"That puts you in rather an unusual position, doesn't it?" Mason asked.

"Oh, I'm always in an unusual position," Brogan said. "I don't mind that. People are always trying to misunderstand me, but I'm very much the same way you are, Mason. I protect my clients. That's my creed. Once I've done that I don't care a snap of my fingers about the rules of the game, the conventional rules that is. I'm here to protect my client."

Mason nodded.

"And that's what I'm going to do."

"Just who is your client?" Mason asked.

"Why," Brogan said, "you are."

"I wasn't aware of it."

"Well, you're acting for Mrs. Atwood, and I consider that I'm acting for Mrs. Atwood, that is, I want the privilege of acting for her, and I may say to both of you that I would consider it a privilege."

"And just what is it you expect to do?" Mason asked.

"I want to do whatever you folks think should be done. There is only one thing that I must insist on, Mr. Mason. In my profession I deal with all sorts and classes of people. Sometimes I deal with ethical people, sometimes I deal with crooks, but I always keep faith. My word is my bond. Now I have assured J.J. that nothing is going to happen to that recording, that it won't leave my possession except on terms that are satisfactory to him.

"Of course, you understand it took quite a bit of manipulating in order to get Fritch to let me have the custody of the only thing he has in the world by way of evidence. Naturally he didn't want to let the recording out of his possession, but I persuaded him that he certainly couldn't get anyone to put up money for him unless he was willing to play fair in return."

"That's the original and there aren't any copies?" Mason asked.

Brogan's eyes grew solemn. "I feel that I can assure you of that."

"What is the ground of your assurance?"

"Well, now, Mr. Mason, you may have to say that it's predicated on a long experience in such matters and on dealing with various types of people. But I feel completely certain that this is all the evidence that exists in the world."

"And what is the position of J. J. Fritch? By the way, is he your client?"

"Mr. Mason, I want to assure you that I am not going to take one cent of compensation from Fritch. Neither am I going to represent him. I am interested in this matter only to the extent that I can protect the interests of innocent people. As far as Mr. Fritch is concerned I do not approve of his methods. I wouldn't represent him. I wouldn't touch him with a ten foot pole. I think the man is resorting to tactics that are closely akin to blackmail, Mr. Mason.

"I am willing to act as intermediary. I am willing to represent Mrs. Atwood in securing possession of certain evidence which she feels, or which she should feel, might be very embarrassing to her family. I certainly am not going to identify myself in any way with that man Fritch. I don't like him. I don't like his tactics. I would certainly never permit my professional reputation to be smirched by engaging in any such nefarious activity."

Mason said, "Suppose we buy this tape recording. Would that be the equivalent of suppressing evidence in a criminal case?"

The smile faded from Brogan's face. His pale eyes

23

studied the lawyer carefully. Then he said, "Goodness, Mr. Mason, that idea has never occurred to me."

"Perhaps it should," Mason said.

"Well, of course," Brogan said, "I'm not a lawyer. I'm only an investigator. In this case I'm only being asked to act as an intermediary. I will only continue to act as an intermediary if I am employed by Mrs. Atwood or by someone in the Bain family. If they employ me to carry on negotiations with Mr. Fritch, I will do my best.

"Now that an attorney has entered the case, Mr. Mason, perhaps *you'd* better be the one to decide on the legality of the transaction.

"Of course, you know and I know that it sounds very bad to talk about suppressing evidence, but on the other hand you know and I know that it is no crime to destroy a forgery.

"Now I am firmly convinced in my own mind, Mr. Mason, that Fritch doesn't have a leg to stand on. I think this recording is a complete forgery, but I'm afraid, Mr. Mason, that it's such a clever forgery it would convince a court or a jury. I hope it wouldn't. But it might, you can't tell.

"Now, of course, Mr. Fritch isn't putting it up to us on a basis of destroying evidence. He's simply asking that Mr. Bain or Mrs. Atwood, if she doesn't want to go to her father, loan Fritch sufficient money so that he can have the means of defending himself against a charge which he claims is completely erroneous."

"The charge has been outlawed under the statute of limitations, hasn't it?"

"I believe it has, Mr. Mason, but there again I'm not an attorney. The point is that Mr. Fritch feels he is being falsely accused, that as a good friend Mr. Bain should advance him sufficient money to see that he is capable of carrying on an investigation and a defense."

"Who would make that investigation?" Mason asked. "Would you?"

"Mr. Mason, I'm sure I don't know. You keep insisting on getting the cart before the horse. Of course, it is

24

possible that Mr. Fritch might retain me to make an investigation for him. I don't know. If he retained me *after* this matter had been completely terminated I might accept the employment. I really can't say at this time. But I do know this. I wouldn't even discuss the matter with him until this transaction is entirely cleared up."

"How much money does Fritch want?"

"Just enough to carry on his investigation and to clear himself of a charge that he insists is false."

"And does he have some idea of what that would be?"

"Well, of course, it means running down a lot of old trails, Mr. Mason, and digging into a lot of musty records. It's not going to be an easy matter. Fritch feels that the minimum, the very minimum, would be twenty-five thousand dollars."

"That," Mason said, "is a *lot* of money."

"Well, Fritch doesn't consider it in terms of money. He considers it in terms of service, of what it would cost him to defend himself against a false accusation."

"That seems to be rather high," Mason said.

"Well, of course, it may be. You know more about those things than I do. If Mrs. Atwood retains me to present the matter to Mr. Fritch, I certainly will do everything I can to get him to accept the smallest amount possible."

"And what happens after the amount is paid?"

"Well, of course, Mr. Mason, I don't know. I frankly haven't gone into that matter with Fritch. Fritch came to me. I told him that I wouldn't work for *him* under any consideration, but that I would get in touch with Mrs. Atwood, and if she wanted to employ me I would be glad to accept the employment. However, I warned Fritch that in case I accepted employment from Mrs. Atwood my activities would be wholeheartedly devoted to her, and that if I thought this tape recording was a complete falsification I would endeavor to prove that it was."

"And what did Fritch say to that?"

"He said that I could take the tape recording on my

professional assurance that nothing would happen to it, and take any steps I wanted to prove that it was genuine. Now I think I've made my position plain."

"Very plain," Mason said dryly. "Now let's hear the tape recording."

Brogan regarded Mason for a moment with an appraisal that was silently hostile.

"Go ahead," Mason said, "let's hear what you have."

"I think we'd better understand each other first, Mr. Mason," Brogan said. "We're not going to get anywhere by trying to question one another's motives. You're an attorney. I assume you have received a retainer from Mrs. Atwood. Now before I take one step in this matter, one single step, I am going to insist that Mrs. Atwood give me a retainer to act on her behalf, and that you, as her attorney, approve of that retainer. Do I make myself plain?"

"In other words, you're going to protect yourself," Mason said.

"You're damn right I am," Brogan said.

"All right," Mason told him. "Let's hear the recording. I take it you're authorized to go that far."

"That far and no further."

"All right, let's listen to it."

Brogan set up a tape recorder, plugged it into a wall socket, went over to the wall, swung back a section of what seemed to be solid wall disclosing a wall safe. He spun the combination on the safe and took out a spool of tape.

"Now, Mr. Mason, as I told you, I have my own professional reputation at stake. I have assured Mr. Fritch that nothing is going to happen to this recording while it is in my hands and that nobody is going to touch it. I'm going to ask you to stay on that side of the table. I want you and Mrs. Atwood to keep entirely away from this machine. I don't want you to try to touch this tape or to inspect it in any way. Now is that understood?"

"You're making the conditions," Mason said.

"I shall expect you to abide by them."

"Any time we don't want to abide by them," Mason said, "we're quite free to walk out."

"You are indeed."

An embroidered silk throw was over the table. Brogan placed the spool of tape on this silk throw beside the transcribing machine. He saw that the controls were adjusted, then put the spool on the machine, and fed the tape through the recording head on to the empty spool.

"Of course," Mason said, smiling, "I wouldn't want to question a man's hospitality, but I for one certainly could use a drink."

"Excuse me, excuse me," Brogan said. "I was so intent on what I was doing I was entirely neglectful of my duties as a host. What would *you* like, Mrs. Atwood?"

"A Scotch and soda," she said.

"I'll have some whisky and water," Mason said, "and if you don't mind I'd like to mix my own."

"Quite all right, quite all right," Brogan said, and his grin disclosed a mouthful of big teeth. "I can appreciate your position, counselor. You have to be suspicious. Now you'll pardon me if I am just as suspicious as you are. You said you wanted to mix your own and I'll take you at your word. If you'll just precede me into the kitchen, Mr. Mason, and if you and Mrs. Atwood will stay in the kitchenette while I'm there we won't have any trouble. In other words, Mr. Mason, I wouldn't want you to use the subterfuge of having me go out to get a drink to create an opportunity to tamper with this tape. Now the kitchen is right through that door and if you and Mrs. Atwood will precede me, please."

Mason and Mrs. Atwood moved dutifully toward the door indicated.

"Some day," Brogan said, "I'm going to get one of these portable bars that manufacture ice that you can keep in the living room, but in the meantime all of my ice is in the refrigerator and the refrigerator is in the kitchen. I hope you understand, Mr. Mason."

"I understand."

"No hard feelings?"

"No hard feelings," Mason said.

In the kitchen Brogan produced glasses. He opened the refrigerator, took out a tray of ice cubes, pressed a lever and the ice cubes popped out into a dish. He stepped toward a butler's pantry and opened a door, disclosing a closet the back of which was lined with shelves that were filled with various bottles.

"Quite an assortment," Mason said.

"It is, indeed, counselor. I make much of my income by buying bankrupt stocks. I had a chance to buy up a bankrupt restaurant a few months ago. I turned the deal to my financial advantage. In fact, the entire wine cellar was left in my hands after a resale of the fixtures. The sale of fixtures got me even on the deal.

"I could, of course, have sold the liquor and made a sweet profit on the transaction, but then I'd have had to pay income tax. As it is the transaction just balances on a cash basis, leaving me with the contents of the wine cellar, which, of course, I am carrying on my books at a most nominal value."

And George Brogan, not only pleased with himself, but pleased at having such an opportune moment to impress Mason with his business shrewdness as well as the legitimate nature of his business activities, rubbed his hands together.

"Help yourself," Brogan invited. "Pour your drinks the way you like them. I appreciate your suspicions, Mr. Mason, and the way you take precautions. I'm taking the same precautions. Each one pours his own drink. Each one puts in his own mixer. Each one drinks from his own glass without putting it down. I'd hate to have you slip a knockout drop in my glass, Mr. Mason, and I'd hate to have you think that I'd slip one in yours."

They put ice cubes in the glasses, poured drinks. Mason went over to the sink and let water from the faucet dribble in on top of the whisky and ice.

"Here's mud in your eye," Brogan said.

"Confusion to our enemies," Mason corrected as he raised the glass to his lips.

Brogan sputtered into dry, cackling laughter. "You're a card, Mr. Mason, you really are, but it's just what I expected. Now shall we go into the other room and listen to the recording?"

Mason stepped hurriedly toward the door.

"Just a moment, just a moment," Brogan said, his voice suddenly cracking like a whip. "I think you don't give me proper respect, Mr. Mason. *I'll* leave the room first. You're not to be in the room with that recording machine unless I'm there—not even for an instant. Do you understand?"

"Oh, pardon me," Mason said. "As a matter of fact I'll have a little more water in my drink anyway."

He stepped back toward the sink.

Brogan stalked into the living room, followed by Mrs. Atwood.

Over the drainboard on the sink was a magnetic knife holder. It was some three inches wide and eight inches long. Eight or nine knives were fastened to it, held in place by magnetic attraction.

Mason pulled off all of these knives. He put his fingers under the flat magnet, raised it from its position and put it in his hip pocket. Then he hurried into the living room, arriving but a few steps behind Mrs. Atwood.

"Now if you'll just stay on that side of the table," Brogan warned, "I'll stay over here. That way there won't be any temptation on your part to do anything that might cause trouble, Mr. Mason. You understand I'm for you one hundred per cent, but I'm forced to protect my own professional reputation for fair dealing."

"Quite commendable. You understand my attitude and I understand yours," Mason said. "If I can wreck Fritch's scheme I'm going to do so."

He placed his glass on the table, drew up a chair, seated himself, and as he did so, surreptitiously slipped the flat magnet out of his hip pocket and under the cloth on the table.

He picked up his glass, took a sip from it, put it down so it was behind the flat magnet. By manipulating his glass slowly from side to side he moved the magnet a few inches toward the recording machine.

"Go right ahead. We're ready any time you are," Mason said.

Brogan flicked a switch, then settled back to watch Mason and Sylvia Atwood.

The recorder gave a few preliminary squawks, then voices that were startlingly clear and distinct filled the room. For fifteen minutes Mason and Sylvia Atwood listened to what purported to be a conversation between J. J. Fritch and Ned Bain relating to the original partnership which had been founded by the men. From that recorded conversation there could be no question but what Ned Bain knew definitely and positively that the money which had been advanced by Fritch was money that had been derived from the robbery of the bank.

"Well," Brogan said, unable to keep a note of triumph from his voice when he had finished the recording, "are you satisfied?"

"Satisfied with what?" Mason asked.

Brogan caught himself quickly. "Satisfied that it is your father's voice?" he asked Mrs. Atwood. "Because if it isn't, that's all there is to it. We'll go right ahead and have Fritch arrested for attempted extortion."

"And if it *is* her father's voice?" Mason asked.

"Then, of course, we're going to have to be more careful."

Mason stood up, his hand resting on the table. He slowly leaned toward the machine, looking down at the recorded tape, pushing the flat magnet ahead of his fingers as his hand slid forward over the cloth.

"Now just a moment, Mr. Mason, just a moment," Brogan said, suddenly wary. "That's far enough."

Mason said, "I want to look at that spool. I want to see whether it's been spliced."

His finger tips pushed the magnet under the cloth.

"Spliced?" Brogan asked. "What difference would that make?"

"It might make a lot."

"Well, it hasn't been spliced. I can assure you of that, although I still don't see what you're getting at."

Brogan rewound the tape back on its proper spool, lifted it off the machine.

Mason abruptly leaned forward, giving the magnet a last push as he did so.

"Let me look at that spool, Brogan," he said.

Brogan put the spool on the table, said, "Mason, don't try anything. I'm going to have to ask you to step back, then I'll show you the whole spool."

"Certainly," Mason said, stepping well back out of the way. "I want to see if it's been spliced."

Brogan said, "After all, this is a business matter with both of us. You're representing a client. I'm hoping to represent that same client. Our interests are in common. You've been through deals of this sort before and so have I. Now let's keep our heads and discuss this matter on a logical, adult basis."

Brogan put a lead pencil down through the center of the spool and unwound some fifteen feet of tape, letting it fall on the floor.

"Now, you see," he said, "there isn't a splice in it."

"Not in that much of it," Mason said.

Brogan reeled off another ten or fifteen feet, then with the forefinger of his other hand wound the tape back onto the spool, revolving the spool on the pencil while it was flat on the table.

"Well, that's all that you're going to see right now," he said. "I haven't permission to go any further. I can assure you that tape isn't spliced. So far as I know there's nothing whatever wrong with it. It's absolutely genuine and authentic."

Brogan picked up the spool, said, "Now I'm going to put this spool back in the safe before we do any more talking."

Brogan momentarily turned his back to put the spool in the safe. Mason, leaning forward, ostensibly to inspect the recording machine, slipped the magnet out from under the cloth.

Sylvia Atwood's green eyes suddenly widened as she saw Mason putting something in his hip pocket. Mason motioned her to silence.

"Well," Mason said, "I'll help myself to another drink if you don't mind, Brogan, and then we'll sit down and talk business."

He stepped out to the kitchen, swiftly put the magnetic knife holder back into place, put the knives in their proper place, and was pouring more whisky into his glass when Brogan and Mrs. Atwood appeared in the doorway.

"Help yourself," Brogan said. "I'm sorry if I was a little suspicious, Mason, but frankly, I'm just a little afraid of you. You have a reputation for being damnably clever that I thoroughly respect."

Mason said, "All right, let's get down to brass tacks. Fritch *wants* twenty-five thousand dollars. How much will he *take?*"

"I think twenty," Brogan said, his eyes narrowing. "I think if I were representing Mrs. Atwood I could save her a cool five thousand dollars."

"What would be your terms?"

"Terms!" Brogan said. "Why, Mr. Mason, I'd simply want a reasonable compensation. I'd leave that matter entirely in your hands, absolutely in your hands as an attorney who's experienced in these matters and who can appreciate the gravity of the situation and knows what this record could well be worth."

Mason sipped his drink thoughtfully. "Look here, Brogan, I'm not going to advise my client to pay a cent, or to employ you to act as intermediary in paying a red cent until I'm certain that tape is a genuine recording. Now you don't want me to put my hands on it. I tell you what we'll do. Play the tape once more, but let me sit where I can watch it while it goes through the recording head so I can see there aren't any splices on it."

"Why all this bother about splices?" Brogan asked. "What difference would a splice make?"

"Simply this, there might be parts of two conversations

on there, so blended and scrambled that Mr. Bain's answers might have been to some other questions altogether."

Brogan threw back his head and laughed. "That's such a farfetched idea, Mason. I doubt that it could even be done."

"I know damn well it could be done," Mason said.

"Well, I'm certain it *wasn't* done."

"I don't care about how you feel. *I* want to be certain."

"How? What can I do to assure you?"

"I want you to run that tape again while I'm sitting beside you."

Brogan shook his head. "I couldn't permit that."

"Well," Mason said, "I've got to see the inside of that tape. I've got to see that it isn't spliced."

"I'll tell you what I'll do," Brogan said. "I'll turn the machine around. In that way you can remain on your side of the table yet watch the tape as it unwinds."

"That'll be satisfactory," Mason said. "I want to hear it once more anyway."

"Why do you want to hear it again?"

"Frankly, because I want to become familiar with Ned Bain's voice."

"It's his voice all right."

"I'm sorry I can't accept your assurance."

"I wouldn't ask you to. I'm just telling you. I might save you some work."

"Oh, I don't mind work."

Brogan led the way back to the living room, switched on the tape recording machine, then went once more to the wall safe and twisted the dials, standing slightly to one side so that he could watch Mason as he did so.

Brogan removed the spool of tape, placed it on the machine, fed it through the recording head, turned the machine around so that Mason could see the inside of the tape, and stepped back, his arms folded, his eyes watchful.

The machine made a few preliminary noises. The tape slowly unwound. There was complete silence.

"Well," Mason said, "what's the matter? Start it playing. You haven't put it in wrong, have you?"

Sudden panic seized Brogan. He leaned forward and adjusted the controls of the machine.

"Be certain you aren't erasing that tape as you're feeding it through," Mason warned.

Brogan abruptly shut off the machine, studied the connections carefully, then again threaded the tape through.

"No chance of that," he said. "I've played thousands of tapes on this machine. I know what I'm doing. Keep back, Mason."

"I'm back," Mason said. "I thought perhaps I might help you."

"I can get along without your help."

Once more Brogan started the tape winding through the recording head.

Again there was a period of complete silence. After a long interval a faint sound of a few words emanated in a conversation that was inaudible.

Brogan turned up the volume control to its maximum capacity.

The tape continued to unwind. Occasionally it was possible to hear a very faint word, but not distinctly enough to tell what was being said.

"Good God!" Brogan said under his breath. Beads of perspiration appeared on his forehead. He suddenly looked up at Mason, his eyes suspicious. "What did you do to this machine?" he shouted.

"What *could* I have done to it?" Mason asked.

"I'm damned if I know," Brogan said. He switched the machine off, rewound the tape by hand. "I think you've reversed the magnets in some way. It hasn't done you a damn bit of good, Mason. I'll get another machine. I'll—"

"Do so by all means," Mason told him. "And when you do, and get that playing again to your satisfaction, would you mind calling me? Before I advise Mrs. Atwood to retain you to enter into negotiations with Mr. Fritch, I want to assure myself that that's a genuine tape recording."

Brogan controlled himself by an effort. He wiped perspiration from his forehead. "You don't need to worry about its being genuine."

"It seems to worry you that it might *not* be genuine."

"I have my professional reputation to consider. If anything's happened to that tape I'd be in a tight spot."

"So you've told us a good many times. Well, I can count on you to give me a ring when you've got another tape recorder set up and have the spool ready to put in operation?"

"You can indeed," Brogan said, fighting to keep a semblance of composure. "I'm quite satisfied it'll be all right, Mr. Mason."

"That's fine," Mason told him. "We'll be back."

"It's something wrong with the machine," Brogan said. "It has to be with the machine. The magnets have become polarized or something. I'll get another machine up here, probably some time tomorrow."

"That's fine," Mason said. "Give me a ring and we'll make an appointment. I'm fairly busy in court right at the moment."

Brogan escorted them to the door, took off the safety chain, spun back the knurled knob, opened the door and said, "Well, thank you very much for coming in. It's about lunchtime. Sorry that I can't ask you to have lunch with me, but I'm going to be busy trying to get that machine adjusted, trying to find out just what the devil happened to it."

His pale eyes stared at Mason. "Just what the devil *did* happen to it?" he asked. "I don't think it'll make much difference on the tape recording, Mr. Mason, but it was a damn fine trick. Personally I'd like to know what the trick was."

"Trick?" Mason asked.

"You said it," Brogan said, hesitated a moment, and then slammed the door.

Standing there in the hallway, they heard the chain snap into place, heard the bolt rasp into its socket.

"Well," Mason said to Sylvia Atwood, "that's that."

"Mr. Mason," she whispered, "what *did* you do? What was that you put in your pocket? What was it that was under the silk cover on that table?"

Mason looked at her innocently. "I wouldn't know."

Abruptly she smiled. "No, I'm quite sure you wouldn't."

"Well," Mason told her, "I'll get in touch with you when I hear from Brogan again."

"You think you'll hear from him soon?"

"Oh, certainly," Mason told her. "He'll have some things to do first, a good story to think up, and then he'll be his affable self once more. He'll assure us there was only a minor defect in the playback mechanism. He'll have it all fixed by tomorrow."

"Mr. Mason, what in the world *did* you do? It sounded as though you'd managed to erase every bit of conversation on that tape!"

Mason raised his eyebrows in surprise. "*I* did?"

"Yes."

"How in the world could I have done that with Brogan watching me all the time?"

She led the way toward the elevator. "I presume that question is worrying Mr. George Brogan at the present time."

Mason grinned. "Particularly in view of his assurance that there was only one recording of that conversation in existence and no dubbed copies."

"And," she went on lightly, "your hearing aid seems to have a lot to do with your success in these matters. Do you wear it often?"

"I have a slight cold," Mason told her, and opening the elevator door, stood to one side for her to enter.

4

MASON'S PRIVATE OFFICE looked as if it could well have been the laboratory in some sound studio.

Mason's miniature wire recorder was on the desk. A connection led from it to a tape recorder which was so arranged that a recording could be made on tape directly from the miniature wire recorder. In addition to that, a monitoring attachment enabled Mason and Della Street to hear what was being recorded.

"That certainly comes in good and clear," Della Street said.

Mason nodded.

"What about Brogan?"

"He's going to have to show his hand," Mason said. "He'll rush out to see Fritch. When that happens Drake's men will be on the job. He—"

Mason broke off as a code knock sounded on the door of his private office.

"That's Paul now, Della."

Della Street opened the door.

Paul Drake, good humored in his gangling, double-jointed way, entered the room, pushed the door shut behind him, grinned and said, "What the deuce are you folks doing in here?"

Mason grinned. "I used my little German wire recorder to record the conversation with your friend Brogan, and incidentally, to make my own copy of the tape recording that he had."

Drake listened. "Seems to come in clear enough. What are you doing with that tape machine?"

"Transferring from wire to tape," Mason explained.

"I'll use the tape for reference and lock the wire away as original evidence."

Drake continued to listen, then chuckled. "You seem to have Brogan going. Is this after the recording was played?"

"That's right. I asked him to play it the second time. What's happened with Brogan? Has he led your men to J. J. Fritch yet?"

"Not yet. He hasn't even gone out."

Mason's voice showed his surprise. "You mean he hasn't left his apartment?"

"No. My men are stationed there."

"How long have they—"

"Plenty of time. They were there before you and Mrs. Atwood left. They saw you going out."

Mason frowned, then let a smile erase the frown. "That means Brogan is having one hell of a time trying to find out what happened to his tape recording. He doesn't dare to report to Fritch."

"Gosh, Perry, what actually *did* happen?"

Mason grinned. "I messed up Brogan's evidence."

"How?"

"To be perfectly frank with you," Mason said, "it was an idea that came to me on the spur of the moment. I thought I might ask for a drink and perhaps get him out of the room so I could at least look at the tape and see if it had been spliced. He was too smart for that."

"He would be," Drake said. "Gosh, Perry, the way that guy plays the game he wouldn't have left you alone with that tape recording for a minute. According to his code of ethics it would have been all right for you to have grabbed the tape and thrown it out of the window."

"I know," Mason said. "He insisted on all three of us going into the kitchen. Then he was so afraid I'd put knockout drops in his drink, or that I would think that he might have drugged ours that he insisted on everyone mixing his own drink. I noticed a magnetic knife holder over the drainboard and that was when I got a sudden idea."

"What did you do?"

"Managed to be the last one to leave the kitchen, pulled the knives off the magnetic holder, slipped the holder out of its socket, and had a nice flat magnet which I was able to insert under the cloth on the table just where I felt certain he was going to put the spool of tape. He didn't notice there was anything under the cloth. I raised the point that I wanted to see some of the tape, so he obligingly rotated the spool while it was within the magnetic field and, of course, erased everything on it."

"Did what?" Drake asked incredulously.

"Erased everything on it."

"I don't get it," Drake said. "How did it erase?"

Mason grinned. "A tape recorder is simply an arrangement of molecules on a magnetized tape. You can erase the conversation and use the tape over and over again by bringing it through a magnetic field, which is, roughly speaking, what happens when you use the tape a second time. As it goes through a magnetic field the old conversation is erased just before the new conversation is put on.

"You can take a good horseshoe magnet, run it around a spool of tape and erase everything on it, but a good flat magnet works a lot better."

"Well I'll be darned," Drake said. "I never knew that. That is, I never thought of it in exactly that way. I knew, of course, that conversations were recorded due to pulsations in a magnetic field. What did Brogan do? I'll bet he had a fit."

Mason chuckled. "He certainly was in a panic for a minute. Then he probably remembered that he had means of duplicating the tape, so he rushed us out of there, assuring us it was something wrong with the machine."

"Does he know what you did?"

"He knows I messed it up some way," Mason said, "but he doesn't know how, and that's worrying him a lot."

"But if he's lost that tape recording then what?"

"That tape recording," Mason said, "was synthetic."

"What do you mean?"

"I mean this—Fritch probably got Ned Bain into a long conversation about a lot of things, politics, old times, business, cattle, oil and all the rest of it. Then Fritch went to some sound recording studio. He ran off portions of the tape recording of his conversation with Ned Bain, and some unscrupulous sound technician helped him fix up a master roll of spliced conversation."

"I still don't get it."

"Just this way, Paul. Let's suppose that in their actual conversation Fritch said to Bain, 'You remember that time we killed the big deer up by the point of the mountain?' and Bain said, 'I remember it just as plain as day, J.J. I never will forget it.'

"All right, Fritch goes to a sound studio. They take that answer that Bain made and on another tape Fritch says, 'You remember the time I raised capital for your oil well venture in Texas by holding up that bank, Ned?'

"Then the sound technician cuts out that part of the tape-recorded conversation where Ned Bain says, 'I remember it just as plain as day, J.J. I never will forget it,' and splices that right in so that it seems an answer to Fritch's question."

Drake said, "You mean the whole conversation was put together that way?"

"That's right."

"Then the tape is a mass of splices?"

"The original tape must be," Mason said, "but the splices have been cunningly made. They're handled in such a way that you can't possibly detect them by listening. Then that master tape was boiled down to about twenty minutes of generalized conversation with four or five very incriminating statements incorporated in it. After that was done the whole thing was dubbed on another spool of tape, which is supposed to be the original sound recording of a conversation."

"How are you going to prove all that?" Drake asked.

"That, of course," Mason admitted, "is the problem. I think I have a clue and a good one."

"What's that?"

"The sound technician was too clever."

"What do you mean?"

"The actual conversation between Fritch and Bain took place in a room or in an apartment somewhere. The voices bounced back from the walls. You can hear just the faint sound of an echo whenever Ned Bain is talking. You hear it sometimes when Fritch is talking. But whenever Fritch asks a question to which Ned Bain makes an incriminating answer, Fritch's question comes in without the faintest sound of echo.

"You can see what that means. That question was asked in a soundproof room in a studio somewhere, and while Fritch tried his best, probably with careful coaching, to make it sound like a casual question as part of the other conversation, the fine quality of the recording during those particular periods is manifest even to an untrained ear.

"You see, what happens in an ordinary room, Paul, is that a voice, particularly if it's a man's heavy voice, bounces back in a whole series of echoes, from the floor, the walls and the ceiling. In ordinary conversation we focus those sounds out and the ear doesn't hear them, but when you record the conversation through a sensitive microphone, every one of those echoes is picked up.

"Sound studios naturally can't afford to have that happen, so they use soundproof rooms with specially prepared walls that break up the echoes so there isn't any voice bounce.

"Now I've listened pretty carefully to that tape recording and at no time do I find Ned Bain making any actual admission. All that Ned Bain does is to make statements confirming certain things J. J. Fritch has said. I think for that reason we can prove the tape recording is a fake if we have to, but the method I used today is going to prove it, provided we get a break."

"What do you think happened?"

"I think that just about as soon as we got out of there Brogan phoned Fritch and said, 'Mason managed to do something to erase the conversation on this spool we have. We'll have to make another copy from the master record. Then we'll destroy this tape recording and substitute the new one. I'll tell Mason it was a defect in the machine. Mason will know I'm lying, but there's nothing he can do about it. There's nothing he can prove.' Then Fritch and Brogan will run off another dubbed copy and tell me that's the same one I listened to, that the trouble wasn't with the tape but with the playback."

Drake thought that over. "Can you prove that the substitute is a new recording, Perry?"

"No."

"Then what did you gain by erasing that first recording?"

"It's going to force Brogan to get in touch with Fritch. When he does that we'll have a line on Fritch. It's also going to force them to make another copy of that master recording. They've got that master spool of spliced tape locked away somewhere in a safe-deposit box. By following Brogan to Fritch and Fritch to the bank we'll know where the master spool is located. Then we'll slap a *subpoena duces tecum* on Fritch ordering him to produce the spool of spliced tape from box number so-and-so in the safe-deposit vault at such-and-such a bank. It will scare them to death. They won't know how much we know."

"But Brogan hasn't left his apartment."

"Probably because Fritch is out some place and he's been unable to get in touch with him."

"What about your client? Does she know you sabotaged the tape?"

"She knows it, but she doesn't know how I did it. Brogan knows and it's frightened him. He'd give a good deal to know how it was done."

"Well, my men are on the job," Drake said. "I thought I'd check with you."

Mason nodded.

"You think you can hear the difference in quality of

conversation when Fritch asks one of those incriminating questions?"

"I think," Mason said, "that even this little recorder I have did a good enough job of reproducing so you can hear it on the copy. Of course, you must remember that it was coming in over a loud-speaker and there was a certain amount of echo from the walls and ceiling of Brogan's apartment. However, those voice bounces would be equally distributed over all the conversation so that there'll still be a better quality of recording in the incriminating questions asked by Fritch."

Mason threw a switch on the tape recorder, shut off the wire recorder, spun the tape recorder back for a few minutes, then turned it on to the playback and let Drake listen.

"Now this part of the conversation," Mason said, "is coming in just about equally clear, as Fritch's voice and Bain's voice have about the same number of echoes. They're talking about the cattle business there. Now listen to this."

Suddenly Fritch's voice said, "I'm wondering what will happen if anyone should ever find out that I'm the one who committed the bank robbery." And Bain answered casually, so casually in fact that he seemed to be discussing some routine matter, "How are they ever going to find out, J.J.?"

Mason cut off the machine. "See what I mean, Paul?"

"I'm not certain that I do," Drake said. "I heard Fritch's question very plainly. The thing that impressed me was the fact that Bain took it all so casually."

"He took it casually," Mason said, "because he was talking about something else. I'm going to play it once more. Now you listen. Even in this dubbed copy you can hear the difference in quality if you listen closely. Fritch asked that question in a studio. Now I'll turn it back and you listen carefully."

Mason turned back the machine. Drake closed his eyes so he could listen to better advantage.

This time when Mason shut off the machine Drake was nodding.

"I get you now, Perry. You can sure hear a difference in quality there."

"Of course," Mason went on, "you can't hear it on this dubbed recording anywhere near as well as you can on the original record."

"If that occurs to them couldn't they fix it up?" Drake asked.

"Sure," Mason admitted. "They'd make a new master tape with Fritch's questions asked in an apartment where there'd be a normal voice bounce. Then they'd make a new copy. But, try as they could, they couldn't get Fritch to ask the same questions, even if they used a script. There'd be a word different here and there, a change of pace or of expression.

"That's the advantage of having this recording. If they change it in the least, or change the wording of Fritch's questions, I'll flash this recording on them and claim that they made two different recordings. That's what I was hoping would happen when I went over there this morning. I was hoping I could get a copy of the recording they had and then frighten them into trying to fake a new recording that would have some different element injected into it. Then I'd be able to prove conclusively that the whole thing was a put-up job."

"That, of course, would be better than relying on the difference in quality on the sound recording," Drake said.

"I'll probably do it yet," Mason told him. "But I couldn't resist the temptation to erase that tape recording right under Brogan's nose."

"It'll give him more respect for you," Drake said. "He—"

Della Street's phone rang. She picked up the receiver and Drake waited to see if the call was for him.

Della Street cupped her hand over the mouthpiece and said, "Mr. Brogan is calling you, Chief."

Mason grinned, said, "I'll take it. Tell Gertie to switch it on my line."

Mason picked up his telephone and said, "Hello."

Brogan's voice said, "I just wanted you to know that I've located the trouble in the machine."

"Indeed," Mason said, and added dryly, "I trust that the tape wasn't ruined."

"No, no, no, no, nothing like that," Brogan said. "The tape is *quite* all right. There was nothing wrong with the tape at all. It was simply a loose connection in the machine itself that prevented the conversation from being broadcast over the loud-speaker so that you could hear it. The tape is quite all right. The machine is fixed and everything's working perfectly now."

"That's fine," Mason said. "Where are you now? At your apartment?"

"At my apartment?" Brogan said in some surprise. "Heavens, no. I'm at my office."

"Oh, I thought perhaps you were still tinkering with the machine."

"I took the machine to a repair shop," Brogan said. "They found the loose connection."

"Then you haven't played the tape back?"

"No, I haven't played it back, but I have played other tapes so that I know the machine is working."

"And you're not sure then that the defect in the machine didn't erase the other tape?"

"It couldn't have."

"But you haven't played it back?"

"I've played back just an inch or two of it to make sure."

"And it came in all right?"

"Clear as a bell. It's really a very good recording, all things considered."

"Of course," Mason said, "you understand my position, Brogan. I'll have to hear it again to make sure you're not kidding me about the tape."

"I want you to," Brogan said.

"Where, when?"

"As soon as possible. How about tomorrow morning at nine o'clock at my apartment. Will that be too early?"

"No, that's fine," Mason told him. "The early hour suits me. I'll be there."

"Thank you," Brogan said and hung up.

Mason turned to Paul Drake. "Brogan says he's at his office but he's found the trouble, which was in the loud-speaker attachment on the machine, that everything's all ready to go, that the tape was not hurt in the least, that at nine o'clock tomorrow morning at his apartment he'll give us another playback.

"Now we know he hasn't left his apartment. You know what that means, Paul. It means that the master tape is located somewhere in his apartment, that he has a series of machines there just as I have here, and that he's made another dubbing and has completed it. He said he was at his office, yet we know he's still in his apartment."

"That means he has the master recording and Fritch doesn't," Drake said.

Mason nodded. "Apparently so."

"You want me to keep my men on the job?"

"Keep them on the job," Mason instructed. "I want Brogan shadowed, but we now know that he has the master recording."

Mason's telephone shrilled into noise and Della Street, answering, said, "Yes, Gertie, who is it?... Just a second, Gertie."

She cupped her hand over the mouthpiece of the telephone, said to Mason, "It's Sylvia Atwood. She says it's terribly important. She simply must speak to you right away."

Mason nodded, picked up the telephone, said, "Hello," and heard Sylvia Atwood's voice, sharp with excitement.

"Mr. Mason, you must come at once. Something terrible has happened."

"What?"

"Fritch telephoned Dad and told him that he had to dismiss you or he would sell his story to the bank. J.J. said he felt there was no call for him to have any further loyalty to Dad, that he was going to play the thing for his own best interests. At first, of course, Dad didn't have the faintest idea of what he was talking about, and then gradually Fritch kept on until it dawned on him. Dad's had a terrible upset. He knows now an attempt is being made to blackmail us on the oil property.

"We thought the very best way possible of reassuring Dad would be to let him talk with you. I think you can reassure him and do more good than all the doctor's medicine in the world."

"You want me to see him?"

"Yes, please."

"When?"

"Just as soon as possible. Right away, if you possibly can."

"You're out there with him now?"

"No. I'm downtown. I could be in your office in five minutes, drive you out and bring you back."

Mason said, "Just a minute." He raised his head, frowned in thoughtful concentration for a moment, then said, "All right, come on in. I'll go out with you."

Mason hung up the telephone, said to Paul Drake, "Now why would Fritch pull a stunt like that?"

"Like what?"

"Ringing up Ned Bain and telling him that he had to dismiss me."

"Well, why not?"

"Because," Mason said, "the best hold Fritch had on the family was on the theory that Ned Bain mustn't know anything at all about what was going on. Now then, Fritch has deliberately thrown that card away. Apparently it was a trump card. Why did he do it?"

"Because he thinks he has something to gain by doing it," Drake said.

"That," Mason told him, "is obvious. Now then, the question is, what did he have to gain?"

Drake shrugged his shoulders.

Mason said to Della, "Sylvia Atwood is going to be

here within five minutes. I'm going out to call on her father and do what I can to reassure him.

"In the meantime, Paul, you keep your men covering Brogan. Brogan and Fritch have been in communication, probably by telephone since Brogan hasn't left his apartment. Of course, Fritch *could* have come to Brogan there at the apartment."

"You don't know Fritch?"

Mason shook his head.

"Have we got a description?"

"We could probably get one," Mason said, "but I don't know that it would do any good now. I was thinking that Brogan would go to Fritch and that Fritch must have the master recording. Apparently it's the other way around. Fritch must have gone to Brogan. Brogan must have the master recording."

"That checks," Drake said. "Brogan is the brains behind the blackmail."

"All right," Mason told him, "we'll play it on that basis for a while."

5

MASON, sitting on Sylvia Atwood's right, noticed approvingly the deft manner with which she handled the car in traffic.

The lawyer sat with arms folded, his keen eyes missing nothing, his face granite hard with expressionless impassivity.

From time to time Sylvia stole a quick sidelong glance at Mason's profile, then devoted her attention to driving.

After they had negotiated the heaviest part of the traffic and were rolling along on a boulevard, she said bitterly, "J.J. has thrown off the mask now and shown himself for what he is—a blackmailer, a dirty, vicious blackmailer."

Mason nodded.

"But," she went on, "how can he do anything to hurt Dad without at the same time hurting himself? He's going to have to admit that he was the one who robbed the bank."

"Was *one* of the persons who robbed the bank," Mason corrected.

"Well," she said, "it doesn't make any difference as far as we're concerned."

"Why?"

"Because it's simply a question of whether Dad knew that he was using stolen money, but it would seem to me that J.J. has completely reversed his position. Before this he was trying to protect himself and his good name. Now he's engaged in blackmail, pure and simple."

"Blackmail," Mason said, "is never pure and it's seldom simple."

"No, I suppose not, but why shouldn't he try to protect himself?"

"Because," Mason said, "they've had some very clever attorneys looking up the statute of limitations, and they've decided that the lapse of time has made Fritch immune from prosecution on any charge. That's probably why the police haven't swooped down on Fritch and arrested him for that bank job. It's up to the bank in a civil suit to try to recover its property—"

"But doesn't a statute of limitations run against a bank?"

"There," Mason said, "you're up against a peculiar, tricky legal situation. In certain types of involuntary trust, where the custodian of the property is presumed to have knowledge of the illegal means by which the property was acquired, and the other person has no knowledge and is prevented from having knowledge by the secretive acts of the involuntary trustee, the statute of limitations may run from the *discovery* of the facts rather than the facts themselves."

"Oh, you lawyers!" she said. "You're *so* technical."

"You have to have technicalities if you're going to have law," Mason said. "The minute you lay down a line of demarcation between right and wrong you are necessarily going to have borderline cases. Go down to the border between Mexico and the United States. Stand two inches on this side of the border and you're in the United States. Stand two inches on the other side and you're in Mexico and subject to the laws of Mexico. That means that moving four inches puts you under an entirely different set of laws."

"Well, that's understandable."

"It's understandable to you," Mason said, "because you can clearly see the boundary line between the United States and Mexico and can understand it. The lawyer sees legal boundary lines just as clearly and can readily comprehend the distinction between being barely on one side of the line and barely on the other.

"Tell me something about your family that we're going to see."

"My father is magnificent. He's been a wonderful, wonderful man. But he's a sick man now."

"And there's a sister?"

"Hattie."

"What about her?"

"She's wonderful, Mr. Mason. Just wait until you meet her. As I told you she's a stay-at-home, but she has the most wonderful disposition.

"When the man who was to be my husband showed up and started courting me, Hattie insisted I should go ahead and marry and she'd stay home and take care of the family."

"Your mother was living then?"

"Yes."

"And you did that?"

"Yes, I did. I suppose I was selfish, but I was in love

50

and—well, I did it, and Hattie stayed on, taking care of the folks, running the house.

"She's wonderful—and now she's having her own chance for happiness."

"Tell me about that," Mason said.

"His name is Edison Levering Doyle. You'll meet him. He's clever. I think he's going places. I feel so happy for Hattie—and yet I'm afraid for her."

"Why are you afraid?" Mason asked.

"It's difficult to describe."

"Can you try?"

"Yes, I can try, but I don't want to."

"Go ahead," Mason said. "What is it?"

"Well, I'm afraid Hattie isn't going to be happy with Edison, and I'm afraid it's going to break her heart, but I don't know what I can do about it."

"That isn't what you started to say," Mason told her.

"All right," she said, "I'll put it right on the line with you, Mr. Mason. Perhaps I never saw it clearly before. Perhaps it's because I've been out traveling and meeting people. Perhaps it's something that a sheltered, circum- scribed existence has done to Hattie. I don't know.

"However—oh, I don't know how to tell you—life has a way of doing things to you. You don't realize that the minutes that pass by are shaping your character. You can't—you can't wait things out. Now I'm just making a mess of it. I knew I would."

Mason said, "You mean that Hattie has become some- what drab, colorless, mousy?"

"I didn't say that."

"That's what you mean?"

"It sounds horrible when you say it that way, Mr. Mason, but—and yet I don't know how to tell you *exactly* what I mean. Let's take two girls. Let's suppose that they're absolutely equal and identical, if you could suppose such a thing. One of them makes herself attractive to men. She likes masculine company. She's on the go. Men makes passes at her and she likes it. She wears good clothes, goes to beauty parlors, travels, sees glamorous women, and naturally she has a tendency to become—well, a little glamorous."

"Go on," Mason said.

"Then we'll suppose that the other woman stays home. She doesn't have time to go to a beauty parlor. She doesn't care because no one is going to see her anyway. She does her hair herself. She doesn't go out much to parties. She's constantly waiting on older people. She's constantly associating with them. She—well, after a year or two of that what's going to happen?"

"You mean the stay-at-home girl is going to lose her charm?"

"She isn't going to develop any."

"But you have just told me that Hattie is now going to have her chance with Edison Doyle."

"I *hope* she's going to have her chance, but—well, a man wants a lot of things in a woman. He wants a mate. He wants someone to keep his home. He wants someone to raise his children. He wants a companion. He also wants fun."

"Are you trying to tell me," Mason asked, "that Edison Doyle was happy with Hattie until he began to see more of you, and then lately you felt he was comparing you and Hattie and perhaps becoming a little interested in you?"

"Good heavens, am I *that* obvious?"

"Is that what you're trying to tell me?"

"Well, not exactly, but— Damn it, that's what I was trying *not* to tell you. I don't even know. I can't even . . ."

"It worries you?" Mason asked as her voice trailed away into silence.

"In a way."

"Tell me a little more about yourself. You married, and then what? Were you happy?"

"I married Sam Atwood. We were happy. It was a wonderful life. Then Sam died. It was quite a shock. However, I'm a person who adjusts readily to a new environment.

"Sam left me insurance, stocks, bonds, real estate—

some good investments. I have made a few good investments of my own. I've been lucky."

"How long ago did your husband die?"

"About eighteen months."

"And what have you been doing since?"

"I've been traveling. I had always wanted to travel. After Sam's death there was no reason why I shouldn't."

"You didn't travel before?"

"Not too much. My husband had business interests that kept him pretty well occupied. He couldn't get too far away from those business interests.

"His death was a shock to me. I wanted to get into a new environment, to meet new people, to see new things. I traveled."

"And you learned something from your travels?"

"I suppose so. I think one does. I've been trying to tell you that I think every day of one's life places a stamp on the individual. You select the sort of life you want to live, and living that life in turn leaves its mark, so that you're changing all the time, one way or the other."

"How long have you been back home?"

"About thirty days."

"You came back and found Edison Doyle and Hattie engaged?"

"Not exactly engaged but going together, and I think there's sort of an understanding. Dad's heart is very bad. I suppose he can't last too long. I think Hattie wants to be with him. Dad has grown to a point where he depends on her."

"And when you came back from your travels you saw Hattie through new eyes?"

"Mr. Mason, I was shocked. I didn't realize—it's so hard to explain, so hard to describe, that I'm not even going to try."

"And Edison Doyle, on the other hand, saw in you a glamorous potential sister-in-law. He started out to be nice to you and now you find him perhaps contrasting you and Hattie?"

"I don't know *what's* happening, Mr. Mason. I like Edison. He's a wonderful guy. I think he's taken life a little too seriously. I think he needs to be jolted out of it. He could marry, settle down and become quite a stick-in-the-mud. On the other hand, he could be jarred out of his shell of seriousness and get a broader outlook."

"What does he do?"

"He's an architect."

"You're around home a good deal?"

"I try to be with Dad some. I'd like to take some of the load off Hattie. I'd like to stay with Dad and have her get out. I think she and Edison should go out more. I think she should pay more attention to her clothes, more attention to her personal appearance."

"How does she feel?"

"It's hard to tell how Hattie feels. Of course, Dad's heart is in such shape that he may pass away at any time. It may be rather sudden. I think Hattie wants to be sure that she's with him, that if he ever should call for her she'd be there."

"And you?"

"I don't see things that way, Mr. Mason. Dad may go tomorrow. He may live for years. I've talked with the doctor about it. No one knows. I have my own problems. I have my own apartment. I have my own friends. I have my own life. I try to keep myself well dressed and attractive. I try to be with Dad some. I've repeatedly put pressure on Hattie to hire nurses so that she could get out."

"She doesn't want that?"

"She doesn't want it, and lately she's been just a little— oh, I don't know, sometimes I think she's—well, we don't see things the same way."

"You think perhaps she feels that her boy-friend is becoming attracted by your glamour and is perhaps a little jealous?"

"Good heavens, Mr. Mason, Hattie wouldn't get jealous. She might get hurt but she wouldn't get jealous."

"Well?" Mason asked.

"Well, Mr. Mason, when I'm with Edison I'm not going to sit around with my hands on my lap and look down at my feet. I accepted Edison as a future brother-in-law. I joked with him and laughed. I like life and laughter and—I think you're prying into things that don't necessarily enter into the case, Mr. Mason, or perhaps I'm telling you things that I shouldn't. This discussion is—well, perhaps you're jumping at conclusions. I think you'd better wait until you've seen things for yourself."

"And what about the rest of the family?" Mason asked. "Tell me about the others."

"Jarrett is an archaeologist. He's always around sticking his nose into ruins somewhere. Right at present he's down in Yucatán."

"And his wife?"

"His wife is filthy rich and terribly snooty."

"In other words, she doesn't like you."

"And I don't like her. However, it's been a good match for Jarrett. Because of her money he's been able to go around digging up ruins, looking at old carvings with a magnifying glass."

"I take it he's more like Hattie than like you?"

"He isn't like anyone except Jarrett Bain. He's a character. He'll sit while you're talking and look at you steadily with gray eyes regarding you through spectacles so thick they distort the whole perspective of his face. He won't say a word. He'll sit and listen. Sometimes he's listening to what you say, and when he does he has an uncanny ability to remember everything. Sometimes his mind is two or three thousand miles away and he isn't paying the slightest attention to what you're saying. It's disconcerting because you never know."

"He doesn't contribute to the conversation?"

"He sits and looks."

"Are he and his wife happy?"

"I suppose so. She dominates him but he doesn't realize it. She has the money. She likes to be the wife of an archaeologist. They travel around in various places where they can poke through ruins."

"She likes that?"

"Oh, she goes and pokes and learns a line of patter so she can get the reputation of being very highbrow with people who know nothing about the subject. But she always manages to spend plenty of time in Paris, London, Rome, Cairo, Rio and places like that. While Jarrett is out exploring she'll go some place where she can wait while he's 'establishing headquarters.'

"There, now you know the whole setup, Mr. Mason."

Mason studied her. "If it should transpire that the bank should recover a judgment against your father and be able to show that this oil property is held in trust for the bank, it wouldn't affect Jarrett because he's married money. It wouldn't affect you because you have money. But it would seriously affect Hattie?"

"Well, I suppose so, if you want to put it *that* way, but there's also the family good name. Phoebe can support an archaeologist and loves doing it, but being married to the son of a bank thief is something else. I also have my own reputation to consider."

"And Hattie?"

"It would, of course, mean a great deal to Hattie."

"And Edison?" Mason asked.

"How do you mean?"

"Edison certainly has human intelligence. He must have realized that some day your father is going to die and that Hattie will inherit a very sizable amount of property."

"He isn't that kind."

"I'm not trying to say that he's marrying her because of that, but he must have realized that."

"Oh, I suppose he does."

"And that might make quite a difference to him."

She slowed the car, turned to regard the lawyer. "You *do* have the damnedest way of expressing things," she said.

"I take it," Mason said, abruptly changing the subject, "your brother Jarrett doesn't know anything about this?"

"He does now. I talked with Jarrett last night on the long-distance telephone."

"And told him about this?"

"Yes."

"Why the urgency?"

"Because," she said, "if I'm going to put up money to safeguard the estate, I expect the estate to pay me back. I wanted to be sure that anything I did had the approval of *all* the family."

"He gave his approval?"

"In a limited way," she said, and laughed bitterly.

"What's the limitation?"

"Oh, I guess I'm supposed to be selfish or something. Anyway, he told me to talk it over with Hattie, and that anything Hattie agreed to would be all right with him, but that before any money was actually paid over he wanted to know how much it was and how much of a contribution I was going to expect from him."

"And you told him?"

"Of course," she said caustically. "What he was angling for was for me to tell him to forget it, that I'd advance whatever was required and the estate could reimburse me after Dad died.

"But he was so damned obvious about it that I got mad and told him that I'd expect him to put up a third of whatever we had to pay."

"What did he say to that?"

"He didn't *say* much. That's not his way, but you could almost hear him thinking. Of course, he'd have to go to Phoebe to get the money and in order to do that he'd have to tell her what it was for.

"In a way I can see the thing from his angle. I'm supposed to be the selfish one in the family, but he's just as bad as I am. *He* didn't do anything to help care for the family. He married money and went off photographing ruins and digging into musty old graves.

"If he'd been decent about it, I might have put up the money; as it is he can dig up his own share. I hope he has imagination enough to lie to Phoebe, but I just don't give a damn."

"Well," Mason said, "that seems to give me a pretty fair picture."

She whipped the car savagely around a corner to the right, drove three swift blocks, then braked the car to a stop in front of a somewhat old-fashioned, two and a half story, rambling structure.

"This is it?" Mason asked.

"This is it."

"You've lived here some time?"

"I was born here," she said. "Now the thing is a white elephant, but we love it. Hattie has charge of it. She keeps it running somehow. Now let me tell you something else, Mr. Perry Mason. If you're going to sit there and look at me in that tone of voice, you and I aren't going to get along worth a damn.

"I don't take kindly to having people adopt a holier-than-thou attitude and intimating that I should have stayed home and sacrificed myself for the family, when I have a pair of gams that men notice and get excited over."

"They *do* get excited?" Mason asked.

She flashed him a defiant glance from her green eyes, then stretching her legs out in front of her, put her ankles together, whipped her skirt up as far as the tops of her stockings. "What do you think?" she asked, then added abruptly, "I'm afraid you're bringing out all the hell cat in me, Mr. Perry Mason. Come on, let's go in."

She opened the door and jumped to the sidewalk before Mason had the door on his side opened.

Together they walked up to the big front porch with wooden lattice work ornamenting the eaves in the architectural taste of a bygone generation.

Sylvia opened the front door, called out, "Yoo-hoo, company's coming. Everybody decent? Come on in, Mr. Mason."

She paused for a moment, holding the doorway open, said over her shoulder, half-apologetically, half-defiantly,

"I'm sorry. I'm not usually an exhibitionist, and I'm not usually so nasty. Here's Hattie.

"Hattie, this is Mr. Perry Mason. My sister, Mr. Mason."

Hattie Bain seemed tired. There was a droop to her shoulders, a droop at the corners of her mouth, a worried look about the large, dark eyes set under a high forehead, surmounted by raven-black hair that was swept back in a style of plain severity.

She gave the lawyer her hand.

"I'm *so* glad you're working on this, Mr. Mason," she said. "We can't begin to tell you what a relief it is."

"How's Dad?" Sylvia asked.

"Not too good. He's badly upset. The medicine doesn't seem to be helping him much. Edison's here."

Mason saw Sylvia Atwood's face light up.

A slender, well-knit young man stepped out into the hallway.

"Hearing the sound of my name I thought I'd better flutter my wings," he said, smiling.

He came forward at once toward Mason, hand outstretched.

"This is Edison Doyle, Mr. Mason."

"Mr. Mason," Doyle said, shaking hands cordially, "it certainly is a pleasure to meet you. I've heard a lot about you and have followed many of your cases. I'm sorry that the thing which brings you here today is a potential misfortune for the family, but it's an unexpected honor."

"Glad to meet you," Mason said. "I understand you are an architect."

"Well, I have a license as an architect, and I have an office. I even have a *little* business."

Doyle's grin was good-natured and infectious.

Mason was conscious of the fact that both women were watching him. There was an indulgent something about Sylvia's mouth as though she might be saying to herself, "He really *is* a darling."

Hattie Bain's eyes left no misunderstanding as to her feelings in the matter, although back of the radiant devotion of her expression was something that could have been anxiety.

"Well, come on," Sylvia said to Mason. "Where's Dad, Hattie?"

"Up in his room."

"In bed?"

"No. He gets nervous when he's lying down. The doctor gave him medicine, but Dad's upset and can't seem to get himself under control. I'm terribly glad you could come, Mr. Mason. I think it will mean a lot."

Sylvia said, "Well, come on, let's put this show on the road."

She led the way through a living room, down a corridor.

"Dad had his study and bedroom upstairs," she said over her shoulder, "but after his heart got bad the doctor didn't want him to climb stairs, so we've put him back here on the ground floor."

She paused at a door and knocked.

"Come in," a man's voice called.

Sylvia opened the door, said, "Hello, Dad, how are you?"

She managed to put a note of breezy cordiality into her voice, a cheering confidence that brought an instant response from the white-haired man who was seated in a big reclining chair, propped up with pillows.

"Sylvia! I knew *you'd* be on the job."

"I've been on the job, Dad," she said. "I want you to meet Perry Mason, the famous lawyer."

"Excuse me if I don't get up," Bain said.

Mason strode across and shook hands. "Glad to know you, Mr. Bain."

Ned Bain's voice showed the fatigue brought on by excitement. "This is a real pleasure. I've heard so much about you. I never thought you'd be here. That's one thing about Sylvia, she gets the best—that's what I've always claimed, that it pays to get the best when you want either a doctor or a lawyer."

"Thank you," Mason said. "I'm not going to take up

any of your time or bother you at all, Mr. Bain. We all feel that you should conserve your strength. I just wanted to tell you that I'm working on this situation and I think we're going to be able to clarify it."

"J.J.'s a crook," Bain said. "I used to like him a lot, but he fooled me."

"Don't worry about him. We'll take care of him."

Bain nodded. "I hope you do. I'm terribly worried about this thing. I want to leave my family well provided for. I know that I don't have too long. But I'd much rather they had self-respect than money. If we compromise with that crook it would look as though I'd been a party to that deal. The disgrace would remain long after I was gone. That's too great a price to pay for financial security, Mr. Mason."

Mason nodded.

"Where's Hattie?" Ned Bain asked Sylvia.

"She was right behind us."

Bain said, "I suppose Edison knows all about it?"

"Not through me," Sylvia said.

"Well, I suppose it can't be helped. After all, it is only fair, I suppose, to—"

Hattie Bain bustled into the room, said, "Your office is trying to get you on the telephone, Mr. Mason. They say it's terribly important."

"If you'll excuse me," Mason said, "I'll—"

"There's a phone right here," Bain said, indicating a little stand by the side of his chair. He pressed a button. A sliding shelf moved out, carrying a desk telephone. "This is an extension from the other room."

"Thanks. If it won't bother you I'll take it here," Mason said. "Apparently it's urgent."

He picked up the phone, glanced at Hattie Bain, and she said, "I'll go hang up the other phone, Mr. Mason. Sometimes you don't hear as well when both receivers are off."

Della Street's voice, sharp with excitement, came over the line, "Chief, Paul Drake's man telephoned. Can you find out what J. J. Fritch looks like? Give me a description quick? Paul Drake is waiting here."

Mason turned to Ned Bain. "I'm wondering," he said, "if you can give us a description of J. J. Fritch."

"Certainly," Bain said. "He's a slender man with high cheekbones, a weather-beaten face, deep-set gray eyes, and has a characteristic stoop. He likes to wear broad-brimmed hats, Texas style. He's a little chap."

"How old?"

"Only around fifty-five, but he's stooped."

"What will he weigh?"

"Not over a hundred and thirty."

Mason relayed the description into the telephone, heard Della Street pass it on to Paul Drake.

"Hang on just a minute," Della Street said.

Mason stood holding the telephone.

Mason heard Paul Drake say, "'Pass that on, if you will, Della,'" and then Drake's voice was on the line, "Hello, Perry."

"Hello, Paul."

"I guess we have the answer, Perry."

"What is it?"

"Your friend Brogan just left his apartment house. From your description, the man with him must be J. J. Fritch."

Mason said, "That means he must have gone to Brogan's apartment and—wait a minute, Paul. It probably means that Fritch *has an apartment in the same building, perhaps on the same floor and*—"

"He does," Drake interrupted. "We've checked him. He's living in the apartment right across from Brogan."

"Right across the hall?" Mason asked.

"That's right. Right across the hall."

"Under what name?"

"Under the name of Frank Reedy."

"That means it's regular, orthodox blackmail," Mason said.

"That's all it ever was, just a regular shakedown racket. Brogan is putting up the front and pretending to be highly ethical. He's keeping Fritch in the background."

"Well," Mason said, "that's something. Have you got a tail on them?"

"That's right. I split it up. One of my operatives is trailing Fritch and the other one is following Brogan. Both had an idea as soon as the men walked out that we'd want to know something about the one who was with Brogan because of the Texas hat and the general setup. I had told them there was a Texas angle to the case and to report if anyone looking like a Texan around fifty-five or sixty came to visit Brogan."

"That's good work, Paul. If you need more men put them on the job. We want to find out what's going on."

"Okay, I'm keeping it covered."

"How did they seem, Paul? Could your men tell anything about the expressions?"

"They were both of them grinning, seemed to be enjoying some sort of a joke."

"They probably are," Mason said. "Perhaps the joke will turn out to be on them."

Mason hung up the telephone, grinned reassuringly at Bain's anxious upturned face. "It's all right, Mr. Bain. It's coming along in good shape."

"Can you tell me why you wanted Fritch's description?"

"We've got him located."

A little twitch of excitement stirred Bain's form. "Where?" he asked eagerly. "Where is the two-timing crook?"

"As a matter of fact," Mason said, "he has an apartment right across from the apartment of George Brogan. Fritch is registered under the name of Frank Reedy, and I don't think there's any question but what he has a lot of sound equipment in there so he can dub and duplicate sound recordings.

"What I think happened, Mr. Bain, is that Fritch engaged you in a long conversation dealing with cattle, talking about old times, and things of that sort."

Bain nodded. "I remember the occasion very clearly. We talked for about two hours," he said.

"And," Mason went on, "Fritch and Brogan fixed up a master recording from that conversation. They had that conversation transcribed so that they had everything before them in writing. Then they picked out certain of your answers that they wanted to use. Then Fritch went to a sound studio and asked questions that would fit in with his purpose and to which your answers would seem to be responsive. They had a tape recording of those questions, then with the aid of a crooked sound technician, they started splicing tape, leaving a good part of the conversation just the way it was, but interpolating a question asked by Fritch, tying it in with your answer to some perfectly innocuous question Fritch had asked at the time of the conversation. But, of course, Fritch's original question was cut out of the spool and the sinister question by him was inserted.

"After they'd fixed up this purely synthetic interview, they went ahead and dubbed it on to a tape. Naturally that tape showed no splices and apparently was a genuine recording."

Bain sighed. "I'm not supposed to get angry," he said. "If I do, it may kill me. I can pop out just like that, Mr. Mason."

Bain snapped bony fingers.

"I know," Mason said. "You must take it easy."

"The trouble is it isn't going to do any good for me to take it easy. Now what are they going to do with that recording?"

Mason said, "Frankly I don't think they'll do anything except try to blackmail you. If they *can't* do that they *might* try to make a deal with the bank.

"That's where Brogan enters into the picture. He can go to the bank as a private detective who has been digging around trying to unearth information that would be of value to the bank. He'll suggest to them that if they want to retain him at a fancy price he'll try and get evidence that will enable them to bring a suit against you."

"Of course," Bain said, "you understand, Mr. Mason, that I simply can't afford to have that happen, no matter what the price may be."

"Why not?" Mason asked. "It might be a good plan to air the whole thing in court."

Bain shook his head. "Just filing that suit," he said, "would completely ruin me. It would be picked up by the papers and reported all over the country. Everyone would feel that I had been Fritch's partner in that bank robbery. I simply can't afford to have anything like that happen. That would blacken the name of my family even more than paying those blackmailers something to get rid of them."

"But," Mason said, "you wouldn't ever get rid of them. You can see what's happened. They've got that master recording. They can keep making dubs from it. Brogan assured us that there was only one tape and that was the one we were listening to, but I've now definitely established that the one I was listening to was a copy."

Sylvia said, "Quit worrying about it, Dad. Leave these crooks to Mr. Mason. He'll find a way to fix them. Now you just leave things to him."

"That's what I'm going to do," Bain said. "However, I'd sure like to hear that recording and see if it's my voice."

"It's your voice, Dad," Sylvia Atwood said.

"I think it is," Mason told him. "But I don't think you need to be at all concerned about that. I feel certain we are going to spike their guns. They've secured your voice and then faked questions. I can tell you one thing, Mr. Bain. There isn't anything on that recording that is, in my opinion, at all incriminating. All of the incriminating statements are contained in the questions by J. J. Fritch. Your answers simply are to the effect that you're agreeing with him. I meet Brogan at his apartment at nine tomorrow to hear it again."

Bain's eyelids fluttered. He nodded, then his head

drooped forward, his eyes remained closed. His breathing was slow and regular.

Hattie Bain, who had returned to the room, placed her finger to her lips in a gesture of silence.

Slowly they tiptoed out of the room and closed the door behind them, leaving Ned Bain sleeping in the chair, propped up by pillows.

"The doctor gave him some heart medicine," Hattie said. "Something that's supposed to make it easier on his heart. It relaxes the capillaries. He also gave him some sort of a sedative to keep him quiet because he said Dad was terribly nervous, and the nervousness was having just as bad an effect as an overdose of excitement.

"The trouble was Dad was so worked up he simply couldn't get to sleep. Talking with you has done a lot for him, Mr. Mason. I could see him quieting right while he was talking with you. Couldn't you, Sylvia?"

"Yes, indeed," she said.

"Well," Mason said, "I'll be getting on back to my office. Do you want to join me at nine o'clock tomorrow morning, Mrs. Atwood?"

"Yes, indeed. That's pretty early, however. Suppose I meet you—well, now wait a minute. It's going to be rather difficult for me to drive all the way uptown and then back to Brogan's apartment. Suppose I come directly to Mr. Brogan's apartment? How will that be?"

"That's fine," Mason said. "I'll meet you there."

"At nine o'clock tomorrow morning," she said. "I'll drive you back, Mr. Mason."

"Hey," Edison Doyle said, "you don't need to do that, Sylvia. I'm headed back uptown anyway and I'd certainly like to drive Mr. Mason up to his office. I'd deem it a pleasure."

Sylvia hesitated. "Well, perhaps I *should* stay here with Dad and see what I can do if he wakes up. You won't mind, Mr. Mason?"

"Certainly not," Mason said. "I hope we've been able to reassure your father."

"Oh, I'm satisfied you have," Hattie interposed. "Dad

was, of course, terribly worried. There's something there in the background that we don't know, something that he knows about J.J., something that causes him to fear J.J. I think Fritch must be a very desperate man and Dad must know it."

"Can you imagine him doing anything so utterly reprehensible as ringing up Mr. Bain?" Doyle asked.

Mason said, "That shows that his back is against the wall."

"I'm afraid I don't understand," Hattie said, genuinely perplexed.

"Don't you see," Sylvia explained, "as soon as Mr. Mason entered the picture they felt certain they were going to be defeated, so then J.J. telephoned Dad, trying to frighten him, not caring a thing about the consequences."

"He should be given a damn good thrashing," Edison Doyle said. "I understand you've proven now that he and this private detective are in cahoots."

"They must be," Mason said. "Fritch has an apartment directly across the hall from Brogan. He's going under the name of Frank Reedy. I imagine they're getting hot under the collar."

"Just what can be done?"

"If we can get the evidence," Mason said, "the evidence that I hope I'm going to get, we can have them arrested for conspiracy."

"Dad wouldn't want that," Hattie said quickly. "He wouldn't want any publicity at all."

"Well, come on," Doyle said. "I'll get you back to your office, Mr. Mason. My chariot's outside. It's not the latest or the best, but it gets you there."

Mason said good-by to the others, followed Doyle out and jumped in the five-year-old car as Doyle held the door open for him.

Doyle, getting around behind the wheel, said, "There's one thing I don't understand about the legal aspect of this case, Mr. Mason."

"What's that?" the lawyer asked, as the car eased away from the curb.

"Just how are they going to identify that tape recording?"

"It has to be done by the testimony of J. J. Fritch," Mason said. "In other words, Fritch would get on the stand and swear that he had this conversation and that for his own protection he had made a tape recording."

"And Fritch is a crook?"

"Undoubtedly."

"And a blackmailer?"

"Undoubtedly."

"And if anything happened that Fritch had to skip out and wasn't there to identify that conversation it couldn't be used?"

"That's right," Mason said. "The tape recording would have to be identified. Fritch would have to testify that it was a recording of a genuine conversation that he'd had with Ned Bain."

"And on cross-examination Fritch would have to admit that he'd robbed the bank?"

"As I understand the facts, that's right."

"It would seem to me you could rip him wide open on cross-examination."

"I can," Mason said, "but the point is that the filing of the case would result in a lot of unfavorable publicity. I think that's what's worrying Mr. Bain."

"That's so," Doyle admitted. "I don't suppose Bain is worrying so much for himself. He's thinking about the daughters—a couple of fine girls—and to have that thing hanging over their heads— No, we just can't let that happen, Mr. Mason, no matter what we have to do."

Mason nodded.

"A couple of fine girls like that!" Doyle repeated. "Gosh, you don't find them any better anywhere in the world.

"There's Hattie, she's the most loyal, considerate, self-effacing girl you can imagine. And—well, no one needs a press agent for Sylvia Atwood."

68

Mason smiled and nodded.

"She's a real beauty," Doyle said, "and full of fun and—there's something so alive, so vital about her. You feel like a new man when you're around her.

"I don't mind telling you, Mr. Mason, that I've probably taken life a little too seriously. I've had my nose stuck too close to the drafting board. That's probably a good way to lay the foundation for architectural skill, but it's a darned poor way to start life."

"I think you'll find it'll pay dividends," Mason said.

"Oh, I suppose so, but when you see what happens to people who take life too seriously, and contrast them with a girl like Sylvia—I don't know, Mr. Mason, I think life, like money, was meant to be spent. You can't hoard money and ever get any good out of it. And life was meant to be lived. Somehow—it's hard to express, but I don't think there's anything more perishable than the seconds that are ticked off by the second hand on a watch. You can't save them. You have to spend them. You have to live them."

"It's not quite as simple as that," Mason said. "A person has to prepare himself. You have to lay a foundation for life. The time you spend in study is an investment, as good as money in a bank."

"Yes, I suppose so," Doyle observed, and lapsed into silence.

After a moment Mason said, "I suppose the girls confided in you as soon as this came up?"

"Hattie did," Doyle said. "She's terribly conscientious. She—well, if there was anything that was going to affect the family, any old scandal or anything, she wanted me to know it before—well, before I committed myself."

He laughed nervously.

"I wasn't trying to pry into your private affairs," Mason said.

"No, no, not at all. I'm glad to have an opportunity to explain matters. I'd do anything for those two girls, Mr. Mason, anything."

"For the *two* girls," Mason said.

There was a moment's silence, then Doyle nodded. "That's right, Mr. Mason."

After that he was silent until he had deposited the lawyer in front of his office building and squeezed the attorney's hand in a parting gesture of cordiality.

"It was wonderful meeting you, Mr. Mason, simply wonderful. It's an experience I won't ever forget. Having you in our corner gives one a feeling of complete invincibility."

Mason laughed. "'Don't overestimate me," he said. "I think we're making progress, but that's the most I can say at the moment."

6

∎

It was almost eight-fifty the next morning when Mason parked his car in front of the apartment house. Della Street opened the door on her side, jumped to the sidewalk.

"You want me to go up with you?" she asked, as Mason walked around the car to join her.

Mason nodded.

"And just what am I supposed to do?"

"Keep your eyes and ears open," Mason said.

"How are you going to explain to Mr. Brogan the fact that I'm with you?"

Mason said, "We don't have to explain anything to Brogan. From now on he's going to be on the defensive."

"I take it I'm to be a witness?"

"That's right."

"But you have Sylvia Atwood."

"That's right. I want a witness I can depend on."

"You don't think you can depend on her?"

"I don't know," Mason said. "Come on, let's go up. I see that Sylvia is already here. That's her car parked up ahead."

Della looked at her wrist watch. "She's early."

"Not too early. It'll take us two or three minutes to get up in the elevator. Come on, let's go."

They entered the apartment house, took the elevator, walked down the corridor. Della Street, who was a step in advance, said, "There's a note here, Chief. It's addressed to you."

Mason looked over her shoulder.

An envelope had been fastened to the door with a thumbtack. The envelope was addressed simply in red crayon, "Mr. Perry Mason."

Della glanced back over her shoulder and the lawyer nodded.

She pulled out the thumbtack, opened the unsealed envelope, pulled out the note. She held it so they could both read it.

It was scrawled in pencil.

Mr. Mason:

Occasionally I indulge in a poker game with some of the boys. It happens tonight is the night. We're starting early, about ten o'clock I understand, and I'm hoping to be finished in ample time to keep our appointment. If, however, I should be a few minutes late please go on in and make yourself at home. I'm leaving the apartment unlocked so you can go on in and wait. I promise you that if I'm not there promptly at nine I won't be over ten minutes late.

George Brogan

Mason regarded the note thoughtfully, then he carefully folded it, put it back in the envelope, used his cigarette lighter to look for the exact hole which had been made by the thumbtack.

"You're suspicious?" Della Street asked.

"It's a trap," Mason said. "I want to get this back in

the original hole made by the thumbtack so no one can prove we've read it. We—oh-oh."

"What is it?" Della Street asked.

"Two holes here," Mason said. "Someone else has taken it off, read it and put it back, but didn't realize the necessity for putting it back in the original hole."

"So what do we do?"

"Well," Mason said, "we don't make a third hole, that's certain. We put it back but—I guess Brogan was smart enough to know I might do just that, so he made two thumbtack holes so I couldn't say I hadn't read it. And since he's gone to that trouble and I'm trapped, I may as well put the note in my pocket."

Mason viciously jabbed the thumbtack into the panel of the door, put the envelope and note in his pocket.

"And we go in?" Della Street asked.

Mason shook his head.

"Why not?"

"I tell you it's a trap. He wants us to go in and search the apartment. He's too damned anxious."

"Why?"

"Nothing for our good," Mason said. "Whatever reason will be for his good."

"Such as what? What could he possibly gain by—?"

Mason said, "Suppose we go in the apartment and find someone has smashed open the safe?"

"So we wait right here?"

"I don't know," Mason said. "Having left the apartment unlocked, he can always claim we went in and—we'll be waiting right here when he comes, and we'll tell him just what we think of his traps and—wait a minute, Sylvia's up here somewhere. She—"

He broke off as a jarring thud from the interior of the apartment shook the floor under them.

"What was that?" Della Street asked, startled.

"I don't know," Mason said. "It sounded as if someone had been—"

He broke off as a woman's terrified scream came from the interior of the apartment.

Della Street instinctively raised a gloved hand to the doorknob, started to turn it.

Mason slapped her hand away.

"Chief, someone's in trouble in there. Someone's screaming."

Mason nodded.

"But, Chief, we can't leave that person in danger. That was a scream of terror. That—"

The door was abruptly jerked open from the inside. A woman's hurrying figure started to dash out into the corridor, then straightened in a rigidity of dismay as she saw Mason and Della Street standing on the threshold.

"Well, Mrs. Atwood," Mason said calmly, "you seem to have gone exploring."

"Oh it's you!" she exclaimed. "Thank heavens. Oh, quick. Good Lord—"

"What is it?" Mason asked.

"J. J. Fritch. He's been killed."

"How do you know?"

"His body was in the liquor closet. It toppled out on its face."

Mason jerked a handkerchief from his pocket, held it over the palm of his hand, grabbed the knob of the door, pulled the door shut. He said to Sylvia Atwood, "You're wearing gloves. Did you have them off when you were in there?"

She shook her head. Her face had gone white under the make-up, causing the rouge to flare into bizarre prominence even there in the dim light of the hall. "I had my gloves on all the time."

"It was Fritch?" Mason asked.

She nodded.

"You're sure he was dead?"

"Good heavens, yes. He toppled forward—"

"How's he dressed?"

"He isn't dressed."

"Naked?"

"He has on underwear. A sleeveless undershirt and shorts."

73

"No socks?"

She shook her head.

"No shoes?"

Again she shook her head.

Della Street looked at Mason anxiously. "Shouldn't we—?"

Mason shook his head. "This is a trap. We've walked into it. Let's try to get out of it."

Still with the handkerchief over his palm, he gently tried the door of the apartment directly behind them and across the hall from the door of Brogan's apartment.

The knob turned smoothly. The apartment door opened.

Mason turned back to the two young women.

"Listen," he said, "I want you to get this and get it straight. Brogan will show up any minute now. He'll be all flustered and in a hurry, claiming that he was detained in a poker game. I want you to tell him that I am downstairs parking the car. His natural inference will be that we all three came together, that I stopped in front of the apartment house to let you two girls out, that I then cruised around to find a parking place for the car, that I'll be up immediately."

"Won't he question us on details?" Della Street asked.

"I'll show up before he gets a chance to question you," Mason said, "provided you do *just* as I say.

"Della, here's the note that was on the door. Be holding that in your hand. Have the paper open as though you had just read it. That will give you an excuse to know that the door is open and unlocked."

She nodded.

"As soon as you have told him that I'm parking the car," Mason said, "turn the knob and walk in just casually and naturally, saying you were about to do so anyway because you'd read the note addressed to me, that I'll be right up."

Della Street nodded.

"Now then," Mason said to Sylvia Atwood, "while that

74

is taking place you'll have an opportunity to step into the background. Don't turn so that you face this apartment, but put your hand behind your back, grope until you find the bell on this apartment. Ring it twice. Two short, quick rings. Then follow Della and George Brogan into the apartment. Manipulate it so you'll be the last one in—"

"Won't Brogan stand to one side for us two to enter first and—"

"See that he doesn't. Brogan is a crook and a black-mailer. He never was a gentleman. He isn't too concerned with the niceties of etiquette."

"And what will you do?"

Mason said, "There's one chance in a hundred I may have that master spool of tape before Brogan turns up. I'll hear your signal. I'll give you just about three seconds to get through the door, after I hear the two rings, then I'll slip out into the corridor, close this door behind me and ring Brogan's bell, or I *may* be able to get here just as you're closing the door and come on in. In that way Brogan can't prove where I've been. Perhaps he'll think I really was parking the car. Now, have you folks got that straight?"

"I have," Della Street said.

Sylvia Atwood said, "I don't understand just how—"

"You don't have to," Della said briskly. "I'll tell you what to do. Do exactly what Mr. Mason says. Go ahead, Chief."

Mason slipped open the door of Fritch's apartment, which had been rented under the name of Frank Reedy, and closed the door behind him.

The drapes were drawn across the windows. The lights were on. In a corner of the room a television set was flickering a commercial.

Mason slipped through the living room, entered a bed-room.

Here again drapes were drawn across the windows. The bed was freshly made and apparently had not been slept in. A dressing gown was thrown across a chair by the bedside. There were also bedroom slippers neatly arranged under the chair.

Mason looked in the bathroom. It was entirely in order, but here again an electric light was on and a shade was pulled.

Mason retraced his steps, pushed open a door into the kitchenette.

Immediately he sensed a peculiar situation. Every shelf was loaded to the brim with canned goods. Mason opened the icebox. It was filled with food. At one end of the kitchen a deep-freeze unit had been installed, a huge affair some seven feet in length.

Mason opened the lid and whistled in surprise. It was jammed to the brim with frozen foods, meat wrapped in packages and labeled, ice cream, frozen strawberries, frozen cherries, package after package of frozen vegetables, packages of biscuit dough which needed only to be put in the oven and baked, pound after pound of butter, several pies and cakes.

Mason lowered the lid, snapped the latch into place.

Apparently J. J. Fritch had been prepared for a siege. He had been in a position to close the door of his apartment and completely retire from the world. There would have been no necessity for him to go out. He could have remained in hiding for weeks or months as the occasion might require.

Mason left the kitchen, returned to the living room, opened the door of a huge closet.

It was well filled with clothing, shoes and sound recording equipment.

Mason tried the closets in the bedroom, being careful whenever he touched anything to have a handkerchief over his hand.

The bedroom closet held a conventional array of men's clothing.

Mason was just about to try a dresser drawer when the bell of the apartment gave two quick, sharp rings.

Mason dashed to the door leading to the hallway, stood there and listened.

He heard feminine voices, heard the booming of a masculine voice. He waited about three seconds, then eased the door open.

The door of the apartment across the way was just closing. Sylvia Atwood was standing in the doorway, gently pushing it shut.

Mason jumped into the corridor, pulled the door of Fritch's apartment shut behind him, pushed on the door of the Brogan apartment, said to Sylvia Atwood, "Well, I guess I'm not late after all."

George Brogan grinned at Mason, walked on across to the windows, pulled back the drapes letting in morning sunlight.

Brogan was a disreputable-looking spectacle. His face had a shadow of dark stubble. The collar of his shirt was wilted down in front where his perspiring chin had been resting against the top of the collar. The skin of his face had that peculiar oily appearance which in some men is an indication of a sleepless night. His eyes were weary and a little bloodshot. There was an odor of alcohol on his breath.

"I'm sorry," he said. "Did you get my note, Mason?"

Mason looked blank.

Della Street said, "Here it is, Chief. It was on the door," and handed Mason the note.

Brogan looked inquiringly at Della Street.

"Miss Street, my confidential secretary," Mason said. "I brought her with me this morning. She came up ahead of me."

"Oh," Brogan said, and then, bowing, muttered the conventional formula of pleasure at making her acquaintance, but his eyes, anxious and furtive, rested apprehensively on Mason's face as Mason read the note.

Brogan waited until he was certain Mason had finished reading, then said, "I'm terribly sorry, Mason. I like to be right on the dot. When I make an appointment I like to keep it, but—well, as you can see, I didn't even stop to get a shave. I dashed up here, stopped long enough to just gulp down a cup of coffee and a couple of eggs. I was getting a terrific headache and wouldn't have been good for anything without some coffee. As it is, I'm only—" he looked at his wrist watch—"five minutes late.

"You know how it is, Mason. I intended to get away from the game early, but I started losing pretty heavily and got mad and began plunging. Then I began to recuperate. Got my losses back and a little more to boot, and—well, when a man gets in that position he keeps thinking—well, just one hand more. And, of course, the others are sore that you're winning. They want an opportunity to get it back. They don't want to see you get up and take their money out of the game.

"So I kept postponing my departure for one hand at a time until finally I just had time enough to make a dash for it. I'm terribly sorry. Won't you folks sit down. I trust you young women will pardon my appearance.

"Now I know what you're thinking, Mason. I know you're thinking that the fault wasn't with that machine yesterday, but that something had gone wrong and the recording had been erased. I'm going to play that tape for you once more so you'll see that nothing has happened to it. First, if you'll pardon me, I'll put on some strong black coffee in the kitchen. I've been up all night and I—"

Brogan started for the kitchen.

Sylvia Atwood flashed Mason a warning glance.

Brogan stepped through the door, then suddenly stopped and stood rigid.

"What's the matter?" Mason asked after a moment.

Brogan slowly turned, closed the door behind him, came to stand directly in front of Mason. His eyes were cold, hard and accusing.

"What the hell's the idea, Mason?" he asked.

"What are you talking about?" Mason asked.

Brogan said, "I left that note on the door before I went out. The apartment was open all night. You came here early. You got that note. You—I think under the circumstances this is the thing to do."

Brogan walked over to the telephone, jerked up the

receiver, dialed Operator and said, "Get me police head-quarters quick. There's been a murder and I'm holding three people here. One of them is probably the murderer."

7

SERGEANT HOLCOMB of Homicide could, when he chose and without apparent effort, be exceedingly nasty, sarcastic and disagreeable.

This time he was in rare form.

"I tell you," Mason said angrily, "I can't wait around here all day. I've been here two hours now."

Sergeant Holcomb, who had commandeered the manager's apartment and was holding all witnesses incommunicado, had taken his time about sending for Perry Mason. Now his eyes glittered ominously.

"Don't pull that line with me," he said. "It's overworked. You've done it too much. You've discovered too many corpses."

"I didn't discover this corpse," Mason said.

"That's what you say."

"Does anyone say I did?"

"*I'm* asking the questions."

"Go on and ask them then."

"Did you know J. J. Fritch in his lifetime?"

"I never met the man that I know of."

"What do you know about the manner in which his body was discovered?"

"George Brogan started out for the kitchen to put on some coffee, stopped, turned around and called the police."

"What were you doing here?"

"I had an appointment with Brogan."

"About what?"

"A matter of business."

"Tell me about it."

Mason shook his head.

"Why not?"

"It's confidential."

"Nothing's confidential in a murder case."

"That's where you and I have a difference of opinion. We've had them before and I dare say we'll have them again."

"I understand you told Brogan you were deaf and had to wear a hearing aid."

"Wrong again."

"You were wearing a hearing aid."

"No. That's a pocket-size wire recorder. The microphone is held against my temple. If Brogan thought it was a hearing aid that was his mistake."

"Let's see it."

"There's nothing on it now. I hadn't switched it on today. I was waiting until my conversation with George Brogan—"

"Let's see it."

Mason took the device from his pocket, passed it over.

Sergeant Holcomb examined it for a few minutes, then opened his brief case and dropped it in. "You'll get this back after it's been examined. I'm not taking your word for anything."

"There's nothing on it today."

"What was on it yesterday?"

"That's my business, or rather my client's business."

"I can find out," Holcomb threatened.

"Then do so, by all means."

"Brogan tells me he left a note on the door for you."

Mason nodded.

"Your secretary, Della Street, had the note in her possession."

"What did *she* tell you?" Mason asked.

Holcomb merely grinned and said, "I'm asking *you* the questions now."

"Very well," Mason said, tightening his lips, his face granite hard. "Go ahead and ask them."

"And remember you're an attorney at law, an officer of the court," Holcomb went on. "Don't think you can get smart and arbitrarily withhold information."

Mason said, "I am sworn by my oath of office to protect my clients. I am going to protect them to the best of my ability. Don't think you can use your authority to browbeat information out of me that I don't think it's proper to give."

"Did your client murder J. J. Fritch?" Holcomb asked sneeringly.

"How the hell do I know," Mason said.

"How's that?" Holcomb asked in surprise.

"I said I wouldn't know."

"Why?" Holcomb asked, his eyes narrowing. "What makes you suspicious?"

"I'm not suspicious."

"Well, your statement implies there's a possibility a client of yours murdered Fritch."

"Certainly there's a possibility."

"You don't know?"

"I don't know."

"Why?"

"For one thing I haven't been permitted to talk with my client. I haven't been permitted to talk with anyone."

"Do you think I'm dumb enough to leave all the witnesses together so they can fix up a story that will account for all of the facts and leave me holding the sack? I wasn't born yesterday."

"Do you think I'm dumb enough to give you information that may betray the interests of a client before I've talked with my client?" Mason retorted.

Holcomb's face darkened. "You'll either give me the information or you'll wish you had."

"Go ahead, ask your questions."

"What were you doing here?"

"I had an appointment."

"With whom?"

"George Brogan."

"When?"

"Nine o'clock."

"What time did you get here?"

"I didn't look at my watch."

"Brogan left a note on the door."

"So I understand."

"Your secretary says she read it."

"Thank you."

"For what?"

"For telling me what my secretary said."

"I'm not telling you all she said."

"Then I'll withdraw my thanks."

"This isn't going to get you anywhere."

"It isn't going to get *you* anywhere."

"When did you first know Fritch had been murdered?"

"I still don't know he's been murdered."

"I told you so."

"I heard you."

"You mean you're not going to take my word?"

"I didn't say that."

"You intimated it."

Mason shrugged his shoulders and lit a cigarette.

"When did you last see J. J. Fritch alive?"

"I haven't seen him alive."

"When did you first see his body?"

"I haven't seen his body."

"What are your relations with Mrs. Sylvia Atwood?"

"She's my client."

"When did she get here?"

"I don't know."

"By here I mean to Brogan's apartment."

"I don't know."

"When did she tell you she got here?"

"I haven't had an opportunity to question her."

"That isn't what I asked you."

"That's what I told you."

"When did she tell you she got to the Brogan apartment?"

"I haven't had an opportunity to question her."

"I'm asking you for a certain specific piece of information."

"I'm giving you a certain specific piece of information."

"When did your secretary get here?"

"I haven't had an opportunity to talk with her."

"She came with you, didn't she?"

"I haven't had an opportunity to question her."

"She isn't your client, she's your secretary."

"How do I know she isn't my client? How do I know what you're going to do? You're crazy enough to charge her with first-degree murder."

"By God, Mason," Holcomb said, jumping to his feet, "I've got nerve enough to charge *you* with first-degree murder, and don't think I haven't.'"

"That's a threat?"

"You're damn right," Holcomb shouted, "that's a threat. I'll do it."

"Very well," Mason said, "in view of the statement you have just made I refuse to make any more statements until I have an opportunity to consult with counsel."

"With counsel?" Holcomb yelled. "You're a lawyer, and a damn good one, even if I hate to admit it."

"A lawyer," Mason said, "should never be his own client. If I'm going to be charged with murder I must have the advice of counsel."

"Well, how do I know whether you're going to be charged with murder or not?"

"You said you were going to."

"I said I could."

"You said you would."

"Well, I will if I think the facts warrant it."

"Do the facts warrant it?"

"Hell, I don't know."

"Then," Mason said, "I don't know whether I care to

make any statement. I've told you that I had an appointment with Brogan for nine o'clock, that I came here to keep that appointment. I might have been a few minutes early. I might have been a few minutes late. I just don't recall looking at my watch. I don't even know if my watch is right. I understand Brogan left a note on the door telling me to go on in and sit down. I was delayed in getting to the apartment. As I entered the apartment I saw that my secretary, Della Street, had gone on in, that Brogan was following her, and that Sylvia Atwood was following Brogan. I was there in time to bring up the rear of the procession and close the door of the apartment behind us.

"Almost immediately Brogan explained that he had been engaged in an all-night poker game and had only stopped to grab a cup of coffee and a couple of eggs, that he felt pretty rocky, that he was sorry to be a few minutes late. I didn't look at my watch to check his statement, but I assumed from what he said that it was then a few minutes after nine o'clock."

"Then you yourself were late getting there," Holcomb charged.

Mason said nothing.

"Did you go directly up to Brogan's apartment when you left your car?"

"When I left my car?"

"Yes."

"Yes."

Holcomb frowned. "There's something funny about this, something that doesn't dovetail."

Mason shrugged his shoulders.

"You went directly to the Brogan apartment?"

"To the outer door, yes. Where did you expect me to go?"

Holcomb said, "You had to find a parking place for your car. The women went up first."

Mason yawned.

"Didn't they?" Holcomb asked.

Mason smiled. "I've made my statement, Sergeant Holcomb. In view of the fact that you have announced that you intend to file a first-degree murder charge against me I do not intend to make any further statement except in the presence of an attorney. I think my statement covers the ground sufficiently so that no important item of information that would assist in any way in carrying out your investigations has been withheld from you. I do not propose to tell you anything that might be considered the betrayal of a professional confidence."

"You can't tell us the nature of your business with Brogan?"

"I won't tell you."

"You can't tell us whether Mrs. Atwood was your client?"

"I can."

"Was she?"

"Yes."

"What were you doing for her?"

"Attending to a business matter."

"What sort of a business matter?"

Mason shrugged his shoulders.

"Brogan tells us it had to do with a tape recording."

"Does he indeed?"

"He says he's looked for that tape recording and can't find it. He thinks you must have taken it."

"Indeed."

"Did you take a tape recording out of Brogan's apartment?"

"No."

"Did you know J. J. Fritch had the apartment across the hall under the name of Frank Reedy?"

"You mean he had the apartment directly across from George Brogan?" Mason asked, surprise in his voice.

"Yes."

Mason raised his eyebrows and whistled.

"Evidently you didn't know it then."

Mason said nothing.

"Well," Holcomb said, "go on and talk."

"I've talked."

"You haven't answered my questions."

"I don't intend to answer all of your questions. I have to draw the line."

"Well, tell me where you draw it," Holcomb said. "Let's get it straight for the record."

Mason said, "I draw a very sharp line of demarcation, Sergeant Holcomb. Your questions resolve themselves into two main categories."

"All right," Holcomb said, "what are they?"

"The questions that I choose to answer and the questions that I choose not to answer. The one classification I am quite willing to answer, the other I am not."

Holcomb's face reddened. "That's a hell of an attitude for an attorney at law to take."

"Isn't it?" Mason said, smiling. "What attitude would you suggest, Sergeant?"

"I'd suggest that you answer questions or you may find yourself in a hell of a predicament."

"You've already outlined that to me. You have even gone so far as to specify the predicament," Mason said, "that is, that I will be charged with first-degree murder. Now then, Sergeant, I feel that I have granted you every consideration and every courtesy. I have been kept waiting here while other witnesses have been interrogated. I think your ruling that no one could leave the apartment house is completely, utterly asinine. I am an attorney at law. I have an office here in the city. I can be found there whenever you want me. Now I'm going to get up and walk right out of here."

"That's what you think."

"I repeat," Mason said, "I am going to get up and walk right out of here unless I am forcibly restrained. If I am forcibly restrained it will only be because I am under arrest. If I am under arrest I want a charge to be preferred and then I want an opportunity to secure bail."

"You don't get bail for first-degree murder."

"That's fine. Then accuse me of first-degree murder."

"I'm not ready to."

"In that case," Mason said, "I'm walking right out of

here, Sergeant. When you get ready to charge me, you know where to find me."

Mason got up and started for the door.

"Sit down," Holcomb shouted. "I'm not done with you."

"I'm done with you," Mason said and opened the door of the apartment.

"Hold him," Holcomb shouted.

A uniformed officer grabbed Mason by the arms.

"Bring him back," Holcomb said.

Mason said, "If you want to charge me with first-degree murder, Sergeant Holcomb, I'm here ready to be charged. If you want to put me under arrest, take me to headquarters. If you forcibly restrain me without putting me under arrest, or if you arrest me without charging me with a crime, I'm going to sue you for false arrest and for assault. Now make up your mind which you want."

The officer dropped his hands to his sides, looked perplexedly at Sergeant Holcomb.

"Hold him," Holcomb said. "He can't pull that stuff."

"Are you charging me with anything?" Mason asked.

"I'll tell you one thing," Holcomb blazed. "Your story doesn't check with the other stories I've heard. *I* think you were in Brogan's apartment and then backed out again."

"I've told you repeatedly," Mason said, "that I had just entered Brogan's apartment on the heels of Brogan and the two young women."

"For the *first* time?"

"For the first time today. I was here yesterday."

"I think you're lying."

"Go to hell," Mason said and started for the door. "You'll either charge me or let me go. I won't tell you another thing."

The officer took a step after him.

Sergeant Holcomb abruptly changed his mind. He said wearily, "Oh, let him go," and sank back into his chair.

8

■

PAUL DRAKE slid into his favorite position in the big overstuffed leather chair in Mason's office. His body was crossways in the chair, the knees were draped over one rounded arm, the other was supporting the small of his back.

The detective raised his long arms, clasped his fingers back of his head, crossed his ankles.

"Go ahead," Mason said. "Give us the low-down, Paul."

"J. J. Fritch was killed by repeated stabs with an ice pick," Drake said. "There was very little external bleeding. Quite an intensive internal hemorrhage because two of the stabs penetrated the heart."

"How many wounds in all?"

"Eight."

"Someone wanted to make a good job of it."

"Apparently. Of course, with a small weapon like an ice pick—"

"Did they recover the ice pick?"

"Not yet."

"Was there an old-fashioned icebox in Brogan's apartment?"

"No, there wasn't. Brogan used an electric icebox and had ice cubes for his drinks. So did Fritch. Police aren't absolutely certain the weapon was an ice pick, but they think it was."

Mason's eyes narrowed.

"I'll tell you something else that hasn't occurred to the police—as yet," Drake went on.

"What?"

"The Bain household has an electric icebox, but it also

has an old-fashioned ice chest on the back porch. Ned Bain sometimes has to have ice packs. They use about fifty pounds a day."

"Holcomb hasn't been out to the Bains' yet?"

"No."

"Della's out there now," Mason said.

"Perhaps she'd better look for the ice pick," Paul said.

Mason was silent for a few minutes.

"When was the murder committed, Paul?"

"Apparently between midnight and three o'clock in the morning, some time in there. The autopsy surgeon says he's positive it wasn't before midnight and he's positive it wasn't after three in the morning. That's the best he can do."

Mason's eyes narrowed thoughtfully.

"Where were you last night between midnight and three o'clock this morning, Perry?"

"In bed."

"That's what comes of being a bachelor. You should get married. As it is, you haven't any alibi. You only have your unsupported word."

Mason said, "The apartment house has a man on duty at the desk twenty-four hours a day."

"Would he have seen you if you went out?"

"I assume so."

"And when you came back?"

Mason nodded.

"He's probably being interrogated."

"You mean they're serious in thinking that *I* killed the man?" Mason asked incredulously.

"Well," Drake said, "here's the dope. Brogan has a perfect alibi."

"How perfect? It's going to have to be completely ironclad before I'll believe it. The whole thing looks too much like a setup to suit me. That poker game was *too* opportune. I think Brogan killed him."

Drake shook his head. "I tell you he has an alibi. He started playing poker at ten o'clock at night. He didn't

leave until five o'clock in the morning. He had been losing
heavily. At five o'clock he had to go out and raise some
money. He was gone about half or three-quarters of an
hour, came back, got in the game, and about eight o'clock
kept trying to make a breakaway, claiming that he had an
appointment on a very important business matter at nine
o'clock, that he had to get shaved and had to change his
shirt."

"When did he leave?"

"No one knows exactly, but it was somewhere around
eight-thirty. He went and had breakfast and got up to the
apartment just as Della Street and Sylvia Atwood were
standing there. What did Della tell them, Perry?"

"Nothing," Mason said. "She adopted the position that
she was my secretary, that under the law any information
she might have affecting the rights of a client was confidential, that because she didn't know all of the details of
the business I was transacting there, she might inadver-
tently disclose something that would be inimical to the
best interests of the client I was representing, and which
would in the nature of things be confidential. Therefore,
she refused to make *any* statements whatever."

"Good girl," Drake said. "I understand Holcomb really
gave her a going-over."

"Apparently he did. He tried everything under the sun.
Della simply sat and smiled at him and told him that if
she could first talk with me she'd be very glad to then
disclose any information she had which was not confidential, but until she could talk with me she didn't know what
information was confidential, and therefore she would tell
him nothing except that she got up in the morning,
dressed and waited for me to pick her up, that I picked
her up at the appointed time. She won't even tell them
what time that was."

Drake nodded. "What about Sylvia Atwood?"

"Sylvia Atwood," Mason said, "was the first one questioned. She told her story and Holcomb let her go. I got
her on the phone and told her I wanted to see her, but she
hasn't come in as yet."

"Did you interview her over the telephone?"

"Only generally. Della's checking exactly what was said."

"I assume you asked Sylvia what she told Holcomb?"

Mason nodded.

"What did she tell you?"

Mason said, "She gave me the story she'd given Brogan, that she came up to the apartment, that she found Della Street at the door reading a note, that the note said Brogan might be detained, that the door was open and we were to go in. Della Street didn't want to go in but Sylvia Atwood said, 'Why not?' "

"You weren't there at the time?"

"She said that I was parking the car," Mason went on, "and was coming up later. Brogan arrived while she and Della were talking things over, and I was following right on Brogan's heels. She didn't notice the time in particular."

Drake said, "The officers found someone who has an apartment on the same floor that swears a woman screamed in one of the apartments a little before nine o'clock. The witness thinks the scream came from the Brogan apartment. The tenants in the apartment below heard a heavy thud in Brogan's apartment and the sound of a woman screaming. That was shortly *before* nine o'clock. They fix the time because they were waiting for a nine o'clock radio program.

"A witness in a ground floor apartment saw Mrs. Atwood trying to park her car and having the devil of a time getting it backed into a small parking space between two cars. Then the owner of the car that was parked behind the place she was trying to get in came out, saw her predicament, spoke to her, telling her he was pulling out.

"He pulled out and Mrs. Atwood backed in. The witness says the time was eight-thirty."

"Eight-thirty!" Mason exclaimed.

"That's right, eight-thirty."

"What about the man who drove out and gave her a chance to park?"

"He thinks it was about eight-forty. He drove uptown and reached his office at five of nine. It's a good fifteen minute drive at that hour."

Mason thought that over.

"Now then," Drake went on, "it looks as though your friend Brogan really came clean with the police."

"What do you mean?"

"He told them the exact nature of your business with him."

"The hell he did," Mason said.

"That's right. They asked him and he had no alternative but to tell them. At least that's the line he handed them."

"What did he tell them?"

"Told them that Fritch had a tape recording that contained evidence in a case that might be filed against Ned Bain, that you were negotiating to buy that evidence."

Mason's face darkened.

"Brogan said that something went wrong with the dictating machine when he was playing the record for you yesterday, that you had insisted on a replay of the tape in order to be certain that Brogan could deliver the merchandise if your client could pay the price, that Brogan told you it was only something wrong with the machine, that actually you had managed to slip one over on him, that you had gummed up the works in some way.

"Brogan told Holcomb that he's satisfied you managed in some way to polarize the recording tape so that anything that was on it completely disappeared. He thinks that you listened to the tape once in order to find out what was on it, then worked your hocus-pocus so that the tape went blank.

"He told Holcomb that he reported all this to Fritch, that Fritch at first seemed very much concerned and then said that it would be all right, that Brogan should make an appointment for nine o'clock in the morning, that some time during the night Fritch would dig up a duplicate original of the tape recording."

"How?" Mason asked.

"Brogan claimed he didn't know."

"Innocent, isn't he?"

"Of course, Brogan is trying to claim that it wasn't blackmail. He also says that this is the first he knew that the tape recording he had wasn't the original tape recording, that he now realizes, of course, that it must have been a dubbed copy and Fritch was holding some sort of an original spool of tape."

"Have they found that spool?"

"They've torn Fritch's apartment to pieces. They can't find a damn thing. They can find lots of blank tape and quite a few machines for playing and recording, but that's all."

Mason frowned. "Then if Fritch had a master spool some place, it's disappeared."

"It's disappeared. Is *your* nose clean in this thing, Perry?"

Mason grinned.

"I'm simply telling you," Drake said, "not because I want to pry into your business, but because I think they've got something on you."

"I'm playing them close to my chest," Mason admitted.

"Well, keep playing them close to your chest, Perry. Don't, for heaven's sake, make any statement that is contrary to fact because I think Holcomb has laid a trap and I'm afraid you've already walked into it."

"Then I'll have to walk right out again."

"It may not be that simple. Is Della in the clear?"

"I think so. I told her to go out to the Bain place. I want to find out about things out there before Sergeant Holcomb starts sweating the family."

"Well," Drake said, "you may have something there. Holcomb isn't working on that angle at the moment. He seems to be getting some dope on you. Right at the moment he's giving Brogan the works."

"He should," Mason said dryly.

"He's doing that all right, and Brogan is sweating blood. And, of course, they're going through the Fritch apartment, the one he rented under the name of Reedy. Did you know that the guy was all prepared for a regular siege? He could hole up in that apartment and just never go out."

Mason raised his eyebrows.

"He had enough food in there to last him for a year," Drake went on. "Frozen food that would keep him living like a king. He had everything for a balanced diet. Meat, potatoes, fruits, vegetables, ice cream, frozen biscuits, flour, bacon, eggs, butter. In short, everything a guy could possibly want. Now here's something, Perry. I can't get the low-down on it, but the police have been finding fingerprints out there in Brogan's apartment. They're not Fritch's fingerprints. They're not Brogan's fingerprints. Someone has been in there and has been going through things."

"The deuce," Mason said.

Drake looked at him sharply. "You wouldn't have been dumb enough to have left any fingerprints, would you, Perry?"

"I tell you I didn't go in there," Mason said. "I *was* in there yesterday, however."

"Of course, the prints may have been made yesterday," Drake said. "But they *could* have been made when the murder was committed."

Mason frowned thoughtfully.

Abruptly his telephone shrilled, breaking the silence.

Mason grabbed for the phone. "Excuse me, Paul. That's the unlisted number. Only you and Della Street have that. Hello."

Mason heard Della Street's voice, sharp-edged with excitement.

"Chief, you'd better jump in your car and get out here just as fast as you can."

"Where?"

"The Bains'."

94

"What's happened?"

"Ned Bain."

"What about him?"

"Dead," she said, "and there are some things I think you should know about before Sergeant Holcomb gets here."

"Good Lord," Mason said, "it isn't a case for Holcomb, is it?"

"No. It's a natural death—in a way," Della Street told him, "but his death *could* have been tied in—in a way."

Mason said, "I'll be right out. Wait for me."

He slammed down the telephone, said to Drake, "Don't get more than two feet away from a phone, Paul. I may need something in a hurry. I'm on my way."

"Where?"

"Bains'."

"Is there another corpse out there?"

Mason nodded. "This one is a natural death."

"Try telling that to Holcomb."

"I'm going to try telling nothing to Holcomb. Find out everything you can about Fritch and Brogan. Put as many men on the job as you have to. Get busy. I'm on my way."

Mason grabbed his hat, dashed out through the exit door of his private office, sprinted for the elevator, jabbed at the down button, and when he had entered the cage said to the operator, "Can you shoot it all the way down? This is an emergency."

"Yes, Mr. Mason," the girl said, and threw the control over, dropping the cage to the ground floor. Two or three other passengers looked at Mason curiously as the lawyer dashed into the lobby and made a run for the parking lot where he kept his car.

Fifteen minutes later Mason was running up the cement walk to the old-fashioned, gingerbread-studded porch of the Bain house.

Della Street, who had been waiting for him, opened the door and said, "Come on in, Chief. The doctor's here."

"What doctor is it, Della?"

"Dr. Flasher. He's the one who had been treating Mr. Bain. Here he is now."

Sylvia Atwood showed up with a tall, tired-looking man in his middle fifties, who peered at Mason from under bushy eyebrows. Suddenly his face lit up. "Well, well," he said, "Mr. Mason. They told me they'd sent for you."

"This is Dr. Flasher, Mr. Mason," Sylvia said.

Mason and the doctor shook hands.

"And this is my brother, Jarrett Bain."

A tall, heavy, slow-moving man peered at Mason through thick-lensed spectacles, took the lawyer's hand and squeezed it with powerful fingers. "Glad to know you, Mr. Mason."

Mason said, "This is a surprise. I thought you were prowling around in the ruins at Yucatán."

"I was. I got Sis's telephone call and decided I'd better be here. Luckily I managed to pick up a cancellation and came right through."

Mason said, "You made a quick trip. When did you get here?"

"This morning," Sylvia Atwood interposed quickly.

"I haven't had a chance to talk with you, Sylvia," Jarrett said. "I guess you're still relying on my wire. I got here—"

Mason looked at his watch. "Tell me about Mr. Bain," he said to Dr. Flasher, trying to appear unhurried, yet conscious of every passing second.

"There's not much to tell, Mr. Mason. The heart muscle was seriously impaired. The only thing that I could do was to prescribe absolute, complete rest, hoping that the heart muscle might pick up again, but the muscle had pretty much lost its tone. Excitement would have proven fatal, and—well, after all, Mr. Mason, the man has gone, so there's no use second-guessing."

Sylvia Atwood interposed quickly, "Dr. Flasher is trying to tell you that death was quite normal and was rather to have been expected. Dr. Flasher is going to sign a death certificate so there won't be any necessity for a lot of red tape."

96

"You've established the cause of death?" Mason asked.

"Yes, yes, certainly," Dr. Flasher said. "It was simply that a tired heart muscle couldn't carry the load any longer. We all have to go some time. Mr. Bain had had a focal infection which didn't do his condition any good. If I could have caught that a few years earlier things might have been a lot better, but—well, that's the way it is, particularly with these men who have had an outdoor background. They think they're rugged, tough and indestructible. Perhaps they might be if they'd only continue living outdoors. But experience teaches us that an outdoor man seriously jeopardizes his health when he decides to alter his mode of living and remain within four walls."

Mason turned to Sylvia Atwood. "I hope this discussion isn't hurting you too much," he said. "I'm not asking questions simply because of idle curiosity."

"I understand," she said. "I shall miss Dad terribly. I'm shocked, of course, and I have a great sense of loss, but it hadn't been unexpected. I understand your interest, Mr. Mason."

"Apparently he died quietly and without pain," Dr. Flasher interposed. "There was a telephone by the side of his bed. There's no indication that he even made any motion toward it. He died quietly, probably in his sleep."

"Well, that's a relief," Sylvia Atwood said.

Dr. Flasher, keeping his eyes on Perry Mason, went on, "I've been very much interested in following your career, Mr. Mason. I hardly expected to meet you here, although Mrs. Atwood told me that she had consulted you. You will, I suppose, have charge of the legal details in connection with the estate."

"I think," Mason said, "it's a little early to discuss that as yet, but I came out here as soon as I learned what had happened. I have met Mr. Bain and I am handling some business for the family."

"Yes, yes. Well, I must be getting on. I'm terribly sorry about what happened, but it couldn't have been avoided. If I had been here right at the moment, I might—I just *might* have prolonged life for a little while, but I think frankly it's better this way. I don't think your father knew what happened, Mrs. Atwood. I think he simply slipped off in his sleep. It's rather a surprise too, because when I saw him yesterday I felt that there had been some definite improvement. Of course, at his age and with his history you can't expect a heart muscle to be completely rejuvenated, but there had been very satisfactory progress. As a matter of fact, I was very much surprised at the news when you telephoned."

"When did he pass away, doctor?"

"I would say some time early this morning, perhaps five or six o'clock. It isn't particularly important to determine the exact time in a case of this sort."

"No, I suppose not. Tell me, there won't be any postmortem, will there?"

"Oh, I hope not!" Sylvia exclaimed.

"No, no, no, don't worry about that, my dear. It's perfectly natural. I'll sign a death certificate. You can notify the mortician, or would you prefer to have me do it?"

"Do you know someone who is good and dependable?" Sylvia asked.

"Yes, yes, of course, my dear. I'll be glad to do it for you."

"I think that would be the better way," Sylvia said. "Don't you, Jarrett?"

They paused, looking toward Jarrett Bain, waiting for his answer.

Jarrett, a vague, indefinite smile on his face, stood there with his arms folded, looking down at them, saying nothing.

"Don't you think so, Jarrett?" Sylvia asked.

"Eh, how's that? I beg your pardon."

"That Dr. Flasher should arrange for the mortician."

"Oh, yes, yes, of course."

Sylvia Atwood flashed Mason a glance, said to Dr. Flasher, "This is rather a harrowing experience. I'm worried about Hattie and—"

"It's been a shock to her all right," Dr. Flasher said. "I've given her a hypodermic. I gave her a good dose. I want her to sleep and be undisturbed."

Sylvia nodded quickly. Her eyes flashed another quick glance at Mason, then she was looking at Dr. Flasher earnestly.

"I think," she said, "if we can expedite arrangements just as much as possible it will help. If you can explain to the mortician that while this death wasn't unexpected it has, nevertheless, come at the end of a long battle and that some of the family are quite upset. In other words, rush things as much as possible. I'd like to have the body moved and the embalming done and everything before Hattie wakes up."

Dr. Flasher said, "I know a mortician who will be most considerate. I'll notify him."

"At once?" Sylvia asked.

"Yes, yes, of course. Just as soon as I get back to my office."

"And there won't be any difficulties, any red tape, any formalities?"

"No, absolutely not, my dear. Don't worry about it. You're getting yourself in something of a state. I'll sign a death certificate, the body will be moved, they'll go right ahead with the orderly process of embalming, and you can make arrangements for the funeral services."

Sylvia moved toward his side, took his arm. "You're wonderful, Dr. Flasher, simply wonderful."

Dr. Flasher turned to look back over his shoulder, smiled and waved at Mason, said, "It was a real pleasure, Counselor. I'll see you again."

Mason nodded.

Sylvia Atwood escorted Dr. Flasher to the door. Mason watched her for a moment, then turned to look at the tall archaeologist standing beside him.

"Rather a shock to you," Mason said.

"Eh, how's that?"

"I said it was a shock to you."

"Oh yes, of course. Poor Dad. I wanted him to take life

99

easier some time ago but he was always full of drive. You wonder why.

"After you've been prowling around through ruins erected by people who lived, loved and died a thousand years ago, and see the way the jungle has crept up over their temples, obliterated their market places, destroyed their works of art, smothered their culture, you realize that the individual shouldn't make life a rat race but a dignified and leisurely journey into the field of universal knowledge.

"Well, if you'll excuse me, Mr. Mason, I'll be seeing you."

Jarrett Bain turned and stalked slowly away.

Della Street said in a low voice to Perry Mason, "Gosh, *his* head's in the clouds! Sylvia's putting something over."

"What?" Mason asked.

"I don't know. Here she comes now."

Sylvia, having let Dr. Flasher out of the front door, came hurrying up to Mason. She gripped his arm with fingers that were tight with agitated suspense and trembling a little.

"I *must* see you, Mr. Mason," she said in a low, intense voice.

"You're seeing me," Mason told her.

The green eyes flashed quickly at Della Street, then away.

"There won't be any delay, any post-mortem, any red tape?" she asked.

"Not if Dr. Flasher signs the death certificate, not unless someone in authority interposes an official question."

"That police sergeant can be very, very disagreeable."

Mason nodded.

"He might—well, of course . . . ."

Mason said, "You wanted to see me about something. Get it off your chest."

She looked around her to make certain no one was in a

position to overhear, glanced once more at Della Street, then said under her breath, "Dad did it."

"Did what?" Mason asked.

"Killed J.J."

"What?" Mason exclaimed.

She nodded.

"Look here," Mason said, "let's get this straight. Your father was home in bed. Fritch was killed apparently between midnight and three o'clock this morning and——"

"Mr. Mason," she said, "Dad did it. I *know* that. I can prove it if I have to. I don't want to be the one to do it. But you must remember that's the fact and I don't think we should try to conceal it. I'm afraid we'll get in trouble if we do try to conceal it."

"Well," Mason said dryly, "you hardly wish to be placed in the position of discovering your father's death and then babbling to the authorities he murdered the man whose corpse you found this morning."

"No one knows I found it," she said quickly, sharply. "I stuck by the story that we had all met together there in front of Brogan's apartment. That was the way you wanted it, wasn't it?"

"That was what you told Holcomb?"

"Yes."

"Then," Mason said, "we can't change it very well, can we?"

"No. There's no reason why we should."

"Of course," Mason told her, "you should be doing everything you could legitimately do to protect your father's memory and——"

"Listen, Mr. Mason, you and I are practical people. Now I'm telling you I may not have a chance to talk to you again for some little time."

"Why?"

She said, "Don't be stupid, Mr. Mason. I'm going to be prostrated with grief and I can't discuss these things in the presence of other people. They don't know what we know. And, of course, none of this can come from me without making it appear that I'm an undutiful daughter, but Dad brooded over what you had told him about Fritch and Brogan. He couldn't sleep. Last night about twenty minutes past twelve he got up and took the car. He wasn't supposed to drive. He wasn't even supposed to go out. He wasn't supposed to have any excitement, but he had been taking medicine that made him feel better and he was strong enough to do what he felt had to be done."

"And what was that?" Mason asked.

"He went up to face J.J., to call him a liar and a scoundrel, and demand that record."

"What record? The one that Brogan had?"

"No, no, please don't be so difficult, Mr. Mason. The one you told Dad that Fritch had, the master record, the one that had been spliced."

"Go on," Mason said.

"He and Fritch had an argument. I suppose Dad lost his temper. No one will ever know what happened now, but I know Dad was up there. Dad got back here around half-past one or two this morning. He parked the car and went in to bed.

"Apparently the strain he had put on his heart had been too much. There had been excitement and—well, you wonder why Dad didn't die right there in his tracks, but somehow he managed to carry through and get back here."

"Go on," Mason said, making no effort to conceal his skepticism.

"That's what happened," she said. "Dad killed him. I can't be the one to let the authorities realize that, but somehow, Mr. Mason, you must see that they do understand it."

"I must?"

"Yes, someone has to."

"Why not let them find out for themselves?" Mason asked.

"They might not find out and they might—well, they might try to pin it on someone else."

"You, for instance?" Mason asked.

"Possibly."

"Your father," Mason said, "is dead. He's not here to defend himself. He can't speak for himself. How do you know that he went out last night between twelve and three?"

"It was about twenty minutes past twelve. I know because I followed him."

"You did?"

"Yes."

"Where?"

"To that apartment house."

"Why didn't you stop him?"

"I—I thought for a while that I would, and then I thought it might be better for Dad to get it off his chest and handle it in his own way. To tell you the truth, Mr. Mason, I wasn't certain, I couldn't be certain, that—that there *hadn't* been some association between Dad and J.J.

"Even if you are correct about that recording and even if J.J. had faked it, there still *could* have been something, some previous tie-up between him and Dad. Oh, I tell you, I did a lot of thinking, but I finally decided to let Dad go ahead and handle it his own way."

"Did anyone else see your father leave?" Mason asked.

She shook her head.

"Anyone else know that he had gone?"

Again she shook her head.

"I'm afraid," Mason said coldly, "there would have to be some other proof, something that—"

She moved close to him. "Mr. Mason," she said, "I have the proof."

"What?"

"I have the *proof!*"

"Go on," Mason said.

She said, "A few minutes before Dr. Flasher came I went in to say my own private last farewell to Dad. I put my hand under the pillow of his bed to straighten it out a little bit, to straighten out his head."

"Go on," Mason said. "What happened?"

"There was something under the pillow."

"What?"

"The spool of tape."

"Are you telling me the truth?" Mason exclaimed.

"Of course I am. It was the spool of tape, the original recording that Fritch had. It's been spliced where it had been put together just like you said it would be. Dad had got hold of it in some way. He carried it back with him and put it under his pillow. It was there."

"What did you do with it?"

She said, "I put it in a safe place—that is, the only place where it's safe for the moment. I'm going to get it and give it to you, then you must use your own judgment.

"But please, Mr. Mason, please don't misunderstand what I say. Dad has gone. I don't know whether he killed J.J. in self-defense or not. Dad is the one who was responsible for the death of J. J. Fritch. Fritch is dead and Dad is dead. They can't punish him. We *must*, simply must see that somehow the authorities get the lead that will start them investigating Dad. I don't want to be the one that gives them that lead, but if necessary I will break down and tell them."

"Go on," Mason said. "You have that spool of tape. What else?"

"Isn't that enough?"

"Do you have anything else?"

"Why do you ask?"

"Because I want to get the whole story."

"I have—I have the ice pick."

"And where did you get that?"

"This morning, when the body fell out of that liquor closet and rolled right at my feet. It was terrible! Horrible!"

"Never mind that," Mason said. "You can pull the dramatic part later. Where was the ice pick?"

"Still in J.J.'s body."

"Where?"

"In his body."

"I mean what part of his body?"

"The chest."

"What did you do with it?"

"I pulled it out and put it in my purse."

"Why did you do that?"

"Because it was our ice pick."

"How did you know?"

"I could recognize it. Ours is a distinctive ice pick. Edison Doyle gave it to us. He found a place where they were on sale. They're big ice picks with a distinctive metal band around the top so you can use them as a hammer to crush ice if you want."

Mason said, "You talk as if there were more than one."

"Yes, Edison saw them on sale. He bought three. He was laughing about it at the time. He said he was giving us one, was keeping one and was going to save the third as a wedding present for whichever one of us girls got married first."

"And you recognized this ice pick?"

"Yes."

"When you first found the body this morning?"

"Yes. Can't you see, Mr. Mason? At that time I was trying to protect Dad at any cost. I didn't know he'd gone on to a higher court. So, much as I hated to touch the thing, I pulled that ice pick out of the body and put it in my purse. Then I ran to the door and met you and Miss Street."

"And Sergeant Holcomb didn't search your purse?" Mason asked.

"Oh, of course, but I didn't have it then."

"What had you done with it?"

"Put it in the coiled fire hose on the lower floor where no one would think of looking for it, but where I could pick it up again after they'd finished questioning me."

"So," Mason said, "you discovered the body, and you have the murder weapon?"

"That's right. I've hidden it temporarily where no one

will look for it, but I wanted to ask you what I should do about it? I—"

Steps sounded behind them. Edison Doyle came rushing up to them.

"Hello, Mr. Mason," he said, and then all in one breath, "Sylvia, what the devil's this?"

"What?" Sylvia asked.

Doyle thrust forward a spool of tape.

"*Where* did you get that?" Sylvia flared.

"From the drawer in Hattie's dresser."

"What were you doing looking in there?"

"At Dr. Flasher's suggestion I was to stay with her until she dropped off to sleep. He gave her a hypo, you know. There were tears on her face and when she dropped off to sleep I looked for a handkerchief. I opened the top drawer in the bureau and this was lying right on top."

"Oh, Edison," Sylvia said, "you—you've done something now—I—I don't know."

"But what *is* it?" Edison Doyle said.

"You shouldn't have found it there," Sylvia Atwood said. "I had found it earlier. It was under Dad's pillow. I put it there until I could ask Mr. Mason about it. Because Hattie had been given a hypo and put to sleep and wasn't to be disturbed I felt certain no one would go in there. I didn't want anyone to know until I could ask Mr. Mason—"

Abruptly she put her hands to her face and started to cry.

"There, there," Doyle said, putting his arm around her shoulders and patting her reassuringly. "It's all right, Sylvia. Mr. Mason is here. He'll tell us what to do. You poor girl, you're all unstrung!"

Her shoulders shook convulsively with sobs.

Della Street wordlessly reached out and took the spool of tape from Edison Doyle's fingers.

As soon as she had done so, Edison Doyle, finding both hands free, promptly and naturally circled Sylvia Atwood with his arms, held the sobbing figure close to him.

"Poor little kid," he said, "you've had more than you can take."

Sylvia sobbed for a moment, then said, "Oh, Edison, you're *such* a comfort! Mr. Mason, will you please take charge of things—of everything?"

"Everything's going to be all right," Edison Doyle went on. "You come with me. You're going to have to lie down and keep quiet."

He gave Mason a significant look, slipped his arm around Sylvia's waist and led her out of the room.

"Well," Della Street said, looking at the spool of tape, "that's that!"

"I think," Mason said, "that we'll see if it is."

"You mean we listen to it?"

"I mean we listen to it."

"And then what?"

"And then," Mason said, "if it turns out to be that master spool of spliced tape we find ourselves in a hell of a fix."

"And if it shouldn't be?"

Mason grinned. "We're in a hell of a fix anyway."

"And," Della Street said bitterly, "not being a woman you can't break out crying on Sergeant Holcomb's shoulder and have him solicitously put you to bed."

"No," Mason said, "but he can solicitously put me out of circulation, and don't ever kid yourself but what he's damned anxious to do just that."

"And the murder weapon?" she asked.

"Fortunately she didn't tell me what she'd done with that. Washed it and put it in the ice box, I suppose."

"Should you find out?"

He shook his head. "Then I'd be an accessory after the fact. This tape recording is evidence, but not of murder. But a murder weapon is something altogether different. We'll let our little green-eyed minx take care of that."

"She won't," Della Street said. "She's too busy stealing her sister's boy-friend."

"No, she's just giving her sex appeal its morning exercise," Mason said.

"That's what *you* think. Come on, Chief, if we're going to listen to that tape recording let's do it before there are any more murders."

"More murders? How many do you think there have been already?"

"*I* count two to date," she said.

9

MASON ESCORTED Della Street to the place where their cars were parked.

"Take your car, Della," Mason said, "and follow me to the office."

He helped her into her car, closed the door.

"Chief, let me take it."

"What?"

"The spool of tape recording."

Mason shook his head.

"They wouldn't search me."

"You forget," Mason told her. "You're in this thing too. You were up there at Brogan's apartment this morning."

"Chief, I wish you wouldn't—"

"It's all right, Della," he told her. "There are times when an attorney has to take chances if he's going to represent his client."

"Who's your client?" she asked sharply.

"Technically, I suppose it's Sylvia Atwood, but actually I think we're representing the cause of justice."

"Well," Della Street said, "personally I don't think they're the same."

"Perhaps they aren't," he conceded. "We'll try to find out. Meet me at the office. Try not to get pinched for speeding. I'm going fast."

"I'll be right on your tail," she told him.

Mason jumped in his car, started the motor, pushed it into speed. From time to time he looked in his rearview mirror. Each time he looked Della Street was pounding along right behind him.

Mason swung his car into the parking space at the office and Della Street parked her car directly beside his.

Mason walked over to join her. "Okay, Della, we've made it so far."

"So far, so good," she said.

They went up in the elevator in silence, walked down the corridor to Mason's private office.

Della Street opened the door with her latchkey. Mason entered the office. Once inside they moved with the silence of conspirators. Della Street pulled a tape recorder from the closet, connected it up, turned it on and motioned to Perry Mason for the spool of recorded tape.

Mason handed it to her. Della Street put it on the tape recorder, ran the free end of the tape through the recording head, put it on the take-up spool, glanced at Mason.

Mason nodded, said, "Keep the volume down, Della."

Della Street turned the volume down low, started the machine on playback.

There was a moment of silence, then a few sounds of electrical static. Suddenly the voice of J. J. Fritch came out of the loud-speaker.

Della Street immediately turned down the volume another notch.

In silence they sat listening to the conversation between the two men who were now dead, the voices startlingly lifelike.

After some five minutes Mason said, "Okay, Della, switch it off. There's no question but what this is it. Also there's no question in my mind but what it's a fake recording."

"Yes, you can hear the difference in some of those

questions, the ones that have been spliced in when J. J. Fritch went to a sound studio and—"

The door from Mason's outer office opened.

"I'm not seeing anyone, Gertie," Mason called out sharply.

The door continued to open.

Della Street jumped to her feet. She gave an expression of annoyance and started toward the door.

The door swung all the way open. Lieutenant Arthur Tragg of the Homicide Squad stood on the threshold.

"Hello, Perry," he said. "Hello, Miss Street."

"You!" Mason said.

Della Street promptly pulled the plug which shut off the current from the tape recording machine, wound up the connecting wire and started to put on the cover.

"Leave it," Tragg said.

"How come?" Mason asked.

"As it happens," Tragg said, "I have a search warrant."

"A search warrant?"

Tragg nodded.

"For what?"

"This office."

"And what the devil do you expect to find in this office?" Mason asked.

Tragg said, "I'm sorry, Mason, I hate to do this to you. I came myself instead of letting Holcomb come because I didn't want any trouble and I was afraid Holcomb might rub it in."

"What's the occasion of the search warrant?"

Tragg said, "I am searching for a certain master spool of spliced tape which was stolen from the apartment of J. J. Fritch this morning.

"I have a couple of my men in the outer office keeping your receptionist occupied. She felt certain you weren't in so she didn't try to ring the phone and tip you off."

"We just came back," Mason said. "I hadn't reported to her that we were in the office."

"So I gathered," Tragg said. "I started in here armed

110

with my search warrant, got as far as the door, heard the sound of a tape recording being played back, so I eased the door open a crack and listened. Now if you don't mind I'll take that spool of tape into custody as evidence."

"Evidence of what?" Mason asked.

"Evidence of motive in the murder of J. J. Fritch. And if you can keep your shirt on, Perry, I'm going to take a chance and tip you off to some valuable information."

"What?" Mason asked.

"I'm sticking my neck out," Tragg said. "I shouldn't do it."

Mason started to say something, then, at the expression he saw on Tragg's face, held his comment.

"Go ahead," he invited.

Tragg said, "You are in a spot."

"I've heard that before," Mason told him.

"You've been in spots before and got out of them. This time you're going to have a job getting out."

"Go on," Mason said.

Tragg said, "Your client, Sylvia Atwood, got to George Brogan's apartment this morning right around eight-forty to keep a nine o'clock appointment. She was twenty minutes early. She went in and did a lot of prowling."

"And that puts *me* in a spot?" Mason asked.

Tragg grinned. "You haven't heard me out yet."

"Go ahead," Mason said. "Let's hear the rest of it."

"Sylvia Atwood," Tragg went on, "entered that apartment around eight-forty. She was in there searching for a spool of tape that was purported to have a conversation between her father and J. J. Fritch on it, the spool of recorded tape that you and Miss Street were just listening to on your machine."

"Go on," Mason said, "we're listening."

"Sylvia Atwood will eventually admit," Lieutenant Tragg went on, "that at about nine o'clock she came to the liquor closet. She opened the door, and then gave a terrific scream, turned and ran in panic to confront you and Della Street at the door of Brogan's apartment."

"How very, very interesting," Mason said. "I suppose you're going to claim that after having been in there for twenty minutes she suddenly discovered the body of J. J. Fritch?"

"No, I'm not," Tragg said. "That's just the point. *She* is."

"Go on," Mason said.

"The point is that she knew you and Della Street would be there at the door of the apartment at about nine o'clock. She waited until she heard you outside the door, then she moved to the liquor closet, climbed up on a chair, jumped to the floor so as to give a jar, let out a terrific scream, turned and ran toward the door."

Mason said, "I'm listening, Tragg."

"And then," Tragg went on, "she told you and Miss Street that the body of J. J. Fritch was in there, and you told her to stand at the door with Della Street, reading the note that Brogan had left on the door for you, pretending that you had just come to the place.

"You told them that you were going into Fritch's apartment and search for a master tape recording, that there was about one chance in a hundred you might find it, that as soon as Brogan showed up Sylvia Atwood was to press the bell button on Fritch's apartment twice.

"As soon as you heard that signal you were going to come to the door of Fritch's apartment. You would wait until the two young women and Brogan had entered Brogan's apartment, and then you'd come along treading on their heels, pretending that you'd been parking the car."

Mason's eyes narrowed.

"Well?" Tragg said.

"I suppose," Mason said, "from all of the detail with which you are giving this conversation, you must have heard it from the lips of some witness?"

"That's right," Tragg said, "although I'd probably be disciplined if anybody knew I'd told you."

"And, under the circumstances, the witness could be none other than Sylvia Atwood. Since she's my client

112

I won't comment on her veracity or the motives which might have prompted her."

"You're wrong," Tragg said.

"Wrong in what?"

"Wrong in guessing the identity of the witness who told us this, who related the conversation."

"Well, who *was* the witness?" Mason asked.

"Perry Mason."

"Oh, I see. Talking in my sleep again, eh?" Mason observed jocularly.

"No," Tragg said, "you'll have to think a long while before you get the answer, Perry."

"What's the answer?"

"Brogan had laid a trap for you. He wanted to find out what you and Mrs. Atwood really felt about the evidence he had, about whether you were planning to pay off, or whether you were going to fight. So he arranged to be in a poker game which would keep him out all night. He left his apartment door unlocked and left a note on it for you stating that if he happened to be a few minutes late you were to go on in and sit down.

"And then he installed a tape recorder with a microphone so ingeniously placed that it would pick up sounds from within the apartment and sounds on the outside of the door in the corridor. He plugged in an electric clock of the type used to turn on radio or television sets and set the time control at eight-fifty.

"You'd be surprised to find how clearly the sounds of Sylvia Atwood jumping on the floor, her scream and the subsequent conversation among the three of you come in on that tape recording.

"George Brogan broke down under Sergeant Holcomb's questioning and told Holcomb the whole business, and gave him the tape."

"I see," Mason said. "My answer is, 'no comment.' "

"I thought that would be your answer," Tragg said. "As a matter of fact I like you, Mason. I think your methods are too damn unconventional. I think you go too far to protect your clients. I think you've skirted the edge of the penitentiary before, and I don't like to see you do it again. I'm telling you this as a friendly tip-off so you won't make a statement that is at variance with the facts of the case. Remember those facts can be established by the sound of your own voice, the sound of Della Street's voice and Sylvia Atwood's voice."

"Thanks," Mason said dryly.

"No thanks at all," Tragg told him. "Now, under the authority of this search warrant, I'm going to take that spool of tape recording which you were clever enough to find in the Fritch apartment."

"Suppose I didn't find it there?" Mason said.

Tragg grinned. "Don't be silly, Perry. In view of Brogan's tape recording stating that you were going in there to look for that specific piece of property, you stand a fat chance denying how you happened to acquire it. As a matter of fact, it was on the strength of Brogan's tape recording that I was able to get an order to search your office.

"Quite naturally the judge who issued the search warrant wasn't particularly keen about it. It wasn't until after he'd listened to the tape recording that he rather reluctantly issued the warrant.

"I decided to serve it myself because I was afraid Holcomb would be so keen on trapping you that he might goad you into making some statement that would prove embarrassing later, when you were confronted with that tape recording."

Mason got up from behind his desk, hesitated a moment, walked over and shook hands with Lieutenant Tragg.

"Now then," Tragg said, "I'll take the tape recording."

"Go ahead," Mason told him. "And incidentally, Tragg, while you're about it, check the whereabouts of George Brogan every minute of the time last night."

"Don't worry," Tragg said, "that's been done."

"He has an alibi?"

"Ironbound, copper-riveted, a lead-pipe cinch. He was

playing poker with seven men. One of them happens to be a friend of the Chief of Police."

"What time did the game start?"

"About ten o'clock and it lasted until Brogan broke away this morning about eight-fifteen, stating he had an important appointment, that he was going to have to hurry to get a cup of coffee and a little breakfast, that he wouldn't have time to clean up. He'd been trying to break away ever since seven o'clock, but he was winning and they kept holding him on for one more round."

"He was there all the time?"

"He was out of the game about thirty minutes around five o'clock in the morning," Tragg said. "He had a losing streak, had dropped all of the money he had, and went out to call on a friend to get some cash. He returned at about five-thirty with fifteen hundred dollars. The murder was committed between midnight and three o'clock this morning."

"You're certain?" Mason asked.

"I'm certain," Tragg said. "At least the autopsy surgeon is. Now use your head on this thing, Perry, and don't get in over your necktie."

"Thanks for the buggy ride," Mason told him.

"Not at all," Tragg said.

He took the spool of tape recording, scribbled a receipt to Mason, turned and left the office.

Della Street looked at Mason with wide eyes.

Mason shrugged his shoulders.

"Chief, can't you tell them—shouldn't you tell them where you *really* got that tape recording?"

"Not yet," Mason said.

"Later on no one will believe you."

"They won't believe me now."

"But, Chief, Sylvia can't help you if you wait to tell your story. They'll think it's something you've hatched up between you. You should protect yourself now by telling the whole truth and calling on Sylvia and Edison Doyle and—"

"We tell the police nothing," Mason interrupted. "This is a law office, not an information bureau."

"It will get you in bad," she said.

"Then I'll have to be in bad. I've been in bad before, and I probably will be in bad again."

"What do we do?"

Mason motioned toward the telephone. "Get Sylvia Atwood on the line. Tell her to get up here just as fast as she can make it."

10

SYLVIA ATWOOD sat in the client's chair in Mason's office. Her eyes were fixed steadily on the lawyer now. There were no more flickering glances. She was regarding him as cautiously as a poker player appraises someone who has just shoved a stack of blue chips into the pot.

"Go ahead," she said.

"That's all of it," Mason said. "We were playing the tape recording to make sure what it was and Tragg walked in with a search warrant."

"So the police have it now?"

"That's right."

"Mr. Mason, you should have done as I told you."

"What?"

"Told them that my father got that tape recording, that he—that he is responsible for what happened up there in the apartment."

"The death of J. J. Fritch?"

"Yes."

"I couldn't tell them that," Mason said.

"Why not?"

"Because I don't know that he was."

"Well you know it now."

"No, I don't. That's why I asked you to come here. I want to know *exactly* what happened. I want to get the *complete* details. You tell me exactly what happened and be careful what you say. Della Street is going to take notes and, in addition to that, I'm going to have a tape recorder taking down everything you say."

"I'm your client," she flared at him. "You've no right to treat me as though I were an adverse party—a suspect."

"You're a client," Mason admitted, "and you also may be a suspect. Now start talking."

Her eyes flashed for a moment, then she said, "Very well, I'll tell you the facts, the true facts, and I'll tell you all of them."

"Go ahead."

She said, "After your conversation with Dad yesterday afternoon he was very upset."

"Naturally," Mason said, "but you must remember that the thing that upset him was not my conversation but what J. J. Fritch had told him."

"Please don't misunderstand me, Mr. Mason. I'm not blaming you. Actually *your* conversation with him quieted his nerves and helped him a lot, but I'm simply trying to fix it from the standpoint of time. It was after you had left yesterday afternoon that we realized Dad was in such a terribly nervous state."

"Go ahead."

"We tried to reach Dr. Flasher and couldn't. He was out on an emergency case, but he had left medicine for Dad and we gave him some of that medicine. It was medicine that was supposed to quiet him and do something to make it easier for the heart to work."

"All right," Mason said. "Then what happened?"

"Dad was nervous. He didn't want to sleep. We sat in the room with him. He dozed from time to time. He didn't think he was sleeping at all. Sometimes he dozed as much as half an hour. By ten o'clock he had quieted down a lot."

"Go ahead," Mason said.

"Edison Doyle had been there earlier in the evening. He, of course, knew all about what was happening. We talked it over and decided we'd take turns keeping an eye on Dad. We thought he might—well, we thought he might take a turn for the worse and might want somebody there on the job."

Mason nodded.

"Edison had some sketches that he had promised against a deadline. They simply had to be out this morning. He said that he'd go up to his office and work until a little after midnight, that he'd come out then and be in a position to take over."

Again Mason nodded.

"We had it agreed that Hattie was to go to bed and get some sleep, that I'd sit up until Dad went to sleep, that then I'd get a couple of hours' sleep. We left a key to the back door under the mat so Edison could come in whenever he got through with his work. He felt that would be one or two o'clock in the morning.

"He was to tiptoe up to one of the guest rooms and go to sleep. I was to fix my alarm clock so I could look in on Dad every hour and a half. If he became restless I'd call Edison and let him keep a steady watch for two hours, then I'd watch for two hours.

"We agreed Hattie needed all the sleep she could get. She was right on the ragged edge. We weren't going to call her unless we had to. We got her to agree to take a sleeping pill."

"What happened?" Mason asked. "Go ahead."

"Hattie went to bed. The house quieted down. Everything was perfectly quiet. I looked in on Dad. He seemed to be asleep. I checked to see that the house was locked up, before heading for bed. Then I heard a car being started in the garage. Whoever was driving it was driving very carefully so that it wouldn't disturb anyone. The car came out with the lights off."

"What did you do?"

"I ran to the window. I saw Dad in the car."

"You're sure?"

"Just as sure as I can be, but I verified it."

"How?"

"I ran into his room. He wasn't in the bed. The covers had been thrown back."

"So what did you do?"

"I followed. I dashed out to where I'd left my car parked at the curb, jumped in and followed the car ahead."

"Why didn't you stop him?"

"I don't know why I didn't, Mr. Mason, but I wanted to find out what it was he had in mind, and—well, I guess I was terribly curious. I knew that Dad wouldn't have gone out except on some matter of the greatest emergency, something that was life and death, and I wanted to find out what it was and where he was going."

"Where did he go?"

"I've already told you. He went directly to that apartment house."

"What did you do?"

"I waited, thinking that he'd come out within a few minutes. After about half an hour or so, when he didn't come out, I became very worried and entered the apartment house."

"Then what?"

"You know it's one of those apartment houses where the outer door is always open. There's no one on duty on the inside. You go right up to the apartments without being announced."

"Go on," Mason said.

"The outer door is supposed to be kept latched, but all you have to do is push against it hard and it opens."

"I know," Mason said. "Tell me what you did."

"I went in and started for the elevator. I saw that it was on the floor where Brogan had his apartment. I felt certain Dad was up there. I was just about to press the button for the elevator when I heard the elevator coming down."

"What did you do?"

"I ran for the stairs and ran part way up the first flight of stairs."

"What happened?"

"I heard someone get out of the elevator. I realized, of course, that it probably was Dad. I ran back down the stairs and was able to glimpse the figure just as it went out. The figure was silhouetted against the door. It wasn't Dad, at least I didn't think it was at the time. I thought it was a woman."

"Go on."

"So I took the elevator back up, walked down the corridor and stood fairly near the door of Brogan's apartment, listening. I couldn't hear any voices. I went back to the end of the corridor and waited. When I'd been waiting for about half an hour or so I again walked back down to the apartment. I was good and worried then. This time I went closer and saw there was a note on the door. I looked at the envelope and saw it was addressed to you. I pulled it off, read the note, realized the apartment was unlocked. I put the note back on the door, trying to push the thumbtack into the same hole that it had occupied, but the light wasn't good and I'm not certain I did it."

"Go on."

"I tried the door of the apartment. It was unlocked. I just wanted to find out if Dad was in there. I opened the door and stepped in."

"Go on," Mason said.

"A light was on in the living room. There was no one in there."

"What did you do?"

"I went through the apartment, switching on lights, looking for Dad. He wasn't there."

"Where was J. J. Fritch?"

"At the time, I don't know."

"He wasn't there then?"

"Of course he was, but I didn't know it. His body must have been in the liquor closet, Mr. Mason."

"You didn't open that door?"

"Not then, no."

"So what did you do?"

"At first I felt Dad must be in J.J.'s apartment across the hall. I tried that door. It was locked. I listened. There was no sound, no voices, no noise of any sort.

"I started to ring, then started to wonder if my eyes could have deceived me and if it had really been Dad who had gone out of the door of that apartment house.

"So I went back down to the street and sure enough our car was gone. So then I hurried back home. Dad was in bed, sound asleep, so I went up to bed and went to sleep myself, setting my alarm so I could look in on Dad every hour and a half until seven-thirty.

"Then I dressed, jumped in my car, drove to a restaurant, had breakfast and went to George Brogan's apartment for my appointment with you. Only, knowing that I'd probably find the apartment unlocked, I went about twenty minutes early."

"Then you didn't see anyone after you got back to the house?"

"No. Edison had gone to bed. Jarrett got in on a plane at four o'clock this morning, rented one of those cars you drive yourself so he'd have his own transportation, and let himself in and went to bed."

"You haven't said anything to anyone else about this?"

"Not so far, but I'm going to."

"Why?"

"Because it's the only fair thing to do, Mr. Mason. If Fritch was killed when the police say he was, that was at the time Dad was up in that apartment house.

"Please understand me, Mr. Mason, as long as Dad was alive I did everything I could to protect him, even going to the extent of taking that murder weapon out of the body. Think of the spot I'd have been in if that horrid Sergeant Holcomb had caught me with that ice pick."

"I've been thinking about that," Mason said.

"Well, I cheerfully took all that risk to protect Dad, but now that he's gone we'd be terribly foolish to run risks trying to conceal the facts. Why, they might even try to pin the murder on one of *us!*"

Mason frowned deeply as he gave the problem his full attention.

"Don't you see, Mr. Mason," she went on, "Dad is dead. He can't be punished. I am willing to assume that he acted in self-defense, but I am not willing to try to protect his memory by concealing essential facts."

"You haven't told Sergeant Holcomb anything about this?"

"Not yet. Of course, at first I didn't have any proof. Later on I found that tape recording under Dad's pillow."

"And what did you do with it?"

"I thought I'd conceal it some place where no one would look until I could ask you about it. I was in something of a panic."

"Go ahead," Mason said.

"I knew that Dr. Flasher had given Hattie a hypo, told her to undress and get into bed. I slipped into her room pretending I wanted to make sure she was all right. She was undressing. I hid the tape recording in the top dresser drawer where she keeps her handkerchiefs. I felt that no one would look in there because they wouldn't want to disturb Hattie."

"Then what?"

"Well, Hattie was still nervous even after the hypo. Dr. Flasher thought it would be a good thing for Edison to go in and sit by the bed and talk with her. He said to talk quietly, in a low, even voice, talking about things that weren't connected with Dad's death, using long sentences and using a monotone as much as possible. He thought that would help her go to sleep.

"You know the rest."

Mason said, "Brogan had a tape recording made of our conversation in front of the door of his apartment this morning. He's turned that over to the police. They know that you discovered the body. They know that I announced I was going into Fritch's apartment and see if I could find that spool of tape recording."

Sylvia Atwood thought that over for a few minutes.

Abruptly she got to her feet. "That settles it," she said. "I've made up my mind what I'm going to do."

"Now wait a minute," Mason said. "You haven't made up your mind to anything. If you want me to represent you, you're going to have to follow my advice."

"But you're not representing me."

"You retained me."

"That was to represent the family, not me. *I'm* not in any trouble, not now—particularly not after what I'm going to do."

"You may think you're not in any trouble," Mason said, "and you may be kidding yourself."

"But I'm not. That's ridiculous. Personally, Mr. Mason, I think you're being altogether too conservative about this thing, and I think you've held your own counsel entirely too long. I think you should have passed the information along to the police."

"What's happened to Hattie?" Mason asked.

"She's still asleep. She'll probably be asleep until midnight or later. Dr. Flasher was particularly anxious that she get a good sleep. She's lost a lot of rest lately and she's terribly nervous."

"Now wait a minute," Mason said. "Let's get a few things straight. I want to know the real truth about that body. What happened when you found it?"

"I told you the truth."

"Tell it again, then."

"I was searching. I wondered if Dad had talked to J.J. in there or in J.J.'s apartment. I felt certain you and Miss Street would arrive before Brogan. And since Brogan had no way of knowing that I would know the apartment was unlocked, he wouldn't have expected me to get there much before nine.

"So I got up there about twenty minutes to nine and I started looking around. Well, frankly, I was searching. That's why I kept my gloves on so I wouldn't leave fingerprints.

"I opened the door of the liquor closet. That is, I turned the knob. As soon as I turned it and the latch

123

clicked the door flew open. The body must have been pressing against the door from the inside.

"It was terrible, horrible. It—"

"Never mind all that. Was the body stiff? Had *rigor mortis* set in?"

"I—I can't be sure. I *think* the arms were held up very rigid—bent at the elbows, but I *think* the legs sprawled. There was a sort of bruise on the back, just above the undershirt. Mr. Mason, no one must ever know about that ice pick being in my possession."

"Where is it now?"

"I'm going to get it. Won't it be better if you don't know some of these things? I'll do what is necessary."

"Now just a moment. Where are you going now?" Mason asked, as Sylvia Atwood picked up her purse and got to her feet.

She started to say something, then changed her mind, looked at him with her eyes wide and innocent.

"Why, home, of course," she said. "That's my place, to be with Hattie."

She hurried to the door.

"Wait a minute," Mason said.

"There isn't time," she retorted, and jerked the door open.

11

PAUL DRAKE phoned Mason at about three o'clock.

"Hear the latest, Perry?"

"What?"

"From a quote, undisclosed but authentic source, unquote, the police have been advised that Ned Bain got up from his sick bed last night, kept a midnight appointment with J. J. Fritch; presumably murdered him in order to obtain possession of a master tape recording, which Fritch was using in an attempt to blackmail Bain into paying a large sum of money."

"That's been announced to the press?"

"That's right. It just came over the radio in a news-cast."

"Who gave them the information?" Mason asked.

"A quote, undisclosed source, unquote. Was that you?"

"No."

"It would be a slick move, making a dead man a murderer. It would get the live ones out from under."

"I didn't do it," Mason said. "Anything else now, Paul?"

"The police recovered the tape recording in question through quote, vigorous, intelligent work, unquote. They ran down a series of clues, decided that the tape recording was in the possession of quote, a prominent downtown lawyer, unquote.

"Police secured a search warrant and entered the office of this lawyer. They found him and his attractive secretary in the lawyer's private office listening to the very tape recording that has become such a valuable piece of evidence in the case."

"The lawyer wasn't named?" Mason asked.

"Wasn't named," Drake said, "but the newscaster announced that his initials were *P. M.*"

"That makes it nice," Mason said. "Thanks for calling."

Mason hung up the telephone, said to Della Street, "Well, the beans are spilled all over the stove. Now we'll have to see what happens."

"She told the police?" Della Street asked.

"The police announced that an undisclosed source of information gave them the tip-off."

"They're investigating?"

Mason nodded.

"Sylvia Atwood might at least have done us the cour-

125

tesy of telling us what she was going to do," Della Street said.

"Sylvia Atwood," Mason observed, getting up from behind the desk and starting to pace the floor, "is adopting the position that she knows more than her attorney."

"Not *her* attorney," Della Street corrected. "The family attorney."

Mason grinned. "That's right."

He continued pacing the floor.

"This," Della Street said, "will get you off the spot, won't it, Chief?"

"It might if the police believe her."

"Do you think they'll believe her?"

"I would say," Mason said, "that there was only about one chance in ten. They'll think that she's concocting a story in order to get herself out of a jam and get me out of a jam. The public will resent the fact that she was altogether too eager to pin a murder on her dead father before the body was even cold.

"That's going to have the effect of making for very poor public relations, Della."

"I'll say it is," Della Street blazed, "and when they photograph her with those cold eyes of hers, and when it seems she tried to make her dead father the fall guy just as soon as she knew he'd passed away— Gosh, Chief, when you stop to think of it that way it really ties together, doesn't it?"

Mason nodded moodily.

"Of course," Della Street said, "she had the tape recording and—"

"You mean *I* had it."

"Well, she gave it to you."

Mason said, "That's something I'm afraid we can't admit, Della."

"Why not?"

"She's our client."

"But you can at least tell where you got it."

"I can't. Of course, we have Edison Doyle. Presumably

he'll tell the police where *he* found it. Police, however, have publicly adopted the position that shrewd detective work enabled them to find the tape recording after I had purloined it from Fritch's apartment.

"If they had to back up on that and if it turned out the tape recording had been given me by someone who had found it, their faces would be red.

"Sergeant Holcomb doesn't like to have his face become red. Tragg will find the facts and face them. Holcomb will move heaven and earth to keep everyone believing I broke into that apartment and purloined that tape."

"And where is that going to leave you?" she asked.

He grinned. "Right behind the eight ball, as usual, but we have to protect our clients, Della, regardless of any other consideration."

"Do you think Brogan really did have the tape recording of what took place in front of his apartment?"

"Sure," Mason said. "Tragg couldn't have repeated that conversation as accurately as he did unless they did have such a tape recording."

The buzzer of the telephone on Della Street's desk sounded.

Mason said, "Tell Gertie I can't see any clients today. Tell her to filter out everything except the important calls. Tell her I'm tied up on an emergency matter of the greatest importance."

Della Street nodded, picked up the telephone, said, "Gertie, Mr. Mason is . . . What? . . . Who? . . . Just a minute."

She turned to Mason.

"Jarrett Bain's out there. He says he simply has to see you, and he seems to be all worked up."

"Is he alone?"

"He's alone."

"I'll see him," Mason said. "Go out and bring him in, Della."

She nodded, hurried through the door to the outer office.

Jarrett Bain, following Della, came striding into Mason's office, his manner radiating indignation.

"Good afternoon, Mr. Bain," Mason said. "Sit down. Tell me what's on your mind."

Bain didn't sit down, but stood towering over Mason's desk, looking down at the lawyer with blazing, angry eyes.

"What's all this about trying to blame the murder of J. J. Fritch on Dad?"

"I don't know," Mason said. "I received a telephone call just a moment ago from the Drake Detective Agency telling me that the police had announced that a quote, undisclosed but authentic source, unquote, had given them a tip-off."

"Wasn't that undisclosed source you?" Bain asked.

Mason shook his head.

Bain glowered at him for a moment, then walked over and sat down in the client's chair as though some of the anger and much of the strength had eased out of him.

"I should have known it," he said, disgustedly.

"Known what?" Mason asked.

"Sylvia," Jarrett said, and there was a world of contempt in his voice.

"You think *she* was the one who told the police?"

"Of course she was," Jarrett said. "She had to do it either through herself or through you. I didn't find out until just an hour or so ago that the tape recording had been found in the drawer of Hattie's dresser. I wish someone had told *me*.

"I guess I'm supposed to be a theorist, Mr. Mason. I'll admit that lots of times I don't keep up with all the gabble-gabble-gabble of conversation that goes on around me, but—my God, if she'd *only* talked with me."

"Just how would that have helped?" Mason asked.

"Why, hang it," Bain said, "Dad didn't go out last night. That's all poppycock."

"How do you know he didn't?"

"Because I was sitting with him," Bain said.

"You were!" Mason exclaimed. "Why, I understood

you got home shortly after four this morning and never saw your father alive."

"That was the surmise," Bain said, "because no one took the trouble to ask me anything. Sylvia took things for granted and Hattie had been given a hypo."

"You did see him?"

"Of course I saw him. That's what I came home for. Sylvia told me on the long-distance telephone that Dad was in bad shape. She told me that this other matter was pending, and if he got word of it the shock might prove fatal. Of course I came home. What would any son have done under the circumstances?"

"Go ahead," Mason said.

"Well," Jarrett said, "I got home. I had a latchkey and let myself in. Naturally I didn't want to break in on Dad. I looked around to try and find one of the girls."

"Go ahead," Mason said, his eyes narrowed with interest.

"Neither one of the girls was there," Jarrett Bain said. "No one was there. Personally I thought that was a hell of a way to take care of a man who had heart trouble."

Mason exchanged glances with Della Street.

"Go ahead," Mason said, "tell us exactly what you did. Describe your movements in detail if you can."

"Well, that's a big house. It's full of rooms. There are several guest rooms. I lugged my bags up to the first guest room, trying to be as quiet as possible. I saw at once that that was being occupied by Sylvia. She had some things on the dresser. Her overnight bag with her creams and stuff was there, and a nightdress laid out on the foot of the bed.

"So I went on into another guest room and put my things in there. Then I went back downstairs and thought I'd better wake Hattie up and let her know I was home. I knew where she slept.

"I got to the door of her room. It was ajar. I knocked gently. No one said anything. I listened, couldn't hear any breathing, so I went in and switched on the light. Hattie wasn't there."

"Then what did you do?"

"Then I became alarmed about Dad. I tiptoed down the corridor to his room and opened the door just a crack and looked in."

"Your father was there?"

"Dad was there, awake, reading," Jarrett said. "He heard the door, looked up and caught my eye and gave a start of surprise and said, 'Jarrett, what in the world are *you* doing here?' "

"He hadn't expected you?"

"Apparently not," Bain said. "Apparently no one expected me. I had sent a wire stating that I was going to be in on the plane that arrived at four o'clock in the morning, but that wire wasn't delivered until the next morning."

"But you got in *before* four o'clock?" Mason asked.

"Fortunately I was able to catch an earlier plane. By flying from New Orleans to Dallas on a local line I was able to pick up a through plane and got in earlier than would have been the case if I'd waited over in New Orleans and taken the direct plane on which I had reservations."

"Go ahead," Mason said. "What happened?"

"Well, Dad and I talked for a while and—well, I could see Dad was terribly worried. He hadn't been able to sleep much. He said the doctor had given him some medicine to quiet his nerves, but after he'd gone to sleep, he'd wakened and felt pretty jittery. He apparently had no idea he was alone in the house. He said he had a bell that he could ring and one of the girls would bring him anything he needed, but he was doing all right. He had everything right near his hand and he decided to sit up and read a little bit."

"So then what?"

"Well, I knew I shouldn't keep Dad up long, but I sat down and talked with him for about half or three-quarters of an hour. Of course *I* avoided the subject of this blackmail because I didn't think he knew anything about it, but he brought it up himself, told me about Fritch telephoning and threatening him, about you coming into the picture and all that."

"Then what?" Mason asked.

"I persuaded Dad to take another one of the capsules that quieted his nerves and told him I'd see him in the morning. He was just as wide awake as could be, but I felt he should try to quiet down, particularly after that capsule I gave him, so I told him *I* was tired and *I* was going to bed."

"Then what?"

"Then I went out and fixed myself a sandwich and a glass of milk in the kitchen, and while I was doing that Edison Doyle showed up."

"You'd met Edison Doyle before?"

"No, I hadn't. I'd been away from home and—well, of course, I'd heard about Edison Doyle and I knew who he was, and that he was interested in Hattie."

"And what happened?"

"Edison Doyle told me that the girls had been a little bit worried about their dad and decided to have someone on duty all night, to look in on him every hour or so. I could see that he assumed I had come home and had taken over the job of watching and that the girls were asleep."

"Did you tell him they weren't home?"

Jarrett shook his head. "No, it wasn't any of his business. I just didn't say anything one way or another."

"And what happened?"

"Well, Edison and I got acquainted and he told me that he'd come up to help watch, that he'd had some work that had to be out that morning, that he'd been up working in the office. His eyes were pretty tired. He'd been straining them over a drawing board making some preliminary sketches and plans. So I told him to go on up and go to bed."

"Where?"

"In the third guest room."

"Did he?"

"That's right. It didn't take much urging."

"Then what?"

"Then," Jarrett said, "after he went to bed, I tiptoed down the corridor, opened the door a crack and looked in on Dad. He had the reading light turned out, just the night light was on and he was sleeping peacefully. I tiptoed back, sat around for a while, began to feel drowsy myself and decided that there was no need having anyone looking in on Dad. I felt certain the girls would be in pretty quick anyway, so I started on up to bed. I decided to set my alarm clock so I could wake up in an hour and a half after I crawled in. I thought I'd just look in on Dad and see how things were going at that time."

"And what happened?"

"Just as I started up the stairs I heard the back door being unlocked. I stood there at the top of the stairs wondering what was happening, and Hattie came in."

"You're sure it was Hattie?"

"Yes."

"How was she dressed?"

"She had on a plaid skirt. I remember that. And she must have been wearing a coat because I'd heard her open the door of the hall closet before she came to where I could see her."

"So what did she do? Did you speak to her?"

"She went to her room. I didn't say a word to her. I'd begun to realize by that time I was plenty tired. I'd been flying on a plane. I'd been up all night. I'd talked with Dad, and I knew Hattie would want to tell me all about how wonderful Edison Doyle was and how happy she was, and how worried she was about Dad, so I decided it could keep. I'm fond of Hattie, but I don't like gushing conversation and all this ga-ga business of young love leaves me cold. Hattie was all right. Anything she had to say could wait until morning."

"So what happened?"

"I went back upstairs. I undressed and took a hot shower. Then just as I'd turned my light off and heaved myself into bed I heard a car door slam out in front of the house. I was curious, so I went to my window and looked out. It was Sylvia's car. She was coming up the sidewalk. Well, I felt everything was under control. I understood that Sylvia was helping out with watching Dad, so I decided I could shut off my alarm clock. So I got into bed and went to sleep."

"How long did you sleep?"

"Pretty long. I didn't get up until around ten in the morning. I was tired."

"And what happened?"

"By that time my wire had been delivered stating that I was arriving on the four o'clock plane. Evidently everyone thought that I'd arrived then and had come on in and had gone to bed."

"But Edison Doyle knew what time you got in."

"Edison Doyle knew that I was there when he arrived, which was around one, I guess, perhaps a little later. But you see, Doyle got up at seven-forty-five and dashed up to his office to meet that client. At least he told me that was what he was going to do.

"Doyle said he was to be there and stand by just in case things got bad. He said Sylvia was able to wake up and then go back to sleep instantly and she'd promised to keep her alarm clock set at intervals, would go down and look in on Dad, then call the others if she felt anyone needed to sit up with him.

"I got up at ten o'clock in the morning, shaved, went downstairs and had some breakfast. I saw Hattie, of course, and had a little talk with her, but she was busy doing chores around the house. I didn't realize it at the time, but I found out afterward that she'd received my wire and had assumed that I came in on the four o'clock plane. She told me Dad was still sleeping. I had some telephoning to do and, as I say, Hattie was busy with housework and getting Dad's breakfast ready. Then along about—I don't know, it must have been nearly eleven, she went in to give Dad his breakfast and that was when she found out he'd passed away.

"Well, of course, after that everything was excitement. We were running around in circles and trying to get Dr.

Flasher, and after Dr. Flasher came—I don't know, the house was full of people. You were there, and Miss Street—I don't know exactly when she came. Sylvia had gone out to keep a nine o'clock appointment. She got back in the midst of the excitement. Someone telephoned Edison Doyle and he dashed out. Dr. Flasher gave Hattie a hypodermic and put her to sleep, and—well, that's about it."

Mason nodded.

"Now then," Jarrett said, "I can begin to put two and two together and see what happened. Hattie went out some place. It was pretty cold at that hour of the morning and she may have put on Dad's overcoat. Sylvia may or may not have thought she was following Dad. She might have peeked into his room just as he was in the bathroom, I don't know. But this much I do know—Dad wasn't out of the house, he didn't murder Fritch, and anyone who says he did is a liar."

"What about this tape recording?" Mason asked.

"The one that was supposed to have been under his pillow?"

Mason nodded.

"I don't think it was under his pillow when I was there," Bain said. "It could have been planted there afterward. I don't know. I'll tell you this much, Mr. Mason. Sylvia is a regular little manipulator. She always gets the idea she knows more than anyone else, and she loves to scheme and manipulate things. You give that girl her head and she'll get you into one hell of a mess. Don't say I didn't warn you.

"It never seems to occur to her that someone else may know something. She wants to be little Miss Fix-It and she'll twist and distort and plant false clues and all that trying to have things her way.

"Now I don't know much about law, but I know a lot about Sylvia, and my best guess is that her cute little tendency to manipulate facts and plant clues could raise merry hell in a murder case.

"Am I right?"

Mason grinned. "You're very, very right."

There was silence for a moment while Mason drummed on his desk, then he said, "Let's try to fix the time as close as we can."

"Well, my plane got in at eleven-forty-five. It took me a few minutes to get my baggage cleared. I had rented a car from a drive-yourself agency. It was waiting for me at the airport. I got home around twelve-thirty."

"Did you look at your watch at any time that you remember?"

"I remember it was around—oh, around one o'clock when I was with Dad. I remember after we'd then been talking a little while I thought he should be getting some sleep, so I put on an act of yawning and talking about being tired."

"How long did you stay after that? I mean in the room with your father."

"Not very long, a few minutes perhaps."

"And then you were in the kitchen eating a sandwich and having a glass of milk when Edison Doyle came in?"

"That's right."

"Edison Doyle had a key?"

"He said Hattie had told him the key to the back door would be left under the back doormat. I guess it was. I didn't notice. Anyway, he opened the back door and came in. I remember he locked the door behind him. It's a spring lock, works with a latchkey."

Mason studied the top of his desk in frowning contemplation. He once more began drumming thoughtfully with the tips of his fingers.

"Now then," Jarrett Bain said, "what should we do? It looks as though Sylvia may be trying to confuse the issue. But right now she's certainly started something. Personally I think she has started something she can't finish."

"We have Hattie to consider," Mason said. "*And* Sylvia."

"Don't waste any time worrying about Sylvia," Bain said. "She'll take care of herself. Right now she's managed to put Hattie in something of a spot and has definitely left a great big black mark on Dad's memory. I like her as a sister, but some of the things she does drive me nuts.

"Now then, she's spread a cockeyed story and as soon as they interview me it'll be established that that story's false."

Mason studied him thoughtfully. "It probably won't occur to them to question you. You may not *have* to be interviewed."

Jarrett Bain shook his head. "No dice, Mr. Mason. I'm sorry but I'm a damn poor liar. Moreover, I have ideas about telling the truth. I have to live with myself."

"You intend to tell your story then?"

"Of course. Anyhow, I have a feeling of loyalty to Dad's memory. I'm doing this much, I'm telling you *first*."

"Where are you going to tell it next?" Mason asked.

"I have an appointment with some guy up at headquarters. Let me see, what's his name now?"

Jarrett took a card out of his pocket, looked at it, said, "A Lieutenant Tragg of Homicide. You know him?"

Mason settled back in his chair and sighed wearily. "I know him."

"Well, I'm on my way up there," Jarrett Bain said, heaving up to his feet. "Didn't realize it was so late. Don't want to keep the guy waiting. Good day, Mr. Mason."

"*Good* day," Mason said as Jarrett walked toward the door.

Silently Mason and Della Street watched the door click shut behind the departing archaeologist.

Della Street sighed in dismay. "The damnedest things happen to us, Chief," she said. "I feel like I want to bawl."

"Who doesn't?" Mason said with a wry grin.

12

NERVOUS, almost hysterical knuckles tapped on the hall door of Mason's private office.

Mason glanced at Della Street. "That probably will be Sylvia," he said. "If it is, let her in."

Della Street opened the door a crack, then pulled it all the way open, stood to one side and said, "Come in, Mrs. Atwood."

Sylvia Atwood's eyes showed that she had been crying. She was almost hysterical as she said, "Oh, thank heavens I've found you here, Mr. Mason. Thank heavens. I rang and rang the phone and no one answered—"

"The switchboard is disconnected after the office closes at five," Mason explained.

"They wouldn't give me any other number. They said it was unlisted. Oh, Mr. Mason, I've done the most awful thing, the most terrible thing!"

"All right," Mason said, "tell me just how bad it is."

"I guess I must have been mistaken about one thing, Mr. Mason. It could have been Hattie who went up there to Brogan's apartment. If it was Hattie then she was wearing Dad's overcoat. When that person came down in the elevator and I was waiting on the stairs and looked to see who it was—well, I'm satisfied it was a woman."

"Still wearing an overcoat?"

"No, the overcoat was over her arm at that time."

"So then *you* went on upstairs?"

"Went on upstairs and waited in front of Brogan's apartment."

"For how long?"

"For a little while. Just like I told you. Then I was satisfied that—well, I thought the figure that went out *must* have been Dad. Please understand me, Mr. Mason, I really and truly thought I was trailing Dad all the time."

"Well," Mason said, "the first thing we have to do is to get Hattie's story."

Sylvia shook her head. "I'm afraid we can't, not until after we've determined our strategy."

"Why not?"

"The police have her."

"The police!" Mason exclaimed. "Why, the doctor said—"

"They wakened her, put her under arrest and bundled her off before the poor girl knew what was happening."

"She'd been drugged," Mason said. "They had no right doing that. Who did it?"

"Sergeant Holcomb."

"Go on," Mason said.

"They—they found the ice pick."

"What ice pick?"

"The one that murdered Fritch."

"Where?"

"In the drawer in Hattie's dresser, underneath her handkerchiefs—the same drawer where I'd concealed the spool of tape, only this was *under* the handkerchiefs. I'd put the tape on *top* of them."

"Well now, *isn't* that interesting," Mason said dryly.

Sylvia said, "I know what you must think of me, Mr. Mason. Probably you think I'm the worst little scatter-brained idiot in the world, but—well, we're into it now, and we're going to have to hang together on this thing."

She opened her purse, took out her checkbook. She said, "I gave you one check for five hundred dollars as a retainer. I'm going to give you fifteen hundred dollars more, Mr. Mason. I want you to—to represent Hattie."

Mason watched her filling out the check.

"And please, Mr. Mason," she went on, "please do what I told you. Remember what I said—I don't want to do anything that would be a black spot on Dad's memory, but, after all, Fritch *was* a blackmailer and he *deserved* to die. Under Dad's moral code he would have been perfectly entitled to kill him.

"If this thing had happened years ago in Texas, Dad wouldn't have thought anything about pulling a gun and killing J.J. on sight and no jury would have done anything to him."

"This didn't happen years ago and it isn't in Texas," Mason said. "And the ideas you had about your father's killing Fritch have all turned out to be demonstrable fallacies."

"I know, but—well, Dad's gone now. They can't do anything to punish *him,* and it's better to have a black spot on his memory than to have one of us girls, I mean, Hattie, in a pack of trouble.

"I'm trying to tell you, Mr. Mason, that since I've already said what I did about Dad—well, no one knows *all* the details.

"Jarrett has, of course, messed things up. But if someone would fake a wire to him telling him of a new archaeological discovery in the jungle, Jarrett would go rushing off without waiting for anything. The funeral wouldn't stop him. He's seen so much of dead civilizations, he looks on individual death as just a—"

"Now look," Mason interrupted, "you've messed things up enough. Don't go sending Jarrett any fake wires."

"Why, Mr. Mason! I wouldn't do that. I want you to handle things now."

Mason said, "Just what *do* you want me to do? What's this check for?"

"I want you to defend Hattie."

Mason said to Della Street, "Endorse on the back of that check that it is for the purpose of defending Hattie Bain, and that I have a free hand to handle the case in my own way, and if I have an opportunity I am at liberty to expose the murderer, whoever that murderer may be. Underscore 'whoever that murderer may be.' "

Mason looked up at Sylvia Atwood. "Is that satisfactory?" he asked.

Her green eyes met his steadily. "Why, of course, Mr. Mason," she said. "Why shouldn't it be?"

Mason held her eyes. "We're all in a mess now," he said. "Some of it is due to your desire to be, to quote your brother, little Miss Fix-It. Now try not to send any fake wire or do anything else that will complicate the situation."

"But, Mr. Mason, I think you're terribly conservative. If Jarrett weren't here to testify about seeing Dad they couldn't *prove* it wasn't Dad who went to that apartment. *I* can swear in all honesty and in all good faith I was trailing Dad."

Mason grinned. "Well, thank you for the compliment."

"What compliment?"

"Thinking I'm too conservative. Tell that to the police some time, will you?"

"You're making fun of me now."

"It's not fun. You're dangerous. I want one thing out of you. Keep your mouth shut and keep your fingers out of the pie."

"I think you're horrid. You've been listening to Jarrett. Before this case is over you'll have reason to thank me for thinking ahead and doing the things your stuffy sense of professional ethics keeps you from even thinking of, much less doing!"

And she walked from the office, head high, shoulders squared.

"Heaven deliver us if she tries anything else!" Mason said.

"Want to bet?" Della asked.

"Good Lord, no!" Mason groaned.

13

PERRY MASON sat in the visitors' room in the jail, looking across at Hattie Bain.

Between them was a heavy partition of plate glass. A microphone and a miniature loud-speaker on each side enabled voices to be heard through the glass screen. Aside from that the parties were as much separated as though they had been in different countries.

Hattie Bain's face showed the devastating effects of the grief at her father's death, the nervous strain to which she had been subjected, and the shock of her imprisonment.

"How are you feeling?" Mason asked.

"Pretty bad. How do I look?"

"Not bad."

"My pictures in the papers were terrible."

"You were full of drugs."

"They didn't give me the breaks at all."

"Did you talk to them?"

"Why, of course, I answered their questions," she said simply.

"Well, suppose you tell me what happened. Did you go to see J. J. Fritch the night of the murder?"

"Yes."

"When?"

"After everything had quieted down at the house. I waited until Dad was asleep and Sylvia had gone to bed."

"Why did you go, Hattie?"

"I thought I could make some deal with him."

"Could you?"

"No."

"Where did you see him, in Brogan's apartment?"

"No, in his apartment. He was nasty to me, insulting to Dad. He was a thoroughly despicable man."

"You told the police all this?"

"Certainly."

"All right, tell me just what happened."

"I drove up to that apartment house. I went up to the apartment that was rented in the name of Frank Reedy, the one that was really Fritch's apartment."

"You knew Fritch?"

"Oh yes, I'd known him years ago when he and Dad were in business together."

"Go on," Mason said.

She said, "I rang the doorbell. I had to ring several times before—"

"That was the Reedy apartment?" Mason asked.

"Yes."

"Now how about the apartment across the hall, the one occupied by George Brogan?"

"J.J. took me in there. He wanted to get me out of his apartment. I think he wasn't alone, that someone was in his apartment. He hustled me right across the hall to that other apartment."

"I want you to think carefully about this," Mason said. "Did you notice any note on the door of that apartment? Anything pinned to the door?"

She thought for a moment, then said, "I can't be certain, Mr. Mason. I was thinking about—yes, I guess perhaps there was."

"But you can't be certain?"

"No, I can't be certain."

"All right, what did you do after you reached Brogan's apartment?"

She said, "I told J.J. that I was going to put the cards right on the table, that you were in a position to prove he was a blackmailer, that you were terribly clever, that he had a tape recording and that you were going to be able to prove it was a forgery.

"I told him that what he was doing was killing Dad

without doing himself any good, and I asked him to be a man and not be a sniveling, sneaking blackmailer."

"What happened?"

"He became insulting."

"Then what?"

"He virtually threw me out. He said if we didn't get rid of you we'd all be sorry."

"And then?"

"Then I went home and went to bed."

"Were you wearing your father's coat?"

"Yes, I was. I started out and realized I'd forgotten to bring a wrap, so I opened the closet and grabbed the first thing handy."

"And you told the police all this?"

"Certainly. It's their business to investigate. They have to ask questions. It's the duty of a good citizen to cooperate."

Mason remained thoughtfully silent. Hattie Bain raised dark, steady eyes to his.

"That's the truth," she said.

"And you told it *all* to the police?"

She nodded.

Mason sighed. "Well, we *may* be able to keep the admission out of evidence on the ground that you were filled up with drugs."

"I don't want it kept out of evidence," she said. "I want the truth told just the way it is."

"And what time was this?" Mason asked.

"Between midnight and—I was back about half-past one or two in the morning. I didn't look at my watch."

"What time did you leave Fritch?"

"I can't tell about the exact time."

Mason said, "Now look, I don't want you to make any more statements to anyone. I'm going to try to get you an immediate hearing in court. I'm going to try to at least get the facts straightened out so we know where we stand. Now you aren't lying to protect your father, are you?"

She shook her head.

"Well, we'll do the best we can."

She said, "I haven't any money to pay you, Mr. Mason, unless, of course, you could wait for Dad's estate."

Mason said, "Your sister Sylvia retained me to represent you."

For a moment there was some peculiar expression in her eyes. "You're going to do what Sylvia instructs you to do? You're going to let her direct my defense?"

Mason said, "I'm going to handle your defense to the best of my ability. I'm going to be working for you and for you alone. Look at me, Miss Bain. Look me in the eyes. Do you understand what I'm saying?"

"Yes."

"Do you understand that I mean it? That I mean every word of it?"

"Yes."

"All right," Mason said. "Remember it. You're my client and I'm your lawyer. I'm not representing anybody else. Just you."

"Thank you, Mr. Mason."

14

THE COURTROOM was packed with spectators who appreciated the importance of the legal battle that was about to take place.

Judge Kaylor emerged from his chambers to take his place on the bench. The bailiff rapped the court to order.

"The case of People versus Harriet Bain," Judge Kaylor said.

"Ready for the prosecution," Delbert Moon, a deputy district attorney, answered.

"And for the defense," Mason announced.

"This is the preliminary hearing on a charge of first-degree murder," Judge Kaylor said.

Delbert Moon, suave, quick-witted, adroit, one of the newer and more skillful trial deputies in a reorganized district attorney's office, was on his feet.

"If the Court please," he said, "I'll call Mr. George Brogan as my first witness."

George Brogan came forward and was sworn.

He gave his name and address to the clerk, and his occupation as that of a private investigator.

"You were acquainted with an individual known to you as J.J. Fritch in his lifetime?" Moon asked.

"Yes, sir."

"Where is he?"

"He is dead."

"How do you know he is dead?"

"I saw his dead body."

"That's all."

Brogan started to leave the stand.

"Just a moment," Mason said. "I have some cross-examination."

"Now, if the Court please," Moon said, "I have deliberately framed my questions so that this witness, who will be recalled later as a material witness for the prosecution, has at the present time testified only to one phase of the *corpus delicti*. I insist that Counsel confine his cross-examination to that part of the case."

Mason said, "I don't think Counsel needs to advise me how to conduct my cross-examination. I suggest that the orderly procedure is for him to listen to my questions and object to any question that he feels is not proper cross-examination."

"Proceed," Judge Kaylor said, smiling slightly.

"You say that you saw the body of J. J. Fritch?" Mason asked.

"That is right."

"When did you see it?"

"I saw it at the morgue."

"Who was present?"

"Sergeant Holcomb of Homicide, and Dr. Hanover, the autopsy surgeon."

"You had known J. J. Fritch in his lifetime?"

"Yes, sir."

"For approximately how long?"

"For a good many years."

"Can you estimate the period of time?"

"No, sir, I cannot."

"Why?"

"It's been a long time."

"Five years?"

"Yes."

"Ten years?"

"Perhaps."

"Fifteen years?"

"I don't know."

"More than ten years?"

"I couldn't say."

"Can't you tell when you first met Mr. Fritch?"

"No, sir, I cannot remember."

"Now you state that you saw the body of Mr. Fritch in the morgue?"

"Yes, sir."

"Was that the *first* time you had seen the dead body of Mr. Fritch?"

"Now, Your Honor," Moon said, "I object. The witness has been called solely for the purpose of establishing the fact that J. J. Fritch was known by him in his lifetime, and that J. J. Fritch is dead. Our next witness will be Dr. Hanover, the autopsy surgeon, who will prove Mr. Fritch met his death by violence at the hands of some third person. We will then be in a position to proceed in an orderly way to connect up the defendant with the death of J. J. Fritch. Therefore, this question is not proper cross-examination at this time. Later on, when the witness has appeared and given his testimony in detail concerning other phases of the case, the question may well be proper."

"The question is quite proper at this time," Mason said.

"You asked the witness if he saw the body of J. J. Fritch. I am asking him when he saw the body, and I am asking him when he *first* saw the body."

"The objection is overruled," Judge Kaylor said.

"When did you first see the body?" Mason asked.

Brogan shifted his position slightly, took a deep breath, glanced over Mason's head at the back of the courtroom, then down at the floor.

"Can't you answer that question?" Mason asked.

"I was trying to get the thing fixed in my mind, trying to get it clear in my mind."

"Well, take your time," Mason said. "Take just as long as you want."

Brogan hesitated for a moment, looked at the deputy district attorney, then glanced away, then said, "As nearly as I can remember it, it was approximately five minutes past nine on the morning of the seventh of this month."

"Where was the body?"

"It was lying on the floor of my apartment in front of the door leading to a closet where I stored liquor."

"What was the condition of the body?"

"Now then, if the Court please," Moon said, "I am again going to object. This is all matter which can be brought out when Mr. Brogan is called as a witness on the other phase of our case. It is not proper at the present time."

Mason said, "The witness has been asked on direct examination as to whether he knew J. J. Fritch and whether he saw the body. I am asking him now to describe the body. I certainly have that right."

"I think so," Judge Kaylor said. "The objection is overruled. Answer the question."

"Go ahead," Mason said, "answer the question."

"The upper part of the body was stiff. It was slightly doubled, that is, the elbows were doubled and pressed into the sides. The body was clad in underwear and that's all."

"Anything else you can think of about the body?"

"There were several small puncture wounds."

"You noticed them at that time?"

"No, sir, I did not, but I noticed little stains of dry blood on the undershirt."

"What kind of an undershirt?"

"A ribbed, sleeveless, athletic undershirt."

"What can you say about the color of the body?"

"Why, nothing. It was sort of a grayish color, the color of a corpse."

"What about the back? Did you notice any color on the back?"

"There was—now that you mention it, I think there was a bruise on the back—below the neck—between the shoulders."

"Visible under the undershirt?"

"Yes, sir. The head was twisted a little. The body was on its back."

"Now that's relating to the time you first saw the body?"

"Yes, sir."

"Now let's go to the next time you saw the body, where was that?"

"That was when it was in the morgue."

"What was the condition of the body at that time?"

"It had been stretched out."

"You could recognize the features?"

"Yes, sir."

"Was that before the autopsy or afterward?"

"Immediately before the autopsy."

"Now, Mr. Brogan," Mason said, "when I asked you when you had first seen the body you hesitated perceptibly. Do you remember that?"

"Oh, if the Court please," Moon said, "I think that is not proper cross-examination, and furthermore I don't think the witness hesitated."

Mason said, "The witness did hesitate, and furthermore he stated when I asked him why he was hesitating that he was trying to get the thing fixed in his mind, trying to get it clear in his mind."

"I believe that is correct," Judge Kaylor ruled.

"Why did you hesitate?" Mason asked.

"I was trying to collect my thoughts on the subject."

"Were your thoughts scattered?"

"The expression was figurative."

"Why did you have to stop and study in order to remember what time it was when you *first* saw the body?"

"I wanted to be certain I wasn't mistaken."

"Thank you," Mason said. "Now I want to ask you a few questions about your acquaintanceship with J. J. Fritch. You can't remember the time you first met him?"

"No, sir."

"Had you done any business for Mr. Fritch?"

"I was—no, not *for* Mr. Fritch, no."

"He had consulted you in connection with a business matter shortly before his death?"

"I will express it this way, Mr. Mason. I know what you're trying to get at and I'll say—"

"Now never mind trying to anticipate what I'm getting at," Mason said. "I have asked you a simple question. I want you to answer it."

"Well, I was not representing J. J. Fritch."

"Whom were you representing?"

"I actually was not representing anyone."

"You were trying to get Sylvia Atwood, the sister of the defendant, to retain you?"

"Yes, sir."

"For what purpose?"

"To secure possession of a tape recording which I felt might be quite damaging to the family."

"Who originally approached you in that connection?"

"I approached Mrs. Atwood."

"Who originally approached you?"

"Mr. Fritch."

"What did he want?"

"He thought that it might be possible to get some money out of the Bain family in return for a tape recording."

"You had heard that tape recording?"

"Yes, sir."

"Did you know there was more than one tape recording?"

"Well—there had been—I believe there was only one original."

"But you did know that one or more copies had been made?"

Moon was on his feet. *"Now,* Your Honor, I am quite certain this cross-examination has gone far afield. Counsel is trying to present his own case by cross-examining my witness. Counsel will hear plenty about that tape recording in a short time when Counsel is called to the stand to explain how that tape recording came to be in *his* possession."

Judge Kaylor said, "The Court is going to ask Counsel to refrain from these acrimonious, sarcastic personalities. The objection is sustained."

Mason smiled at the worried Brogan.

"Thank you, Mr. Brogan," Mason said. "That's all."

"No further questions," Moon said. "Call Dr. Hanover."

Dr. Hanover came forward, was sworn, gave his name, residence and occupation, and a brief summary of his professional qualifications.

"I ask you, Dr. Hanover," Moon said, "if you were present when a body was identified by Mr. George Brogan, the witness who has just left the stand?"

"I was. Yes, sir."

"That was the body that he has now identified as being that of J. J. Fritch?"

"Yes, sir."

"Doctor, when did you first see the body in question?"

"At approximately nine-forty on the morning of the seventh."

"Did you at that time make preliminary tests to determine when death had occurred?"

"I did. Yes, sir."

"And what did those tests show?"

"That death had occurred between midnight and three o'clock in the morning of that same day."

"Did you subsequently perform a post-mortem on that body?"

"I did. Yes, sir."

"Doctor, I don't want a technical description of what you found—I want you to just tell the Court in plain, ordinary language as to what you found was the cause of death."

"The cause of death was a series of eight puncture wounds which had penetrated the chest cavity. Four of those wounds had been made from the front and two of them had penetrated the heart. Four of the wounds had been made from behind. One of them had penetrated the heart, two the lung, one had failed to penetrate because of striking the scapula, or shoulder blade."

"Those wounds caused death?"

"Yes, sir."

"An immediate death?"

"That depends on what you mean by the word immediate. I would say that the *immediate* effect of the wounds was to cause the man to fall forward, to become helpless. Death ensued within a relatively short time."

"Now then," Moon said, "I'm going to ask you if you are acquainted with a phenomenon known technically as post-mortem lividity?"

"I am. Yes, sir."

"Will you please explain what is meant by that?"

"Yes, sir. After death, when the blood ceases to circulate in the body, it naturally has a tendency while it is still fluid to settle to the lowest portion of the body. This causes a congestion of the blood vessels in the underside of the body and as the blood undergoes the changes which are associated with a cessation of circulation, I might say a stagnation if I were to use a term that might make it more understandable, there is a discoloration or a lividity in the portion of the body affected. To the uninitiated that may seem to be a bruise."

"Now, Doctor, where does this port-mortem lividity form?"

"Upon the parts of the body that are affected by the settling of blood due to gravitational attraction."

"You mean by that the lowest portions of the body?"

"That is correct. Speaking from a standpoint of body position and not from a standpoint of anatomical structure. In other words, if the body is left lying on its back the post-mortem lividity will appear along the muscles of the back, except the places where the skin is pressing against some object."

"If the body is lying on its stomach the post-mortem lividity will not be on the back?"

"No, sir."

"And if the body is propped in such a position so that it is sitting straight up, would you expect to find a post-mortem lividity between the shoulders or along the back of the neck?"

"No, sir."

"Did you find any post-mortem lividity on the body of J. J. Fritch?"

"I did, sir. A very well defined post-mortem lividity."

"And where was this located? I'm going to ask you, Doctor, just to indicate and explain in ordinary language if you will, please, disregarding anatomical terms as much as possible."

Dr. Hanover placed his right hand to the back of his neck between the shoulder blades, said, "There was some post-mortem lividity here and in two or three places along the back."

"What did this post-mortem lividity indicate to you as an autopsy surgeon and an experienced pathologist, Doctor?"

"That the body had been lying on its back."

"Now what about *rigor mortis?*"

"*Rigor mortis* had set in to the extent that the arms and shoulders were locked in *rigor mortis,* but *rigor mortis* had not as yet proceeded to the legs."

"That is, when the body was found?"

"Yes, sir."

"Returning to post-mortem lividity, Doctor, when does it begin to form?"

"Under most conditions this discoloration will begin to be apparent from one to two hours after death."

"And what can you tell us about the development of *rigor mortis,* Doctor?"

"*Rigor mortis* develops first in the face and jaws. The onset usually takes place in this area in from three to five hours after death. The rigidity gradually extends downward, involving the neck, chest and arms, abdomen, and finally the legs and feet. For the entire body to be involved usually requires a period of from about eight to twelve hours after death.

"However, *rigor mortis* is a variable factor. It depends somewhat upon circumstances, perhaps somewhat upon temperature."

"From your observations, taken as a whole, Doctor, can you fix the time of death of the body in question?"

"Yes, sir. I can fix it within a period of three hours."

"And those three hours are what?"

"Between midnight and 3:00 A.M."

"Cross-examine," Moon said.

"Did you," Mason asked, "fix the time of death solely from the development of *rigor mortis?*"

"No, sir. I did not."

"Did you fix it from the post-mortem lividity?"

"Definitely not."

"Let us suppose that a body had been lying in one position long enough for post-mortem lividity to have formed. Then someone moved the body. Would that change the post-mortem lividity?"

"Definitely that would not. When the blood has once settled there is a certain amount of clotting which takes place in the tissues, so that if the body is moved after this has taken place the original lividity will still be present.

"As one of the outstanding authorities has stated in a book on this subject, when a dead body is found with post-mortem lividity on the upper surface of the body the investigator can be sure that someone has moved that body from its position at a time at least several hours after death occurred. There again, Mr. Mason, when I refer to the upper portion of the body I mean the upper positional portion rather than the upper anatomical portion."

"I understand," Mason said. "As I understand it, Doctor, you are not basing your conclusions as to the time of death entirely on the post-mortem lividity?"

"No, sir. That is a factor, but post-mortem lividity and *rigor mortis* are somewhat indefinite factors. *Rigor mortis* varies considerably in connection with the time of development. If a person dies after a fight, or after extreme muscular exertion, *rigor mortis* may set in very quickly. For myself I consider it rather dangerous to try to predicate a conclusion as to time of death entirely upon *rigor mortis*.

"That, of course, refers to fixing a time of death within the narrow limits of one hour, two hours or three hours. Of course, over a longer period of time a person can make an estimate, and a very accurate estimate, for instance, a six-hour period during which death must have occurred. After twenty-four hours, if certain characteristic changes in *rigor mortis* are present, I would say that it would be possible to draw a conclusion as to a six-hour interval during which death must have taken place."

"But in this case you are fixing it within a three-hour period?"

"Yes, sir."

"Doctor, you probably know your own mind better than anyone. I'm going to ask you if you are prejudiced against the defendant in this case?"

Dr. Hanover gave the question frowning consideration. "Well, of course, I have an opinion as to the guilt or innocence of the defendant."

"You think she is guilty?"

"I do."

"That is a fixed opinion in your mind?"

"It is."

"Due to investigations you have made?"

"Investigations I have made and investigations that have been made by others and the results of which I know."

"Therefore you are prejudiced against the defendant?"

"I don't think I am prejudiced against her. I have an opinion as to her guilt."

"And as a citizen you would dislike to see a guilty defendant escape the penalty of her crime?"

"That is right."

"Therefore, since you feel the defendant is guilty, you are anxious to see that she pays the penalty?"

"I suppose that is true."

"So that in giving your testimony you would naturally try to give it in such a way as to bring about the greatest prejudice to the defendant's case?"

"No, sir, that very definitely is not correct."

"I am not talking now, Doctor, about altering the *facts*. I am talking about the *manner* of giving your testimony."

"Yes, sir."

"Now, Doctor, may I ask you what factors you have taken into consideration in connection with fixing the time of death during this three-hour period?"

"Two factors," Dr. Hanover said. "The time element involved in connection with the ingestion of a meal, which I naturally assume was a normal evening meal, and the temperature of the body. The temperature factor I consider an absolute index."

"You didn't mention either of these matters on direct examination, Doctor."

"I wasn't asked about them."

"You were asked as to fixing the time of death?"

"I was, and I fixed the time of death."

"Now, Doctor, did you know that you were not going to be asked about these two other factors on your direct examination?"

"Oh, Your Honor," Moon said, "I think this is not legitimate cross-examination. This is nagging at the witness, bickering with the witness. This is splitting hairs with the witness. This is dragging in completely irrelevant matters."

"No, it isn't," Mason said. "This is going to the question of the bias of the witness."

"He has already testified that he thinks the defendant is guilty, and he wants to see her convicted," Moon said.

"Exactly," Mason retorted, "but he has also sworn under his oath that the prejudice didn't in any way affect the manner in which he gave his testimony. I now propose to show that it has affected the manner in which he's giving his testimony."

"Just how do you mean, Mr. Mason?" Judge Kaylor asked.

"I propose to show," Mason said, "that Dr. Hanover deliberately refrained from making any statement as to the factors by which he fixed the time of death on direct examination because he had an understanding with the prosecutor that he would carefully refrain from mentioning those two factors on direct examination, thereby trapping me into cross-examining him on the element of time. He felt he would be in a better strategic position to harm the defendant's case by doing this on cross-examination rather than on direct examination."

"The objection is overruled," Judge Kaylor said.

"Can you answer that question, Doctor?" Mason asked.

Dr. Hanover suddenly became uncomfortable.

"Well," he said, "I had, of course, discussed my testimony with the authorities."

"By the authorities you mean the deputy district attorney?"

"And the police."

"But with the deputy district attorney?"

"Yes, sir."

"And did the police tell you anything about the manner in which you were to give testimony?"

Dr. Hanover rose at once to the bait. "Absolutely not, sir. They did not. There is absolutely nothing to justify that insinuation."

"Did the deputy district attorney?" Mason asked.

Abruptly Dr. Hanover became embarrassed. "Well, there was a general discussion as to what my testimony would cover."

"Wasn't there a *specific* discussion that you would say nothing on direct examination as to the manner in which you fixed your time of death, that you would simply give a flat opinion that death occurred between midnight and three o'clock in the morning, that you would purposely refrain from elaborating on your reasons, and that when I cross-examined you you would then be in a position to crucify me?"

"I don't think the word crucify was used."

"But its equivalent?"

"Well, I will say that I was instructed to—no, instructed is not the right word. I am somewhat at a loss for the right word. It was agreed that I would withhold testimony as to details until the questions were asked on cross-examination."

"Forcing me to lead with my chin?" Mason asked.

Dr. Hanover smiled. "That is a slang expression which was not used."

"All right, what was the slang expression that *was* used?" Mason asked.

Dr. Hanover abruptly shifted his eyes and remained silent.

"Oh, Your Honor," Moon said, "I think the exact words are immaterial. Dr. Hanover has certainly given Counsel the point Counsel was trying so laboriously to make."

"I want the exact words," Mason said. "I think I'm entitled to have them. I think it has a bearing on the attitude of this witness."

"The objection is overruled."

"What was the exact slang expression that was used?"

"Nail you to the cross," Dr. Hanover blurted.

"So that when you smiled in rather a superior manner and said that the word crucify was not used, you were taking advantage of a technicality?"

"I object to that question as argumentative," Moon said.

"Sustained," Judge Kaylor ruled. "The facts speak for themselves."

"Now then," Mason said, abruptly shifting his tactics, "you stated that the immediate effect of the wounds was not to cause death but would cause the man to fall forward and become helpless?"

"I believe I so testified. Yes, sir."

"That is your opinion?"

"Yes, sir."

"Fall *forward?*" Mason asked.

"Yes, sir."

"Why do you assume he fell forward rather than backward?"

"Because I am assuming that the four stab wounds in front were the first wounds and that after the man fell forward the other four wounds were inflicted while he was lying on his face."

"And why do you assume that?"

"Why, because it's—it's natural."

"And why do you say it's natural?"

"Well, frankly, there is nothing about any of the wounds that would enable me to tell the order in which the wounds had been inflicted. They were all inflicted at approximately the same time, that is, in what I would judge a rapid sequence, but if the man was stabbed in the heart and fell forward it would be impossible to inflict any more stabs in the front, and the remaining four stabs would have been in the back."

"Unless," Mason said, "the first four stabs had been in the back and the man had fallen over backward, in which event the remaining four wounds would have been in the front."

"Well, have it that way if you want to."

"I don't want to have it either way," Mason said. "All I want to bring out is the fact that beyond mere surmise and conjecture you know nothing as to the order in which the wounds were inflicted or whether the wounds in front were first or those in back were second."

"I was assuming that the wounds in front were made first, but I will admit, Mr. Mason, that I cannot testify to that."

"And yet you have just testified that the post-mortem lividity indicated the body had been *lying on its back?*"

"Well—yes, when the body finally came to rest."

"And death presupposes that?"

"Oh, I suppose so."

"So then the evidence you have uncovered from your examination indicates the first four wounds were the back wounds."

"It could be."

"I am asking you if the evidence you uncovered in your examination doesn't so indicate?"

"Yes, I guess it does."

"Don't guess, Doctor. Does it?"

"Yes, but that evidence isn't sufficient to be conclusive."

"Then you don't know in what position the man died?"

"No, sir."

"But you assume the body had been moved after death?"

"Definitely not. I don't think it had been."

"Then the attack must have been from the rear."

"I won't argue the point, Mr. Mason."

"Don't argue, answer."

"Well—I don't know."

"Then you don't know the man fell forward?"

"No."

"Did you examine the body for poisons?"

"I examined the body for the cause of death. I found the cause of death to be the series of puncture wounds mentioned before."

"You found they were sufficient to cause death?"

"Yes, sir."

"Do you know, of your own knowledge, whether there

was any other contributing cause of death, such as poison?"

"No, sir. I know that these wounds were inflicted during the man's lifetime. I know that the result of those wounds would have been to produce death. Therefore, I assume that those wounds were the cause of death. Whether there was any other factor which would cause symptoms I do not know. I do know that the wounds were the cause of death. That is what I was asked about and that's what I testified about."

"Now, Doctor, you state that you have determined the time of death as being between midnight and three o'clock on the morning of the seventh."

"Yes, sir."

"That is an accurate determination?"

"Understand, Mr. Mason, I cannot tell *exactly* when death occurred, but I *can* fix limits *within which death must have occurred.* I am prepared to state that death did not occur prior to midnight and that it did not occur after three o'clock on the morning of the seventh. I think the probabilities are that death occurred around one o'clock in the morning, but in order to be on the safe side I have established that three-hour limit and am prepared to state that death occurred somewhere within those three hours."

"How do you know?" Mason asked.

"Primarily by taking the temperature of the body and comparing it with certain statistical information we have as to the rate of cooling."

"And," Mason said, smiling, "this is the phase of your testimony that you and the prosecutor's office decided could best be brought out on cross-examination?"

"Well, yes."

"All right then, let's bring it out. What about the rate of cooling?"

"The average normal temperature of a body at the time of death, particularly in the case of a death by violence, may be assumed as ninety-eight point six Fahrenheit. The body will cool at the rate of approximately one and one-half degrees an hour, depending upon surrounding circumstances—for the first twelve hours, that is."

"Why do you say in cases of homicide?"

"Because in cases of natural death the man may have been suffering from a high fever. If, for instance, there was a fever of a hundred and three this would make a difference in the body temperature and so would affect calculations as to the time of death. On the other hand, where a man is apparently in perfect health at the time of death and meets a violent end, we are safe in assuming a temperature of ninety-eight point six."

"So you determined the time of death in this case because of the temperature of the body?"

"Primarily. I also took into consideration the extent to which *rigor mortis* had developed, the state of food in the digestive tract, and the appearance of the post-mortem lividity."

"Did you take into consideration the fact that the body was unclothed?"

"Yes, sir. I took into consideration the various elements of temperature. In other words, the temperature of the surrounding air, and the fact that the body was unclothed."

"But *was* the body unclothed at the time of death?" Mason asked.

"I am assuming that it was."

"That is an assumption like the one you made about the sequence of the wounds, Doctor, simply predicated upon what seems to your mind to be most natural?"

"No, sir. We made a most careful examination of the clothing that was hanging in the closet of the apartment occupied by the decedent."

"That apartment was directly across the hall from the apartment occupied by George Brogan?"

"That is correct."

"You examined that clothing very carefully?"

"All of it, yes, sir."

"Looking for what?"

"For puncture marks or bloodstains."

"You found neither?"

"No, sir."

"Therefore at the time of death you are prepared to state that J. J. Fritch was wandering around the apartment of George Brogan clad only in an undershirt and shorts?"

"No, sir."

"I thought that was the effect of your testimony."

"I can't state that he was wandering around. I will further state this, Mr. Mason, *if* the body *had* been clothed, and if the clothing had been removed at some time shortly after death, the determination as to the time of death because of temperature rate would not have been changed. I am making a sufficient allowance in the three-hour time limit so that I feel certain death did not occur before midnight and did not occur after 3:00 A.M."

"Those are absolute time limits?" Mason asked.

"Absolutely. Yes, sir."

"You are satisfied that it was a physical impossibility for death to have occurred before midnight?"

"Yes."

"Or later than three o'clock in the morning?"

"Yes, sir."

"You are prepared to stake your reputation on that, Doctor?"

"I am testifying to it."

"Thank you," Mason said. "That is all."

Moon said, "Just a moment, Doctor. I have a few questions to ask you on redirect examination covering points that were brought out by Mr. Mason in his cross-examination. Now, Doctor, when you first saw this body, where was it?"

"It was lying on the floor in the apartment of George Brogan."

"Where in that apartment?"

"Immediately in front of a liquor closet, and I may state the person who claimed to have found the body claimed that it had been in the liquor closet and had tumbled out when the door was opened."

"Just a moment," Mason said, "I move to strike the last part of that out as being hearsay."

"Objection sustained. The motion is granted. That part of the testimony will be stricken," Judge Kaylor ruled.

Moon, nettled but realizing that his position was legally indefensible, accepted his defeat as gracefully as possible, and said, "Would it have been possible, Doctor, in your opinion, for this body to have been placed in that liquor closet and to have fallen out when the door was opened?"

"No, sir."

"Why?"

"Taking into consideration the various factors which I have enumerated, that assumption is completely negatived."

"Why?"

"Because, in the first place, it is negatived by the position of the arms. *Rigor mortis* had developed so that the arms were locked in position. The elbows were close to the sides. The hands were near the jaw. Yet there was no evidence that the arms had been tied up in any way."

"And what does that indicate, Doctor?"

"That the body very definitely could not have been propped up in the liquor closet, or anywhere else, immediately after death. The hands and arms in that case would have dropped, and *rigor mortis* would have set in, locking the arms in that lower position. The fact that the hands were elevated, that the elbows were at the side, indicates that the body must have been lying on its back rather than propped up. In my opinion, that was the only way in which *rigor mortis* could have set in with the hands in that position."

"Any other reasons?"

"Yes, sir, the development of post-mortem lividity."

"Thank you, Doctor, that's all."

"Now, just a minute," Mason said. "I'd like to ask the doctor a few more questions about that."

"Very well, go right ahead," Moon said.

"This was testimony that you had previously discussed with the prosecutor?"

"Yes, sir."

"And had agreed between you that if necessary it was to be brought out on redirect examination, but that you would try while you were being cross-examined to slip in the fact that the person who found the body claimed it had tumbled out of the liquor closet?"

"Well, that's a fact. I heard that statement myself."

"At the time the body was discovered?"

"At a later date. I interviewed that witness."

"But it was agreed that you were to try to slip that fact in on cross-examination?"

"Well—I—I pointed out that that statement of the witness was obviously false, and Mr. Moon suggested that if possible I should point that out while I was giving my testimony."

"And was it suggested that you slip that statement in if you had a chance?"

"Oh, Your Honor, I think we've gone into this a dozen times," Moon said. "Let's assume that this witness is favorable to the prosecution."

"On that assumption," Mason said, "I won't insist on an answer. I simply want the Court to understand that the entire testimony of this witness is colored by a prejudice in favor of the prosecution."

"That isn't what I said," Moon said.

"But that's what *I* say," Mason said, "and if there's any question about it I'll continue to bore into this witness until it is established."

"Oh, go ahead. Let's get the case over with," Moon said, sitting down. "It's a minor point. I don't care one way or the other."

"It wouldn't have been possible," Mason asked, "for the body to have been placed in the liquor closet, the hands raised and then the door closed holding the hands in position?"

"You couldn't have held the hands in that position while you were closing the door without the use of some kind of a device that would tie the hands up," Dr. Hanover said, "and even then you wouldn't have a condition of post-mortem lividity such as I found. Taking the two together there is absolutely no question but what the body lay on its back after death in approximately the position in which it was found by the police."

"Did you examine the carpet to see if there were any traces of blood?"

"You mean in front of the liquor closet?"

"Where the body was lying."

"Yes, sir. I did."

"Did you find such traces?"

"No."

"That's all, Doctor."

"Just a moment," Moon said. "Would you have expected to find such traces, Doctor?"

"Not necessarily. The bleeding was very minute due to the small nature of the puncture wounds, which sealed themselves almost immediately. There was some internal hemorrhage but very little external hemorrhage. It is quite possible that the undershirt would have absorbed all of the visible traces of blood."

"Thank you, that's all."

"Just one more question," Mason said, smiling. "You have some very delicate tests for ascertaining presence of blood, do you not, Doctor?"

"Yes, sir."

"Tests that will show microscopic quantities of blood, very microscopic quantities?"

"Well, they're not specific, but they do show blood. They show several things and blood is one of them."

"Were those tests performed on this carpet?"

"No, sir. We looked the carpet over but found no signs of blood."

"Why weren't those tests made on the carpet?"

"Very frankly we didn't think of it at the time, Mr. Mason. It was assumed when the police first saw the body that the statement made by the witness was correct and that the body had tumbled out of the liquor closet when

165

the door was opened. It wasn't until later on that the post-mortem examination indicated definitely that statement could not have been true. By that time there had been quite a bit of trampling around over the carpet, the conditions were not the same as when the body was discovered, and the prosecutor's office felt that that would make any evidence we might try to produce objectionable—the fact that the carpet hadn't been preserved in the same condition and that people had walked over it."

"That's all," Mason said.

"That's all, Doctor," Moon said.

Dr. Hanover withdrew from the stand, obviously relieved that the ordeal was over.

Delbert Moon said, "Call Mrs. Erma Lorton as the prosecution's next witness."

Mrs. Lorton, a tall, angular woman with somewhat close-set eyes and a mouth that was a thin line of determination, came striding forward to the witness stand.

She gave her name and stated that her address was the Mendon Apartments.

"That is the apartment house in which Mr. Brogan and the decedent, Mr. Fritch, had apartments?"

"Yes, sir."

"I'm going to direct your attention to the early hours of the morning of the seventh, Mrs. Lorton," Moon said, arising to his feet, smoothing down his coat, adjusting his hair, looking around at the audience, quite aware of the fact that he was about to explode a dramatic bombshell.

"Yes, sir."

"At about twelve-thirty on the morning of the seventh, what were you doing?"

"I was occupying my apartment."

"And specifically what were you doing?"

"I was waiting up."

"For what purpose?"

"I was waiting for my neighbor to come in."

"By your neighbor, whom do you mean?"

"The one who occupied the adjoining apartment."

"What is your apartment?"

"607."

"And your neighbor occupied what apartment?"

"609."

"Who was this neighbor?"

"A young woman."

"A friend of yours?"

"Yes."

"Now I am not going to ask you anything except a general question to establish the nature of your interest. Had this young woman confided in you as to certain matters? You can answer that question yes or no."

"Yes, she had."

"And was the nature of that confidence such that you would naturally be expected to take an interest in the time she returned home on the night in question?"

"Yes."

"And you were waiting up in order to see what time she returned home?"

"Yes."

"And what, if anything, did you observe?"

"At twelve-thirty-five in the morning I had my door very slightly ajar. I was listening for the sound of the elevator."

"You heard the sound of the elevator?"

"I did. Yes, sir."

"And what happened?"

"When I heard the elevator door clang and steps in the corridor, I assumed it was my friend. I wanted to let her know that I was still up in case I could be of any assistance to her. I opened the door a crack so as to beckon to her."

"And what happened?"

"I found that the steps were not approaching my apartment but that a person was standing in front of the elevator, looking at the numbers on the apartments."

"Can you identify this person?"

"Yes, sir. She was the defendant in this action."

"The one now seated next to Mr. Perry Mason?"

"Yes, sir."

"If the Court please, I'm going to ask the defendant, Harriet Bain, to stand up."

"Stand up," the judge said.

Harriet Bain stood up.

"That is the woman?" Moon asked.

"That is the woman. Yes, sir."

"And did you see what happened to this woman, where she went?"

"Yes, sir. I continued to watch."

"Tell the Court what happened. Where did she go?"

"Down to the end of the hall, to the apartment occupied by Frank Reedy."

"That is, the man whom you then knew as Frank Reedy?"

"Yes, sir."

"And do you now know his real name?"

"Yes, sir."

"What is it?"

"J. J. Fritch."

"I am going to show you a photograph of J. J. Fritch, deceased, and I will ask you if that is the man you knew in his lifetime as Frank Reedy?"

"It is."

"That is his photograph?"

"It is."

"I ask to have this marked for identification, Your Honor."

"So ordered."

"Now, Mrs. Lorton, I am going to ask you what did the defendant do?"

"She rang the bell."

"Of that apartment?"

"Yes."

"And then what happened?"

"Mr. Reedy, that is, Mr. Fritch opened the door and let her in."

"Did you see her leave that apartment?"

"No, sir."

"You didn't see her come out?"

"No, sir."

"Did you continue to watch for some period of time?"

"Yes, sir."

"For how long?"

"For ten minutes."

"And then what happened?"

"The elevator door opened, my friend came in, and I talked briefly with her. I told her that I was still up and that if she wanted to talk things over with me it would be all right. She told me everything had been adjusted satisfactorily, and so I went to bed."

"You may cross-examine," Moon said.

Mason smiled at the witness.

"You identified the defendant without any trouble?"

"Yes, sir."

"You have exceptionally good eyesight?"

"My eyes are very good. Yes, sir."

"Do you wear glasses?"

"No, sir."

"Do you ever wear glasses?"

"Sometimes for reading, yes."

"Do you wear them always for reading?"

"Well, yes."

"You can see without your glasses?"

"Yes, sir."

"But you can't *read* without them?"

"No, sir."

"You have to wear glasses for reading?"'

"It's necessary, yes, sir. I told you that," she snapped angrily.

"And you're not wearing glasses now?"

"No, sir."

"And you were quite able to identify the defendant when she stood up?"

"Yes, sir."

"Was that the first time you had seen the defendant after the seventh of the month?"

"No, sir."

"You had seen her at the jail?"

"Yes, sir."

"In a line-up?"

"No, sir."

"She was by herself?"

"Yes, sir."

"She was pointed out to you?"

"Yes, sir."

"By whom?"

"By Sergeant Holcomb."

"And what did Sergeant Holcomb say to you at that time?"

"Oh, if the Court please, I object to this as not proper cross-examination, as being hearsay evidence," Moon said.

"Sustained," Judge Kaylor said.

"Did someone point out the defendant to you at that time?"

"*I* pointed out the defendant."

"You said that that person was the defendant?"

"Yes, sir."

"But who first directed your attention to the defendant?"

"Well, of course, the police wanted to know if I could identify her. They took me to the jail to see if I could."

There was a slight titter in the courtroom.

"Then the police *first* pointed the defendant out to you and *then* you pointed the defendant out to the police?"

"Well, I agreed she was the person I had seen."

"That was the only person they showed you?"

"Yes, sir."

"Then you were advised at that time, were you not, that that person was Harriet Bain, who had been arrested for the murder of J. J. Fritch?"

"Yes, sir."

"Now then," Mason said, "since you have to wear glasses to read how did it happen that you were able to identify the photograph of J. J. Fritch while you were not wearing your glasses?"

"I—I could see it."

"Could you see it well enough to identify it?"

"Yes, sir."

Mason picked up a law book from the desk, took it up and handed it to her, said, "Just go ahead and read one paragraph, any paragraph, from this page. Read it without your glasses."

She squinted her eyes, held the book far out in front of her, then brought it closer, then back out in front of her again.

"I can't read it," she said. "I can't see it well enough to read it clearly."

"And you couldn't see the photograph any more clearly?"

"I knew whose photograph it was," she replied triumphantly.

"How did you know?"

"The deputy district attorney, Mr. Moon, told me that the photograph he handed me was that of Mr. J. J. Fritch," she said righteously.

"Thank you," Mason said, smiling. "That is all."

Moon, plainly angry, shouted at the witness, "Well, despite the fact you didn't have your glasses on you could see the photograph well enough to know it was the photograph of the man you knew as Frank Reedy, couldn't you?"

"That's objected to," Mason said, "as leading and suggestive."

"This is redirect examination, Your Honor," Moon said.

"It doesn't make any difference what it is," Mason said. "You can't put words in the mouth of your own witness."

"I think you'd better reframe the question," Judge Kaylor said.

"But, of course, Your Honor, in redirect examination it becomes necessary to direct the attention of the witness to the particular part of the testimony brought out on cross-examination that you wish to refute."

"Just ask her the question," Mason said, "but don't put the words in her mouth."

Moon said, "I'm not taking my ruling from you."

"Apparently you're not taking it from the Court either," Mason told him. "The Court has already ruled."

Judge Kaylor said, "Come, come, gentlemen, let's have no personalities. The Court ruled that the objection was well taken. Reframe your question, Mr. Deputy District Attorney."

"You saw that photograph?" Moon asked the witness.

"Yes, sir."

"And recognized it?"

"Yes, sir."

"That's all."

"Just a moment," Mason said. "*How* did you recognize it?"

"Well, I could see that it was a photograph."

"Could you distinguish the features any plainer than you could read the printing in that book I just handed you?"

"Well, I knew it was the photograph because Mr. Moon had told me it was the photograph I'd be called on to identify."

"And you were willing to take his word for it?" Mason said.

"Certainly."

"And similarly," Mason said, "when the officers pointed out the defendant in this case to you and told you that she was the person whom you had seen there in the hallway you were willing to take their word for it, weren't you?"

"Well, it isn't the same situation. I'm *certain* about her."

"Then you weren't certain about the man in the photograph?"

"I could have been dubious. I was taking Mr. Moon's word for it. He'd shown me the same photograph twice before and I'd identified it."

172

Mason smiled. "How do you know it was the same photograph?"

She snapped angrily, "I guess the word of a district attorney is good enough for me!"

"And, by the same token, so is the word of a sergeant of police?"

"Yes."

"That's all."

"Oh, that's all," Moon said irritably. "We'll get this matter disposed of right now. Call Frank Haswell."

Frank Haswell, a tall, thin individual, with a lazy, good-natured manner, settled himself on the witness stand as though he intended to remain for some time and wanted to be comfortable.

Preliminary questions showed that he was a fingerprint expert, that he had been called on to dust the apartment occupied by George Brogan for latent fingerprints, and that he had made an extensive search of the apartment looking for fingerprints. He had found and photographed a large number.

Moon once more stood up in order to attract the attention of the audience, unmistakably rather proud of his own personal appearance, tall, broad-shouldered, slim-waisted, with a wealth of wavy hair sweeping back from his forehead.

"Then, Mr. Haswell," he said, "were you able to identify any of these latent fingerprints that you took?"

"Yes, sir. I was."

"Did you find the fingerprints of any person who is now in this courtroom?"

"Yes, sir."

"Whose?"

Haswell said, "I found the fingerprints of Perry Mason."

Laughter rocked the courtroom despite the attempt of the bailiff to secure order. Even Judge Kaylor permitted himself a smile.

"Where did you find those fingerprints?"

"In three places."

"Where?"

"On the underside of a table in the living room, on the blade of a knife in the kitchen, and on the back of a magnetic knife-holder over the kitchen sink."

"How did you identify those fingerprints?"

"Mr. Mason had previously given a set of prints to the department in connection with another homicide case."

"What other fingerprints did you find?"

"I found the prints of Harriet Bain."

"The defendant in this case?"

"Yes, sir."

"How did you check those fingerprints?"

"By making a direct comparison with original fingerprints from her fingers."

"Where did you find her fingerprints?"

"I could best illustrate that by identifying a photograph of the living room and a photograph of the room where the body was discovered. There are certain places marked on that photograph. Little white circles. Those represent the approximate location of the places where I found the fingerprints of the defendant."

"We would like to offer that photograph in evidence. I will show it to Counsel and—"

"There's no need," Mason said. "I'm only too glad to stipulate that this photograph may be received in evidence."

"Cross-examine," Moon snapped.

"You only found three of my fingerprints?" Mason asked incredulously.

"Yes, sir."

"Why didn't you find more? I was in that apartment for some time."

"Well, of course, Mr. Mason, finding a latent fingerprint is something like finding game in the woods. There may be lots of game but it may be rather difficult to find. It is necessary that the fingerprint be placed on a surface that will retain the latent impression and it must be developed within a certain limit of time."

"What limit?"

"Well, there, of course," the witness said, "you get into

a factor which is governed by a lot of variables. It depends on weather conditions, upon the degree of humidity, the nature of the substance on which the latent fingerprint is impressed. I would say in this case, Mr. Mason, that I could assume that the fingerprints I found were made within a period of seventy-two hours."

"More than that?"

"I don't think so, Mr. Mason. I am, of course, making an estimate, but under the circumstances I would say within a period of seventy-two hours."

"So that your examination indicated that the defendant had been in that apartment some time within seventy-two hours prior to the time your search was made?"

"Yes, sir."

"That I had been there within seventy-two hours prior to the time your search was made?"

"Yes, sir."

"Did you find fingerprints of Sylvia Atwood, the defendant's sister?"

"Yes, sir."

"So that she had been in the apartment some time within seventy-two hours prior to the time the fingerprints were developed?"

"Yes, sir."

"Did you find fingerprints of the decedent, J. J. Fritch?"

"Yes, sir."

"Many of them?"

"Quite a few."

"So he had been in the apartment within seventy-two hours of the time of your examination?"

"Yes, sir."

"And did you find fingerprints of George Brogan?"

"Naturally."

"So he had been in the apartment within seventy-two hours of the time the search was made?"

"Yes, sir."

"Now then," Mason said, "will you kindly tell us

whether you found the fingerprints of Sergeant Holcomb of the Homicide Squad in that apartment?"

Haswell grinned. "As it happened," he said, "I did."

"So Sergeant Holcomb had been in that apartment within seventy-two hours of the time your search was made?"

"Yes, sir."

"Now then," Mason said, "can you kindly tell us whether there was anything in your examination that indicated whether Sergeant Holcomb had been in that apartment *before the murder was committed?*"

"No, sir. I only know I found his fingerprints."

"Do you know whether the defendant was in that apartment prior to the time the murder was committed?"

"No, sir. I only know that I found her fingerprints."

"Do you know that I was in the apartment prior to the time the murder was committed?"

"I only know that I found your fingerprints."

"So far as your testimony is concerned," Mason said, "and let's be perfectly fair about this, I am talking now only about your testimony, there is no more reason to think that the defendant in this case committed the murder than that I committed the murder or that Sergeant Holcomb committed the murder?"

"Well, of course," the witness said, "I can't—"

"Oh, I'm going to object to that question as argumentative," Moon said. "Not proper cross-examination."

"Well, of course," the Court observed, "it *is* somewhat argumentative. However, Counsel is merely trying to point out the application of the time element. I think I will permit it."

"What's your answer?" Mason said.

"The answer is no," the witness said. "I can't tell when those prints were made. I only know that within some time during which those prints could be preserved the defendant had been in that apartment."

"And that I had been in that apartment?"

"Yes, sir."

"And that Sergeant Holcomb had been in that apartment?"

"Yes, sir."

"And as far as anything your investigations disclosed there's just as much reason to believe that Sergeant Holcomb had been in that apartment and committed that murder as there is to believe that the defendant had been in that apartment and committed that murder?"

"Well, of course," the witness said, "I know that Sergeant Holcomb was in the apartment after the murder was committed."

"Do you know whether he was in the apartment before the murder was committed?"

"No, sir."

"Do you know whether the defendant was in that apartment after the murder was committed?"

"I understand that—well, now, wait a minute, if I have to answer that question fairly I will have to answer that I do not."

"Thank you," Mason said. "That's all."

Moon hesitated as though debating whether to ask another question, then decided against it and said, "That's all."

"Now then, Your Honor," Moon said, "I wish to call George Brogan once more, this time to direct his testimony to an entirely different phase of the case. This, if the Court please, is laying the foundation for the introduction in evidence of the spool of tape recording which had been the subject of previous examination and which spool was found by the police under a search warrant."

Brogan once more took the stand. His manner indicated that he knew he was facing an ordeal which was far from welcome.

"Now, Mr. Brogan," Moon said, "I am going to ask you if prior to the seventh of this month you had had occasion to converse with Perry Mason?"

"I had. Yes, sir."

"And where did that conversation take place?"

"In my apartment."

"And did that conversation have something to do with any of the Bain family?"

"It did. Yes, sir. It affected property rights, which, in turn, were important to each member of the family, that is, potentially important."

"And did those conversations have to do with the activities of Mr. J. J. Fritch, the man who was murdered?"

"They did. Yes, sir."

"Can you describe them generally? You don't need to go into detail, but tell what was the general nature of the conversation and the negotiations."

Brogan took a long breath, shifted his position once more, hesitated, seeking to choose his words.

Judge Kaylor glanced at Mason, then turned to Moon. "Isn't this somewhat remote?"

"No, Your Honor. It proves motive and it is laying the foundation for the introduction of this evidence which was discussed earlier, a spool of recorded tape, which the police found *in the possession of Mr. Perry Mason.*"

"Is there any objection?" Judge Kaylor asked, glancing at Mason, who sat completely relaxed, sliding his thumb and forefinger up and down the polished sides of a pencil.

"None whatever," Mason said, smiling affably.

"Very well, go ahead," Judge Kaylor said. "I would suggest, however, that we be as brief as possible. I think that if Counsel wishes to prove motivation this witness can testify generally to the facts in connection with the business negotiations and not go into a lot of detail."

"You have heard what the Court said," Moon said to the witness. "Just be brief. Tell us generally what this discussion was about."

Brogan said, "I happened to find out that Mr. Fritch was involved in a matter which he had effectively concealed for many years. He claimed that there had been some connection between him and Ned Bain, the father of the defendant. If that connection had been established it might well have resulted in a great property loss so far as the Bain family was concerned."

178

"So what did you do?"

"I felt that I might be able to be of some value and offered my services to the Bains."

"All of the Bains?"

"No, a representative of the Bain family."

"Who?"

"Mrs. Sylvia Atwood."

"By Mrs. Atwood you are referring to the sister of the defendant?"

"Yes, sir."

"And what happened?"

"Mrs. Atwood retained Mr. Mason. Mr. Mason called on me and I tried to make my position clear, that I was under the circumstances in a position to act somewhat in the nature of intermediary, but that if I were to do so I wanted it definitely understood that I was representing the Bain family and no one else, that under no circumstances did I wish to affiliate myself with Mr. Fritch."

"May I ask why you adopted that attitude?"

"For ethical reasons. It was a matter of business ethics."

"Was there perhaps something unethical about Mr. Fritch's approach?"

"I felt there was."

"What did you feel was unethical about it?"

"Frankly, I felt it was plain blackmail."

"And you didn't wish any part of that?"

"Definitely not."

"But you did approach Mrs. Atwood?"

"Yes, sir."

"And she in turn retained Mr. Mason?"

"Yes, sir."

"Now was there a spool of tape recording which entered into those negotiations?"

"Yes, sir."

"What was the nature of that recording?"

"It purported to be a recording of a conversation which had taken place between Mr. Fritch and Mr. Ned Bain, the father of the defendant."

"And what happened?"

"Mr. Mason and Mrs. Atwood came to my apartment. They wanted to hear that recorded conversation. I played it for them."

"How did you come to have possession of it?"

"Mr. Fritch gave it to me for that purpose. He thought that it would best serve his own interests to have Mr. Mason and Mrs. Atwood acquainted with the details of his claim, and as soon as he knew Mr. Mason had been retained he knew he was going to have to make out a strong case if he was going to get any money. He knew he had to put all his facts on the table."

"And what happened?"

"I had assured Mr. Fritch that while I would not represent him in any way I would stake my reputation on the fact that nothing would happen to that tape recording."

"Did something happen to it?"

"It did."

"What?"

"It was ruined."

"How?"

"I don't know how. I certainly wish I did. I gather, however, that it was some form of a radio-active polarization brought about by a clever subterfuge on the part of Mr. Mason."

"In what way?"

Judge Kaylor glanced at Mason. "Surely," he said, "we are now entering a field of surmise and something that seems to me to be definitely outside the issues in this case."

"If the Court please, it is showing the motivation," Moon explained, "and it is also laying the foundations for the introduction of this spool of tape recording in evidence."

"Well, there seems to be no objection," Judge Kaylor said. "Proceed. Answer the question."

"I don't know how Mr. Mason did it," Brogan said. "He had a device with him. He pretended it was a hearing aid. I don't know *what* it was. I am assuming that it was a polarizing device which enabled him to erase the recorded tape as it was being played."

"And what happened?"

"Mr. Mason asked me to play the tape back a second time. When I did there was nothing on it, the tape was completely blank."

"What did you do?"

"I assured Mr. Mason, of course, that I felt it must be something that was wrong with the machine, and stated that I wished time to have the machine fixed."

"Why did you state that it was something wrong with the machine?"

"I simply couldn't bear the thought of having something happen to that tape and have to face Mr. Fritch and confess to him that I had been outwitted in the matter. I knew that Mr. Fritch wouldn't accept that explanation, that he would be terribly angry."

"Now at that time did you think this recorded tape was the only tape recording of that conversation?"

"I did. Yes, sir."

"Did anything happen to change your mind?"

"It did. Yes, sir."

"What?"

"I was forced to report to Mr. Fritch what had happened. At the time I learned that the tape recording which I had, and which I assumed to be an original, which I may say Mr. Fritch had repeatedly assured me was the original and only tape recording, was, in fact, a dubbed copy of another master tape recording."

"And where was this master tape recording?"

"In the possession of Mr. Fritch."

"And what did Mr. Fritch tell you about it, if anything?"

"In the presence of the defendant or in the presence of Mr. Mason as Counsel for the defendant?" Judge Kaylor asked.

"Well, no, Your Honor. I am trying to show——"

"No objection, Your Honor. No objection whatever,"

Mason said. "Let him go into this to his heart's content."

"Well, of course, if there's no objection, the Court ordinarily permits evidence to go in. I am assuming that Counsel is familiar with facts that the Court does not know, and therefore there probably is some underlying connection here, but it seems to me that to expect this defendant to be bound by a conversation which took place between Mr. Fritch and this witness, and of which she presumably had no knowledge, is somewhat stretching a point."

"It's quite all right," Mason said.

"Very well," Judge Kaylor snapped. "Answer the question, Mr. Witness."

Brogan said, "Fritch reported to me that he had anticipated something might happen to the genuine recorded conversation which he had, and therefore he had given me a dubbed copy so that I could point out to Mrs. Atwood the position in which she found herself, while he had retained the original so that nothing *could* happen to it. He said that he would make me another copy."

"What was your reaction to this?"

"I was very much embarrassed because I had assured both Mr. Mason and Mrs. Atwood that this recording which I had was the original, and was the only one in existence, that I had Mr. Fritch's assurance that this was the case."

"But Mr. Fritch himself told you that he had another original recording?"

"He did. Yes, sir."

"Did you have occasion to see that recording?"

"I did. Yes, sir."

"Was there anything about it that was distinctive?"

"Yes, sir."

"What?"

"There were numerous splices in the tape itself, that is, indications that two or perhaps more pieces of tape had been spliced together."

"And did Mr. Fritch make another copy or another dubbed duplicate of that original?"

"Yes, sir."

"And what did you do?"'

"I was very much disturbed because I realized I had been jockeyed into a perfectly untenable position."

"In what way?"

"If representatives of the Bain family had made any arrangements with Mr. Fritch to secure the dubbed copy, the original would still have been just as much of a menace as ever."

"I take it that there was something in the recorded conversation which you felt the Bain family would not care to have made public?"

"Yes, sir."

"And do you know from your own observations that Mr. Fritch did on the sixth of this month have the original, which you have referred to as having been spliced and showing evidences of having been spliced?"

"Yes, sir."

"And where was that?"

"In his apartment."

"Where did he keep it in his apartment?"

"I don't know. He went and got it for me and showed it to me. He also showed me a tape recorder on which he could make duplications."

"Now then, you had an appointment with Mr. Mason for nine o'clock on the morning of the seventh?"

"Yes, sir."

"And with Mrs. Atwood?"

"Yes, sir."

"Were you there at your apartment at nine o'clock?"

"Not at nine o'clock. No, sir."

"Will you kindly tell the Court just what you did?"

"Well, I was very much interested in trying to learn the reactions of Mr. Mason and Mrs. Atwood. I was particularly interested in trying to find out the method by which Mr. Mason, without ever having had his hands on that spool of tape recording, had managed to cause the conversation on that tape recording to vanish into thin air."

"So what did you do?"

"I had an engagement for a poker game on the evening of the sixth. I deliberately planned to stay all night at that poker game and to be about five or ten minutes late in getting to my apartment."

"Why did you do that?"

"I wanted to find out what Mr. Mason and Mrs. Atwood said about that tape recording. I wanted to know what their reactions were. I wanted to find out what their confidential thoughts were on the subject."

"So what did you do, if anything?"

"I deliberately planned to absent myself from my apartment. I left my door unlocked. I left a note pinned to the door in an envelope addressed to Mr. Perry Mason. That note told him that I was playing poker and it might be I would be delayed, that he was to enter my apartment and wait for me."

"What else did you do?"

"I planted a tape recorder with a hidden microphone."

"Where?"

"So that it would record any conversation which took place either in front of the door of the apartment or in the apartment itself."

"And did you make some arrangement to have that microphone turned on?"

"I did. Yes, sir."

"How? In what way?"

"By use of an electric clock."

"Can you explain that a little more fully?"

"There are clocks that are run by electricity. They keep accurate time. You can get an attachment on those clocks which is similar to an alarm. When a predetermined time comes that attachment will turn on an electric current, actuating any device that you want. I set this clock for eight-fifty, so that at ten minutes to nine the clock would automatically turn on a tape recorder and start it running.

I left a thirty-minute spool of tape on there so that I could know everything that was said by persons who were standing in front of my door or who had entered my apartment. I left the transom open and the microphone was in the ceiling of the room just inside the transom."

"And how long would that recording device continue to operate?"

"Until twenty minutes past nine. It would start at eight-fifty. It was a thirty-minute spool. I expected to be there before nine-twenty. I expected to give them about five or ten minutes to indulge in conversation and then I would show up."

"Your absence therefore was deliberate?"

"Yes, sir."

"And did you show up?"

"Yes, sir."

"When?"

"About nine-five."

"And you found Mr. Mason there?"

"Mr. Mason, Mrs. Atwood and Mr. Mason's secretary, Miss Street, I believe her name is."

"And you entered the apartment?"

"Yes, sir."

"And what happened?"

"Then was when I discovered the body of J. J. Fritch."

"Now then, did you subsequently turn on that tape recorder to see what conversation had taken place?"

"I did. Yes, sir."

"I am going to ask you if there was anything in that conversation about a previous discovery of the body of J. J. Fritch."

"There was. Yes, sir."

"And were there any comments made by Mr. Mason in connection with that discovery?"

"Yes, sir."

"Advice?"

"Yes, sir."

"Did Mr. Mason say anything about searching for a

185

spool of original tape recording which he was satisfied Mr. Fritch had?"

"Yes, sir. He did."

"Do you have that tape recording here?"

"Yes, sir."

"Is it possible to recognize the voices?"

"It is. Yes, sir."

"If the Court please," Moon said, "I wish at this time to introduce this tape recording. I have here a machine which will play that tape recording, and I think the Court will be interested in hearing it."

"Any objection?" Judge Kaylor asked.

"Lots of objection," Mason said. "This doesn't have anything to do with the crime. It doesn't bind the defendant, Hattie Bain, in any way. *She* wasn't present at that time. *She* didn't hear what was being said. Therefore she can't be bound by it."

"Her attorney was there," Moon said.

"At that time I wasn't her counsel," Mason pointed out. "You can't bind her by something I have said before I was retained to represent her. Otherwise you might as well go back ten years and find something I said."

"I think we're entitled to put this in evidence. It's highly significant," Moon commented.

"You may put it in evidence under certain circumstances," Mason said. "You would have to ask one of the persons present as to whether a certain conversation did not take place. If that person admitted that conversation that's all there is to it. Your tape recording can't be introduced. If the person denied that conversation you'd then be in a position to introduce the tape recording to impeach that person *provided* you could prove that the clock worked, that the tape recording actually was made covering the period between eight-fifty and nine-twenty, and, further, that one of the voices on the tape recording was recognizable by anyone as the voice of the party whom you sought to impeach. Even then the recording would be evidence only of impeaching circumstances and not of a fact."

"I think that's the law," Judge Kaylor said.

"Oh, if the Court please," Moon said angrily. "I expect to show by this tape recording that Mr. Mason himself, knowing that J. J. Fritch was dead, proceeded unlawfully to invade and enter the apartment of J. J. Fritch *for the specific purpose of illegally and unlawfully looking for this spliced tape recording.*"

"Therefore, you mean that I murdered Fritch?" Mason asked.

"You may ultimately become involved as an accessory," Moon snapped.

"Now what tape recording do you want to introduce?" Judge Kaylor asked.

"Right now the one made in front of Brogan's apartment, showing the discovery of the body and Mason's statement that he was going to make an illegal search."

"The objection to that is sustained," Judge Kaylor ruled. "None of the participants in that conversation are being tried in this case, nor is it claimed that conversation took place in the presence of the defendant."

"I also want to introduce the tape recording Brogan has testified to as being the Fritch original tape recording."

"You'll have to lay a foundation first."

"I thought I had done so, Your Honor."

"This witness has merely stated there was such a tape recording. He hasn't identified it."

"If the Court will listen to it, the Court will become convinced that the tape recording contains proof of its own authenticity. It lays its own foundation."

Judge Kaylor shook his head. "Some witness will have to identify it."

"Well, Brogan can state that this recording is similar in appearance to the one Fritch had."

"Look out of the window," Mason said. "You'll see a thousand automobiles in the parking lot below. They all of them are 'similar in appearance.' You'll find some that are identical models. If you're going to identify them you're going to have to get into individual characteristics rather then overall group characteristics."

"You don't need to tell me how to practice law!" Moon flared angrily.

"Someone does," Mason said, and sat down.

Judge Kaylor said, "That will do, Counselor. The Court does not wish to have any sarcastic personal interchanges between Counsel."

"I was merely replying in kind," Mason said.

"Well, I don't want Counsel to reply in kind. I want this hearing kept on an orderly plane. Now then, gentlemen, I have listened patiently to this line of testimony. I think some witness will have to identify that tape recording if it's to be introduced. I suggest you pass this phase of the case for the present."

"That's all for now, Mr. Brogan," Moon said. "I'll recall you after you've listened to this tape recording."

Brogan got up to leave the stand.

Mason said, "I want to cross-examine."

"Go ahead, Mr. Mason," Judge Kaylor said.

Perry Mason arose from his chair, walked around the end of the counsel table and stood waiting for Brogan to look at him.

Brogan glanced up quickly, saw Mason's hard eyes, features which might have been carved from granite, and hastily averted his glance.

The silence became significant.

"Proceed," Judge Kaylor said.

"Did you understand that Fritch had robbed a bank?" Mason asked.

"I gathered there was a possibility that had been the case."

"Did you know him at the time of the bank robbery?"

"I—I think I did."

"Did you know how much Fritch wanted in return for his silence about the details of that bank robbery?"

"I knew he wanted a substantial sum of money."

"You were willing to act as intermediary and negotiate for the payment of that sum of money?"

"Not in the sense your question implies."

"How then?"

"I was willing to do what I could to help Mr. Bain—the Bain family."

"Did you know the Bains?"

"Not personally."

"Why were you so willing to help them?"

"Because I thought they were being—well, I thought they needed—"

"You started to say you thought they were being blackmailed, didn't you?"

"Yes."

"They were being blackmailed, weren't they?"

"Well, it depends. It was rather a peculiar situation taken by and large."

"And you were willing to participate in that blackmail?"

"No, sir."

"You were willing to collect the money from them and turn it over to Fritch?"

"Well that, of course, is a bald statement. That excludes my motives, which, I think, were rather laudable."

"Just answer the question," Mason said. "You were willing to collect money from them and turn it over to Fritch?"

"Well, yes, if you want it that way."

"In a blackmail proposition?"

"I thought it amounted to blackmail."

"You gathered that Fritch was in a position to give certain information to the bank which would make it appear that money which had been stolen from the bank had been used by Mr. Bain to purchase property which subsequently became very valuable through the development of oil, and that Mr. Bain had used this money with the knowledge that it represented the loot taken in a bank robbery. Is that correct?"

"That's substantially correct."

"Now then, during the night when the murder was committed you were not in your apartment?"

"That is right."

"You were intimately acquainted with Mr. Fritch?"

"I was in a way co-operating with him. Mr. Fritch wanted money. He thought I was in a position to get it for him."

"And you were trying to get money for him?"

"I was trying to get the matter cleaned up."

"By getting it cleaned up you mean getting the Bain family to put up enough money to buy the silence of J. J. Fritch?"

"Well—to get it cleaned up."

"Fritch had an apartment right across from yours?"

"Yes, sir."

"Who secured that apartment for him?"

"I did."

"Now Fritch anticipated that he might have to remain out of circulation for a considerable period of time, did he not?"

"I can't tell you what was in Mr. Fritch's mind."

"Didn't he so communicate to you?"

The witness hesitated, said, "Well, I believe that at one time he did say something like that."

"You went into Fritch's apartment from time to time?"

"Yes, sir."

"And he went into your apartment?"

"Yes, sir."

"He had a key to your apartment?"

"Well—"

"Did he or didn't he?"

"Well, yes, he did."

"You had a key to his apartment?"

"He asked me to—"

"Did you have a key to his apartment?"

"Yes, sir."

"You were in there from time to time?"

"Yes, sir."

"Were you familiar with the preparations he had made to keep himself in a place of concealment in the event it became necessary?"

"Just what do you mean by that?"

"Specifically, were you aware of the fact that he had purchased a very large deep-freeze box, that he had stocked that with all sorts of provisions so that in case of necessity it wouldn't be necessary for him to go out for anything, that he wouldn't have to be seen in public, on the street, or even in the elevator of the building?"

"Yes, sir."

"Do you know what that deep-freeze unit cost?"

"Around seven hundred dollars I believe."

"And it was stocked with provisions worth a good deal of money?"

"I believe so."

"More than a hundred dollars?"

"I believe so."

"More than two hundred dollars?"

"I believe around—well, around three hundred or three hundred and twenty-five dollars."

"Who put up the money for that?"

Brogan squirmed. "Of course, I was in a peculiar position and—"

"Did you put up the money which represented the purchase price of the deep-freeze icebox and the material that was in it, the foodstuffs?"

"I loaned Mr. Fritch a certain sum of money."

"How much?"

"Two thousand dollars."

"And do you know that that money, or a good part of it, went toward defraying the expense of moving into that apartment, of installing a television set and purchasing the deep-freeze icebox and the provisions that were in that deep-freeze icebox?"

"I surmised that it did. Yes, sir."

"So by the time we divorce your efforts of all of the protestations of ethical integrity with which you have sought to surround yourself, the fact remains that you financed J. J. Fritch in his blackmailing activities?"

"I don't so regard it."

"You 'grubstaked' him?"

"I do not so regard it."

"I do," Mason said.

"Well, you're entitled to your opinion," Brogan said. "I'm entitled to mine."

"Now then,'" Mason said, "on the night of the murder you *deliberately* stayed away?"

"Yes, sir."

"You were in a poker game?"

"Yes, sir."

"You can prove where you were every minute of the time?"

"Absolutely every minute of the time up until approximately eight-twenty."

"Where were you after eight-twenty?"

"I stopped in for a bite to eat. Frankly, I don't even remember the restaurant. It was some restaurant that caught my eye as I was driving along the street. It happened to be open. I looked in and there were vacant tables and an efficient-looking waitress was standing apparently with nothing to do, so I felt I could get some breakfast without too much delay. I stopped in for some hot coffee and something to eat."

"You had been engaged in playing poker all night, that is, all the night of the sixth and all the morning of the seventh up until eight-twenty?"

"Yes, sir."

"With how many people?"

"There were seven people in the game, and every one of them can and will vouch for the fact that I was there all night."

"You had arranged this poker game deliberately?"

"No, sir. I—well, perhaps I did have something to do with arranging it."

"Then you did it deliberately so you would have a legitimate excuse for being away from the apartment, so that you in turn could leave a note on the door and use this tape recorder in order to learn what Mrs. Atwood and I were talking about?"

"Perhaps so. I could have had several motives."

"But that was one of them?"

"Yes."

"Primarily you wanted to know whether we were going to pay Fritch money for the recording?"

"I was *primarily* interested in seeing how you had managed to erase the voice recording on that tape without going near it."

"But you did deliberately arrange to be absent during the period the murder was to be committed?"

"Yes, sir. I—now wait a minute, wait a minute! I didn't mean that."

"Then why did you say it?"

"You said it. You put the words in my mouth."

"You gave yourself an alibi, didn't you?"

"I had a perfect alibi, Mr. Mason. You can't involve me in that murder no matter what you do."

"Why not?"

"Because the murder was committed while I was seated in the presence of seven witnesses."

"You left the poker game in order to get some money, didn't you?"

"That's right."

"When was that?"

"At about five in the morning. I was only gone for approximately twenty minutes."

"Where did you go?"

"To see a friend."

"What friend?"

"I don't care to tell."

"Why not?"

"It might embarrass him."

"What did you do?"

"I got fifteen hundred dollars."

"And what time was that?"

"Five in the morning, Mr. Mason," Brogan said angrily. "Two hours after the extreme limit that the doctor says J. J. Fritch must have been killed."

"How far," Mason asked, "was it from your apartment to the place where the poker game was in progress?"

"Approximately—oh, I don't know, five blocks."

"You could have driven it in a car in five minutes?"

"I suppose so. If I weren't tied up in traffic."

"There wasn't any traffic to tie you up at five o'clock in the morning?"

"No," Brogan said sarcastically, "I could have driven from that poker game to my apartment at five o'clock in the morning. I could have been there at five minutes past five. I could have stayed there until fifteen minutes past five. I could then have returned to my poker game at five-twenty. Now then, Mr. Mason, suppose you figure out how I could have possibly committed a murder that was committed between midnight and three o'clock in the morning by leaving a poker game at five o'clock. I have never yet been able to turn back the hands of the clock."

Judge Kaylor said with some annoyance, "The witness will refrain from asking Counsel questions, the witness will refrain from challenging Counsel, the witness will confine himself to answering questions."

Mason said, "As a matter of fact, Your Honor, if the Court will bear with us I appreciate that question very much. I would like to answer it."

Judge Kaylor glanced at Mason as though he could hardly believe his ears.

"As a matter of fact," Mason said, "the solution is very simple. All he had to do was to drive to his apartment, stab J. J. Fritch with the ice pick, take all of the frozen food out of the big deep-freeze icebox, dump Fritch's body in on its back with the knees and the elbows bent, close the lid and return to his poker game, stay there until eight-twenty, then dash up to his apartment, pull Fritch out of the deep-freeze unit, put him in his liquor closet, dump the food back into the food container, walk around the block, wait until nine o'clock, come hurrying up to his apartment and state that he had been at breakfast. The facts would then match the facts which we have in this case. The temperature would have been so tampered with that the autopsy surgeon would have been fooled into believing that death had taken place at somewhere around one o'clock in the morning, instead of four hours later."

Mason walked back, sat down at the counsel table, tilted back in his swivel chair and smiled.

Judge Kaylor, leaning forward, glanced goggle-eyed from the witness to Mason, then to the deputy district attorney.

"That's a lie!" George Brogan shouted. "I never did anything of the sort!"

"We object to Counsel's statement. It's not evidence. It's not even logical," Moon yelled at the judge.

"Show me where it isn't logical," Mason said.

The courtroom broke into such an uproar that it took the bailiff several seconds to pound it back into any semblance of silence.

"Do you have any vestige of proof for this astounding accusation, Mr. Mason?"

"It's not an accusation," Mason said. "The witness merely asked me a question. He challenged me to show how he could have committed the murder, and I answered that challenge."

"It couldn't have been done that way," Moon assured the Court.

"Why not?"

"The doctor wouldn't have been fooled by any such expedient."

"Call him back on the stand and ask him," Mason challenged.

There was an awkward interval of silence.

"Are there any further questions of this witness?" Judge Kaylor asked somewhat lamely.

"One or two more," Mason said.

"Very well, proceed," Judge Kaylor ordered, but it was quite apparent that he was engaged in deep thought.

Mason said, "You knew that Fritch had robbed a bank some years ago?"

"I knew he was supposed to have done so."

"And that the amount of the loot had been approximately two hundred thousand dollars?"

"So I understood."

"Fritch was not alone in that robbery?"

"I don't know."

"You knew that the reports mentioned that he wasn't alone?"

"So I understand. He had a confederate, perhaps two. I don't know."

Mason said, so casually that for a moment the full import of his question failed to dawn on the spectators, "Now, Mr. Brogan, were you one of the men who participated in that robbery?"

Brogan started to get up out of the witness chair, then sank back down into it.

There was a long interval of silence in the courtroom.

"Oh, if the Court please," Moon said, "this question is insulting. It is without any foundation of fact. It is simply a shot in the dark. It is asked only for the purpose of embarrassing and humiliating the witness."

"Let him answer it then," Mason said. "Let him declare under oath that he wasn't one of the members of that holdup gang. The crime itself has been outlawed, but if he now says under oath that he wasn't a member of the gang he can be prosecuted for perjury."

Again there was an interval of silence.

"I object to the question," Moon said. "It's—"

"Overruled," Judge Kaylor snapped.

The judge glared down at the unhappy witness. "You heard that question?" he asked.

"Yes, sir."

"You understand that question?"

"Yes, sir."

"Answer it."

Brogan shifted his position, glanced at the ceiling, said, "I don't think I care to answer it."

"The Court orders you to answer it."

Brogan shook his head. "I'm not going to answer it."

"On what ground?" Mason asked, smiling.

"On the ground that the answer might incriminate me."

Mason grinned at the discomfited deputy district attorney, then turned back to Brogan.

"You were losing in the poker game, Mr. Brogan?" Mason asked.

"I've already told you I was."

"And at five o'clock you went out to get more money?"

"Yes, sir."

"And returned with a considerable sum of cash?"

"Yes, sir."

"And you can't tell us where you secured this cash?"

"I told you I got it from a friend."

"And you refuse to divulge the name of the friend?"

"That's right."

"Why?"

"On the ground—I don't think I have to."

"I think it's incompetent, irrelevant and immaterial and not proper cross-examination," Moon said.

Mason grinned and said to Judge Kaylor, "Order him to answer the question and he'll refuse to answer *that* one on the ground the answer will incriminate him."

"I object," Moon said. "I don't feel this is proper cross-examination."

Judge Kaylor, watching the witness carefully, said, "I'm going to overrule the objection. Answer the question."

Brogan doggedly shook his head.

"Are you going to answer that question?" Mason asked.

"No, sir."

"Why not?"

"On the same ground, Mr. Mason, you mentioned, that the answer might incriminate me."

Mason said, "As a matter of fact, the friend from whom you secured this money was a close, intimate friend, was it not?"

"Yes, sir."

"A very close friend?"

"Yes, sir."

"Perhaps the closest friend you have?"

"Perhaps."

"In other words," Mason said, "you got that money from yourself. *You* were the friend. You left the poker game and went to your apartment in order to get cash out of the secret wall safe in that apartment, didn't you?"

Brogan fidgeted.

"Answer the question," Judge Kaylor snapped.

Brogan looked at the judge appealingly. "Can't you see, Your Honor, he's just driving me into a position here where he's going to pin this murder on me no matter what happens. I can't combat that kind of stuff."

"You can answer questions," Judge Kaylor said. "If you went to your apartment at that time in order to get money you can say so."

"I don't have to say so," Brogan said. "I refuse to answer."

"On what ground?"

"On the ground that it will incriminate me."

Mason grinned. "That's all," he said. "No more questions. That's all, Mr. Brogan."

"That's all, Mr. Brogan. Leave the stand," Moon instructed.

His face red with anger, Moon said, "If the Court please, insinuations are not proof. Innuendoes are certainly not entitled to the weight of evidence.

"I know, however, *why* they were made and I think the Court knows why they were made. I intend to prevent the garbled reports which I am satisfied Counsel hoped would find their way into the press. I am going to recall Dr. Hanover and spike these rumors immediately and at once."

"Very well, call him," Mason said.

Mason stood up and beckoned to Della Street, who was seated near the back of the courtroom.

Della left the courtroom and shortly returned carrying an armful of books. She placed them on the table in front of Mason, withdrew from the courtroom and a moment later returned carrying another armful of books.

Dr. Hanover, taking the stand, looked down at the array of books which Mason had arranged so that the titles stamped in gilt on the backs of the books were visible to the witness on the stand.

"Now then," Moon said, "I'm going to ask Dr. Hanover a question. Doctor, would it have been possible for the conditions which you found when you examined that body to have been artificially induced by the body having been stored in a deep-freeze unit? In other words, is it at all possible that J. J. Fritch could have been murdered at five o'clock in the morning, the body kept for an interval of some two or three hours in a deep-freeze icebox, so that you would have placed the time of death at between midnight and 3:00 A.M.?"

"Just a moment," Mason said. "Before you answer that question, Doctor, I want to object on the ground that no proper foundation has been laid."

"I have already shown the doctor's qualifications," Moon said.

"I'd like to cross-examine him purely in regard to his qualifications," Mason announced.

"Very well," Judge Kaylor ruled. "That is your privilege."

Mason picked up a book. "Have you ever heard of a book entitled *Homicide Investigation* by Dr. LeMoyne Snyder, Doctor?"

"Yes, sir."

"What is the reputation of that book?"

"Excellent."

"It is a standard authority in the field of forensic medicine?"

"It is."

"Have you ever heard of Professor Glaister's book *Forensic Medicine and Toxicology?*"

"Indeed yes."

"What is its reputation?"

"Excellent."

"It is a standard book in the field of forensic medicine?"

"It is."

Mason started opening the books to pages which had been marked with bookmarks. Dr. Hanover's fascinated gaze followed the lawyer's activity as he spread the books open, piled one on top of the other until he had an imposing array.

"Now then," Mason said, "I am going to object to the question asked by Counsel on the ground that no proper foundation has been laid, that it assumes facts not in evidence, that it fails to state facts which are in evidence."

"What facts are omitted?" Moon challenged.

"Mainly the fact that Dr. Hanover based his testimony in part upon the state of the contents of the stomach and the condition of the meal which he *assumed* had been ingested at the usual meal hour. I am going to point out that Dr. Hanover has no means of knowing when that meal was ingested and therefore his testimony is dependent entirely upon that of body temperature.

"I also want to point out that the witness, Mrs. Lorton, your own witness, by whose testimony you are bound, stated specifically that when the defendant went to the apartment of J. J. Fritch, whom she knew as Frank Reedy, that Mr. J. J. Fritch opened the door and let her in. She didn't say 'some man.' She said that *Fritch* himself opened the door and let her in. Now at that time it is quite apparent that Fritch must have been fully dressed. If the witness Lorton saw him clearly enough to know that he was the one who let the defendant into the apartment, she would certainly have noticed if Mr. Fritch had answered the door in his underwear and admitted a woman to his apartment while he was so attired. It is, therefore, obvious that the only yardstick which Dr. Hanover has for fixing the time of death is that of temperature, and since it now appears in the evidence that Fritch was apparently fully dressed at the time of Miss Bain's call, but was clad in his underwear at the time he met his death, I submit that the witness be not permitted to answer this question as it is now asked."

"Oh, I'll put it to him this way," Moon said. "I'll meet the issue head-on. I'll take the bull by the horns. Dr. Hanover, assuming only the facts that you yourself know, assuming that you don't know the time Fritch ingested the meal which you found in his stomach, predicating your testimony entirely on the temperature of the body, is it or is it not possible that the decedent met his death later than three o'clock in the morning, but the conditions of temperature which you found could have been caused by placing the body in a deep-freeze compartment?"

"Also pointing out," Mason interjected, "the fact that this would absolutely account for the position of the hands at the time that *rigor mortis* of the arms and shoulders set in."

"I don't have to put that in my question," Moon said, testily.

Mason grinned. "I'm merely calling it to the doctor's attention because his professional reputation is at stake, and I may also point out to the witness and to Counsel that before we get done we're going to *prove* what actually happened."

"You don't need to threaten this witness," Moon shouted.

"I'm not threatening him, I'm cautioning him," Mason said, and sat down.

"Answer the question," Moon said.

Dr. Hanover ran his hand over his bald head, glanced once more at the books Mason had opened, said to the deputy district attorney, "That is, of course, rather a difficult question."

"What's difficult about it?"

"I have previously observed," Dr. Hanover said, "that in fixing the time of death from the temperature of the body, it is necessary to take into consideration the manner in which the body is clothed and the temperature of the surrounding environment. When I fixed the time of death as being between twelve o'clock and 3:00 A.M., I took into consideration the fact that the body was unclothed save for an athletic undershirt and boxer trunks. I also took into consideration the temperature of the apartment in which the body was found."

The doctor squirmed uneasily. "I will have to say that if you change any of those constant factors, or factors which I took to be constant, you naturally change my conclusions."

"But would that change your conclusions enough so that it would make that much of a time difference?" Moon protested.

Dr. Hanover, now having the deputy district attorney on the defensive, said quietly, "I'm afraid you would have to tell me, Mr. Moon, what was the temperature of the interior of that frozen-food container."

"I don't know," Moon said.

"Then I can't answer the question," Dr. Hanover said, smiling affably as he realized the avenue of escape he had opened up for himself.

"But we can find out," Moon said. "I suggest, if the Court please, that before there is any opportunity to tamper with the evidence in this case, the Court take a look at the premises, that the Court adjourn so we can take a look at that icebox right here and now, and I suggest that the witness, Dr. Hanover, be required to go to inspect the premises with us."

"I think the Court would like to take a look at those premises," Judge Kaylor ruled. "Under the circumstances it would certainly seem to be advisable."

"Now just a moment, Your Honor," Moon went on. "I suggest that all of this grandstand divertissement has been done for the purpose of staving off the evil moment when Mr. Perry Mason has to account for how he came to have this master record with its splices and its background of murder. I suggest that all of this is a desperate expedient to draw a series of red herrings across the trail so that no one will examine him as to what he did when he entered Fritch's apartment at nine o'clock on the morning of the seventh. We have a tape recording of Mr. Mason's own voice showing that he himself went into Fritch's

202

apartment for the purpose of making a search. I would like to have the Court hear that recording before we go out there."

Mason laughed. "The recording is completely, absolutely incompetent, irrelevant and immaterial. He can only use it for the purpose of impeaching me. He can't impeach me until I have testified to something that is opposed to the matters on that recording."

"Well, let me ask you," Moon said, "did you or didn't you enter Fritch's apartment at nine o'clock on the morning of the seventh?"

"Now, let's see," Mason said, "how long was that after the murder had been committed? Four hours or six hours?"

"That was at least six hours after the latest date the murder could have been committed," Moon shouted. "That's what Dr. Hanover said and I'm sticking by his testimony until he changes it."

"I thought he'd changed it," Mason said. "However, you are now seeking to bind the defendant by some action I took six hours after the murder with which she is charged was committed, at a time when I have assured you I was not representing the defendant in this case. You are seeking to impeach me by introducing a tape recording of a conversation about which the defendant never knew, a conversation which took place in her absence."

Judge Kaylor shook his head. "I am afraid, Mr. Moon," he said, "that the objection is only too well taken. If, of course, you wish to use this tape recording for the purpose of substantiating a charge of unprofessional conduct, of concealing evidence, of becoming an accessory after the fact, or any other thing along those lines, you're entitled to do so, but you certainly can't use it here save for purposes of impeachment, and you can only impeach an answer of a witness that is made in response to a relevant question."

"So," Mason said, grinning, "I suggest we go look at the premises."

Judge Kaylor nodded. "Court will adjourn to reconvene at the premises in question."

The sound of the bailiff's gavel was the trigger which released a terrific uproar, a veritable pandemonium of voices as people engaged in arguments among themselves, called out comments to the various parties, some of them pressing forward to shake Mason's hand.

Hattie Bain glanced at Mason with wide, apprehensive eyes. "Is it—what does this mean—good or bad?"

"You'll have to be patient," Mason told her. "You're going to have to return to the custody of the matron."

"For how long?"

Mason grinned. "Not too long, the way things look now," he reassured her.

15

Sergeant Holcomb unlocked the door of the Fritch apartment. His face was dark with anger.

"Now, of course," Judge Kaylor said, "it is usual in such cases to have all testimony taken in court and no testimony given while we are inspecting the premises. However, in this case since there is no jury I see no reason for enforcing such a rule.

"Now, Mr. Mason, you had reference to a deep-freeze box."

Mason nodded.

"Will you show me that, Sergeant?" Judge Kaylor asked.

Sergeant Holcomb led the way to the deep-freeze and threw back the cover.

"Now, as I understand it, Mr. Mason," Judge Kaylor said, "it is your contention that the body was placed in this deep-freeze."

"The Court will notice that the box is big enough to accommodate a man," Mason said.

"So are a thousand other iceboxes within a radius of a hundred yards," Sergeant Holcomb blurted.

"That will do, Sergeant," Judge Kaylor said. "I simply want to get Mr. Mason's contention. Now, Mr. Mason, is there any evidence, any single bit of evidence whatever that would indicate that the body had been put in here? There is the opportunity. The box is deep enough. However, you're going to have to show more than opportunity."

"In the first place," Mason said, "let's look at this."

He grabbed a pasteboard container of ice cream from the top of the deep-freeze, pulled the cover back, walked over to a silverware drawer in the cupboard, took out a teaspoon and plunged it down into the contents of the ice cream.

"Do you see what I mean?" he asked.

Judge Kaylor frowned. "I'm not certain that I do."

"This ice cream," Mason said, "was melted and then refrozen. See how it has frozen into crystals? It isn't smooth, as would have been the case if it had been stored without having been melted."

"I see, I see," Judge Kaylor said, his voice showing great interest. "Let me take a look at that."

He took the spoon and plunged it into the ice cream. The edge of the spoon rasped on frozen crystals.

"You see there's been a shrinkage in volume and it has frozen in the form of flakes, not as a smooth mixture," Mason said.

"Sergeant," Judge Kaylor snapped, his tone showing sudden interest, "open up another one of those ice-cream cartons."

Sergeant Holcomb pulled back the cover of another.

"The same condition," Mason said.

Judge Kaylor tested it with the spoon.

"Try another one, Sergeant."

Again Sergeant Holcomb took out another container,

and Judge Kaylor plunged the spoon into it, brought up the contents so he could inspect them.

"This certainly is interesting," he said. "Quite apparently this ice cream has been melted and refrozen."

"Any icebox is apt to have trouble," Sergeant Holcomb said. "I'm not certain but what we shut off this icebox when we were inspecting the place."

"Did you?" Judge Kaylor asked.

"I'm not certain."

"Well, you *should* be certain if you shut it off," the judge snapped.

He turned to Mason and there was a new interest in his voice. "Do you have any other evidence, Mr. Mason?"

"Certainly," Mason said. "Take out the packages. Test the bottom of the deep-freeze for blood stains."

"This is only a grandstand," Moon said. "This was done to get newspaper publicity to divert attention from—"

"Sergeant," Judge Kaylor asked, "did you remove the foodstuffs from this deep-freeze unit when you inspected the premises?"

"We didn't touch a thing in there," Sergeant Holcomb said. "We preserved everything just like it was. We looked the place over for fingerprints, that's all."

"Take them out," Judge Kaylor ordered.

"Of course, if we once take them out they'll start melting and Perry Mason will claim—"

"Take them out," Judge Kaylor ordered. "We've already ascertained that the ice cream has been out long enough to at least partially melt. Now get the rest of these things out. Let's look at the bottom of this box."

Sergeant Holcomb started lifting out the packages. He tossed out one package after another, piling them helter-skelter on the floor, mixing up meats, frozen vegetables, frozen fruits. His manner was all but openly defiant.

As he neared the bottom of the box Judge Kaylor leaned over to look.

As the last package thudded to the floor, Judge Kaylor said, "It took you two minutes and eighteen seconds, Sergeant, and—what's that?"

"That's a place where some of the juice leaked out of the meat," Holcomb said.

"Juice doesn't leak out of meat that's frozen hard," Judge Kaylor snapped. "I want—where's Dr. Hanover?"

"He's coming," Moon said. "He—"

"Well, get him," Judge Kaylor said. "I want the police technicians up here. I want to find out if that's human blood. If there's enough of it to type I want the blood typed with that of the victim, J. J. Fritch."

Judge Kaylor turned to Mason. "How did you know that stain was there, Mr. Mason?" he asked.

"I didn't know, Your Honor. I surmised."

"Well, you took a long gamble on it," Judge Kaylor said, his manner suspicious.

Mason grinned at him. "What else was there to take a gamble on?" he asked.

Judge Kaylor thought that over and slowly a smile touched the corners of his stern mouth. "I guess you have something there, Counselor," he said, and turned away.

"Moreover," Mason pointed out, indicating the pile of packages which Sergeant Holcomb had dumped on the floor, "you'll notice a couple of blood smears on the outside of one of those packages. I think if Your Honor will have the fingerprint expert up here you may find there's a latent fingerprint outlined in blood on that package."

"That's where the butcher wrapped it up," Sergeant Holcomb said. "That—"

"Let me see, let me see," Judge Kaylor announced. He peered down at the package, then abruptly straightened. "Everybody clear out of here," he said. "I want everybody out of this apartment. I want this place sealed up. I want the fingerprint expert and the police pathologist in here and then *I'm* going to tell them how *I* want this apartment searched for evidence."

The judge glowered at Sergeant Holcomb and, angered by the surly look on Holcomb's face, added, "And you may consider that a rebuke, Sergeant."

16

MASON, Della Street and Paul Drake sat in Drake's office. From time to time Mason consulted his wrist watch.

"Gosh, it's taking them long enough," he said.

"Don't worry," Drake told them. "They're being thorough, that's all. Believe me, they're really going to go to town this time. Judge Kaylor is mad as a wet hen."

Mason got up from his chair and started impatiently pacing the floor.

"I don't see how you had the thing figured out," Drake said.

"I *didn't* have it figured out," Mason told him. "That's what bothers me. I had to take a gamble. But remember this, Sylvia Atwood is a shrewd, calculating individual, yet she could have been telling the truth about that corpse tumbling out of the closet where the liquor was kept, and falling to the floor. I heard her scream and we could hear the thud of the body falling.

"The streaks of post-mortem lividity were on the back. Therefore, the body must have been lying on its back, but the body couldn't have been lying on its back if it had been in the liquor closet as she said.

"Now why would anyone move the body? The only reason I could think of was that someone didn't want the body found in the place where it had been lying while the post-mortem lividity formed.

"That meant it was to the advantage of someone, presumably the murderer, to see that the body was found in a different place from where it had been lying.

"The body was clad only in underwear. There were no clothes belonging to J. J. Fritch in Brogan's apartment. Therefore, it is reasonable to suppose that Fritch was killed in his own apartment. He was probably getting ready for bed, or perhaps he had already gone to bed and—"

"But the bed was made. It hadn't been slept in," Drake said.

Mason grinned. "Anyone can make a bed."

"Go on," Drake said.

"If the body had been moved," Mason said, "and judging from the peculiar position of the body it must have been crowded into some small space—"

"It would have been crowded in a small space in the liquor closet," Drake pointed out.

"But in that event the post-mortem lividity would have been lower down and not around the back of the neck, and the arms would have been down."

"Yes, I guess that's so," Drake said.

"Therefore," Mason said, "we came to the unmistakable conclusion that the body had been moved. Now Hattie Bain couldn't have moved that body, not by herself. Neither could Sylvia Atwood. Moreover, moving the body wouldn't have done *them* any good. The person who moved that body must have moved it for a reason. The only reason I can think of was that he wanted to establish an alibi. He wanted to establish it by interfering with the normal rate of cooling of a dead body."

"Do you think Brogan had time enough to do all that?" Drake asked.

Mason said, "Let's look at it this way, Paul. *Somebody* moved that body. It was done for a definite purpose. The most logical assumption is that it was done to build up an alibi, therefore we are looking for someone who has an alibi between midnight and two or three o'clock in the morning, but who does *not* have an alibi for a later hour.

"It has to be someone who is strong enough to have picked up a body and moved it. It has to be someone whom J. J. Fritch would have received in his underwear. We *know* that someone made the bed and fixed up Fritch's apartment, probably in order to make it appear

Fritch had been killed earlier before he had gone to bed."

"How do we know that?" Drake asked.

"Because," Mason said, "the body may have been put in an icebox. That would make the autopsy surgeon think the murder had been committed earlier than had been the case. But even the autopsy surgeon fixes the earliest date at midnight. Now when I went in there that morning *the television was on.* Fritch would hardly have had the television on much after midnight. There weren't any programs at that hour. That indicates Fritch either met his death before midnight or that somebody tampered with the evidence."

Drake nodded.

"And since Hattie saw him alive after midnight, it means someone tampered with the evidence."

"Yes, that's logical," Drake admitted.

"Now then," Mason went on, "one of the persons who fits the description of our hypothetical murderer is George Brogan, but there is one defect to our line of reasoning connecting him with the crime."

"What's that?"

"He had no motive."

"What do you mean, he had no motive? Wasn't Fritch sore at him and—?"

"Why should Fritch be sore at him? Brogan was getting money out of Bain for Fritch."

"But couldn't he have stolen that recording and—?"

"No," Mason said, "as soon as Fritch died the menace against the Bain estate was wiped out. The tape recording doesn't prove anything. It would only have been a means of corroborating Fritch's testimony. If Fritch had stated that Bain was his confederate and that Bain knew the money which went into that oil land had come from the bank, that would have been one thing. He could have used the tape recording to bolster his testimony, but without that testimony you certainly couldn't use the tape recording."

"By George," Drake said, "that's so!"

The telephone rang sharply.

Della Street jerked the receiver to her ear, said, "Yes. Hello, Mr. Drake's office. . . . Oh, just a minute.

"It's for you, Paul."

Drake picked up the receiver, said, "Hello. Yes. . . . The devil! . . . You're sure? . . . A good print? . . . The same type of blood? . . . Okay, thanks. Keep me posted."

He hung up the telephone, grinned at Mason and said, "You've hit a jackpot, Perry."

"How come?"

"They've made a test of the stains of blood on the bottom of the icebox. They're human blood. They're blood of the same type as that of J. J. Fritch. It's an unusual and rare type. Therefore, the similarity in typing is significant.

"They've found perfect latent fingerprints outlined in blood on the packages of food that were taken out of the deep-freeze container. There again the blood is the same type as that of J. J. Fritch. They've photographed the bloodstained prints but they can't match them with those of anyone in the case. They're not Sylvia Atwood's. They're not Hattie Bain's. They're not Ned Bain's. They're not yours. They're not George Brogan's."

Mason grinned and lit a cigarette.

"Any suggestions?" Drake asked.

"Lots of them."

"Such as what?"

Mason said, "Let's narrow down our line of reasoning, Paul. We need someone who had an alibi for the hours before the murder was committed but who could have no alibi afterward. We need someone who was strong enough to lift the body of J. J. Fritch. Moreover, we need someone who was scientific enough to realize that the question of body temperature would be considered by the autopsy surgeon as an element in determining the time of death.

"Furthermore, there's the question of motivation to be considered. We need someone who stood to profit by finding that spool of master tape. We need someone who was ruthless enough to have stabbed J. J. Fritch in the back, and we need above all someone who had access to the ice pick in the Bain house.

"Now, the selection of that weapon is an interesting thing. It means that the person who committed that murder wanted a weapon that would do the job, yet it wasn't the most efficient weapcn on earth. It was a weapon that came to hand on the spur of the moment, say some time after midnight on the date of the murder.

"We need someone who could establish an alibi for an entire evening up to around 3:00 A.M., who had opportunity after that to go and kill Fritch, leave his body in the icebox until around eight in the morning and then plant it in some other place. Of course, finding the door of Brogan's apartment unlocked gave him the ideal place.

"So our murderer, Paul, is strong, ruthless, cold-blooded, scientific, interested in the fortunes of the Bain family and one who would have access to the ice pick."

"Good heavens," Della Street said, "do you realize that you're practically putting a rope around the neck of Jarrett Bain?"

Mason stood looking down at her and at the startled face of Paul Drake. He inhaled a deep drag from his cigarette, blew out the smoke, grinned and said, "Well?"

"Good Lord," Drake exclaimed, "when you look at it that way, it's the only possible solution. He came home and talked with his dad, he learned all about what you had said about the probability of the tape recording being forged, of it being spliced tape. Edison Doyle could give him an alibi for the time around two o'clock. Then he *said* he went to bed and slept until about ten o'clock. Good Lord!"

Mason said, "There was nothing whatever to have prevented him from going up to see J. J. Fritch around three-thirty in the morning, sticking an ice pick in Fritch's back, pulling the stuff out of the deep-freeze locker, putting Fritch in there, staying out until about eight o'clock in the morning, then going back and getting Fritch, putting him in the liquor closet where he knew the body would be discovered when Sylvia and I went to keep our nine o'clock appointment. Then he hastily dumped the food back into the icebox and—"

"Wait a minute," Paul Drake interposed, "you're narrowing the circle all right, but what about Edison Doyle? He was one who had to leave, and he was one who had an alibi for around midnight but didn't—"

"And look at the way he's built," Mason said. "Can you see *him* reaching down and picking J. J. Fritch up out of an icebox, carrying him across the hall and propping him in a liquor closet? Doyle is the fox-terrier type, but Jarrett Bain is a great, big, lumbering giant of a man with a bull neck, a huge pair of shoulders, and that peculiarly cold-blooded attitude of utter detachment which characterizes a certain type of scientist."

"So what are we going to do?" Paul Drake asked.

Mason turned to Della Street. "Ring up the Bain residence," he said. "See if you can get Jarrett Bain on the telephone."

Della Street put through the call, then after a moment looked at Mason with wide, startled eyes.

"What is it?" Mason asked.

"Jarrett isn't even going to be here for the funeral," she said. "He left word that he was sorry but he couldn't help the dead. He could only help the living. He said he'd received a wire on some new archaeological remains, and he took off by plane."

Mason pinched out his cigarette.

"Well," he said, "I guess he's gone, then. Do you know, it might be a difficult matter to find him."

Drake seemed uncomfortable. "The police," he said, "are trying to pin this on Brogan. They're claiming the fingerprints are those of Brogan's accomplice, that Brogan engineered the whole thing."

Mason grinned.

"Aren't you going to tip them off," Della Street asked, "so that they can lay off Brogan and catch Jarrett Bain before he disappears into the jungle?"

Mason grinned. "There is such a thing as poetic justice.

213

Let's let Mr. Brogan sweat a little. They can't actually convict him on the evidence they have now. They have evidence enough to arrest but not enough to convict. As far as Jarrett Bain is concerned let's let the police solve their own problems.

"*Our* responsibilities are very definite and very limited, Della. We were representing Hattie Bain, who has now been discharged from custody."

"Hattie Bain and her green-eyed sister," Della said.

"Oh, by all means," Mason grinned, "the green-eyed sister. Little Miss Fix-It. We mustn't forget her!"

"Oh, my Lord!" Della Street exclaimed. "That telegram summoning Jarrett to the jungle on account of that new archaeological discovery! Remember she said—"

She broke off and looked wide-eyed at Perry Mason.

The lawyer lit another cigarette. "Little Miss Fix-It," he said.

3/07

The Case of the
Troubled Trustee

WHENEVER people who are familiar with the outstanding figurés in the field of legal medicine get together for informal shoptalk, the name of Dr. Leopold Breitenecker, of Vienna, will probably be mentioned.

My close friend, Dr. LeMoyne Snyder, who is both an attorney at law and an M.D., who has specialized in the field of forensic medicine and whose book *Homicide Investigation* is one of the most authoritative books on the subject, spent quite a bit of time working and studying with Dr. Breitenecker in Vienna. He has told me much about the man's ability.

Too few people appreciate the importance of legal medicine and very few people appreciate the ramifications of the subject.

The average individual thinks of legal medicine in terms of the investigation of murders; legal medicine not only covers a wide scope but the field is constantly being enlarged.

The expert in legal medicine is being called upon daily to answer questions upon which important issues depend.

A man is smoking in bed. The house burns and the body is charred beyond recognition: Did the man have a heart attack, drop a cigarette and so cause the fire; or was he intoxicated when he met his death through suffocation or from the flames?

The medicolegal expert can give the answers, and where there is a certain type of insurance the answer may be important.

A body is found in bed: Was the body moved from some other place after death and placed in the bed?

The medicolegal expert can usually answer that question.

Were injuries inflicted before death or after death? What was the direction of the bullet wound? Which is the wound of entrance and which the wound of exit? How far was the gun from the body when it was discharged? Was the death murder or suicide?

Many many times in cases when medicolegal experts were not called in, these questions have been answered erroneously. But the expert in the field of forensic medicine not only gives answers to these questions. he is able to demonstrate that his answers are correct. The international recognition of Dr. Breitenecker was expressed when he was sent by U Thant (UNO) into the Congo in 1962 to clarify the circumstances of the death of three members of the International Red Cross, and again, in 1964, when U Thant called him in to investigate the murder of an English officer in the Cypriot conflict.

And since he is one of the world's outstanding experts in this important field,

I dedicate this book to my friend,

LEOPOLD BREITENECKER, M.D.
Professor and present Dean of the Faculty
of Medicine, University of Vienna.

ERLE STANLEY GARDNER

CAST OF CHARACTERS

1

―――――――
■

PERRY MASON, entering his office, grinned at Della Street and said, "What's in the mail, Della, anything startling?"

She indicated the pile of letters on Mason's desk. "The usual, people who want."

"Want what?"

"People who want you to make talks; write letters of endorsement, donate some intimate article for a celebrity auction."

"What else is new?" Mason asked.

Della Street rolled her eyes in an exaggerated pantomime of passionate interest.

"If," she said, "you want any efficiency whatever out of Gertie, your romantic receptionist, you had better get Kerry Dutton out of the office."

"And who is Kerry Dutton?" Mason asked.

"He is a youngish gentleman whose clothes are quietly elegant. He has a cameo-like profile, brown, wavy hair, steel-gray eyes, a very nice mouth, probably a thirty-six chest and a thirty waist. He is driving Gertie half crazy. She can't take her eyes off him."

"What does he want?" Mason asked.

"That," she said, "is the mystery. The man's card says that he is an investment counselor. He wants to see you about a matter that is very personal and exceedingly urgent."

Mason said, "I don't want to make any investments. I don't—"

"A professional matter," she interrupted.

Mason said, "My specialty is murder cases and trial

1

work. What the devil would I want with an investment counselor?"

"I intimated as much," Della Street said.

"He wouldn't tell you what it was all about?"

"No, only that it was a highly personal matter involving something which must be handled in complete confidence and with the greatest of tact."

Mason said, "I'll take a look at him, at any rate that will get him away from Gertie's romantic gaze.

"How old is he, Della?"

"I would say thirty-one or thirty-two."

"And," Mason said, "I suppose his shoes are polished, his nails well manicured, his tie faultless, his appearance impeccable."

"Isn't all that supposed to go with an investment counselor?" Della Street asked.

Mason suddenly became thoughtful. "Hang it," he said, "I may have been doing the guy an injustice. Show him in, Della, and we'll find out what he wants."

Della Street nodded, left the office, and a few moments later returned, leading Kerry Dutton into the office.

"Mr. Dutton, Mr. Mason," she said.

Mason met the unflinching gray eyes, gave the man a brief appraisal from head to foot, then got up to shake hands. "How are you, Mr. Dutton?" he said.

"This is a great honor," Dutton said. "I am sorry I had to come without an appointment, Mr. Mason, but the matter is one of extreme urgency."

"Tell me generally what it's about," Mason invited. "I take it you're consulting me professionally?"

"Yes, indeed."

"My work," Mason said, "is largely in other fields. I doubt that I can help you. You're probably wasting time for both of us."

"You defend criminals, don't you?" Dutton asked.

"Yes."

"That's what I want you for."

"Who's the criminal?" Mason asked.

Dutton touched his breast with his left forefinger.

2

Mason studied his visitor with eyes that were steady and penetrating.

"You've been arrested and are out on bail?" he asked.

Dutton shook his head. "I haven't been arrested. That's why I came to you. I would like to keep from being arrested."

"You have perhaps embezzled money?"

"Yes."

"From whom?"

"From the account of one Desere Ellis."

"How much have you embezzled?"

"Looking at it one way it's a quarter of a million dollars."

Mason shook his head. "Every man," he said, "is entitled to his day in court. Every man is entitled to a lawyer to represent him, but a lawyer is not a partner in crime. From the facts as you tell them, you not only cannot escape arrest but, if I were to represent you, I would pick up that telephone and call the police."

"Wait a minute. You don't know the facts."

"I know enough of them from your own admissions."

"May I tell the story my way?"

Mason looked at his wrist watch. "I'll give you two minutes," he said, "but I'm busy. Your case doesn't appeal to me and your type doesn't appeal to me."

Dutton flushed.

Mason gave him no invitation to sit down, and Dutton remained standing.

"Templeton Ellis, the father of Desere Ellis, was one of my clients," he said. "He died four years ago. At the time of her father's death, Desere was twenty-three and was mixed up with a lot of people of whom her father didn't approve.

"He left a will containing a spendthrift trust. I was the trustee. Desere was to have the income as I saw fit to give it to her for her needs. She could have as much of the principal as I felt was advisable. I was given sole discretion in handling the funds; the right to invest and reinvest. I was to serve without bond."

3

"I see," Mason said. "He left you with absolute power."

"Yes. He did that to protect his daughter from herself."

"And what did he do," Mason asked pointedly, "to protect his daughter from you?"

"Nothing," Dutton said.

Mason's silence was eloquent.

"Now then," Dutton went on, "the amount of money that he left was around one hundred thousand dollars. In the four years since his death, I have given his daughter approximately a hundred and ten thousand dollars."

Mason frowned. "I thought you said you had embezzled a quarter of a million."

"In a way, I have."

"I don't understand."

"Desere's father wanted me to keep intact the securities he had left, but I had the *power* to buy and sell.

"All right. I bought and I sold.

"One of her father's favorite stocks was a dog, the Steer Ridge Oil and Refining Company. I sold that stock without letting anyone know I had done so. I sold some of the other no-goods in the portfolio, stocks the father had held onto more for sentimental reasons than for sound business reasons," Dutton said. "I divided the money I received into three approximately equal amounts. One third I invested in blue-chip securities; the other I invested in securities which I felt had a strong opportunity for gain; and the remaining third, I used in real estate speculation in communities where I felt there would be development. I turned these properties over at a profit, put them in my own name, pyramided profits, and have netted a quarter of a million dollars."

"What about taxes?" Mason asked.

"I had the profit-making properties in my own name. I paid the capital gains taxes from the profits."

"What about annual accountings?"

"I have never made one, and the beneficiary has never asked for one."

4

"Hasn't she wanted to know what was happening to her money?"

"She thinks she knows. She thinks she has just about exhausted all the trust funds. I have given her more than two thousand dollars a month for all the period the trust has been in effect."

"Has she saved any of that?" Mason asked.

"Saved any? Heavens, no! She's spent that and probably has a few IOUs out. She is a pushover for all sorts of worthy and unworthy causes."

Mason caught Della Street's eye. "I see," he said.

Dutton watched him anxiously. "I hope you do," he said.

Mason studied his visitor for a moment, then said, "You have been guilty of all sorts of legal violations. You have mingled trust funds with your own; you have embezzled property; you have defrauded your client and betrayed your trust."

"Exactly," Dutton said. "I felt, however, that it was the thing to do."

"And what do you want me to do about all this?" Mason asked.

Dutton said, "Within three months, the trust will terminate. I have to make an accounting at that time and turn over all of the trust monies to Desere."

"And I take it," Mason said, "you're not going to be able to make restitution."

"Restitution?" Dutton said in surprise. "Why, I have the entire fund intact. I have simply kept the properties in my name."

Mason regarded him thoughtfully. "Sit down," he suddenly invited.

"Thank you," Dutton said, and took a seat.

"Suppose you tell me," Mason said, "exactly what was the idea."

Dutton said, "I tried to do my best to protect Desere's interests. One hundred thousand dollars is not a great deal of money if you look at it in one way; in another way, it is a very great deal of money.

5

"At the time of her father's death, the people with whom Desere was running around had long hair, wore beards, had dirty fingernails, were left-wing idealists, and looked down on her as an heiress. They dipped into her money right and left, patronized her and considered her a square. She went overboard trying to live up to their ideals so they'd respect her. They took her money but always looked on her as an outsider. She's a sensitive young woman who was hurt, lonely, and eager to be accepted as one of the crowd.

"Her father thought four years would give her a more mature perspective."

"And it was to protect her from that type of associate that her father made this spendthrift trust?"

"Yes. He wanted to protect her from herself. Undoubtedly her father's idea was that I would clamp down on the money she was to receive; that I would bring financial pressure to bear to force her to drop her friends and form her friendships from another environment. In fact, he intimated as much to me before his death."

"Why didn't you do it?" Mason asked.

"Because that would have been the wrong way to play my cards," Dutton said. "I realized that if she represented a large sum of money to these individuals, an attempt would be made to exploit her simply to secure a financial advantage. I wanted her friends to believe the trust fund would be exhausted.

"If, on the other hand, I could build up enough speculative profits which she knew nothing about so that I could afford to dish out her money to her with a liberal hand, she would spend it and any prospective fortune hunter would then regard her as a woman who had gone through her inheritance and, as such, she would be ostracized from the beatnik crowd."

"And you risked going to jail for this?" Mason asked.

"I want you to keep me from going to jail," Dutton said. "While I had taken chances on mingling the trust funds with my own assets, I had always held them in my

6

name as trustee without disclosing the beneficiary of the trust."

"Suppose you had died?" Mason asked.

"I am in good health. I have no intention of dying in the near future."

Mason said, "Every week several hundred persons are slaughtered on the highways in a red harvest. None of these people had any intention of dying when they started out."

Dutton grinned. "I am one of those who *didn't* get killed on a weekend."

Mason looked at Dutton and said, "You're a young man."

"It depends on what you consider young. I consider myself quite mature. I'm thirty-two."

"And Desere?"

"She'll be twenty-seven in a few months."

"When you started handling this trust you were still in your late twenties?"

Dutton flushed and said, "That's right."

"Do you," Mason asked suddenly, "love her that much?"

"What!" Dutton exclaimed, snapping back in the chair and sitting very straight.

Mason said, "You have your career ahead of you. Apparently, you have a remarkable aptitude in your chosen profession. In order to protect Desere Ellis and keep her from being the victim of fortune hunters, you have jeopardized your entire professional career and apparently haven't gained a thing by it.

"Now you are talking to a lawyer. Lawyers are not noted for being particularly naïve, so perhaps you had better tell me the *real* story."

Dutton sighed, looked for an embarrassed moment at Della Street, then blurted out, "All right, I love her. I have always loved her, and I don't want her to know it the way things are now."

"Why?"

7

"Because she would never think of me in that way. Her attitude toward me is one she would show to a much older man. . . . Well, I'm sort of a big brother; a species of uncle. I don't talk her language. I don't mingle with the set that appeals to her. At the present time, she regards me only as the custodian of her money. Her set regards me as 'square.' "

"Were you so successful four years ago," Mason asked, "that Desere's father thought his daughter's financial affairs would be better in your hands than in those of some more experienced and older banker?"

Dutton hesitated.

"Go on," Mason said.

"All right," Dutton told him, "her father wanted to— Well, he liked me. He thought I might have a steadying influence on Desere— She was running with that crazy crowd. She went overboard for a lot of fads and fancies."

"And her father hoped that if she had to see a lot of you in connection with money matters she'd fall in love with you?"

"I guess that was partly his idea. He wanted to protect her from herself, and he may have had some idea of having her fall in love with me. He knew how I felt toward her.

"Actually, like so many schemes which fail to take human nature into consideration, the thing worked out just the opposite. She thinks of me as a moneygrubber. Our difference in ages has been accentuated."

"And you've been in love with her for four years?"

"Five."

"And never told her how you felt?"

"Of course I did. That was more than four years ago."

"What did she say?"

"She felt sorry for me. She said it was simply that I'd built up a synthetic feeling for her. She said she'd be a younger sister to me if I'd take her on that basis; that if I was going to persist in this crazy idea of being in love with her it would mean she couldn't see me any more. It would spoil the friendship."

"So you took it on that basis?" Mason asked.

"I've been waiting," Dutton said.

"Did her father have any idea he was dying?"

"Yes. He knew. The doctors gave him eight months. They were too optimistic. He lasted six."

"And now you feel that the will and the spendthrift trust didn't work out the way he had anticipated?"

Dutton said, "It had exactly the opposite effect. For a few months, Desere was so terribly hurt and angry that she would hardly speak to me.

"She felt that her father had repudiated her; that he had insulted her intelligence; that he was trying to dominate her life even after he had passed away and— Well, she's like a wild colt. She doesn't want any restrictions. Show her a fence and she tries to jump it. Come toward her with a halter and she wants to run; and if she gets cornered, she wants to bite and kick.

"After the will was read, she felt her father had crowded her into a corner, so she started biting and kicking."

"And, I take it," Mason said, "you were the target?"

"That's right."

"And you felt that embezzling the trust assets would make everything all right?"

"I wasn't trying to make things all right. I was trying to keep them from going all wrong."

"How?"

"She'd be a target for dead-beat fortune hunters if they knew the truth. Even as it is, she has a beatnik no-good moving in on her. He wants to marry her and 'manage' the few thousand she's going to get on the termination of the trust."

Mason smiled. "You don't approve of him as a husband for Desere?"

Dutton said grimly, "If he marries her, I'll—I don't know *what* I would do, but *someone* should shoot the guy."

Mason regarded Dutton thoughtfully. "Perhaps," he

suggested, "you should be a little more aggressive in your romantic affairs."

"I have to play the waiting game a little longer," Dutton said.

"You've been playing it without any results for four years now," Mason said.

"Five," Dutton corrected. "I felt that as Desere grew more mature the difference in our ages would become insignificant. I want her to stop thinking of me as an older brother—a much older brother."

Mason said, "All right, I'm glad you've come clean. Now, I want you to do three things. First, make me a check for a thousand dollars as a retainer. Second, sign an undated declaration of trust, listing all the securities that are in your name but which you are holding as trustee for Desere Ellis. You don't necessarily need to tell her about it, but get a record that these properties are being held only as a trustee under the will, then if you die she is protected."

"Third?" Dutton asked.

"Try to get Miss Ellis to come in to see me," Mason said. "I want to talk with her."

"Why?"

"Someone has to tell her that there is more money coming to her at the termination of the trust than she had anticipated, and someone has to tell her why. If you try to tell her, you have to sketch yourself as a heel. If I tell her, I *may* be able to put you in the position of a hero."

"Look here," Dutton said, "you can't tell her how I feel toward her. You can't—"

"Don't be foolish," Mason interrupted. "I'm not running a matrimonial agency; I'm running a law office. You're going to pay me to keep you out of trouble. I want to keep you out of trouble.

"Your love life is none of my business except as it affects the job I have to do."

Dutton took a checkbook from his pocket and started writing a check.

10

2

∎

Mason entered his private office the next morning to find Della Street opening the morning mail. He stood for a few moments watching her with appreciative eyes.

"Thanks," he said abruptly.

She looked up in surprise. "For what?"

"For just being," Mason said. "For being so much a part of things, so completely efficient and . . . and all the rest of it."

"Thank *you*," she said, her eyes suddenly soft.

"Any progress?"

"On what?" she asked.

"Come, come," Mason said, smiling. "Don't try to pull the wool over *my* eyes. On the romance, of course."

"The Dutton case?"

"Exactly."

"Nothing so far," she said. "Give the man a little time."

"He may not have as much time as he thinks," Mason said, seating himself in the client's overstuffed chair and watching Della Street's smoothly graceful figure as she stood at the desk opening letters, putting them in three piles—the urgent on the left-hand corner of the desk, the personal-answer-required in the middle, and the general run-of-the-mill for secretarial attention on the right.

"Want some advice?" she asked.

Mason grinned. "That's why I brought the subject up."

She said, "You can't play Dan Cupid."

"Why not?"

"You don't have the build. You wear too many clothes, and you lack a bow and arrow."

Mason grinned. "Keep talking."

"Sometimes," Della Street said, choosing her words carefully as though she had rehearsed them, "a woman will be close to a man for a long time, seeing him in the part in which he has cast himself and, unless he makes some direct approach, not regarding him as a romantic possibility."

"And under those circumstances?" Mason asked.

"Under those circumstances," Della Street said, "nature gave the male the prerogative of taking the initiative; and if he isn't man enough to take it, it is quite possible the girl will *never* see him as a romantic possibility."

"Go on," Mason told her.

"But the one thing that would definitely wreck everything would be for someone else to try and take the initiative on behalf of this individual."

"Longfellow, I believe, commented on that in the poem dealing with John Alden and Priscilla," Mason said.

Della Street nodded.

"All right," Mason told her, "I've been forewarned. You want me to keep my bungling masculine touch under cover, is that it?"

The phone on Della Street's desk rang.

She flashed him a quick smile, picked up the receiver and said, "Yes, Gertie," to the receptionist.

She said, "Wait a moment. Hold on, Gertie, I'll see."

Della Street turned to Perry Mason. "Desere Ellis is in the office," she said.

Mason grinned. "Let's take a look, Della."

"Just a moment," Della Street said. "She is accompanied by a Mr. and Mrs. Hedley, apparently a mother and son."

"They are all three of them together?" Mason asked.

Della Street nodded. "As Gertie whispered confidentially, the mother is a determined creature with a rattrap mouth and monkey eyes; and the son is pure beatnik with a beard and a cool-cat manner which makes her flesh crawl. You know how Gertie is and how she loves to make snap appraisals of clients."

"And generally she's right," Mason said. "Have Gertie send the three of them in."

Della Street relayed the message, then went to the door communicating with the outer office and held it open.

Hedley came in first—a broad-shouldered young man with a spade beard, calmly contemptuous eyes, a sport shirt open at the neck disclosing a hairy chest, a pair of rather wrinkled slacks, and sandals over bare feet. He was carrying a coat over his arm.

Behind him was his mother, a woman of around fifty, not as tall as her son. She was rather dumpy and had a sharp pointed nose on each side of which alert brown eyes glittered as she made a quick appraisal of Mason; the eyes darted to Della Street, then around the office.

Behind Mrs. Hedley, Desere Ellis—slightly taller than average, her skin deeply tanned, honey-blonde hair, steady blue eyes and a figure a little on the spare side— seemed paled into insignificance.

"How do you do?" Mason said. "I'm Perry Mason."

The man, stalking forward and pushing out a hand, said, "I'm Fred Hedley. This is my mother, Rosanna, and my fiancée, Miss Ellis."

Mason nodded. "Won't you be seated?"

They found chairs. Desere looked at Della Street.

"My confidential secretary," Mason explained. "She takes notes on interviews, keeps things straight, and is my right hand."

Fred Hedley cleared his throat, but it was his mother who hurriedly interposed to assume the conversational initiative.

"Desere was told to come and see you," she said. "We gathered it was about her trust."

"I see," Mason said, noncommittally.

"We'd like to know about it," Mrs. Hedley said.

"Just what was it you wanted to know?" Mason asked.

Fred Hedley said, "The reason why Desere should be told to come and see you."

"Who told her?" Mason asked.

"The trustee, Kerry Dutton."

13

Mason's eyes locked with Hedley's. "Do *you* know him?" he asked.

"I've met him," Hedley said in a lukewarm voice. And then added as though disposing of Kerry Dutton for all time, "A square, a moneygrabber. He's an outsider."

"He's a very dear friend," Desere Ellis interposed, "and my father had the greatest confidence in him."

"Perhaps too much confidence," Mrs. Hedley snapped.

"You see," Desere explained, "my father thought I was not to be trusted with money. There was rather a fair sum of money, and Father left it to Kerry as trustee so that I could have enough each year to keep me going for four years, but not enough to go out and splurge and wake up broke. I think Daddy was more afraid of my gambling than anything else."

"I see," Mason observed noncommittally, and then asked, "Do you have any predilection for gambling, Miss Ellis?"

She laughed nervously. "I guess Daddy thought so. I guess he thought I had a predilection for just about everything."

Mrs. Hedley said, "The reason we're here is that we understand the trustee has finally come around to the idea for an endowment."

"An endowment?" Mason asked.

"Fred's idea," she said. "He wants to have it so that—"

Fred Hedley held up his hand. "Never mind telling him the details, Mom."

"I think Mr. Mason should know them."

"Then *I'll* tell him," Hedley said.

He turned to face the lawyer. "Get one thing straight, Mr. Mason, I'm not a visionary; I'm not a goof. I play around with a bunch of poets and artists but I'm essentially an executive type."

Warming to his subject, he got up from the chair, leaned forward and placed his hands on Mason's desk.

"I think we are beginning to realize that every country needs to develop geniuses; but here in this country we

14

can't do it because the genius can't develop; he starves to death.

"Look at the artists, the poets, the writers I know who could be developed into geniuses. I don't mean. Mr. Mason. that anybody has to develop them. All they need is to be left alone—just be free to develop their own talents."

"And they can't do it?" Mason asked.

"They can't do it," Hedley said, "because they can't make a living while they're doing it. They're starving to death. You can't develop anything on an empty stomach except an appetite."

"And you have some idea?" Mason asked.

"I want to endow up-and-coming poets, writers, artists. thinkers -principally, thinkers."

"What kind of thinkers?"

"Political thinkers."

"What kind of politics?" Mason asked.

"Now, there you go, Mr. Mason. You're trying to pin me down. Probably because of the beard. You think I'm a goof. I'm not. I go with a beat crowd, but I don't just want to drift along with the stream. I stay cool, but I want to *do* something."

"Such as what?"

"I want to *think.*"

"You called Dutton a square," Mason said. "Why?"

"Because he *is* a square."

"What's a square?"

"He doesn't belong; he's narrow-minded; he's all wrapped up in a conventional concept of moneygrubbing.

"Times are changing. The whole world has changed. You can't get anywhere any more with the conventional type of thinking—not in art, not in writing, not in poetry, not in political thinking."

Mason glanced at Desere Ellis. "You are planning to finance this idea he has?"

"I wish I could." she said. "but I don't see how I can. As I told the Hedleys, Dad's money is just about used up. I wish now I hadn't been quite so extravagant. Sometimes I even wish Kerry Dutton had been more firm with me and had done more of what Dad wanted him to."

"In what way?" Mason asked.

"Not giving me money to throw away."

"You threw it away?"

She made a little gesture. "Oh, I was always taking off for Europe, or someplace, and buying new cars, new clothes, living it up. Once you start in, you can go through money pretty fast, Mr. Mason."

"And Dutton gave you the money?"

"I think his idea was that he'd take the money Dad left and pay it out in installments so that I would have a steady income until the time came when the trust was terminated."

"And then you'd have nothing?" Mason asked.

"Then I'd have nothing," she said. "Then I'd have to consider seriously how I was going to make a living."

"Did you remonstrate at all with Dutton?" Mason asked.

"Remonstrate with him?" she said, and laughed. "I remonstrated with him all the time."

"About giving you so much money?"

"About not giving me enough. I asked him how did he or anyone else know if I would live until the trust terminated. Why not go through life seeing what there was to see, living what there was to live, and then cross the bridge of the trust termination when I came to it."

Fred Hedley said, "If you ask my opinion, Mr. Mason, it was one hell of a way to handle a trust. Particularly, a spendthrift trust of that sort. Her father recognized that tendency in his daughter and wanted to guard against it. If Dutton had been on the job, we'd have a lot more money now for our foundation."

Mason smiled affably, the smile taking some of the sting from his words, and said, "But I didn't."

"Didn't what?" Hedley asked.

"Ask your opinion," Mason said.

Hedley flushed.

"Well," Mrs. Hedley said, "we're here. What do you have to tell us, Mr. Mason?"

"Nothing," Mason said.

"Nothing?"

Mason spread his hands in a gesture.

"Well, why are we here?" Fred Hedley asked.

"I thought perhaps *you'd* tell *me*," Mason said.

The trio exchanged glances.

Desere Ellis said, "Kerry Dutton called me last night. He told me that the time was approaching when the trust would be terminated, that he had retained you as his attorney and suggested that it might be a good plan for me to drop in and see you just to get acquainted."

"He suggested you bring the Hedleys?"

"No, that was my idea."

"Why," Mrs. Hedley asked, "would he need an attorney to terminate the trust if the money is all gone and—I suppose, of course, there will be accurate accounts submitted Then all he has to do is to turn over whatever balance there may be and Desere will give him a receipt."

"Oh, there are lots of legal gimmicks in a thing of this sort," Fred Hedley said. "I can see why he thought he'd need an attorney, but I don't see why he wanted Desere to come in at this time."

"Perhaps it didn't occur to him that the three of you were coming," Mason said.

"Well you may have a point there," Hedley admitted. "We thought, of course, from the way the message was received that you were going to make some announcement There is, as I figure it, somewhere around fifteen thousand dollars left, and while that's not enough to carry out the plan we had in mind, it could be a start in the right direction. Desere, of course, would have to make some sacrifices, but she's going to have to anyway. Personally I think it's a damn shame Desere frittered away all this money on frivolities when it could have served a really useful purpose."

"You estimate there's fifteen thousand dollars left?" Mason asked.

"In the trust? Yes."

"Just how do you figure?"

"Well, we know the amount of the original trust. We know what Desere has taken out and we can figure just about what the income should have been."

"How much have you been getting during the last twelve months?" Mason asked Desere. "I take it there's no secret about it."

"Heavens, no," she said. "I've had just about all of it." And then looking at him sharply, said, "You should know, as Kerry's attorney."

"I've just had one preliminary talk with him so far," Mason said. "I haven't gone into details."

"You're preparing an accounting?"

"Not yet."

"Well," she said, "I've been getting just about two thousand dollars a month for the past four years. But the last couple of months Kerry has intimated there will be a balance to be distributed on the termination of the trust. So I did a little figuring and believe there should be around fifteen thousand dollars—perhaps a little more—because Kerry has intimated there may be a little surprise for me."

"You haven't asked him specifically?"

"I haven't asked him much of anything," she said somewhat wistfully. "He calls me over the telephone and sends me checks and . . . he doesn't approve."

"Of what?"

"Of the Hedleys, for one thing," she snapped. "Of the way I do things, for another."

"Look here," Mason asked, "have you been spending two thousand dollars a month?"

"Not lately," she said; and then after a moment, added, "I'm running scared."

"What do you mean?"

"I'm trying to save a little."

"If you'd give up your apartment and live more simply, that last money that's coming in could go a long

18

way toward getting Fred's foundation started," Mrs. Hedley said.

Desere Ellis shook her head. "I'm sold on it, but I'm going to use my money to take a business course and fit myself so I can make a living. I've been a playgirl long enough."

Fred Hedley looked at her in surprise. "You mean you're going to join the herd? You're going to become a key-pounding square?"

"I mean that I'm going to fit myself to take the responsibilities of life."

"You would be simply a cog in a business machine," Hedley told her reprovingly. "In no time at all you'd lose track of your friends who are original thinkers. You'd become just another wage slave taking pothooks and slanting lines. You'd be on the outside."

Mason grinned "Don't disparage secretaries. Mr. Hedley," he said. "They are pearls of great price and I can assure you that good ones are hard to find. These days you have to get them and train them over a long period of time. Miss Street is my right hand. I'd be lost without her."

"Wage slaves," Hedley snapped. "Human dignity is entitled to something more than machine routine."

Mason said, "Dignity means greatness. Look it up sometime."

He turned to Desere Ellis and said, "I don't know why Mr. Dutton suggested you come and see me. I am going to represent Mr. Dutton. I will be glad to talk with *you* at any time."

Mason placed a subtle emphasis upon the "you."

She nodded.

"But," Mason said, "I am acting as Dutton's attorney and at the moment I am not in a position to disclose anything about our relationship or about his affairs. I would want to have him present at any conversation with you."

"Heavens," she said, "you don't need to keep things

19

confidential as far as anything in connection with the trust is concerned. It's dead open and shut. I've kept books on it; I know how much I had and how much I've spent."

"Were there any new investments?" Mason asked.

"I don't think so. Dad left the property in stocks and bonds. Kerry has had to sell them a little at a time to keep up my allowance, but there have been some dividends, some increases in value. That's part of the bookkeeping I've been doing—just checking up."

"We've gone back over the bonds and stocks," Hedley said, "and figured the dividends, interest payments and selling prices."

"I see," Mason commented noncommittally; and then asked, "When are you going to enroll in this business course, Miss Ellis?"

"Tomorrow," she said.

Mason nodded approvingly and then, by his continued silence, indicated that he had nothing more to offer.

Hedley got to his feet and was promptly joined by Desere. Mrs. Hedley hesitated for a moment and then slowly arose from her chair.

"Thank you for calling," Mason said.

Della Street held open the exit door and they marched out.

When the door had closed, Mason turned to his secretary with a worried look. "I am probably violating all sorts of professional ethics," he said. "I'm afraid I'm getting swept along on the same current which has caused Kerry Dutton to lose his footing."

"Meaning you're falling in love with the girl?" Della Street asked, smiling.

Mason said, "I guess there's always the temptation to play God. . . . Here's a woman who has frittered away her life and, as far as she knows, all of the money that her father left her. She's tied up with some radicals who are writing intellectual poetry, espousing theoretical political views predicated upon limited experience and less

20

knowledge; and she's now just at the point of coming to grips with herself."

"Well," Della Street asked, "what should you do? Tell her the truth?"

Mason said after a moment's thought, "I am not my client's conscience—only his lawyer."

3

■

IT WAS the next morning when Della Street handed Mason the folded newspaper as he entered the office.

"What's this?" Mason asked. "The financial page?"

"Right."

"What's the trouble?"

"Read it," she said. "Unless I'm mistaken, there's plenty of trouble."

Mason read the paragraph she indicated.

It was announced last night that Steer Ridge Oil & Refining Company had brought in a gusher proving up an entirely new territory in the Crystal Dome area. Market value of the company stock had been steadily declining and according to Jarvis Reader, president of the company, the news of this strike will reverse the downward trend. The new gusher is reported in an entirely new field which had previously been abandoned by one of the major oil companies as non-productive.

Mason gave a low whistle. "Better get our client, Kerry Dutton, on the phone, Della."

She nodded. "I looked up his number. I felt perhaps you'd want to call him."

She picked up the instrument, said, "Give me an outside line, Gertie." And then her fingers flew over the dial.

She held the phone for several seconds, then her eyebrows raised. She made a little gesture to Mason but she continued holding on for another ten seconds.

At the end of that time, she dropped the telephone back into place.

"No answer?" Mason asked.

"No answer."

Mason said, "Ring up my broker, Della. Tell him I want fifty shares of Steer Ridge Oil and Refining."

Della Street put through the call, transmitted the order, then said, "He wants to talk with you personally, Chief."

Mason nodded. "Put him on."

The lawyer picked up the telephone on his desk and said, "Yes, Steve, what is it?"

"You know something in particular or are you just playing a hunch on that paragraph in the paper this morning?"

"Well, it's a little of both," Mason said. "Why?"

"I don't know about that Steer Ridge stock," the broker said. "It's skyrocketed. Somebody apparently has been snapping up stock for the last few days and the thing has climbed sky high. It had been down to almost nothing."

"What do you know about the company?" Mason asked.

"Nothing much. It got along pretty well for a while; then the stockholders were reported to be fighting among themselves. There may be a proxy battle. A fellow by the name of Jarvis Reader is president. He's a queer sort of a duck, apparently a wild-eyed gambler who committed the company to taking up all sorts of leases on territory that had lots of acreage and not very much else. Under his management the stock has been steadily declining for some time. Recently someone started trying to get proxies.

"Now, whenever that happens in a low-priced stock the management tries to counter with news that will put the stock up in price. Hence a good reason for this paragraph in the paper; or they may *really* have a new field and the insiders have kept the news. from the public so as to buy up stock; or it may be just a rumor.

"I was wondering if *you* have any inside information."

"Not me," Mason said. "I was hoping you had some."

"I've told you mine."

"Okay," Mason said, "buy me fifty shares at the market, regardless of what it costs. I want to be a stockholder in the company."

"Okay, if you say so," the broker said. "But I'd advise you not to go overboard simply on the strength of that newspaper report. That security has been a dog. A lot of people who had held it for years have sold out during the last year and some of them have taken quite a loss."

"Keep your eye on it," Mason said. "If there should be any really startling developments, let me know."

The lawyer hung up the telephone, glanced at Della Street, and said, "I wonder how our client is feeling about now?"

"That," Della Street said, "is a good question. Of course, he said he had the power to buy and sell, but the beneficiary *thinks* she has a block of that stock and that it's skyrocketing. On the strength of that feeling, she may be committing herself to all sorts of beatnik endowments."

The telephone on Della Street's desk rang.

Della Street picked it up, said, "Yes, Gertie?" Then after a few moments, said, "Just a minute. Have him wait on the line."

She turned to Perry Mason and said, "Fred Hedley is calling. He says that it's on a matter of the *greatest* importance and that he *knows* you will want to talk with him. He has some important information for you."

Mason hesitated a moment, then nodded and picked up his phone.

Della Street threw the switch which put both phones on the same line.

Mason said, "Hello. Perry Mason speaking."

Fred Hedley's voice was so excited that the words were all but telescoped together.

"Mr. Mason. Mr. Mason. I've got some wonderful news. This is *really* something! Have you seen the financial page of the morning paper?"

"What about it?" Mason asked.

"They've struck it rich. Steer Ridge Oil and Refining has proved up a new territory and brought in a big gusher."

Mason said, "This is Fred Hedley talking?"

"That's right, Mr. Mason. You remember me. I was in your office with my mother and Desere Ellis. I'm the one that's establishing the foundation."

"Oh, yes," Mason said. "What does the Steer Ridge Oil and Refining Company have to do with your foundation, Mr. Hedley?"

"Everything in the world," Hedley said. "Some of the stock that's held in the trust for Desere Ellis is a big block of the Steer Ridge Oil and Refining. It's going up in value like a skyrocket."

"Well, that's interesting," Mason said. "How do you know it's still in the trust?"

"It has to be. That was the stock that Desere's father wanted Dutton to hang on to and sell only as a last resort."

"Was it a condition of the trust?"

"I don't know," Hedley said with·a trace of irritation in his voice. "*You* should know. You're representing the guy."

"I am not familiar with the terms of the trust as far as *all* of the securities are concerned," Mason said. "I gathered from what you have told me that you were, and I was just asking the question. You folks told *me* he had distributed all but about fifteen thousand dollars. That means he must have had to sell some of the securities."

"Not the Steer Ridge," Hedley said confidently. "There's some sort of a proxy fight on, and a man called on Desere just a couple of weeks ago to get her proxies. She sent him to Dutton.

"That stock is going up like a rocket. It'll be worth thousands, hundreds of thousands!"

Mason said, "I fail to see just what difference all this makes—to you."

"This simply means there will now be adequate funds for us to carry out the work we want. Desere can give me the financial backing and I'll go to work on that endowment. It's going to be one of the biggest things in the whole world of creative art, Mr. Mason.

"Don't you understand what it's going to mean? My Lord, here are potential geniuses starving to death and being forced into some kind of a commercial treadmill occupation simply because they can't hang on until an unappreciative society recognizes their talent.

"We're going to create future Rembrandts. That is, they won't be stuffy like Rembrandt—they'll be truly creative in every sense of the word. We're going to develop writing geniuses. We're going to develop poets. We're going to emancipate American art and talent."

"Have you told Desere about this new development?" Mason asked.

"I haven't been able to get her thus far, but I certainly hope I can be the first to tell her. This was the day she started school, you know—business school."

"I see," Mason said. "Well, thank you very much for calling."

"Can you tell me where I can get in touch with Kerry Dutton?" Hedley asked.

"No," Mason said.

"I should talk with him right away in case he doesn't know about developments."

"You don't have his address?"

"I wasn't interested enough to ever ask for his address. Frankly, Mason, I think your client is a square, and I think he handled that trust like a fool."

"How should he have handled it?" Mason asked.

"He should have conserved the assets so there'd be enough money for Desere to do something that would really make a mark. Why, if he'd been careful and held her down to earth on expenses, she could have lived on just the income from the securities, and the principal could have been intact for something of this sort."

"All right," Mason said. "Thank you for calling but I'm not permitted to give out my client's address. I think the proper procedure would be for you to call Miss Ellis, have Miss Ellis call Dutton, and Dutton call me."

"All right," Hedley said, "if that's the way you want it. I was just trying to do you a favor."

"I appreciate your interest," Mason said. "Good-by." And the lawyer hung up.

Della Street, who had been monitoring the conversation and taking shorthand notes, looked up from her book and said, "Well, that's that. The fat seems to be in the fire."

Mason said, "Hang it, you have to sympathize with Dutton's viewpoint despite the fact it's irregular. However, if it comes to a showdown on a strict legal basis, we can probably keep him in the clear.

"He had every right on earth to sell any securities that he wanted to and invest the money in other securities. He *didn't* have any right to mislead his beneficiary and he *should* have made accountings. He had no right to mingle his own funds with those of the trust. Somehow I have an idea that when Mrs. Hedley finds out about all this and finds out that the stock in the Steer Ridge Oil and Refining Company was sold a year ago, there's going to be a fine, large mix-up and I am going to be right in the middle of it."

"That," Della Street said, "seems to me to be the understatement of the week. What are we going to tell Desere?"

"The same thing we tell everybody," Mason said. "We are representing Dutton. We are not representing anyone else. We can give out no information. Let them get in touch with Dutton, and Dutton, in turn, will get in touch with me."

"When this news gets to him," Della Street said, "he'll— Well, he may take to the tall timber."

"How do you know he isn't there now?" Mason asked.

She looked at the lawyer for a long, thoughtful moment and then said, "That's right. We don't."

4

◼

SHORTLY AFTER lunch Mason said, "Della, write out Kerry Dutton's name, address and telephone number on a card, will you please? And call Paul Drake at the Drake Detective Agency. Ask him if he can come in for a minute.

"Also, ring up my broker and make certain I am now a stockholder in the Steer Ridge Oil and Refining Company."

"If there's anything going on behind the scenes with inside information," Della Street said, "the insiders certainly had a wonderful opportunity for stock manipulation."

Mason said with a smile, "That's why I chose to become a stockholder, Della. As a stockholder of record, I'm entitled to protect my interests."

Della Street typed out the card with Dutton's address and telephone number; called the Drake Detective Agency, which was on the same floor with Mason; and a few moments later, Paul Drake's code knock sounded on the door of Mason's private office.

Paul Drake, head of the Drake Detective Agency, as tall as Perry Mason, broad-shouldered and good-looking, tried always to minimize his appearance.

He dressed in quiet clothes; always drove a car that was three to five years old— one of the more popular makes; and tried by every means to be self-effacing.

"Hi, beautiful," he said to Della; nodded to Perry; slid into the overstuffed, leather chair for clients and settled himself for a cigarette. "Shoot," he said.

"Paul," Mason told him, "this is on me. I want you to find a client. I am footing the bill."

"Client skipped out?" Drake asked.

"Could be."

"Owing you money?"

"No."

"Witness to something you want hushed up?"

"No."

"Witness to something in favor of one of your clients and you want his testimony?"

"No."

"What then?"

"Can't tell you," Mason said.

"Think he skipped out?"

"He could have."

"What do I tell him if I find him?"

"Nothing. Just let me know where he is."

"And I take it I'm not supposed to leave any back trail?"

"Try not to leave any back trail that leads back to me," Mason said. "Otherwise, you can go as far as you want. I realize that if you're going to get a guy located fast you can't go and ask questions without leaving *some* sort of a back trail. We'll have to take a chance on that."

"Starting now?" Drake asked.

"Yes," Mason said, handing Drake the typed card.

"You're in a hurry?"

"Yes. However, I have one other thing. This is something you should be able to get a routine check on. I want to find out something about Jarvis Reader, president of the Steer Ridge Oil and Refining Company."

"There was an article about them in the paper," Drake said. "Seems they struck it rich."

"You read that article, too?"

"Uh-huh. You can't believe too much of what you hear

28

in deals of that sort, but I understand the stock is going up out of sight."

"You don't have any, do you, Paul?"

"Detectives don't get rich buying and selling stock. They don't get rich, period."

"Okay," Mason told him. "On your way, and let's see what you can turn up. Keep me posted."

Less than fifteen minutes after Paul Drake had left the office, the telephone on Della Street's desk rang, and Della Street, answering it, said, "All right, tell him to sit down a moment, Gertie. I'll see if Mr. Mason can see him."

Della Street turned from her telephone. "Speaking of angels," she said, "Jarvis Reader is in the outer office."

"He wants to see me?" Mason asked.

She nodded.

"Go bring him in, Della."

Della Street said, "Tell him Mr. Mason will see him, Gertie. I'm on my way out to get him."

Della Street left the office to return a moment later with a powerful, somewhat stoop-shouldered man in his middle fifties. He had a weather-beaten face, bushy eyebrows, piercing gray eyes, and a belligerent manner.

"Hello," he said. "You're Mason?"

Mason grinned. "You're Reader?"

"Right."

"What can I do for you?"

Reader said, "You're representing Kerry Dutton, I understand."

"Who told you that?"

"Never mind. I want a straight answer. Are you or are you not representing Kerry Dutton?"

"Mr. Dutton has retained me to represent him in one matter. Yes."

"In *one* matter?"

"That's right."

"Well, there are going to be several matters."

"Such as what?"

"I have learned," Reader said, "that Dutton made

29

statements that I was crooked; that my management of the company was manipulated for my own purposes; that I didn't know straight up about oil; that I was primarily interested in bilking people into investing in stock so I could keep myself in power as the head of the company at a darn good salary."

"When did you hear all this?" Mason asked.

"Some time ago, but I haven't done anything about it because I wanted to wait until I could prove what a liar Dutton was.

"Now then, my management has been vindicated, and I'll bet Dutton wishes he had the twenty thousand shares of stock he sold a while ago."

"Sold it?" Mason asked, inquiringly.

"That's right. That's when he made the statements. He was reported to have sold the stock to a purchaser and warned him that it probably wasn't any good; that I didn't know straight up about the oil business; that I was just working a flimflam getting a lot of sterile acreage tied up so I could make a big showing to people who knew nothing about the oil business and keep drawing a nice salary, having an expense account, a private airplane and all that sort of stuff."

"If," Mason said, "you're really intending to sue my client, you shouldn't be talking with me, and I certainly am not going to talk with you. You can get an attorney and have him call on me if there's anything you want to adjust."

"I don't need an attorney," Reader said. "Not right away. I'm not here to sue. I'm not here to threaten. I'm simply here to tell Dutton that I will accept an apology— a public apology which I can print in the papers."

"Why don't you tell him?" Mason asked.

"Can't find him. He's hard to catch."

"You've tried?"

"I've tried. . . . I wanted to be the first to tell him about our oil strike before he read it in the papers. I couldn't find him. Then the news was released on the radio and the papers picked it up. Now he's heard all about it and I'm the last person in the world he wants to see."

Mason said, "Just as a matter of curiosity and not talking about any claims you may have against Mr. Dutton because I don't care to discuss them, you folks were friendly at one time?"

"Friends!" Reader exclaimed, drawing a forefinger across his throat. "Oh, yes, we're friends. That guy has done everything he could to make it tough for me."

"What I meant was that you knew him?"

"Hell yes, I knew him."

"And have for some time?"

"Ever since he became trustee under that will. I went to him and wanted him to invest more money in Steer Ridge Oil. He laughed at me. I'll bet he wishes now he'd followed my advice. That trust would have been worth a lot of money today.

"I was friendly with Templeton Ellis. He had faith in me. He was one of my first backers. He put money into Steer Ridge on four different occasions; left a tidy bloc of stock, and just because it started going down in value, that smart-aleck trustee sold it out. Not only sold it out, but shot off his big mouth that the management was crooked; that no one in the company knew anything about the oil business and that I was getting leases on land that nobody else would touch with a ten-foot pole."

Reader paused for a moment, then went on, "Now, there's something else you'd better know about if you're getting yourself tied up with Dutton: The beneficiary of that trust thinks he still has the twenty thousand shares of Steer Ridge stock in the trust. She doesn't know he sold her out."

"What makes you think that?" Mason asked.

"I don't think, I know. I'll tell you something else. Dutton will be frantically trying to buy that stock back. He's willing to pay almost any price for it. I'm personally going to see he can't get it back.

"When you see him, tell him that I know everything he's doing. And tell him that his stool pigeon, Rodger

Palmer, who's trying to pick up stock and proxies, isn't going to get to first base.

"I've forgotten more about corporate management of oil properties than these birds ever knew. . . . Tell Mr. Kerry Dutton that whenever he's ready to buy a page ad in the daily papers apologizing to me, I'll think about letting him off the hook. Until that time, he can fry in his own grease."

Mason smiled. "I think you'd better tell him that yourself, face to face, Mr. Reader."

"I will if I can find the guy."

Reader turned on his heel and started for the outer office, paused to say, "And when Desere Ellis finds he's sold her out, there's going to be hell to pay."

"You can go out this way," Della Street said, holding open the exit door.

Reader hesitated a minute and said, "Thanks, I'll go out the same way I came in. I like it that way."

He strode out through the door to the entrance room.

5

IT WAS after seven-thirty. Mason and Della were closing up the office, and Mason was just holding the exit door open for Della when the unlisted phone rang stridently.

Mason said, "That's the unlisted telephone. That'll be Paul Drake."

Della Street nodded and hurried across to the instrument, picked it up and said, "Yes, Paul?"

She nodded to Mason, who picked up the extension phone on his desk.

"Hi, Paul," Mason said. "What's new?"

"This fellow Dutton is something of a problem, Perry."

"What about him?"

"He's being hard to find."

"I didn't think he'd be easy or I wouldn't be paying you fifty dollars a day to look him up."

"Well, he's trying to be *real* hard to find. Someone is looking for him and I have an idea that someone is a process server with some papers to put right in the middle of Dutton's hot little hand."

"And you think Dutton's hiding out to avoid that?"

"He's hiding out to avoid something."

"Where are you now, Paul?"

"I'm in a telephone booth across the street from a service station about four blocks from Dutton's apartment. I have an idea I'm going to pick up his trail. While I was waiting I thought I'd telephone for instructions."

"How come?"

"Well, I became pretty well convinced he wasn't intending to go back to his apartment. There's a man sitting outside waiting. I looked up the license number on his car. He's a chap named Rodger Palmer. From the way he acts, I think he's a process server. He's sure anxious to see Dutton and he has lots of patience. He's just covering the entrance to the apartment house. Also, the girl at the switchboard said Dutton had been in and out several times earlier in the day, carrying a big briefcase each time."

"Both in and out?" Mason asked.

"Both in and out."

"Could be he was moving stuff out and stashing it in the trunk of his automobile," Mason said.

"That's the point," Drake said. "I figured he'd buy his gasoline around here somewhere, so I covered all the gasoline stations around and finally not only hit pay dirt but I may have hit a jackpot, as far as Dutton is concerned. I found the place where he buys his gasoline and has the service work done on his car. The car is there now being serviced. He told the attendant to change the oil, give it a good lube job and check all the tires—that he was going on a long trip."

"Didn't say where?"

33

"No, but the car is there and I have a stakeout on it."

Mason said. "I want a line on Dutton, Paul. I'm mixed up in something with him and I may be skating on rather thin ice, ethically. A great deal depends on what kind of a guy he is, whether he's on the up-and-up or whether he's taking people for rides."

"Well. I think he's getting ready to skip out."

"All right. sit on the job," Mason said. "Follow him and find out where he's headed."

"How strong do I go?"

"As strong as you have to."

"Suppose he heads out of town?"

"Head out of town right after him, Paul."

"I'll probably need some help."

"Get it!"

"Suppose he buys a plane ticket and heads for Brazil?"

"Get the plane; get the flight number; wire your correspondent in Brazil and pick him up when he lands."

"In other words. the sky's the limit?"

"That's right. But what with his having the car serviced and all of that, you can be pretty sure he's going to start out by automobile."

"And you want me to stay with him?"

"Like glue," Mason said.

"Okay," Drake told him. "I'll be reporting. I'll need at least one assistant on the job. I'll phone for one now."

Mason hung up the phone and faced Della Street with a puzzled frown.

"How much are you mixed in all this, Chief?" she asked. "I mean, how deep?"

"Let's put it this way," Mason said, "Dutton tells me he's embezzled money from the beneficiary of the trust. The way *he* tells it, he's made restitution; and the way he *says* he did it, it was technically legal within the terms of the trust, provided he told me the truth about the trust.

"But the way he's acting doesn't coincide with his story to me. Unless you have something on for tonight, Della, let's go tie on a nosebag, then come back to the

34

office and sit around for a while. I have an idea we may have a showdown somewhere along the line. We'll keep in touch with Paul Drake's office and let them know where we are."

Della Street smiled. "If you can promise an extra cut of rare roast beef for me, with baked potato, onion rings and a green salad, I'm with you until midnight."

"We'll double it," Mason said. "I know just the place where they specialize in that kind of food."

6

HALFWAY THROUGH the meal, the waiter approached the table and said, "You're accepting calls, Mr. Mason?"

"Yes, I told the headwaiter when I came in," Mason said.

The waiter nodded, and plugged in the telephone. Mason picked it up and heard Paul Drake's voice.

"Where are you now, Paul?"

"The office told me where you were," Drake said reproachfully. "I'm sitting in my automobile munching on a candy bar to keep my stomach from getting corns where it rubs against my backbone, I'm that hungry."

"What's the score?"

"Well, I picked up Dutton, all right."

"Where did he go?"

"Right now, he isn't going anyplace. He's sitting in a car, watching."

"What's he watching?"

"He followed a guy here who looks like a dressed-up beatnik."

"Tall, broad-shouldered, with a beard?" Mason asked.

"That's the fellow."

"And where is the place he's waiting?"

35

"It's the Doberman Apartments on Locks Street. Does that mean anything to you?"

"It means quite a bit," Mason said. "That's where Desere Ellis lives, and the man with the beard is probably calling on her."

"And Dutton is checking?"

Mason thought for a moment; then said, "No. Dutton probably is waiting to be sure the coast is clear when he talks to Desere Ellis. He probably has decided to tell her something rather important and he wants to be certain he isn't interrupted. The beatnik's name is Fred Hedley. He tries to ape the crowd and be a cool cat. Actually he wants to promote a deal with Desere Ellis whereby he can play God to a lot of artists, poets and writers.

"I can tell you that much, but it's in confidence.

"If my hunch is right, Paul, Dutton will wait there until Fred Hedley comes out and drives away. Then Dutton will go on up to the apartment."

"Then what?"

"When Dutton comes out," Mason said, "shadow him. Have you got a relief yet?"

"I had a little difficulty getting an operative I could trust," Drake said, "but I finally got one and he's on his way here. My men are tied up today. That is, the good men.

"I went out on this job myself, because the man I first sent out reported he couldn't get any trace of Dutton. I didn't like to hand you a failure, and I figured there'd be a lead if a man put in enough time looking for it. So I went out and started covering the service stations. I hit pay dirt there and got stuck with the job."

Mason said, "Get a relief. Put the finger on Dutton and go get a good dinner. Be sure you get a good man."

"The one I have coming is okay," Drake said.

Mason said, "We're going to be here at this café for another half hour; then we'll go up to the office and wait for your call there. Try to give us a report by ten-thirty, because we'll knock it off shortly after that."

"Okay," Drake said, "will do."

Mason hung up the phone and related what he had learned to Della Street.

She made a little grimace.

"Meaning?" Mason asked.

"Meaning that Desere Ellis is or has been infatuated with Hedley and that's not the way things should be. I'm pulling for Dutton."

"And so?" Mason asked.

"So," she said, "Dutton is waiting for Hedley to go home. As soon as Hedley leaves, Dutton will go up to Desere Ellis' apartment and she'll know intuitively that he was sitting outside waiting for Hedley to go home. That puts two strikes against Dutton as far as any woman is concerned. A woman wants a man who will chart his own course and assert himself; not one who will skulk in the shadows and wait until the coast is clear before he makes a move."

"Of course," Mason pointed out, "it may be that Dutton isn't afraid to face Hedley for a showdown, but he's planning to tell Desere the whole business and he doesn't want Hedley to know about Desere's financial affairs."

"In that case Fred Hedley's mother will step into the picture and things will move fast after that," Della Street said. "That is, if she has an idea there's more money in the trust than appears to be the case at the present time."

Mason raised his wineglass. "I give you the Mexican toast," he said, *"salud y pesetas y amor sin suegras."*

"What is that?" Della Street asked.

"That," Mason said, "is a toast that Mexican gentlemen give to each other in the privacy of their clubs."

"What does it mean?"

"It means health, wealth and love without mothers-in-law."

Della Street burst out laughing. "The man who invented that must have known Mrs. Hedley," she said.

"Or someone pretty much like her," Mason agreed.

They finished a leisurely dinner, and Mason was just signing the check when the waiter came hurrying up

37

with the telephone. He plugged it in and said, "An emergency, Mr. Mason."

Mason picked up the phone, said, "Yes. What is it?"

Drake's voice said, "You'd better get up here, Perry. Quick!"

"Where is here?"

"That address I gave you, the Doberman Apartments. If you want to protect your client, you'd better get here. There's hell to pay."

"We'll be right there."

"I'll be waiting," Drake told him. "I'll be at the front of the apartment house. It's on Locks Street."

"Coming right away," Mason said.

Mason grabbed Della Street's arm. "Emergency," he told her.

"What's happened?"

"Paul didn't say. Just said we'd better get up there, quick, if we wanted to protect our client. Come on, let's go."

Mason signaled the headwaiter, who in turn signaled the doorman, and the lawyer's car was in front waiting by the time Mason and Della Street reached the outer door of the restaurant.

Mason, an expert driver, jockeyed for position at the traffic signals, but they encountered some heavy traffic and it was some twenty minutes before they reached the address.

Drake was waiting for them on the curb.

"Well," he said, "you're too late."

"What happened?" Mason asked.

Drake said, "The fellow with the beard came out, got in his car and started off. Just as you had predicted, Dutton didn't follow him. He jumped out of his car and hurried into the apartment house.

"Now, I don't know whether Hedley knew that Dutton was waiting and wanted to trap him, or whether Hedley had forgotten something, but Dutton hadn't been in the house five minutes when Hedley came driving back, double-parked his car, jumped out and went into the apartment house like a guy carrying the mail."

"And what happened?"

"Plenty," Drake said. "A woman ran out on a balcony on the third floor and started screaming for the police. I guess someone telephoned. . . . Anyhow, a police radio patrol car came driving up, and about that time Dutton came out of the apartment. He was hurrying, but he took one look and saw that police car and his gait slowed to a saunter and he came idling across the street while the cops jumped out of the radio car and went dashing into the apartment house."

"Then what?"

"Dutton drove off and—"

"Hang it, Paul," Mason said, "I wanted Dutton followed."

"He's being followed. I had a relief here. I thought I'd make a report myself because the relief wouldn't have any opportunity. They were going—fast."

"What happened?"

"Well, I talked with one of the cops when they came out. They had Hedley with them, but Hedley was pretty much the worse for wear. I think he's going to have a sore nose for a couple of days and there's blood all over his shirt. He's also got one eye swelling shut, and the way he talked, his lips were pretty well puffed up.

"As nearly as I can get the story, Hedley started the brawl. He caught Dutton up in this girl's apartment and there were words, and then Hedley took a swing and from that point on the party got rough."

"And Hedley got the worst of it?" Mason asked.

"Well, he certainly didn't get the best of it. Dutton didn't have a mark on him, but Hedley looked as if he'd been put through a washing machine."

"What did the cops do?"

"They turned him loose after they got him outside, but I heard enough of the conversation to learn that they figured he was the one who started it."

"What was Hedley saying?"

"He was going to swear out a warrant for Dutton's arrest for assault and battery and anything else. The officers didn't seem too much impressed, however, and told Hedley he'd better pick up the tab for damages on the apartment of a Miss Ellis in 321, or he might find himself facing trouble."

Mason turned to Della Street, who was smiling broadly.

"Well, Della," Mason said, "I guess things turned out the way you wanted them to, and on that note, since the crisis seems to have passed, since Dutton is being tailed, we'll call it a day."

"And," Della Street said, demurely, "thank you for a lovely dinner."

"Dinner!" Drake said. "That damn candy bar has been repeating on me for the last hour."

Mason said, "I suggest the café where you reached us, Paul. It has wonderful extra-cut rare roast beef, baked potatoes, onion rings and salad. And, of course, since you're still on duty, the cost of the dinner would be an acceptable expense in the eyes of the Bureau of Internal Revenue."

Drake's eyes were anguished. "A couple of hours ago," he said, "I could have eaten a live horse. Now, with the taste of that synthetic chocolate in my mouth, I don't want anything except a glass of warm milk and later on a little bicarbonate of soda."

7

∎

THE NEXT MORNING Mason stopped in at Paul Drake's office on the way down the corridor to his own office.

The receptionist said, "Mr. Drake's down in your office, Mr. Mason, waiting to see you on an important matter. He telephoned Miss Street and she said you were expected in about this time so he went down to wait."

"I'll go on down," Mason said. "But tell me first, where's our quarry?"

The girl at the telephone desk smiled and said, "I'm not supposed to know, but Mr. Drake received a telephone call from Ensenada, Mexico, just before he telephoned Miss Street."

"That," Mason said, "will make a nice vacation."

The lawyer was smiling as he walked down the corridor and opened the door of his private office.

"Good morning, Della," he said. "Hi, Paul, how are you? I've been thinking we're working too hard. How would you folks like to break away from routine for a day and drive down to Ensenada, Mexico?

"That's a wonderful Mexican city, wonderful food, sweet lobsters, the *caguama,* or big turtle from the Gulf, enchiladas, chile con carne, refried frijoles, ice cold Mexican beer—"

"Hush," Della Street said, "you're breaking Paul's heart. He had stomach trouble last night."

"How come?" Mason asked.

Drake shook his head. "I knew when I was getting into this business what the occupational hazards were. Like a surgeon who lives under tension and usually develops heart trouble by the time he's fifty-five, a detective lives on hamburgers and bicarbonate of soda. . . . How the devil did you know about Ensenada, Perry?"

"Stopped in your office on the way down," Mason said. "Your telephone operator told me you had a call from Ensenada."

"Well," Drake said, "my man lost Dutton."

"Lost him!"

"That's right."

"For how long?"

"About an hour."

"What happened?"

Drake said, "My man who relieved me took up the tailing job."

"And what did he do?" Mason asked.

"Well, Dutton left the apartment house just as the cops came up. He drove around aimlessly for a while; then after about ten or fifteen minutes stopped at a service station and—"

"I thought you said his car was filled up," Mason said.

"That's right, he'd filled it up where he had it serviced, but this time he was only interested in the telephone. He went into the telephone booth and dialed a number. My man had to be a little careful. He parked across the street and watched with binoculars but he couldn't get the number.

"Anyhow the fellow either got the wrong number or a busy signal, because he just held the phone to his ear for a few seconds; then hung up, waited a few seconds, then dialed again."

"What happened this time?"

"Well, my man figured that telephone conversation was pretty damn important. He wanted to get it the worst way, so he took a chance."

"On what?"

"He approached the booth while the fellow was in there, acting as though he wanted to make an important call. Dutton waved him away, but my man had one of those pocket battery-powered wire recorders and some adhesive tape. I've been using them lately and they work pretty well. He had parked his car around the back of the booth and he ostensibly walked back to wait by his car. What he actually did was fasten the wire recorder on the back of the booth, using adhesive tape, and then he got in his car and drove away. He didn't drive very far but waited where he could watch Dutton's car.

"When Dutton came out of the booth after that last call, he was going like a house afire. My man figured he'd retrieve the wire recorder later on or ring the office and tell somebody to go and get it. He stayed with Dutton."

Mason nodded. "That was the thing to do."

"But Dutton drove like crazy. He went through three red lights that my man followed him through, hoping that a traffic officer would tag both of them. On the fourth red light, Dutton almost had a collision. The intersection was blocked. Dutton got away and my man was stymied by traffic."

"Going through red lights that way, didn't Dutton know he was being followed?"

"Probably," Drake said. "He may even have been trying to shake pursuit, but somehow the way my operative felt, Dutton was going someplace in too much of a hurry to give a hoot about anything—and that's the way it turned out."

"Go on," Mason said.

"Well, after my man lost him and knew he'd lost him for good, he went back to the phone booth and picked up the wire recorder, turned back the wire recorder to the starting point and then listened to the conversation. Of course, he could only hear one end of the conversation. It was brief and to the point."

"What was it?" Mason asked.

"The first thing Dutton said was a question. 'What's new? You know who this is.' Then he waited for the answer and then said, 'I called the other number and was told to call you at this pay station. . . . I'll pay over the five thousand if you're acting in good faith.' Then there was a period of silence while he was evidently getting instructions, and then he said, 'Give me that again . . . the seventh tee at the Barclay Country Club, is that right? . . . Why pick that sort of place?' Then he said, 'All right, all right, it's nearly that time now. . . . Yes, I've got a key. . . .' Then he hung up the phone and that was the end of the conversation."

"Your man followed up that lead?" Mason asked.

"My man went to the Barclay Country Club. It's a key job, and my man didn't have a key, and at that hour of the night there wasn't any chance of getting in without one, but there were three or four cars parked and one of them was Dutton's. My man checked the license number."

"So what did he do?"

"Put himself in a position where he could pick up the car when it left, and waited it out. He got there at ten minutes after ten o'clock."

"How long did he have to wait?"

"About twelve minutes."

"Then what?"

"Then Dutton came out at ten-twenty-two and started driving south. My man tailed him without headlights for a while and it was pretty damn risky. But Dutton stopped after a short distance and got out of the car. My man went on past, then pretended to have tire trouble, jacked up the car and waited until Dutton came sailing past.

"Dutton drove to the border, kept on driving down to Ensenada. He had no idea he was tailed. He's staying at the Siesta del Tarde Auto Court. He is registered under the name of Frank Kerry."

Mason said, "He doesn't need any credentials in the way of tourist cards or anything of that sort as long as he's no farther south than Ensenada, eh, Paul?"

"That's right. If he gets below Ensenada, he's going to need a tourist card or an entry permit of some kind; but as far as Ensenada he's on his own."

"Your man still tailing him?"

"That's right. He's doing the best he can. Of course, one man isn't much good on a twenty-four-hour-a-day job. . . . Do you want me to send a relief down?"

Mason was thoughtful. "Might as well, Paul," he said. "And I think the time has come for me to assume the role of a Dutch uncle."

"Doing what?" Drake asked.

"Getting this thing cleaned up before I get too deeply involved," Mason told him. "After all, Dutton is a client of mine but— Well, I may have to insist that he surrender himself or go to the police."

"And then what?"

"Then," Mason said, grinning, *"I'll* try to beat the rap."

The lawyer turned to Della Street. "How," he asked, "would you like to take a couple of notebooks, plenty of pencils, a briefcase and a quick trip down to Ensenada, Mexico? This time I think we'll get the real story."

8

◼

MASON AND Della Street left Tijuana behind, took the smooth new road to Ensenada.

"The old road," Mason said, "was more scenic."

"Wasn't it? But these days one sacrifices everything to speed. However, it's nice to get where you're going without fighting the steering wheel around a lot of curves. Do you think he's really embezzled money, Chief?"

"I don't know," Mason said. "The way he acts, I'm afraid he's leaving me to hold the sack."

"In what way?"

"There'll be a hue and cry," Mason said, "and I'll be in there pitching, assuring everybody that things are going to work out all right; that I have every confidence in my client; that I know the facts; that I have advised him and that he hasn't committed any crime; that in due course everything will be explained and cleared up."

"And then?" she asked.

"And then," Mason said, "after a while it may dawn on me that my client is being hard to find."

"You mean in Ensenada?"

"Ensenada," Mason said, "could be simply the first stop. He's going to stay there long enough to get out from under the telltale registration of his automobile and all that. He'll probably leave the car where it can be found; double back to the United States; grab a plane

45

for Brazil or someplace, and leave me behind to make explanations."

"You think he's that kind?" she asked.

"No," Mason said shortly, "I don't."

"Then what?"

"That," the lawyer told her, "is the reason we're making this trip, Della."

They drove into Ensenada, threaded their way down the busy main street, and Mason asked directions to the Siesta del Tarde.

"Will you know Drake's man?" Della Street asked as they drove up in front of the auto court.

"He'll know *me,"* Mason said.

The lawyer got out and stood stretching and yawning, looking around at the scenery, soaking up the sunlight, before helping Della from the car.

The two of them walked toward the office of the auto court, then paused and looked back toward the car. Mason caught the eye of the man who was sauntering down the street.

The man winked at Mason, put a cigarette in his mouth, fumbled through his pockets and said, "Pardon me, could you let me have a match?"

"I can do better than that," Mason said. "I have a Zippo lighter."

The lawyer snapped the lighter into flame, held it toward the man with the cigarette.

"In Unit nineteen," the detective said. "He hasn't been out, unless he sneaked out while I was telephoning a report to Los Angeles.

"That's his car over there, the Chevvy with the license number, OAC seven, seven, seven."

"Okay," Mason said, "we're going in and talk with him. Keep an eye on things. I may want you as a witness. . . . How you are feeling? Pretty well bushed?"

"Staying awake is the hardest part of a job like this, Mr. Mason. I was up all night and sitting here in the car where it's warm, I kept wanting to take forty winks.

If I had, I'd be apt to wake up and find the bird had flown the coop."

Mason said, "You can either check out within the next thirty minutes, or we'll have a relief for you. Paul Drake got in touch with a relief operative in San Diego this morning and he's on his way down."

"That'll help," the detective said. "I'm not complaining, I'm just trying to stay awake and sometimes that's just about the hardest job a man can have."

"Okay," Mason told him, "we're going in."

The lawyer nodded to Della Street.

A long driveway led to the office; then down to a parking place by the cabins. Palm trees and banana trees shaded the units of the court.

Mason, ignoring the sign which said *Office,* guided Della to the unit occupied by Kerry Dutton.

The lawyer turned to his secretary and said, "When I knock on the door, say, 'Towels.' "

The lawyer knocked.

A moment later, Della Street said, "Towels."

"Come in," a man's voice called, and a hand on the inside turned the knob on the door.

Mason pushed his way into the room, followed by Della Street.

Kerry Dutton stared at them in speechless amazement.

Mason said, "When I'm representing a person, I like to do a good job, and in order to do a good job I have to have the *real* facts. I thought perhaps you could tell me a little more about your problem."

Dutton's eyes went from one to the other.

Mason moved over to a chair; held it for Della, then seated himself in the other chair, leaving the bed for Dutton.

Dutton's legs took him over to the bed and seemed to give way as he settled down on the counterpane.

"Well?" Mason asked.

Dutton shook his head.

"What's the trouble?" Mason asked.

"It isn't what you think," Dutton said.

"How much of what you told me was untrue?"

"What I told you was generally true," Dutton said. "It was the things I didn't tell you that—oh, what's the use?"

"There isn't any," Mason assured him. "That is, no use in trying to hold out on your lawyer. Sooner or later the facts will come to light, and if your lawyer doesn't know what they're going to be in advance, he's pretty apt to be caught at a disadvantage."

Dutton simply shook his head.

"Now then," Mason went on, "no matter how legal your actions may have been in the first place, you weakened your position by resorting to flight. In California, flight is considered evidence of guilt, and a prosecutor is permitted to introduce that evidence in a criminal trial."

Dutton started to say something.

There was a knock on the door.

Dutton looked at Mason, then at Della Street, apprehension on his face.

"Expecting visitors?" Mason asked.

Dutton got up from the bed, started for the door, stopped.

The knock was repeated, this time in a more peremptory manner.

"Better see who it is," Mason said.

Dutton opened the door.

Two men came in, one in the uniform of a police officer; one in plain clothes.

The man in plain clothes sized up the occupants of the room, bowed, and said, "The señorita, I hope, will excuse me. I am the *Jefe* of *Policia*. May I ask which one of you gentlemen is Kerry Dutton from Los Angeles?"

"And the reason for the request?" Mason asked.

The chief of police regarded him with appraising eyes. "I do not think," he said pointedly, "that I have the honor of your acquaintance, sir."

"I am Perry Mason, an attorney at law," Mason said, "and this is my secretary, Miss Della Street."

The chief bowed deferentially. "It is such a pleasure

to make your acquaintance, sir, and I am so sorry that I have to interfere with what was perhaps a professional conference—no?"

"That is right," Mason said. "I am conferring with my client, and my secretary was preparing to take some notes. If you could spare us perhaps a half an hour, I am quite certain that we will be at your service at that time."

The eyes softened into a smile. "That is what you would call a good try, but unfortunately, Señor Mason, the business that I have with Mr. Dutton is of the urgency."

He turned to Dutton. "Señor Dutton, it is with great regret that it is necessary for me to inform you that you are in custody of the *policia*."

"And the charge?" Mason asked.

"A warrant of first-degree murder which we will honor here to the extent of declaring that Señor Dutton is an undesirable alien. As such, we will escort him to the border and ask him to leave Mexico immediately."

"Murder!" Mason exclaimed. "Who was killed?"

"That information will, I trust, be forthcoming when Señor Dutton reaches the border. It is my unpleasant duty to see he is promptly escorted to the border."

"And at the border?" Mason asked.

The officer smiled. "At the border," he said, "I feel quite certain that police from your country will be waiting. What would you do if you were a police officer in the United States, and you knew that a man whom you wished to arrest for murder was to be deported as an undesirable alien?"

"That procedure seems a little high-handed to me," Mason said.

"Doubtless, it does," the officer announced, "but we do things in our country the way we wish to do them in our country, just as you are permitted to do things in your country the way you wish to do them in your country. That is, we do not interfere with you and we do not care to have you interfere with us.

"I am going to ask you to withdraw, if you will please be so good."

Mason said, "I am an attorney at law. My client is accused of a crime and I demand the right to represent him and consult with him."

The chief smiled. "You are an attorney in the United States?"

"Yes."

"And in Mexico?"

Mason hesitated.

"In Mexico," the chief of police went on, "attorneys in good standing are referred to as *licenciados*. That means they have a license granted by the Mexican government to practice law. You perhaps have such a license, Señor Mason?"

Mason grinned. "All right, it's your country, your customs and your prisoner."

"Thank you," the chief said, "and there is no reason why we should detain you further, Señor Mason."

"But this man is charged with murder," Mason asked, "and his attorney can't talk with him?"

The chief shrugged his shoulders. "You are licensed in your country. You can talk with your client there at any time. Here he is charged only with being an undesirable alien. We do not wish undesirable aliens in our country any more than you do."

"What's undesirable about him?" Mason asked.

The chief smiled and said, "He is a fugitive from justice in the United States. This makes him very undesirable as a Mexican visitor."

"There are legal proceedings looking to his deportation?" Mason asked.

"Only the proceedings necessary to get him transferred to the border. Here in Mexico we expedite the process of justice as much as possible."

Mason looked at Dutton, then back at the chief of police. "Zip the lip," he said.

The chief raised his eyebrows. "I'm afraid I didn't understand you."

"Pardon me," Mason said, "it was just a bit of American slang."

"Oh, yes—you Americans. And now, Señor, if you and your so charming secretary will just step this way, please—and I strongly recommend the restaurants here. You will find the service excellent and the food beyond compare. As tourists, we will try to make you happy."

"But not as an attorney?" Mason asked.

The chief shrugged expressive shoulders. "Unfortunately, you are not an attorney in Mexico. If you would reside in Mexico and comply with the requirements, I have no doubt but that you could become a *licenciado,* but until then . . ."

There was another expressive shrug of the shoulders.

The police officer held the outer door open.

Mason put his hand on Della Street's arm, and together they stepped out of the room into the shaded walkway which was filled with the sound of white-winged doves, the scent of flowers and the beauty of semitropical foliage.

9

As MASON and Della Street walked down the little sidewalk in front of the auto courts, Drake's detective came running toward them, motioning frantically.

Mason quickened his step.

"What is it?" he asked.

"I called Drake to report, and he's on the phone. Something he wants to tell you about right away. Says it's terribly important; that I should get you. He's going to hold the line until you can come."

Mason nodded to Della Street, hurried down the walkway under the palms and banana trees, his long legs making the detective trot to keep up, while Della Street made no attempt to match the pace.

In the phone booth, where the receiver was off the hook, Mason closed the door, picked up the receiver, said, "Yes? Hello."

Drake's voice said, "That you, Perry?"

"Right."

"All right," Drake said, "there's a rumble. I don't know how bad it is as far as your client is concerned, but it's pretty bad at this end."

"Murder?" Mason asked.

"Right. How did you know?"

"The officers moved in on Dutton while I was talking with him."

Drake said, "Here's all I know. An early golfer found a body on tee seven at the Barclay Country Club. The man had been shot once."

"Did they find the weapon?" Mason asked.

"I don't know," Drake said. "This much I do know. An attempt had been made to keep the police from identifying the victim and apparently that attempt has succeeded to date.

"Everything in the man's pockets had been taken. There isn't so much as a handkerchief. The labels had been cut from the inside of the coat pocket and on the little hanging strap at the back of the neck.

"The cutting had been skillfully done with a very sharp knife or a razor blade.

"The time of death hasn't been officially determined as yet, but it could be at just about the time our man tailed Dutton out to the golf club—that's within the general over-all time limit that they've mapped out for the murder. After they have a complete autopsy, they may let Dutton off the hook. Right now I understand the tentative time is fixed between nine-thirty last night and two-thirty this morning."

"All right," Mason said. "Now, your man couldn't get into the club because it was a key job?"

"That's right. You have to go in through the club-house to get to the court."

"There must be a service road," Mason said.

"There is, somewhere. I haven't looked it up."

Mason said, "At that hour of the night, the murdered man probably let himself in with a key. It's a cinch that Dutton did."

"Dutton's a member of the club," Drake said.

"All right, probably the other man is, too. Get photographs from the newspaper reporters and start covering members who are regular players and—"

"We're way behind on that," Drake said, "the police have five detectives interviewing all the members whose record of greens fees shows that they've been playing regularly. They have photographs of the dead man and they're trying to make an identification."

"Have you seen a photograph?"

"No," Drake said. "I have a general description."

"Shoot."

"A man about fifty-five," Drake said, "with dark hair, powerful broad shoulders, slightly stooped, black eyes, about six feet one inch in height, weight two hundred and five pounds, very hairy hands, big powerful wrists."

"No keys on him?" Mason asked.

"No keys, no coins, no knife, no handkerchiefs, no pens, no pencils—nothing."

Mason said thoughtfully, "Paul, you talked about a man you thought was a process server who was waiting to serve papers on Dutton?"

"That's right, he— By George, Perry, it could be the same man. The description fits."

"You'd recognize the man if you saw him?"

"Sure."

"Stay away from the morgue," Mason said. "Let's see if you can get a look at the police photographs."

"Gosh, Perry," Drake wailed, "if I make the guy, I'll have to go to the police. That's evidence a private detective can't withhold."

"You can't make a positive identification from a newspaper photograph like that," Mason said. "You'd have to see the corpse."

"Well, you were talking about police photographs."

"I was," Mason said. "Now I am talking about newspaper photographs. . . . Della and I are on our way back just as fast as we can get there. I'll leave my car here. I'll get my friend Munoz to fly us to San Diego. You have Pinky waiting at the San Diego airport with a twin-motored job to bring us in to the Tri-City Airport, and sit tight until we get there. Meet us at Tri-City Airport."

"Even if there's a very good resemblance in the newspaper photographs, I'd have to run it down," Drake said. "In a murder case my license wouldn't be worth a thin dime if I held out an identification."

"You and your license," Mason said.

"Me and my living," Drake told him. "I'll have the plane in San Diego by the time you get there."

"We'll get there pretty darn fast," Mason said and hung up.

10

■

"PINKY" BRIER, the famous aviatrix, brought the twin-motored plane in at the Tri-City Airport as gracefully as a bird coming in to a landing.

A worried Paul Drake, who had been anxiously waiting, came out of the late afternoon shadows to meet Perry Mason and Della Street as they disembarked.

"You left your car?" Drake asked.

"Left it down there," Mason said. "We'll get it later on. Right now we're working against time."

"We're working against time and against a condition you aren't going to like," Drake said.

"What's the condition?"

"I've seen the photograph in the papers."

"What about it?"

"Perry, I *think* that man is the one that I took for a process server—perhaps he is, perhaps he isn't, but in any event, he was hanging around keeping cases on this Dutton apartment."

"But you can't make a positive identification from a newspaper photograph of that sort," Mason said.

"I know I can't, but I've got enough of an identification to tell Lieutenant Tragg that I might be of some assistance and should go down to the morgue and take a look at the body."

"Then, if you identify him," Mason said, "you're going to have to tell Tragg where you saw him and when."

"That's right."

"And that," Mason said, "is going to put our client in a hole."

"Your client is in a hole now," Drake said.

"Well, you'll put him deeper in the hole."

"He's in just about as deep as he can get right now," Drake said, "or he will be when my operative testifies.

"You remember my operative was shadowing Dutton. He put a wire recorder up against the telephone booth and heard one side of the conversation in which Dutton arranged to meet someone out at the Barclay Country Club on the seventh tee.

"That's where they found this murdered man."

Mason said thoughtfully, "Your operative is in Ensenada now?"

"No, he's started home," Drake said. "By the time he gets here he'll know what his duty is. He'll report to the police, and the police will confiscate that wire recording."

"Who has the wire recording?"

"He does. It's in the trunk of his car.

"You've got a responsibility here, too, Perry. You can't suppress evidence. You can represent your client regardless of what the evidence against him may be, but you can't conceal evidence of a murder."

"All right," Mason said, "let's face it before they smoke us out. Let's call Lieutenant Tragg. Then Pinky can take us in to the Los Angeles Airport, and Tragg can meet us."

Drake said, "We'll have cars scattered all over the country. Your car in Ensenada; mine here at Tri-City."

"We can rent cars if we need them," Mason said, "but we're fighting against time. Della will drive your car to Los Angeles."

"What does your client tell you?" Drake asked.

"Nothing," Mason said.

Drake said, "The only defense that's going to be open to you in the long run is trying to prove self-defense. Your client went out there to meet this guy. Whoever it was, the man was blackmailing Dutton. The party got rough. Your client had to shoot to kill in order to get away. The police found five thousand dollars in fifty-dollar bills in your client's possession when he was arrested at the border. They think this was money for a blackmail payoff."

"That's what they *think*," Mason said. "How do they know it wasn't getaway money?"

"They believe it was a blackmail payoff. They know things we don't know."

"I suppose so," Mason said. "There's so much about this that I don't know that it bothers me. The best defense is the truth, but in this case I don't know what the truth is, and I'm not at all certain my client is going to tell me."

"Why not?"

"There's just a chance he's protecting someone, or trying to."

"That would mean a woman, wouldn't it?" Drake asked.

Mason said, "Come on, let's get hold of a telephone."

Mason went to a telephone, called the Los Angeles Police Department, got Lt. Tragg at Homicide on the line.

"I see you're investigating a death at the Barclay Country Club," Mason said.

"You saw that in the papers?"

"I heard it was in the papers."

"Yes. Yes," Tragg said, "and I suppose you have some information in connection with it that you've been sitting on for several hours, and now that you've decided it's too dangerous to hold out any longer, you've decided to be co-operative."

"You do me an injustice," Mason said, grinning.

"I know. I always do," Tragg said dryly.

"As a matter of fact," Mason told him, "I have just this minute arrived by plane from Mexico. I have been talking with Paul Drake, and Paul Drake tells me that from the picture of the murdered man that was published in the paper he has an idea he may have seen the individual in question sometime last night."

"Where? When?" Lt. Tragg asked, snapping the questions like the crack of a whip.

"Not so fast," Mason said. "We don't know as yet that it's the *same* person."

"Well, you'd better find out, and find out pretty damn quick," Lt. Tragg said. "If Paul Drake has any information that's going to help us clear up a murder case, he'd better get it in our hands fast."

"That's what we want to do," Mason said. "We're even going to charter a plane and fly in to the airport. We'll meet you there in about half an hour. We'll go to the morgue with you. If it turns out it's the same man, Drake will be only too glad to give you all the information you want."

Tragg said, "We're bringing a suspect in for questioning on that murder. Do you suppose there's any chance—of course, I know it's only a one-in-a-million shot—but is there any chance, Mason, that this man is a client of yours?"

"The victim?"

"No, the one we're bringing in."

"Well, that would depend," Mason said, "on the identity of the man you're bringing in."

"His name," Lt. Tragg said, "is Kerry Dutton. He's a young man who's had quite a spectacular success as an investment counselor."

"What connects him with the murder?" Mason asked.

Tragg said, "I had my question in first. Is he, by any chance, a client of yours?"

"He's a client of mine," Mason said.

"That," Tragg said, "explains a lot. Where are you now?"

Mason told him.

"You think you can get here within twenty-five or thirty minutes?"

"Yes. We have a twin-motored plane all ready to go."

"Get in it, and get started," Tragg said. "I'll meet you personally with a radio car at the airport, and I want one-hundred-per-cent co-operation— Now, get that, Mason, I want one-hundred-per-cent co-operation. We're not playing tiddlywinks. This is murder."

"We'll meet you there," Mason said.

Mason hung up the phone. "How bad is it?" Drake asked.

"Just as bad as Tragg can make it if things don't work out so well."

"And if they do work out well?"

"It's just about as bad as I could make it for my client," Mason said.

"Well, there's one advantage about giving the officers the information they need to clinch a case against someone," Drake pointed out, "they don't catch you unprepared."

They gave Pinky only time enough to finish a cup of coffee; then were flown in to Los Angeles where Lt. Tragg met them.

"All right," Tragg said, "start talking."

"We have to go to the morgue before we talk," Mason said. "We don't *know* that this is the same person."

"You tell me what the highlights are on the way,"

Tragg said, "and then if it turns out to be the same person, we won't lose any time; and if it isn't the same person, I'll keep the facts in confidence."

"I'm sorry," Mason said, "we can't do that. It's a matter of a professional obligation to a client."

Tragg said, "Under those circumstances, you boys can prepare yourselves for a ride. We're going places very, very fast. You'd better strap yourselves in with those seat belts, because they might come in handy. And hang onto your hats."

The trip to the morgue was made in record time. Lt. Tragg and the officer who was with him led the way into the big, silent room where the wall was lined with steel drawers, looking for all the world like some huge sinister filing cabinet.

The officer knew the number without looking it up, took hold of the handle and pulled out the sliding cabinet.

Drake stood looking at the corpse for nearly ten seconds.

"All right," Tragg said at last, "is it or isn't it?"

Drake looked at Mason and shrugged his shoulders, then turned to Tragg. "It is," he said.

"All right," Tragg said, "let's get started. We've lost enough time already—perhaps too much."

Drake said, "I had the job of shadowing Kerry Dutton yesterday."

"Go on."

"Someone else was on the job."

"Who?"

"This man," Drake said, indicating the still form on the slab.

"What do you know about him?"

"Nothing. I thought he was a process server."

"He was tailing Dutton?"

"He was waiting for Dutton. That is, he was casing Dutton's apartment and I had an idea he was a process server."

"What gave you that idea?"

"Just something about the way he acted."

"All right," Lt. Tragg said, "I don't want to pull it out of you a piece at a time, minutes are precious. We're trying to build up a case and we don't want to get the wrong man but we sure do want to get the right one."

"I can't tell you much about him," Drake said, "except I can give you the license number of his automobile. I looked it up and have the owner's name."

Tragg's face lit up. "What was the license number?" he asked.

Drake pulled out his notebook and gave Tragg the number and the name of Rodger Palmer.

Tragg dashed to the telephone, exploded into action, telephoned orders to trace the license application, to wire in a descriptive classification of the thumbprints, and to check identities.

When he had finished, he returned to where Drake and Perry Mason were standing.

"Just why were you shadowing Kerry Dutton?" Tragg asked.

Drake started to say something, caught Mason's eye, hesitated; then said, "Because Perry Mason told me to."

Tragg flushed. "Let's not try any run-arounds," he said.

"That isn't a run-around," Mason said. "It's a straight-forward answer. That's all Paul Drake knows about it."

"All right, then I'll ask you. Why did you tell Paul Drake to shadow Dutton?"

"That," Mason said, "is something I'm not at liberty to disclose."

Tragg said, "You'll disclose everything you know about the murder, or you'll find yourself in hot water up to your necktie."

"I'll disclose everything I know about the *murder*," Mason said.

"Well, what you know about Dutton fits in with what we know about the murder."

"I don't think it does," Mason said. "As a matter of

fact, I was having Paul Drake shadow Dutton because I was worried about my own responsibility in the matter."

"So I gathered," Tragg said. "You don't ordinarily have a detective agency shadow your own clients."

"Sometimes I do."

"Now then," Tragg said, "here's the important question, and I want an answer to it. Did any of this shadowing take Kerry Dutton to the vicinity of the Barclay Country Club?"

There was a period of silence. Then Mason said cautiously, "I believe I should answer that question. I can state that it did."

"The hell it did!" Tragg said, his face lighting up. "At what time?"

"What time, Paul?" Mason asked.

"Right around ten-ten to ten-twenty," Drake said.

"Now then," Mason volunteered, "in order to keep you from feeling you're having to draw information out of us a bit at a time, I'm going to tell you that before Dutton went out to the country club he had a conversation with someone and apparently arranged to meet that person out at the country club."

"How do you know?"

"He went into a telephone booth and called someone. One of Drake's men was shadowing him. He put a wire recorder on the outside of the telephone booth and walked away. It's a very sensitive recorder, compact but highly efficient. After Dutton drove away, Drake's man came back and picked up the recorder, ran it back, found out what the conversation was about and went out to the Barclay Country Club."

"He didn't follow Dutton out?"

"No, Dutton went through red lights and generally drove like crazy. So, after trying to follow him, Drake's man went back and picked up the recorder, ran it back to the starting point, listened to the conversation, and was able to make out that an appointment had been made at the Barclay Country Club."

"And he drove out there right away?"

"Yes. He went right out there."

"And Dutton's car was out there?"

"That's right. Dutton's car and two or three other cars."

"Was one of them this car that you gave me the license on?" Lt. Tragg asked Drake.

"I don't know as yet, but we will know," Drake said.

The telephone rang—a sharp strident sound in that room of eternal silence.

Tragg strode over to the instrument, picked it up, said, "Yes . . . speaking."

The officer listened for several seconds; then a slow grin spread over his face. "That does it," he said. "Okay."

Tragg hung up and said, "All right, we've got our corpse identified. His name is Rodger Palmer all right. He was an employee of Templeton Ellis until Ellis died; then he went to work for the Steer Ridge Oil and Refining Company.

"Now then, do any of those activities tie in with what you fellows know?"

Mason chose his words carefully. "Templeton Ellis was the father of Desere Ellis. Kerry Dutton is the trustee of money which was payable to her under her father's will. Some of the stocks, I believe, which were included in the estate at one time were shares of the Steer Ridge Oil and Refining Company."

Tragg turned to Drake. "What's the name of your detective, the one with the wire recorder?"

"Tom Fulton."

"Where is he now?"

"On his way up from Ensenada."

"Where's he going to report when he reaches the city here?"

"To my office."

"I want to see him as soon as he reports," Tragg said, "and I want to be very, very certain that nothing happens to that recording. That is evidence in the case and I want it."

"You'll have it," Mason promised.

"Getting facts out of you two," Tragg said, "is like pulling hen's teeth with a pair of fire tongs, but thank you very much for your co-operation."

"We gave you what we had," Mason said.

"You gave me what you *had* to give me," Tragg amended, "but I appreciate it just the same. It's bad business when we can't get a corpse identified."

"But even without the identification, you felt you had a case against Kerry Dutton?"

Tragg grinned and said, "We brought him in for questioning."

Mason said, "They told me down in Mexico that he was under arrest; that there was a warrant out for him, charging first-degree murder."

"Tut, tut," Tragg said.

"You didn't extradite him?"

"We couldn't have extradited him without preferring a charge."

"But he is under arrest?"

"He's been brought in for questioning."

"He's my client," Mason said. "I want to see him."

"If he's charged with anything, you can talk with him. As soon as he's booked, he can call an attorney."

"Where is he now?" Mason asked.

Tragg said, "I'll put it on the line with you, Perry. As far as I know he's between here and there."

"There meaning?"

"Tecate," Lt. Tragg said, grinning. "It was a lot easier for us to pick him up there than it would have been in Tijuana, so when the Mexicans deported him as an undesirable alien, they put him back into the United States at Tecate."

Mason turned to Paul Drake. "Okay, Paul," he said, "let's go to the office. Della should be there by now with your car."

"Better hang around your office," Tragg said. "If Kerry Dutton wants to call you, we'll give him *one* telephone call."

"One should be enough," Mason said.

11

PERRY MASON and Paul Drake found Paul's car in the office parking lot. "Your man Fulton, Paul?" Mason asked.

"What about him?"

"You know what about him. We've got to get in touch with him."

"He's on his way home from Ensenada. Police will be laying for him and want to grab that wire recording."

"I know they will," Mason said. "We've got to get to him before the police do."

Drake shook his head. "What do you mean?" Mason asked. "You mean it can't be done?"

"I mean it's not going to be done," Drake said. "I have a license to consider. We can't play hide-and-seek with the police in a murder case. You're a lawyer; you know that."

Mason spoke slowly, giving emphasis to each word as he enunciated it. "Paul, I'm an attorney. I have a license, the same as you do. I'm not going to suppress any evidence. You're not going to suppress any evidence. We're not going to tamper with evidence, but I'm representing a client. The police are going to try to convict that client of first-degree murder. They're moving pretty fast in this thing. That means there's some evidence that we know nothing about. I want to find out about it. I want to know what it is. Your operative is going to be a witness for the prosecution. We can't help that, but we sure have a right to get a report from him at the earliest possible moment. You're paying him, and I'm paying you. Now then, what kind of a car is he driving? What route is he going to take?"

Drake shook his head. "I don't like it."

Mason said, "You don't have to like it. I know what I'm doing. I'm not asking you to violate any law."

"Well," Drake said, reluctantly, "there's a service station out on the corner of Melwood and Figueroa. It's a big service station with plenty of pumps and employees on duty, and every operative who has been on a long, out-of-town trip is instructed to fill his gas tank at this station when he comes in.

"The big thing in the private detective business is to be sure you don't run out of gas when you're on a tailing job.

"The man who runs that service station knows most of my operatives. I know he knows Tom Fulton. We can ask him if Tom has been in there yet. If he has, it means that Tom has parked his car and reported to the office and the cops have probably grabbed him by this time, or, at any rate, they will before we can get hold of him now."

"There's a phone booth, Paul. Put through the call."

Drake entered the phone booth, put through the call, came back and shook his head, "He hasn't been in yet. You can't tell just when he will come in. The guy has been up all night on a tailing job and it's a long drive from Ensenada up here. He was entitled to get some sleep."

"The police will have a stakeout on your office, Paul, and I don't dare take any chances. You're going to have to go down to that service station and wait— Hang it, we'll both go. They probably have a stakeout on my office as well as on yours. They may figure we'll try to head Fulton off. Come on, Paul, we'll just have to go and wait."

Drake drove through traffic and into the service station. He caught the eye of the manager. "Going to wait around awhile, Jim," he said.

"He hasn't been in yet," the manager said, looking curiously at Perry Mason.

"We want to speed matters up as much as possible," Drake said. "He's a witness, and we want to—"

"Put him in touch with the police at once," Mason interpolated.

"Okay, there's parking room over there next to the grease rack," the man said. "Make yourselves comfortable. You any idea when he's going to be in?"

"He'll be in shortly," Drake said.

Drake backed the car into the space so that they had a commanding view of the gas pumps.

"Want to phone Della Street and let her know where you are?" Drake asked.

Mason shook his head. "We'll keep everyone guessing for a while."

An hour and a half passed; then Drake suddenly gripped Mason's arm. "Here he comes, Perry," he said. "Now remember we can't do anything that will serve as a peg on which the police can hang a complaint."

Mason's eyes were wide with candor—too wide. "Why, certainly not, Paul! We're only co-operating with the police. Call him over."

While the attendant was putting gasoline in Fulton's car, Drake caught his eye and called him over.

"Why, hello, Mr. Drake. What are *you* doing here?"

"Waiting for you," Drake said.

"Gosh, I'm sorry. I took just a little shut-eye down in Ensenada before I pulled out. I was afraid I couldn't keep awake and—"

"That's all right," Drake said.

The operative's eyes twinkled. "You certainly get around, Mr. Mason."

Drake said, "He wants to ask you a few questions."

"Go ahead."

Mason said, "You lost Dutton last night on the tailing job?"

"That's right. He drove like crazy. He went through signals, right and left and darn near got me smashed up trying to follow him. I was hoping we'd both get pinched and I could square the pinch by explaining to the officer. It's a chance we have to take."

"And how did you pick him up again?" Mason asked.

66

"He went to a phone booth and I bugged the phone booth with a little bug that fits right up snug against the glass. A transistor wire recorder is suspended underneath."

"And what did you find?"

"He said he was going out to the Barclay Country Club and would meet someone on tee number seven. I've reported all that."

"I want it official this time," Mason said. "You didn't spot him out there?"

"Not right away. His car was there."

"You tried to get in?"

"I tried the door to see if it was unlocked."

"Was it?"

"No. There was a spring lock on it."

"So you waited?"

"That's right."

"How long did you wait?"

"Twelve minutes."

"And then what?"

"And then he came out."

"How did he act when he came out, excited?"

"He seemed to be— Well, he was in a hurry. He knew exactly what he wanted to do."

"He didn't pay any attention to you?"

"I was sitting pretty well in the shadows back in my car. That is, I'd crawled over in the back seat so I wasn't at all conspicuous."

"There were other cars parked around there?"

"Half a dozen, I guess."

"You didn't take the license numbers?"

"No, I spotted Dutton's car there, and he was the one I was tailing so I didn't pay any attention to the others —no one told me to."

"That's all right," Mason said. "We're not blaming you, but can you describe the cars?"

"Why, they were just—just ordinary cars."

"No car that stood out, not a sport job, or some big flashy job?"

"No, as I remember it, they were all rather mediocre —I took them for cars belonging to employees who slept in on the premises. There weren't too many of them—I guess three would just about hit it, but there may have been four."

"All right," Mason said, "we don't have much time. We have to hit the high spots. Dutton came out, got in his car and drove away?"

"That's right."

"You tailed along?"

"Yes."

"Any trouble?"

"Just once. I started following him with my lights off. Dutton stopped his car rather suddenly and then backed up. There was nothing for me to do but to keep on going."

"So you lost him again?"

"No, I didn't lose him. I got down the road, pulled off to one side, put out a red blinker, got out a jack and jacked up the rear bumper. I made as if I was changing a tire. I kept my eye on him all the time."

"How far away was he?"

"Oh, half a mile, I guess."

"His lights were on?"

"Yes."

"You couldn't see him, you could only see the headlights?"

"That's right."

"He just stopped?"

"Yes."

"Then what happened?"

"Well, then he got in his car and went on."

"What did you do?"

"I stood there helpless and let him pass. Then when he got ahead of me, I let the car down off the jack fast, threw the jack in the rear seat, jumped in and took off after him. In a case of that sort the subject hardly expects a crippled car to come to life and take off after him, so he isn't suspicious."

"And you tailed him, how far?"

"All the way to the border and then on to Ensenada."

"Did he make any stops?"

"Once for a cup of coffee and a hamburger."

"What did you do?"

"Sat outside the place, parked in my car, and drooled," the detective said. "That coffee looked so darn good, I would have given a week's pay for a cup, but I didn't dare let him spot me so I had to sit outside and wait until he came out."

"Do you think he knew he was being tailed?"

"I don't think so. I would drop behind for a way and then come up, and I passed him once or twice where I could keep his headlights in my windshield and pulled in to a coffee joint as though I was getting coffee, but as soon as he passed me I took up the chase again."

"Now, that wire recording," Mason said, "you have it?"

"Yes."

"The police want it."

"I wondered if they would. I was going to ask Drake what to do with it."

Mason said, "Go to the office. Don't tell anyone that you have seen either Drake or me unless you are asked specifically. If you are asked by the police, don't lie. Tell them that I was waiting for you and that I told you I wanted you to take your evidence to the police at once; that they were anxiously awaiting it."

"I don't say anything about Mr. Drake?"

"Not unless they ask you specifically. If they ask you if you've talked with anyone, tell them you talked with me. If they ask you if anyone was with me, you can tell them Paul Drake was, but just don't volunteer any information. On the other hand, appear to be very cooperative."

Fulton nodded.

"Now then," Mason said, "why did Dutton bring his car to a stop and back up? Any idea?"

"No, I haven't," Fulton said, "but I checked on my speedometer."

Mason's face brightened. "You did?"

"That's right. He was on Crenmore when he stopped, exactly one and three-tenths miles from the entrance to Barclay Country Club."

Mason turned to Paul Drake. "Paul," he said, "get this man a bonus of the best dinner in the city for himself and his wife— You married, Fulton?"

"Not yet," Fulton said, grinning. "I was, but it didn't take. I played the field for a while and now I'm getting ready to go overboard again. This time it's going to be different."

"Get your girl friend and take her to the best restaurant in town," Mason said. "Get everything you can eat, have a bottle of champagne with dinner and turn in the bill on your expense account."

Fulton shot out his hand. "That's mighty fine of you, Mr. Mason."

"I always like to see a good job well done," Mason said.

Fulton looked at Drake. "Anything else?"

Mason shook his head.

"Okay," Fulton said, "I'll be on my way. I'm to go in to the office and start making out a report in the usual way?"

"That's right," Drake said. "Take a typewriter and start tapping it out."

"Do I say anything about the subject stopping there on the road?"

"You sure do," Mason said. "Don't conceal *anything*. Remember, those are my instructions. Don't conceal a single piece of evidence from the police."

Fulton signed the ticket for the gasoline and drove out.

"Well," Drake said, "I guess we may as well—"

"Go to that culvert and see what's there," Mason interjected.

"Culvert?" Drake asked.

"Sure," Mason said. "That's why he stopped and backed up. We'll take a look at whatever is in that culvert."

"And then what?"

"Then," Mason said, smiling, "we don't touch anything. We call Lieutenant Tragg and tell him that Fulton reported to us that the subject had stopped a mile and three-tenths from the country club; that we went out to see what had caused him to stop and back up. Much to our surprise, we found a culvert. We looked in the culvert and it appeared that something had been stashed in there and so we're calling the police."

"Tragg will be hopping mad," Drake said.

"Let him hop," Mason pointed out.

"Suppose there isn't a culvert? Suppose it was something in the road?"

Mason said, "I'm willing to bet ten to one it was a culvert."

"Suppose the police have checked it?"

"They could very well have done so," Mason said. "Whenever a crook has evidence to dispose of, he looks for the first culvert he comes to, and if Lieutenant Tragg is as smart as I think he is, he has probably instructed his men to look at the first culvert on every road leading away from the country club."

"In which event he will have been one jump ahead of us."

Mason grinned. "But only one jump, Paul. Come on, let's go. If you don't mind, I'll drive. We don't have much time."

Mason drove to the country club, checked the speedometer, turned and drove a mile and three-tenths.

"Well, you're right," Drake said. "It's a culvert."

"You can see marks where a car was braked to a sudden stop," Mason said. "Well, we'll take a look, Paul."

The lawyer parked the car, got out, raised the hood of the car, took a flashlight from the glove compartment, and walked down the embankment to the culvert. He looked up and down the road, said, "Let me know when the coast is clear, Paul."

"Okay," Drake said, after two cars had passed, "you've got an open road now."

Mason dropped to his knees, peered into the culvert.

"See anything?" Drake asked.

"Footprints," Mason said, "and nothing else."

"Car coming, Perry."

Mason hurriedly arose, walked over to the side of the road.

A passing motorist stopped. "Having trouble?" he asked, noticing the upraised hood.

"Just a vapor lock," Mason said, smiling. "I think it will straighten itself out if we let it cool off a minute. Thanks!"

The motorist waved his hand. "Good luck," he said, and drove away.

Mason thoughtfully lowered the hood of the car, got in, and started the motor.

"Now what?" Drake asked.

"Now," Mason said, "I'm going to try and see my client—and ask him what it was he concealed in that culvert."

12

MASON SAT looking across the dividing partition at his client's worried face.

"How much did you tell them?" Mason asked.

"Not a thing," Dutton said. "I told them that I resented the way they had made the arrest and taken me out of Ensenada; that I thought I had been kidnaped by the police; that I was indignant, as a citizen, and I put on the act of being too damn mad to co-operate."

"It's all right," Mason said. "It's a good act. The only thing is, it doesn't fool anyone. What have they got on you, do you know?"

"No."

"They've got something," Mason said. "Suppose you tell me the real story."

"I wanted to tell it to them," Dutton said, "but I was going to follow your instructions because you're my attorney. If I'd told it to them, I'd have been free by this time."

"You think you would have?" Mason asked.

"Very definitely," Dutton said. "They don't have a thing on me."

"Well, tell me your story," Mason said, "and if I'll buy it, I'll have you pass it along to the police and the district attorney."

"There isn't much to tell," Dutton said.

"Did you know the dead man?"

"I've talked with him on the phone. That is, if he's Rodger Palmer."

"What do you know about him?"

"Not too much. But he had me in kind of a peculiar position."

"Blackmail?"

"Well, not exactly. Palmer was engaged in a sneak attack on the management of Steer Ridge Oil and Refining Company. He wanted to get rid of the management and put his own crowd in."

"You knew that?"

"I knew that—at least, he told me."

"Go ahead," Mason said. "What happened?"

"Well," Dutton said, "Palmer knew that Desere Ellis had a big block of stock in the oil company. At least, he assumed she did. He knew that her father had bought it and that it had gone into the trust fund."

"And so?" Mason asked.

"And so he went to Miss Ellis and wanted her to give him a proxy. She told him that she couldn't do it because the stock was in my name as trustee. So then he asked her to write a letter to me as trustee, instructing me to give him a proxy on stock."

"And she did?"

"She did."

"And then?" Mason asked, his eyes showing his keen interest.

73

"Then, of course, I was in a spot," Dutton said. "I didn't have the stock. I didn't want her to know I didn't have the stock. That would have caused her to ask for an accounting. Therefore, I didn't want to tell him I'd sold the stock."

"This was at a time when the value of the stock was low?"

"That's right. It was just before the strike in the new field. Palmer could have bought up control of the company if he could have found the stock and had the money, but he was working on a shoestring."

"So what did you do?"

"I told him I would have to know more about what he had in mind, and what his plans for developing the company's property were before I'd honor Miss Ellis' letter.

"He insisted on seeing me; I refused to give him an interview. Then he played his ace in the hole. He told me he had something to tell me about Fred Hedley. He said it would eliminate Hedley from the picture as far as Desere Ellis was concerned. He said he needed money to carry on his proxy campaign and that if I'd bring him five thousand dollars in fifty-dollar bills, he'd give me an earful of facts on Hedley that would put Hedley out of circulation."

Mason regarded his client skeptically. "And he also wanted proxies?"

"Yes."

"He was a blackmailer then?"

"I guess that's the word for it. However, I'd have done *anything* to prevent Desere marrying Hedley."

"What about proxies?"

"That's the strange, incredible thing," Dutton said. "When he made me that offer, I decided to take him up. I went out and bought up twenty thousand shares of Steer Ridge Oil stock in my own name. I got them at from ten to fifteen cents a share. I intended to let Palmer think they were the original shares of stock from the trust.

"Then within a couple of days the new strike was made and the stock started climbing sky high."

"And the stock is in your name, and not in the trust?"

"That's right."

"You have no letters from Palmer, no evidence to back up your story?"

"No."

Mason shook his head. "Tell that story to a jury and add it to your handling of the trust fund and you'll be crucified."

"But I did what I felt was best."

"For whom? For you or for Desere?"

"For everyone."

Mason shook his head. "A jury will think you sold out the Steer Ridge Oil stock from the trust fund; that you had a tip the new wells were in oil sand; that you acted on that tip to feather your own financial nest; that Palmer found out what you were doing, or rather what you had done, and was blackmailing you."

There was dismay on Dutton's face. "I hadn't thought of it that way."

"Better start thinking of it that way now," Mason said.

"Good heavens, *everything* I've done can be misinterpreted," Dutton said.

"Exactly," Mason agreed.

"You, yourself, don't even believe me," Dutton charged.

"I'm trying to," Mason said. And then added, "That's part of my job. A jury won't have to try so hard."

There was an interval of grim silence, then Mason said, "So you agreed to meet Palmer surreptitiously at a spot that wasn't particularly convenient to pay over blackmail, but was ideal for murder."

"He was the one who picked the spot," Dutton said.

"Too bad he can't come to life long enough to tell the jury so," Mason observed.

"Why in the world did you ever consent to go out there to meet him?" Mason asked after a few moments.

"That's where he wanted me to meet him."

"Why?"

"He didn't say why, but I gathered that he had to be pretty furtive about what he was doing. He didn't want it to come out into the open that he was trying to round up proxies on the stock or get control of the corporation. He wanted to get himself pretty firmly seated in the saddle before he turned the horse loose and let it buck. And he seemed afraid to let anyone find out he was selling me information."

"All right, you agreed to go out there," Mason said, wearily, "and you went out there."

"That's right."

"For your information," Mason told him, "the police have a wire recording of your conversation from the telephone booth. The one in which you agreed to go out there. You—"

The lawyer stopped before the expression of utter consternation on Dutton's face.

"How in the world could they get a wire recording of *that* conversation?" Dutton asked.

Mason regarded the man with thought-narrowed eyes. "It seems to give you a jolt."

"Good heavens, yes. Of course, it gives me a jolt. I picked out a telephone booth and— Wait a minute, there was some fellow snooping around on the outside."

"He planted a bug and a wire recorder," Mason said. "I thought you should know it."

Dutton lowered his eyes, then suddenly raised them. "He bugged the conversation in the telephone booth, he didn't tap the line?"

"No," Mason said. "Wire tapping is illegal."

"I see," Dutton said. "Then he only has my end of the conversation recorded on wire?"

"That's right."

"Just that end of the conversation?"

"That's right, but your end was pretty incriminating. You said that you would go out there and meet him on the seventh tee at the Barclay Country Club."

76

"Yes, I did," Dutton said, slowly, "and the police have that recording?"

"The police have that recording."

Dutton shrugged his shoulders.

Mason said, "All right, Dutton, you've stalled around now long enough to have thought over all the angles. You've had plenty of time to think up a pretty good story; you have an idea of what the police have against you, so why not try to give *me* the facts? The *real* facts might help."

"He was dead when I got there," Dutton said.

"How long did you hang around?"

"Too long!"

"Why?"

"I had a key to the clubhouse," Dutton said. "All members have keys. Palmer knew that. He'd borrowed a key from a friend. Palmer wasn't a member. I went in through the clubhouse, out the back door to the links and walked down to the seventh tee. That's about a hundred yards from the clubhouse.

"All the time I was walking down there, I thought I was making a darn fool of myself. That was no way to meet a man and carry on a legitimate business conversation or a legitimate business transaction."

"You can say that again," Mason observed dryly.

"What do you mean?"

"If it embarrasses you to tell me about it," Mason said, "think how you're going to feel when you have to tell twelve cold-eyed, skeptical jurors about it and then be cross-examined by a sarcastic district attorney."

There was a long moment of silence.

"You may as well get on with it," Mason said.

Dutton said, "I stood around the seventh tee expecting to see Palmer there. I was, of course, watching the skyline for a man to show up. After some ten minutes, I started walking around and then I saw something dark on the ground. At first I thought it was a shadow. I moved over and my foot struck against it."

Dutton stopped talking.

"Palmer's body?" Mason asked.

"It was Palmer's body."

"What did you do?"

"I got in a panic. I almost ran back to the clubhouse; got in my car and drove away."

Mason said, "You didn't have a flashlight?"

Dutton hesitated a fraction of a second, then said, "No."

"You went out there in the dark?"

"Yes. A flashlight might have attracted the attention of the club watchman. He's paid to watch the locker rooms and not the golf links, but a flashlight could have attracted his attention."

"Then that's your story?"

"That's it."

"You're willing to stick to it?"

"Absolutely. It's the truth."

Mason regarded the man in thoughtful silence.

"Well?" Dutton asked, at length, squirming uncomfortably.

Mason said, "What about the gun?"

"What gun?"

"The gun you hid in the culvert."

Dutton's eyes widened.

"Go on," Mason said. "What about the gun you hid in the culvert?"

"You're crazy!"

Mason said, "Look, let's quit kidding each other and kidding ourselves. The police picked you up. They had enough evidence against you to contemplate charging you with murder.

"That can only mean one thing. They found the murder weapon and they traced it to you.

"You may not realize it, but the average amateur criminal always regards a culvert as a wonderful place to hide incriminating objects. They run true to form with devastating regularity.

"Therefore, when the police encounter a murder, one

of the first things they do is to start looking in culverts on all roads leading away from the scene of the crime.

"Now, I'm willing to bet that you made a stop at a culvert, got out of your car and tossed the murder weapon and perhaps some other incriminating evidence into the culvert."

"And the police have *that?*" Dutton asked in dismay.

"The police have that."

"Then there's nothing left for *you* to do," Dutton said, "except have me plead guilty and put myself on the mercy of the court."

"Did you kill him?" Mason asked.

"No, I didn't kill him," Dutton said, "but I did find a gun by the body. I picked it up and when I got to my car, I examined it by flashlight and found it was my gun."

"You had a flashlight in the car?"

"Well, it was the dash light," Dutton said.

Mason said, "You're indulging in the most expensive luxury a man *can* indulge in."

"What's that? Being tried for murder?"

"No, lying to your lawyer."

"I'm not lying."

Mason said, "Don't be silly. A detective was watching you when you came out of the club. You jumped in your car and drove away at high speed. You went a mile and three-tenths, passed over a culvert, slammed on your brakes so you left tire marks on the surface of the pavement, put your car in reverse; went back, got out and tossed something under the culvert. You didn't turn on the dash light; you didn't use any flashlight."

"A detective was watching me?"

"Yes."

"Then why wasn't I arrested?"

"It was a private detective and no one knew anything about the murder, as yet."

"All right," Dutton said. "You have me convicted in your own mind and—"

"I don't have you convicted in my mind," Mason said.

"I simply suggested that you had better tell your lawyer the truth. How did you know it was your gun?"

"I looked at the gun on the ground."

"Then you must have had some light. What did you do, strike a match?"

"I had a small pocket flashlight in my coat. A very small, flat light which has a rechargeable battery. It gives a small field of illumination."

"Then you *did* have the means of looking around when you got out on the tee for the seventh hole?"

"Yes, I guess so, if I had used it."

"Why didn't you use it?"

"There wasn't any occasion to use it."

Mason said, "After you discovered the body, you did use it?"

"Yes."

"I was wondering," Mason said, "how you identified the body, and how you identified the gun."

"Well, that was it. I had this flashlight with me."

"As soon as you recognized the gun as yours, you pocketed the gun and made a beeline for your car?"

"Yes."

Mason said, "I don't think you're that big a damn fool, Dutton. I think you're protecting someone."

"Protecting someone!" Dutton exclaimed.

"That's right."

"I'm trying to protect myself. I wish I could."

"Not with that story, you can't."

"Well, it's the only story I have."

Mason looked at his watch and said, "I have things to do. I'm going to tell you one thing. If you tell that story on the witness stand, you're going to be convicted."

"But why? The story is the truth."

"It may be the truth," Mason said, "but if that's so, it isn't all the truth. You're skipping over some incidents that might make your story convincing. You're trying to conceal things that you think might be against you. Hell, I don't know what you're doing, but every instinct I have as a lawyer tells me that once someone starts cross-examining you on that story, you're going to find yourself boxed in."

"No lawyer can cross-examine me and confuse me when I'm telling the truth," Dutton said.

"Exactly," Mason told him. "That's why I think you're going to be confused."

"Try it," Dutton invited. "Try cross-examining me."

"All right," Mason said, adopting a sneering, sarcastic attitude, "I'll pretend I'm the district attorney. Now, you answer questions. You're on the witness stand."

"Go right ahead," Dutton said.

"You had this flashlight in your pocket?" Mason said.

"Yes, sir."

"Why did you have it?"

"So I could— Well, I thought I might have to use it."

"For what purpose?"

"To identify the man I was to meet."

"You knew him?"

"I'd— Well, I talked with him over the telephone."

"Oh," Mason said, "you were going to use the flashlight then to identify his voice, is that right?"

"Well, I thought I'd take the flashlight along. It might come in handy."

"And it did come in very, very handy, didn't it?" Mason said sarcastically. "It enabled you to identify the body, to make sure he was very, very dead. It enabled you to search the body, to cut the labels off his clothes, to be certain you left nothing at all on the body so the corpse could readily be identified."

"I didn't say I had made sure he was dead."

"Well, then you didn't feel for a pulse?"

"No."

"In other words, the man might have been wounded and you simply took off for Ensenada on a vacation leaving a badly wounded man dying there on the golf course?"

"I could tell he was dead."

"How?"

"By— Well, he'd been shot."

"How did you know he'd been shot?"

"The gun was there."

"You found the gun with the aid of the flashlight?"

"Yes."

"And you knew it was your gun as soon as you saw it?"

"Yes."

"How? Did you check the numbers on the gun?"

"No, I . . . I recognized it."

"What was there about it that enabled you to recognize it?"

"The size, the shape."

"A thirty-eight-caliber Smith and Wesson short-barreled revolver?"

"Yes."

"Any distinguishing features about it?"

"Well . . . I just knew it was my gun, that's all."

"Certainly," Mason said, "you knew it was your gun because you had it in your pocket when you went out on the golf links. You knew it was your gun because you had loaded it and intended to murder the man who was trying to blackmail you. You knew it was your gun and you knew that you didn't dare to be caught with it in your possession. So you stopped your car in the middle of your flight and threw the gun under the culvert, hoping that it would remain there undiscovered."

Dutton cringed under Mason's sarcastic manner.

The lawyer got to his feet. "All right," he said. "That's a very weak sample of what you'll have to contend with. Hamilton Burger can be a demon when it comes to cross-examination.

"Think it over, Mr. Dutton.

"Whenever you're ready to change your story, send for me."

"What are you going to do?" Dutton asked. "Quit the case? Plead me guilty?"

"Are you guilty?" Mason asked.

"No."

"I never let a client plead guilty if he isn't guilty," Mason said. "I don't believe in it. I try to find the truth."

"You think I'm telling the truth?"

"No," Mason said, "but I still don't think you're a murderer. I think you're just a rotten liar. I hope you either improve by the time you get on the witness stand, or else have a different story to tell."

And with that, Mason signaled the officer who was waiting at the door of the conference room.

The lawyer walked out, and the barred door clanged shut.

13

DESERE ELLIS said, "Oh, Mr. Mason, I'm so glad to see you. Isn't this simply too terrible for anything?"

Mason said, "These things nearly always look blacker at the start; then after the facts begin to come to light the case looks better. Are you willing to talk with me?"

"Willing? Why, I'm anxious! I've been wondering how I could get in touch with you. Tell me, how is the case against Kerry? Does it look bad? All I know is that he's been arrested."

"That," Mason said, "is something I can't tell you. I'm Kerry's attorney. I want you to understand that. I'm here as Kerry Dutton's lawyer. I'm representing him and no one else.

"Now, Dutton may be representing you, in a way, but that doesn't mean that *I'm* representing you. My whole interest in this case is to protect Kerry Dutton against the charges that have been made against him and to get an acquittal, if possible. Do you understand that?"

"Yes."

"All right," Mason said, "let's talk."

"Won't you be seated?" she asked, indicating a comfortable chair.

Mason said, "Thank you," and dropped into the chair.

"May I get you a drink?"

"No," Mason said, smiling, "I'm on duty and when I'm on duty I prefer not to drink. Now then, tell me about Dutton's gun."

"About . . . Dutton's . . . gun!"

"That's right."

Her eyes were wide with panic. "What about it?"

"Did he loan it to you?"

"Why . . . why, yes."

"Where is it?" Mason asked.

"In the drawer, in my bedroom."

"Let's go get it," Mason said.

"All right. I'll bring it to you."

"If it's all the same with you, I'd like to go with you," Mason said.

"Why?"

"One might say, to see how good an actress you are."

"What do you mean?" she flared.

"If you're telling the truth," Mason said, "I think I can detect it. If you're not, I think I can also tell that. It may make a big difference."

"In what way?"

"Let's get the gun first and then I'll tell you."

"All right," she said, "come with me."

She led the way down a passageway, opened the door of a typically feminine room, walked over to a dresser by the bed, triumphantly opened the drawer and then recoiled with her hand on her breast.

"It's . . . it's not here!"

"I didn't think it would be," Mason said dryly. "The gun was used in killing Rodger Palmer. Now, perhaps you'll tell me how *that* happened?"

"I don't know," she said, "I—I— Why, I just can't imagine. I would have sworn the gun was here."

Mason eyed her narrowly. "That," he said, "is exactly what I want you to do."

"What?"

"Swear that the gun was there."

"But . . . but what could have happened to it?"

"Someone took it," Mason said. "Unless you took it and used it."

"What do you mean?"

Mason said, "Did you, by any chance, go out to the Barclay Country Club the night of the murder?"

"No, why?"

"You are a member of the Barclay Club?"

"Yes."

"And, as such, have a key?"

"Heavens, I suppose so. There's one around here somewhere. Wait a minute, I had that in the drawer with the gun."

"You say you *had* it?" Mason said. "That's past tense."

"All right, if you want to be technical about it, I *have* it."

"Let's take a look."

She rummaged through the back of the drawer and then triumphantly produced a key.

"Now then," Mason said, "is there any chance that last night you took this key and that gun, went out to the Barclay Country Club, met Rodger Palmer on the seventh tee, had an argument with him over blackmail and shot him?"

"Good heavens, what are you talking about? Are you crazy?"

"I don't think so," Mason said. "I'm just asking you if that happened."

"No!"

Mason said, "There's a pretty good chance that the Palmer murder was committed with Dutton's gun. Now then, as far as you know, that gun was here in this drawer until the day of the murder?"

She regarded him with white-faced emotion. "Of course it was here. Only . . . only someone must have taken it, because it's gone."

"And you don't know when it was taken?"

Her forehead puckered into a contemplative frown. "I saw it here two days ago, or was it three days ago. I

85

was cleaning out one of the other drawers and wanted a place to put some things. I debated whether to put them in the drawer with the gun. I remember I opened the drawer and saw that the gun was there."

"And you haven't opened the drawer since then?"

"Heavens, Mr. Mason, I just don't know. I'm trying to think. I come in here a dozen times a day. This is my bedroom. I keep things in the drawers. I open them and close them. I—I'm only telling you what I can remember."

"All right," Mason said, "remember that the gun was there two days ago; remember that you *thought* it was there when I asked you about it. You're going to have to swear to it."

"And this man, Palmer, was shot with Kerry's gun?"

"Apparently so. He was killed sometime during the night of the twenty-first."

"Can they . . . fix the time any more definitely than that it was just sometime during the night?"

"I think perhaps a little more definitely," Mason said, "but they *want* to fix it as being around sometime between nine-thirty and two-thirty, because that's when Kerry Dutton was out there at the golf club."

"He *was* out there?"

"Yes."

She was thoughtfully silent.

"Now then," Mason said, "is there any chance that Kerry Dutton could have been here in the house; could have gone into your bedroom and repossessed that gun from your bedroom drawer?"

She shook her head emphatically.

"Think it over," Mason said. "You see Kerry Dutton from time to time?"

"Mostly I talk with him over the telephone. He . . . he seems to avoid me."

"Has he been here within the last two days at any time that you can remember, prior to the time he had the fight?"

"No."

"You're sure?"

"Of course, I'm sure. He . . . he just wouldn't come near me. He was terribly hurt."

"Now, the night of the fight was the night of the murder. . . . Was he in your bedroom at any time prior to the start of the fight?"

"Not before the fight started, but afterwards they were all over the place."

"What happened?"

"Fred had been here to see me. He was elated. He wanted me to marry him and to use all the Steer Ridge Oil stock to give him some money with which to carry out that pet project of his."

"What did you tell him?"

"I told him I'd have to think it over."

"Then what happened?"

"Then he went home and, shortly afterwards, Kerry was at the door."

"And what did Kerry want?"

"He said he wanted to talk with me privately."

"You invited him in?"

"Yes, of course."

"What was the situation between you? Were relations strained or cordial?"

"I tried to be cordial, but he was terribly standoffish. Finally I asked him what was the matter with him and why he had been so distant during the past few weeks, why he had been avoiding me.

"He said he had something to tell me, that it was going to be difficult. I thought he was going to tell me again how much he loved me and ask me to marry me."

"And you had told him prior to that time that the subject was distasteful to you, that you would be his young sister, but that if he wouldn't be content with that, you couldn't continue being friends?"

Her eyes shifted from Mason's, then she said suddenly, "I wish I'd bitten my tongue off before I'd told him that."

"Why? Had you changed your mind?"

"Frankly, Mr. Mason, I don't know. But it made such a difference in Kerry. It was just as if all the lights had gone off."

"All right, getting back to the night of the twenty-first," Mason said, "what happened? You asked him why he had been so distant?"

"Well, I . . . I was glad to see him but had the impression he'd been waiting outside watching Fred's car and waiting for Fred to drive away, and somehow there was something about that that I didn't like."

"And then what happened?"

"Fred had either forgotten something or else he knew that Kerry was waiting. I don't know which. But Kerry was just telling me that he had something to tell me, that he hoped I wouldn't tell Fred or tell Fred's mother. He said they were trying to dominate my thinking and said I should quit running around with that type of person."

"And then," Mason prompted, as she hesitated.

"And then, all of a sudden, Fred's voice came from the doorway. He'd come back and hadn't knocked or pressed the button or anything. He just opened the door and stood there sneering."

"You said you heard his voice from the doorway?"

"Yes. He started telling Kerry a lot of things—that it was moneygrubbers like Kerry who were running the world, that really constructive thinkers stood no chance."

"Then what?"

"Then Kerry walked up to him, told him to shut up and get out, that he was talking to me and had some information that was for my ears alone."

"Go on," Mason said.

She said, "Fred's face got flushed with anger. Usually, he tries to appear to be cool, to hide his emotions beneath that attitude of calm contempt.

"This time, he got mad and said, 'Why, you little moneygrubbing pipsqueak,' and made a swing at Kerry."

"Did the blow land?"

She said, "I can't tell you everything that happened. I never saw anything in my life as fast as Kerry Dutton. He was all over the place, in and out, avoiding Fred's swings and punching Fred all over.

"Then Fred made a dash for the bedroom, and Kerry was right after him. Fred was screaming, and some woman in the adjoining apartment was shouting for the police. They were making a terrific noise; and in the bedroom some furniture got smashed."

"How did that happen?" Mason asked.

"They broke the nightstand, I guess, when someone fell against it; and someone jerked open a bureau drawer —not the upper one that had the gun, but one of the lower ones where I keep clothes and lingerie."

"And then?" Mason asked.

"Then Kerry really flattened him, because Fred was lying on the floor, and Kerry came running by me. He said, 'I'm sorry, Desere. I'll see you later.'

"I had already telephoned for the police while they were struggling in the bedroom. The woman in the adjoining apartment had been screaming for the police; and just a few minutes after Kerry left, and while Fred was getting himself together and trying to get to his feet, the police came and asked a lot of questions about what had happened.

"Fred told his story. But he lied, Mr. Mason. He lied about several things. My opinion of him went down when I heard the way he told the police what had happened."

"Did the police believe him?"

"At first, I think they did. Then they asked him to describe Kerry, and when he told them how tall he was and how much he weighed and how old he was and they looked at Fred Hedley standing over six feet and broad-shouldered, one of the officers said to Fred, 'Well, you wouldn't have had any trouble if you'd landed that first punch.'

"And Fred walked right into the trap and said, 'You can say that again. The shifty little pipsqueak ducked that punch and slammed me in the stomach so hard it knocked the wind out of me. Then he was climbing all over me while I was half paralyzed from the solar plexus punch.'

"Then the officer grinned and said, 'So you really did start the fight? It was you that took the first punch.' "

"And then?" Mason asked.

"Then the officers told him he'd brought it on himself and refused to give him a warrant for Kerry's arrest."

Mason said, "Tell me a little more about what Hedley was talking about—what he wanted."

"What he wanted was an endowment for this art center of his."

"What is it—an art gallery, a school, or what?" Mason asked.

"Oh, it varies from time to time. It's one of his rather nebulous ideas. And yet, in some ways, it isn't so nebulous. What he wants is to encourage artists to start a whole new school."

"A *new* school?"

"Well, more along the lines of a branch of modern art. Something that's a cross between the so-called modernistic school and the primitive school, interpretive art."

"He's quite definite in his ideas as to what he wants?"

"Well, as to *what* he wants, but not exactly how he intends to go about getting what he wants.

"Mainly he thinks that art is decadent; that color photography has made pictorial art, in the conventional sense, passé; that the so-called modernistic school is, at times, too lacking in the proper subject matter. So what he wants is to get people to paint things the way they see them, particularly portraits."

"He paints, himself?"

"Only vague outlines illustrating his technique."

"Do you have some of his paintings?"

"Not here, but— Well, he goes in for portraits. He encourages students to paint them with exaggerated facial characteristics.

"If you went to a conventional portrait painter, he'd

smooth out all of your lines, and— Not that there *are* any lines, of course, I'm just talking figuratively—and soften the whole contour of the features so that you would be better looking.

"Hedley doesn't believe in that. He wants it done just the other way around. He emphasizes the predominant features. His paintings are something like colored cartoons. As he says, he paints the character rather than the flesh."

"And he wants you to endow that school of art?"

"Yes, to have it take its rightful place as the modern type of portrait painting."

"Do you think he could ever sell portraits of that sort?"

"Who knows? After the vogue catches on, he probably could. But that's why he needs to have an endowment, just to get started. You see, people probably wouldn't pose for their portraits—that is, not for that kind of a portrait . . . unless it became stylish."

"I can readily understand that much," Mason said.

She hurried on. "His first subjects would be prominent men that he'd get from the newspapers. You see very good pen-and-ink, black-and-white cartoons, but what he wants to do is to make something that is almost a cartoon—not quite. It stops just short of being a cartoon but it would be in color and would be beautifully done."

"Does he have the ability and technique to do it beautifully?"

"Not now. He wants to develop. Really, Mr. Mason, I don't know why you started cross-examining me about Fred Hedley."

"Because I'm trying to get certain facts and I want to have those facts straight. Now, when Hedley talks about an endowment, he really means he wants to give financial aid to certain aspiring artists who can't make a living otherwise. Is that right?"

"I guess so, yes."

"And *he's* an aspiring artist who can't make a living?"

"He *may* be the founder of a whole new school of painting."

"And he intends to subsidize himself?"

"He says he'd be untrue to his art if he didn't."

"With *your* money?"

"Of course. What other money would he have?"

"That's a good question," Mason said.

"Well, of course, he despises moneygrubbing."

"All right," Mason said, "the police are going to question you."

"But I can't understand how anything like that could have happened. I mean, how Kerry could have taken the gun."

"He had plenty of opportunity," Mason said, "but if we're going to save Dutton's neck, we've got to find out *how* it happened. Unless, of course, Dutton killed him."

"Do you think he did, Mr. Mason?"

"He's my client," Mason said with a wry smile. And then after a moment, "Thank you very much for your co-operation, Miss Ellis."

14

PAUL DRAKE sat in Mason's office with a notebook balanced on his knee and said, "Our men have uncovered a lot of stuff. None of it is going to help."

"Go on," Mason said, "give me the facts."

"Well, Rodger Palmer was a great believer in the Steer Ridge Oil stock, but he hated Jarvis Reader, the head of the company.

"I don't know whether you noticed it or not, Perry, but there's a lot of similarity in the appearance of the two men. Reader is perhaps a few years younger, but both men were two-fisted oil men who had worked as roughnecks, who believed in direct action but who had ideas that were diametrically opposed.

"Palmer believed in developing a company working along proven structures, taking a chance on wildcatting after scientific exploration of the structures indicated there was a reasonable chance.

"Jarvis Reader is a plunger. He wants to be a big shot, the bigger the better. He made his money, not by operating oil wells but by selling stock, paying himself a fancy salary and making his reports to the stockholders look good by tying up huge blocks of acreage.

"Now, of course, you can't tie up acreage like that in really good oil country, and the Steer Ridge Oil Company was going steadily downhill until it had that lucky strike.

"Reader is a flashy dresser, a big spender, regards himself as the big executive type, has a twin-motored airplane at his beck and call and is *always* the big shot.

"After Rodger Palmer got out of the company, he had periods of pretty lean living. He hung around cheap hotels. Sometimes he would be in rooming houses where shady characters lived. Once he was even questioned by the police in connection with the nylon stocking strangling of a prostitute. He had been in the rooming house at the time, but fortunately had an alibi. He had been talking with the clerk at the time the actual murder must have been committed.

"But that gives you a general idea of the guy's background. His clothes were seedy, he was pretty much discredited in the oil game.

"Then he started calling on stockholders in the Steer Ridge Company, telling them that they were being bilked, and he put up a pretty convincing argument. I understand a group of stockholders, who controlled a large block of the stock, gave him money to try and get proxies so that Reader could be ousted.

"Now then, you asked about Fred Hedley the night of the murder and whether he could possibly have been out there at the country club at the time the murder was committed.

"There's not a chance. At the time the murder must

have been committed, Hedley was in a drugstore having his face patched. After that fight he was out of circulation and pretty badly messed up.

"He found an all-night drugstore, and the clerk helped him put on disinfectants and patched him up."

"All right," Mason said, with a sigh. "We go to trial tomorrow and, so far, every single thing we've uncovered not only hasn't helped us but is ammunition the district attorney can use."

"And he'll sure use it," Drake said. "He'd rather win this case than any case he's ever tried. The way he looks at it, he's running downhill all the way."

Mason said, "It looks that way, Paul, but we'll give him a fight for every inch of ground we have to hold."

15

∎

JUDGE EDUARDO ALVARADO opened the second day of the trial by saying, "Gentlemen, I hope we can get a jury today."

"I see no reason why we can't," Perry Mason said.

"The peremptory is with the prosecution," Judge Alvarado said.

"The prosecution passes."

Mason arose, bowed and smiled. "Let the jury be sworn," he said. "The defense has no further peremptories and is satisfied with this jury."

Judge Alvarado smiled as he said, "Well, I hardly expected such prompt action. I thank you, gentlemen. The clerk will now swear the jury and then Court will take a ten-minute recess."

At the conclusion of the recess, Judge Alvarado nodded to the table of the prosecution where Stevenson

Bailey, one of the trial deputies, sat next to Hamilton Burger, the district attorney.

"Make your opening speech, Mr. Prosecutor," the judge said.

Bailey said, "If it please the Court, and you members of the jury, this is going to be perhaps the briefest opening statement I have ever made.

"For the most part I am going to let the facts speak for themselves, but because they are somewhat complicated I will give you a brief outline.

"The defendant, Kerry Dutton, was trustee under a so-called spendthrift trust created by Templeton Ellis in favor of his daughter, Desere Ellis.

"Under the terms of this trust, the defendant, Dutton, had the right to sell securities as he saw fit, purchase other securities, and to pay out such money as he saw fit to the beneficiary of the trust.

"Now then, ladies and gentlemen, we expect to prove that in the three years and some months, almost four years, during which this trust had been in effect—" And here Bailey held up four fingers in front of the jury— "during all of those four years, the defendant in this case *never made a single accounting to the beneficiary of the trust.*"

Bailey paused to let that statement sink in.

"Furthermore, ladies and gentlemen of the jury, we propose to show that the defendant, Dutton, had systematically looted that trust, using income from it to feather his own financial nest until he had built up an independent fortune in his own name through shrewd investments and manipulations but *he never—made—an—accounting!*"

Again there was a moment of silence.

"As a part of the holdings of the trust, there had been stock in the Steer Ridge Oil and Refining Company. This stock was highly speculative. At one time it was rather high; then it went to a low where the value was only nominal; and then when oil had been struck, the property skyrocketed.

"We expect to show that Rodger Palmer, the decedent, had known the executive officials of the Steer Ridge Oil and Refining Company for some time, had also known Templeton Ellis, the father of Desere Ellis.

"We expect to show that Rodger Palmer wanted the defendant to give him a proxy enabling the decedent to vote the trust stock in the Steer Ridge Company. The defendant refused, because he had to refuse, since he had sold the Steer Ridge stock. The decedent didn't know of this sale, but we can show by inference at least that he did know of a purchase of a large block of Steer Ridge stock the defendant had made in his own name.

"The decedent, Rodger Palmer, was threatening the defendant with exposure unless he received a proxy and the sum of five thousand dollars with which to carry on his proxy fight.

"Now, we expect to show this and to show that Rodger Palmer made a final appointment with the defendant at approximately ten o'clock on the night of the twenty-first of September.

"I say that it was a final appointment, because the defendant kept that appointment and, at that time, killed Rodger Palmer. The decedent, Rodger Palmer, had demanded five thousand dollars as the price of his silence. The defendant had been prepared to pay that price if he had to. He had drawn five thousand dollars from his bank and had the money on him in cash when he was apprehended.

"But the defendant knew that blackmail was endless. The blackmailer's attitude would be even more eager, his appetite the more voracious by receiving this payment.

"So after due consideration, after careful deliberation, Kerry Dutton decided on murder as his best way out.

"The murder, ladies and gentlemen, took place at the seventh tee of the exclusive Barclay Country Club. The body was not found until the next morning.

"By that time the defendant had fled to Mexico and was registered at an auto court under the name of Frank Kerry.

"We may never know all the information Palmer was holding over the defendant's head. We can surmise some of it. The circumstantial evidence screams to heaven of blackmail.

"We further propose to show that along the path of his flight, the defendant paused long enough to throw the gun, the murder weapon with which Rodger Palmer was killed, under a culvert.

"On the strength of that evidence, ladies and gentlemen of the jury, we expect to ask for a verdict of first-degree murder.

"We thank you."

Bailey bowed with courtly dignity, strode back to the counsel table, and sat down.

"Do you wish to make an opening statement at this time?" Judge Alvarado asked Perry Mason.

"We will defer our opening statement until the defense is ready to put on its case," Mason said.

"Very well," Judge Alvarado said, "call your first witness, Mr. Prosecutor."

Bailey called the autopsy surgeon who testified to having performed an autopsy on the body of Rodger Palmer. The death had been caused by a single gunshot wound in the head, which had been fired into the right temple from a gun which ,had been not more than six inches away from the man's head at the time of its discharge.

Asked as to the time of death, he fixed the time of death as between nine-thirty o'clock and two-thirty A.M. on the night of the twenty-first and twenty-second of September.

"Cross-examine," Bailey snapped at Mason.

Mason said, almost casually, "Death could have been at nine o'clock, Doctor?"

"I doubt it."

"At eight-thirty?"

"I don't think so."

"But it *could* have been at eight-thirty?"

"It's possible but not probable. I fix nine-thirty as the earliest hour."

"But it's *possible* death occurred at eight-thirty?"

"But not probable. You can't fix the time of death with a stop watch."

"That's all, Doctor, thank you."

In rapid succession, Bailey called witnesses who testified to Rodger Palmer's interest in the Steer Ridge Oil and Refining Company, to his friendship with Templeton Ellis, and to the fact that he had, shortly prior to his death, been engaged in a quiet campaign to secure proxies in the Steer Ridge Oil and Refining Company in his name.

Mason brushed all of these witnesses aside with the casual comment, "No questions," when he was asked to cross-examine.

Judge Alvarado watched the lawyer with thoughtful curiosity as it became apparent Mason did not intend to engage in routine cross-examination.

"Call Miss Desere Ellis to the stand," Bailey said, in the manner of one making a dramatic announcement.

Desere Ellis came forward, her manner subdued, her eyes purposely avoiding those of Kerry Dutton.

She took the oath, seated herself on the stand, and faced the prosecutor with the manner of a courageous woman who is facing an ordeal and is determined to be brave.

Under skillful questioning by Bailey she told about her father's death, the reading of the will, the initial conversations with the defendant about the trust.

"Now then," Bailey said, "when did the defendant make his first accounting under the trust?"

"He never made any accounting."

"Never—made—any—accounting?" Bailey repeated.

"No, sir, no *formal* accounting."

"Well, were there any other accountings, any *informal* accountings?"

"Well, he discussed, from time to time, the securities which he had had sold in order to give me my allowance."

"And did he make any comments at that time in regard to the principal of the trust?"

"He said at one time that he had sold nearly all of the securities which my father had left."

"Thereby giving you the impression that there would be no funds available to you after the termination of the trust?"

"I had that impression, yes."

"Did the defendant, at any time, tell you that there was a large sum of money in the trust which he would have to pay over to you or to which you would be entitled on the termination of the trust period?"

She shifted her position on the witness stand, started to glance at Dutton, then lowered her eyes.

"No," she said.

"Did he ever tell you he had sold your Steer Ridge stock at a dollar a share, then, later on, purchased a similar block of Steer Ridge stock *in his own name* at from ten to fifteen cents a share?"

"No."

"Did he tell you he had made this purchase only a few days before the stock had skyrocketed in value?"

"No."

"Did he tell you he had secured inside information that Steer Ridge was drilling in a most promising formation?"

"No."

"Did you have any reason to believe your Steer Ridge stock had been sold?"

"No."

"The defendant never told you so?"

"No."

Bailey said to Perry Mason, "Cross-examine."

Mason arose and approached the witness, his manner courteous, pausing when he was some five steps from the witness stand, waiting until she raised her eyes to his.

Mason said in a kindly voice, "You had the impression that your trust funds would be exhausted when the time came to terminate the trust?"

"Yes."

"That was an impression you had in your mind?"

"Yes."

"Now then," Mason said, holding up his left index finger, "please follow this question very closely. Are you prepared to do so?"

"Yes, sir," she said, her eyes on his finger.

Mason moved the finger, slowly, beating time to the words, "Did you get this impression from your own thinking, or *did the defendant ever tell you in so many words that the trust fund would be exhausted at the time the trust terminated?*"

"I . . . I had that impression."

"I know you did," Mason said, "and it is quite possible that the defendant knew you did, but I am asking now if the defendant ever *told you in so many words* definitely, positively, that the trust fund would be exhausted at the time the trust terminated?"

"I can't remember his ever having said that."

"That's all," Mason said.

"Just one more question on redirect," Bailey said. "Did the defendant ever tell you in so many words, Miss Ellis, that there would be a large sum of money coming to you on the termination of your trust?"

"No, sir," she said, promptly.

"That's all," Bailey said.

"Just one more question on recross?" Mason asked. "Miss Ellis, did you ever ask the defendant?"

"No, I can't remember doing that."

"In other words, you took the situation for granted?"

"Yes."

"That's all," Mason said.

Bailey was again on his feet. "I'm going to ask one more question on redirect. Isn't it a fact that the defendant was fully aware of your feeling that the trust fund would be exhausted?"

"Objected to," Mason said, "as calling for a conclusion of the witness."

"All right, all right, if I have to do it the long way around, I'll do it the long way around," Bailey said in exasperation. "Isn't it a fact that the defendant let you know by his own words that he understood you felt the termination of the trust would leave you with no funds?"

"Objected to as calling for a conclusion of the witness and on the further ground that it is leading and suggestive."

"It's redirect examination," Bailey said.

"I don't care what it is," Mason said. "A man has no more right to lead his witness on redirect than he does on direct. Furthermore, this calls for a conclusion of the witness as to what the defendant said. Let's have a question calling for the defendant's exact words."

Bailey waved his hands in a gesture of dismissal. "I think the jury understands the situation. I'm not going to bicker with counsel. That's all, Miss Ellis."

Mason smiled. *"That's all."*

"I'll call Mrs. Rosanna Hedley to the stand," Bailey said.

Mrs. Hedley assumed her position on the witness stand with a very visible chip on her shoulder. She didn't intend to be confused by any attorney.

"Did you ever hear a conversation between Desere Ellis and the defendant in which she asked him about the condition of the trust funds?" Bailey asked.

"Yes, sir."

"Do you remember when that was?"

"I remember exactly when it was. That was on the fourth day of July, on the evening of the fourth of July."

"Who was present?"

"My son was present, that is, he had been present."

"And by your son, you mean Fred Hedley?"

"That's right," she said. "Fred Hedley, the artist."

Bailey smiled almost imperceptibly. "Exactly," he said. "Was Fred there at the time of this conversation?"

"No, he had left the room."

"Then who was present?"

"Just Miss Ellis, the defendant, and myself."

"And what did Miss Ellis say?"

"She asked the defendant how the trust was coming, what she could count on."

"And what did the defendant say in response to the question?"

"He told her that he thought the trust funds would last out the duration of the trust, letting her have the same allowance she'd been having."

"Move to strike the answer," Mason said, "as not being responsive to the question and as being a conclusion of the witness. The witness should state the exact words used by the defendant as nearly as she can recollect."

"The motion is granted. The answer will go out. The witness will answer the question as to exactly what the defendant said."

"You mean I have to give his exact words?" Mrs Hedley asked.

"As nearly as you can," Judge Alvarado explained, not unkindly. "When you give your impression of his words, you are not giving the exact words but a conclusion you drew from the conversation. Can you remember exactly what he said?"

"Well, as nearly as I can remember, he said, with one of those oily smiles, 'Don't worry, Desere, there will be money enough in the trust fund to keep your allowance until the trust expires.' "

"Cross-examine," Bailey snapped.

Mason smiled. "His smile was oily, Mrs. Hedley?"

"Oily," she repeated.

"What do you mean by an oily smile?" Mason asked.

"You know what I mean, a smirk, a simper."

"Greasy?" Mason asked.

"Oily!" she snapped.

"That gives a pretty good picture of your feeling for the defendant, does it not?" Mason asked.

"A feeling which events have amply justified," she said acidly.

"Now then," Mason said, "he told her there would be enough money to last out the trust?"

"Yes."

"In other words," Mason said, "he was predicting the

102

future. We might have had another crash in the security market."

"Yes," she said, "the world might have come to an end."

"And there *was* enough money in the trust to carry through Desere's allowance to the end of the trust, was there not?" Mason said.

"That much and nearly two hundred and fifty thousand more."

"Then he didn't lie to her, did he?"

"He deceived her."

"But he didn't lie to her."

"Objected to as argumentative, as calling for a conclusion of the witness," Bailey said. "If the defense is going to be technical, *I'll* be technical."

Mason smiled blandly and said, "I'll withdraw the question. I think the jury has the picture in mind," and sat down.

Bailey called a ballistics expert, who identified the Smith & Wesson revolver introduced in evidence as the murder weapon. He then called a firearms dealer who identified the gun as having been sold by him to the defendant, and introduced in evidence the certificate of purchase, bearing the signature of the defendant.

Bailey also introduced maps showing the scene of the murder; photographs of the terrain; of the body, and of the clothes worn by the decedent. He introduced the coat worn by Palmer when the body was discovered and called attention to the fact that the labels had been cut from the garment.

The coroner testified there were no keys, no money, no handkerchief, no knife, nothing in the pockets.

Bailey called Lt. Tragg to the stand. Tragg testified to having been advised of the murder, going to the golf club, inspecting the body and the premises; then looking in the culverts along the road leading from the golf club.

"Why did you do this?" Bailey asked.

"It's a routine police procedure."

"What did you find, if anything?"

"I found this gun, tagged People's Exhibit A-G, in a culvert, one and three-tenths miles from the entrance to the golf club."

"And what did you do with that gun?"

"I traced the registration on it."

"How long did that take you?"

"Only a few minutes after it was found. We ran down the serial number."

"What else did you do, if anything?"

"When we connected the serial number with the defendant, we got the license number of his automobile and put out an all-points bulletin."

"And did that all-points bulletin include certain cities in Mexico?"

"We have an arrangement on important homicide cases by which the Mexican police in Ensenada, Tijuana and Mexicali co-operate with us."

"And what did you find?"

"We found the defendant registered in Ensenada—"

"Just a moment," Mason interrupted. "is the witness testifying as to what he found or what the Mexican police found? In the latter event, it is hearsay."

"Quite right," Bailey said. "Don't testify to anything you have been told, Lieutenant Tragg."

"Well, then I can't testify to his being in Mexico," Lt. Tragg said with a smile.

"Where did you, personally, find the defendant?"

"At the international border, just outside of Tecate," Tragg said.

"And how did you happen to find him there?"

"The Mexican police pushed him across the line."

"And what did you do?"

"Took him in custody."

"Did you have any conversation with the defendant at that time?"

"Yes."

"Did you tell him that he was accused of murder?"

"I told him that he was wanted for questioning in connection with the murder of Rodger Palmer."

"Did you ask him where he had been at the time the murder was committed or approximately that time?"

"I asked him many questions, and his answer was the same to all of them."

"What was his answer?"

" 'I refuse to make any statement until I have consulted my attorney!' "

"That was his answer to all questions?"

"Well, I asked him why, if he had nothing to conceal, he had registered under the name of Frank Kerry in Mexico, and he stated that actually Kerry was his middle name, that Frank was his first name and his full name was Frank Kerry Dutton."

"I see," Bailey said. "Cross-examine."

"Why, no questions at all," Mason said, with a gesture of his hand.

There was a note of triumph in Bailey's voice as he said, "Call Thomas Densmore Fulton to the stand."

Fulton came forward and was sworn.

"What is your occupation?"

"I am a private detective."

"By whom are you employed?"

"Mostly by the Drake Detective Agency."

"On the twenty-first day of September last, by whom were you employed?"

"Paul Drake."

"What were your instructions?"

"To shadow a subject."

"Who was the subject?"

"The defendant, Kerry Dutton."

"And in connection with your duties, did you follow Kerry Dutton anywhere?"

"I did. Yes, sir."

"Where?"

"I followed him to a telephone booth."

"Where was that telephone booth?"

"At a service station on the corner of Figueroa and Boulevard Way."

"Was the service station open or closed?"

"The service station was closed. It was a big service station with quite a bit of parking space, but the telephone booth was open."

"What did you do?"

"I saw the defendant enter the telephone booth and I drove my car from across the street and into the parking station. He dialed a number, then hung up the phone and after a short interval, dialed again. I ran up to the booth as though I were in a hurry to use the telephone."

"What did the defendant do?"

"He motioned me away."

"What did you do?"

"I surreptitiously planted a wire recorder with adhesive tape so that the microphone, which is very sensitive, would pick up sounds within the booth."

"Then what did you do?"

"Returned to my car."

"And what happened after that?"

"The defendant emerged from the telephone booth, jumped in his car and took off."

"What did you do?"

"I tried to follow him."

"Were you able to do so?"

"No, sir."

"Why?"

"The defendant drove like crazy. He went through three or four red lights, through a boulevard stop, nearly had a collision with another car, left me stymied in cross-traffic and got away."

"So, what did you do?"

"I returned to the telephone booth to pick up the wire recorder and see if I had a clue there."

"And you picked up the wire recorder?"

"Yes, sir."

"Then what did you do?"

"I rewound the wire to the starting position and turned the key over to listening and listened to the recording."

"Do you have that wire recorder here?"

"I do."

"If the Court please," Bailey said, "I believe the conversation on the wire recorder is the best evidence. It is not as clear as I would like to have it, but it is, nevertheless, understandable. I have arranged for an amplifier and I would like to have this conversation played directly to the jury."

"No objection," Mason said.

Rather dramatically, Bailey set up the wire recorder, in connection with the amplifier, and turned on the current. A buzzing sound filled the courtroom, then the sound of a man's voice. "Hello, what's new? You know who this is."

There was a brief interval of silence, then the voice said, "I called this other number for instructions; I was told to call you here at this pay station. . . . Yes, I have the five thousand and will pay it over if things are as you represented—if you're acting in good faith."

There was an interval of silence; then the man's voice said, "Give me that place again. The seventh tee at the Barclay Country Club . . . why in the world pick that sort of a place? . . . When? . . . Good heavens, it's nearly that time now . . . All right. All right! I'll get out there. Yes, I've got a key to the club. I'll be there."

There was an abrupt click as the recording ended.

"That, if the Court and the jury please," Bailey said, "is the termination of the conversation."

Bailey turned to the witness. "What did you do after hearing that conversation?"

"I went at once to the Barclay Country Club."

"What did you find there?"

"I found the defendant's automobile parked there."

"How long did it take you to get there from the time you listened to that conversation on the tape recorder?"

"Probably fifteen minutes."

"And what did you do?"

"I tried the door of the club, but it was locked. I waited until the defendant came out."

"How long was that?"

"I arrived at ten-ten. The defendant emerged at ten-twenty-two."

"Now, let's get this time element straight," Bailey said. "You tried to follow the defendant?"

"That's right."

"He was driving, as you said, like crazy. He went through red lights and boulevard stops?"

"Three red lights; one boulevard stop."

"You lost him?"

"That's right."

"You returned to the telephone booth?"

"Yes, sir."

"You picked up your recording device and listened to the conversation?"

"Yes, sir."

"How long, in your opinion, was that from the time you had left the telephone booth following the defendant?"

"Probably five minutes."

"And then you went directly to the Barclay Country Club?"

"Yes."

"And you waited at the Barclay Country Club for how long?"

"Eleven minutes . . . nearly twelve minutes."

"And then the defendant came out?"

"Yes, sir."

"And what did he do?"

"He drove down the road for a mile and three-tenths."

"And then what?"

"Then he brought his car to an abrupt stop and started backing up."

"What did you do?"

"I had to drive on past him so he wouldn't be suspicious."

"And then what?"

"I went half a mile down the road, jumped out of the car, put a bumper jack under the rear bumper and acted as if I had a flat tire."

"And what happened?"

"Within a matter of seconds the defendant's car went past me again, going at high speed."

"What did you do?"

"I hurriedly removed the bumper jack, tossed it in the back of the car, and stepped on the throttle."

"And were able to follow the defendant?"

"Yes, sir."

"How far did you follow him?"

"To Ensenada."

"Where in Ensenada?"

"To the Siesta del Tarde Auto Court."

"And then what did you do?"

"I telephoned Paul Drake that the subject was registered at the Siesta del Tarde Auto Court under the name of Frank Kerry."

"And then what?"

"Then Perry Mason and his secretary, Della Street, showed up and I told them where the defendant was and they went to his room."

"Then what?"

"Then the Mexican police came."

Bailey smiled. "Cross-examine," he said to Mason.

Mason said, "Your wire recording gives only one side of the conversation?"

"That's right."

"You don't know whom the defendant was calling?"

"No, sir."

"You don't know what words were used on the other end of the line?"

"No, sir."

"That's all," Mason said.

Judge Alvarado said, "It is now time for the evening adjournment. I congratulate counsel for both sides on the speed with which this trial is progressing.

"During the evening the jurors will not converse among

themselves or with anyone else about the case, nor will they read newspaper accounts of the trial or listen to anything on radio or television pertaining to the trial. They will avoid forming or expressing any opinion until the case is finally submitted for a decision. If anyone should approach any of you jurors to discuss the case, report that matter to the Court.

"Court will take a recess until ten o'clock tomorrow morning."

16

MASON SAT in the visiting room of the jail and let his eyes bore into those of his client.

"This," he said, "is your last chance."

"I'm telling you the truth."

"You can't ever change your story from this point on," Mason warned. "If you ever get on the witness stand, tell your story and then are forced to change it under cross-examination, you're a gone goose."

Dutton nodded.

"And don't discount Hamilton Burger's ability as a cross-examiner."

"Do you think I'm going to have to get on the stand?"

"You're going to have to get on the stand," Mason said. "They have a dead open-and-shut case against you. You're not only going to have to get on the stand, but you are going to have to persuade the jury that you're telling the truth.

"Now then, if they catch you in some little lie—just anything—the time you get up in the morning, how many lumps of sugar you had in your coffee, just anything that is false, they're going to hold it against you all the way down the line."

"I've told you the truth," Dutton said.

"You aren't trying to protect someone? You aren't shading the facts in order to make it easy on Desere Ellis?"

He shook his head.

"And you aren't trying to protect yourself?"

"No, I've told you the truth."

"Palmer had given you a number to call on the dot at nine-forty-five?"

Dutton nodded.

"You went to the telephone booth, called this number and were given another number, both numbers were pay stations, a voice told you to meet Palmer at the seventh tee at the Barclay Country Club when you called the second number?"

"Right."

"Now, was that last voice a woman's?"

"I don't know. At the time I thought it was a man trying to talk in a high-pitched voice so as to disguise it; now I just don't know. All I know is it was high-pitched for a man's voice, low-pitched for a woman's."

"What was the number you called?"

"It was a phone booth. I've forgotten the number. Palmer told me that he'd have someone there to take the call and tell me where he could meet me; that it would be a pay station I was calling so not to try to do anything funny."

"Now then, you remained in the phone booth and called a number?"

"Right."

"That was the number of a pay station?"

"That's right."

"And what happened when you called that number?"

"A voice answered, said, 'Take a pencil, write down this number and call it in exactly ten seconds—no more, no less.' I feel sure that first voice was a man's voice— Well, I'm not absolutely certain. It was sort of disguised."

"And you wrote down the number?"

"Yes."

"What was the idea of the two numbers?"

"Apparently so I couldn't locate the number in time to have police or private detectives get on the job and find out where I was to meet Palmer or in time to set up recording devices so they could catch him."

"But if you knew that it was Palmer you were going to be meeting . . ."

"I knew it was Palmer. I also knew he was supposed to have evidence that was going to discredit Fred Hedley."

"And why did you want that evidence?"

"You know why."

"I'm asking you so I can hear it in your words just the way you'll be telling it to a jury."

"I wanted to protect Desere Ellis."

"Why?"

"Because . . . well, because that was my job under the will."

"Whom were you protecting her from?"

"From herself, largely; and also from a man who was trying to take advantage of her."

Mason regarded his client thoughtfully, abruptly got to his feet. "All right, Dutton, I don't want you to think I'm rehearsing you. I don't want you to rehearse yourself. I don't want you to get on that witness stand and act as if your story had been rehearsed. I want you to tell the truth and it had better look as if you're telling the truth."

"I'll do my best, Mr. Mason," Dutton said.

Mason nodded. "Get some sleep. It's going to be an ordeal, and don't think it won't be."

■

17

WHEN PERRY MASON returned to his office, Della Street said, "Paul Drake has a witness, Chief."

"Where is he?"

"They're in Paul's office."

"Who's the witness?"

"A man who lives within about a hundred yards of the fairway at the Barclay Country Club. His house is not too far from the tee-off position on hole number seven.

"He heard a shot on the night of the twenty-first and it was earlier than the time the prosecution thinks the murder was committed."

Perry Mason's face lit up in a smile. "I've been waiting for a break in this case," he said, "and this may be it. Get him in here, Della."

Della manipulated the dial of the phone and a moment later she said, "He's on his way."

"Now then," Mason said, "get me a blank subpoena on behalf of the defense. As soon as I ask this fellow his name, you take it down, slip out to the other office, fill the name in on the subpoena and return it to me.

"No matter what happens we aren't going to let this man leave this office without having a subpoena slapped on him as a defense witness."

Della Street nodded, moved over to the filing case, took out the folder in the case of People of the State of California vs. Kerry Dutton, removed the original subpoena and a copy; then stepped out to the other office to place them out of sight.

"All ready," she said.

Drake's code knock sounded on the exit door.

Mason nodded to Della Street, who opened the door.

Paul Drake ushered in a tall, somewhat loose-jointed man in his middle fifties; a man with keen eyes, bushy eyebrows, prominent ears, a long thin neck.

"This is Mr. Mason," Drake said. "Mason, this is George Holbrook. Mr. Holbrook lives out by the Barclay Country Club."

"George Holbrook, is it?" Mason asked, shaking hands. "Any middle initial, Mr. Holbrook?"

"Sure," Holbrook said, grinning. "A conventional one. George W. Holbrook. The 'W' standing for Washington."

Della Street silently slipped from the room.

"Well, sit down, Mr. Holbrook," Mason said. "I understand you know something about this case?"

"Maybe I do and maybe I don't," Holbrook said, sitting down in the chair and crossing his long legs in front of him, then after a moment clasping bony fingers around his upthrust right knee.

"Trouble is, Mr. Mason, you can't tell these days what you hear. There are so many sounds, so many noises, among them sonic booms, a fellow never knows quite what he *does* hear."

"Suppose you tell me about it," Mason said.

"Well, I got to reading about this thing in the paper and all of a sudden it struck me right between the eyes. I said to my wife, 'Hey, wait a minute, wasn't that the night I heard the shot?' "

"You're not certain of the date?" Mason asked, his voice showing his disappointment.

"Now, wait a minute," Holbrook said. "I *think* I can fix the date all right. I was telling you what I'd said to the wife."

"Go ahead," Mason said.

"We'd just got a wire from my wife's sister that she was arriving on the ten-fifty plane and we were sitting there talking it over. Then my wife went out in the kitchen and I stepped out on the front porch for a little breath of air—and a puff or two on a cigarette."

Holbrook grinned. "The wife doesn't like smoking in the house. She has a very sensitive nose, and tobacco smell just doesn't agree with her, so I kind of step out when I'm smoking and— Well, she'd like to have me swear off. I guess she thinks I have. So what with one thing and another, I kind of sneak out when I'm smoking."

"Go ahead," Mason said.

"Well, I heard this shot. I'm pretty darn sure it was a shot. I've done hunting in my time and I think I know a shot when I hear one."

"And what happened?"

"Well, I stood there looking, trying to see where the shot came from."

"You couldn't locate it from the sound?"

"I think it was out on the golf course somewhere. That's where it sounded like."

"You checked the date because of the arrival of your sister?"

"That's right. She came on the twenty-first."

"How did it happen," Mason said, "that the next morning, with the papers full of a body having been found on the golf course, you didn't connect up the shot with the murder?"

"That was simple," Holbrook said. "The wife's sister had always wanted to take a motor tour and she was due in at ten-fifty. We picked her up at the airport and, of course, she was all packed, so my wife suggested we take the motor trip she'd been wanting. I guess the women had had it planned that way all along. They'd been using the long distance phone back and forth. You can't get ahead of a couple of women—can't get ahead of one, for that matter.

"Well, anyway we started off at six o'clock the next morning, had breakfast along the road, and took a swing up through Northern California around the Redwood Highway, then came back through Yosemite Park. What's more, with the excitement of the sister coming, and going down and meeting the plane and all that, I just pretty nearly forgot about that shot. It wasn't until I got to reading in the paper about this case that I got to thinking about it again."

"You hadn't heard about the murder?" Mason asked.

"Why, sure we'd heard about it," Holbrook said. "Talked about it, as a matter of fact.

"I first heard it on the radio when we were between Modesto and Sacramento, somewhere along in there. I didn't pay too much attention to it the first time I heard it, just a murder that had been committed on a golf course. Then the second time, my wife perked up and said, 'Why, George, that's the golf course near our house.' And I got to thinking and said, 'I guess that's where it was all right.'

"Then we got to Sacramento and stayed there overnight. Then went on up to Redding and I got a San-Francisco paper in Redding and— Well, I just sort of like to keep in touch with the comic strips."

Holbrook broke off to grin amiably at Mason. "Wife says I'm just a grown-up juvenile; but doggone it, I *do* like to read the comic strips."

Mason nodded.

"Well, there was something in the paper there about the body being found on the seventh tee. I didn't pay much attention to what that meant because, until a few days ago, I didn't know where the seventh tee was. I'm retired and the income isn't enough to afford golf.

"It was after this trial started that one of the newspapers published a map of the golf course. That's a long course. It stretches down quite a ways and has about six holes strung out one right after the other."

"And this map showed the location of the body?"

"That's right. Showed it with reference to the seventh tee and showed the seventh tee with reference to the streets—the cross streets out there."

Holbrook shifted his position. "You see, when the golf course was first laid out, that was all open land out there but they only owned just so much of it so they kept the golf course on the land they owned. Then with the golf course there, the subdividers moved in and it seems like in no time at all the thing was all built up.

"We bought our house right after the big boom—and that was fifteen years ago, I guess. I was working then. Been living there ever since."

"Have you ever played golf?"

"Got no use for it. As far as I'm concerned, it's just taking a bunch of sticks, going up to a ball, hitting the ball where the sticks aren't, then packing the sticks up to where the ball is and repeating it all over."

Mason said, "Can you fix the exact time that you heard the shot?"

"Now, that's what I'm talking about," Holbrook said. "I'm really certain that it was way before ten o'clock."

"How do you know?"

"Because I listen to news at ten o'clock and I'm pretty sure the news hadn't come on yet."

"How long before ten o'clock?"

"Well, I was out there on the porch taking a smoke and—"

"Was it dark?" Mason asked.

"Yes, it was dark. I remember the cigarette glowed when I threw it away out there on the front lawn, and I got to wondering if my wife had maybe seen the end of the cigarette glowing when I threw it—but she hadn't. That doesn't mean she didn't know what I went out there for, but I guess she was excited over her sister coming and all.

"And all of a sudden, I realized it was time for that ten o'clock news I like to listen to on TV. I was just starting to go in the house to turn on the TV when I heard this shot."

"Did you turn on the television?"

"Sure did. Seems to me I missed the first couple of minutes of it. Remember I was mad that I turned it on in the middle of a commercial."

Mason said, "Your testimony may be very valuable, Mr. Holbrook. There was just the one shot?"

"Just the one shot. That's why I figured it wasn't a

backfire. Usually you get a backfire and there'll be an interval of a second or two and then two or three more backfires, and then an interval and maybe one big backfire—something like that. This was just the one single explosion."

Mason said, "I'm going to ask you to come to court as a witness. Do you have any objection?"

"Well, I don't want to get mixed up in things," Holbrook said. "But I don't want to be a party to an injustice."

Mason glanced at Paul Drake. "Would your wife's sister get a kick out of seeing your picture in the paper?"

Holbrook grinned. "Now, I'll say she would! She's a good sport. If she thought that there'd been a murder committed out there and she just missed it— Well, she'd get a kick out of it, but . . ." And here the smile left Holbrook's face. "I'm not so sure about Doris."

"That's your wife?" Mason asked.

"That's my wife, for better or worse. She's it."

Holbrook was thoughtful for a moment, then went on. "She's awful nice. Good housekeeper; mighty neat and considerate—can't say that I complain, but she isn't like Edith."

"Edith is the sister?" Mason asked.

"Edith is the sister."

"You drove to the airport to meet your wife's sister?"

"That's right."

"How far do you live from the airport?"

"Takes us twenty-five minutes."

"And she arrived on the ten-fifty plane?"

"That's right."

"Then you could have hardly listened to the ten o'clock news that night," Mason said.

A sudden frown creased Holbrook's forehead. "Now, wait a minute. Wait a minute," he said. "Oh yes, the plane was a little late. I remember we called up about ten o'clock. They said the plane would be fifteen minutes late. I'm pretty sure I watched both the nine o'clock and the ten o'clock news that night."

"You're sure about the nine o'clock news?"

"That's right. I was mad because I missed the first minute or two of the nine o'clock news, so I turned the set on again at ten."

Mason said to Della Street, "I think we're going to have to rely on Mr. Holbrook as a witness, Della."

Della Street nodded, handed Mason the subpoena.

Mason said, "Just to make it formal, Mr. Holbrook, I'm giving you a subpoena. This is made out for ten o'clock tomorrow morning. If you'll just be in court at ten o'clock, I don't think we're going to detain you very long because I think the prosecution is about ready to rest its case."

"Well, whatever's right is right," Holbrook said. "I just thought you ought to know about it. I called the office and they said you were in court but the Drake Detective Agency was investigating anything in connection with the case, so I told my story down there at the agency. That was right?"

"That was right," Mason said.

"Well, I was awfully glad to meet you people. I guess I didn't get your name, young lady."

"Della Street," she said, "Mr. Mason's confidential secretary, and have been for many years."

"I figured as much," Holbrook said, putting forth a big bony paw. "Even if you look young, you seem to know what's what. Pleased to meet you, Miss Street."

Then Holbrook solemnly shook hands with Mason and with Paul Drake. Della Street held the door open and Holbrook walked out.

Mason waited until the door had clicked shut; then he executed a little jig, grabbed Della Street around the waist, whirled her into a few steps of a dance, then released her to grab Paul Drake's hand and pump it up and down.

"Saved by the bell!" he said.

"You think that'll do it?" Drake asked.

"That'll do it," Mason said. "That's going to create a reasonable doubt."

"Suppose the prosecution comes up with someone who swears the shot was later?"

Mason grinned and said, "I'll then claim there were *two* shots, and the prosecution can't prove which shot was the fatal shot from the standpoint of time."

"It'll create a reasonable doubt?" Drake asked.

"It'll do better than that," Mason said. "It'll probably result in a verdict of acquittal on the theory that Dutton is telling the truth and Palmer was dead when he got there. Dutton just walked into a trap."

"It still would have been a lot better if he hadn't taken that gun and hidden it," Drake said.

Mason's face lost its smile. "Are you telling me?" he said. "I'm going to have to do quite a bit of arguing to get around that, but I'm going to make it appear that when he saw that gun, he naturally thought the woman he loved was involved."

"Desere Ellis?"

Mason nodded.

"Going to let him say that he's in love with her on the witness stand?" Drake asked.

Mason shook his head. "Heavens, no, I'm not going to let him *say* it. I'm going to let him try to keep from saying it; and then when the district attorney takes him on cross-examination, it's all going to come out and come out reluctantly. We'll have a romantic and dramatic scene in the courtroom."

"And, I take it," Drake said, "no defense attorney ever got an unjust verdict when there was a romantic and a dramatic scene in a courtroom?"

"Not one involving heartthrobs," Mason said, "and this is going to involve heartthrobs, orange blossoms, wedding bells and what have you.

"Come on, we're closing up the shop and I'm going to buy you folks the best dinner to be had anywhere in the city—a dinner with all the frills, including ice-cold vintage champagne."

18

■

THE NEXT MORNING as Judge Alvarado took his place on
the bench and looked over the courtroom, it was quite
apparent that the prosecution was discussing strategy on
a matter which they considered to be of considerable
importance.

Bailey and Hamilton Burger had their heads together
in a whispered conference, as soon as the bailiff had
rapped his gavel and Judge Alvarado had seated himself
on the bench.

"The case of People versus Kerry Dutton," Judge Alvarado said. "The defendant is in court; the jurors are
all present. It is so stipulated, gentlemen?"

"So stipulated," Perry Mason said.

"Yes, Your Honor," Hamilton Burger said. "It is so
stipulated. May we have just a moment?"

Again there was a whispered conference; then Burger
nodded his head somewhat reluctantly, apparently.

Immediately Bailey jumped to his feet. "If the Court
please, that concludes the evidence of the prosecution.
We rest our case."

A murmur of surprise ran through the spectators in
the courtroom.

Judge Alvarado frowned. "It would have been perhaps
fairer to the defense if the decision had been announced
at the close of the courtroom session yesterday."

"We didn't know it at that time. We have just this
minute reached our decision," Bailey said.

"Very well," Judge Alvarado said. "I will, however,
be willing to grant the defense a reasonable recess so
that it may meet this somewhat unexpected development."

"If the Court please," Mason said, arising and smiling

at the jury, "the defense is not only willing but eager to proceed immediately."

"Very well," Judge Alvarado said. "Go ahead."

"And we do not wish to make an opening statement at this time," Mason said. "Our first witness is Desere Ellis."

"Come forward to the stand, Miss Ellis," Judge Alvarado said. "You have already been sworn and so it is not necessary for you to take an oath once more."

Desere Ellis came forward. This time she met the defendant's eyes with a quick flicker of a smile; then seated herself on the witness stand and turned to face Perry Mason.

"You are, of course, acquainted with the defendant and have known him for some time?" Mason asked.

"Yes."

"Did the defendant ever give you a gun?"

"He loaned me a gun, yes."

Mason said, "I show you the People's Exhibit A-G, a Smith and Wesson snub-nosed, thirty-eight-caliber revolver, number K524967, and ask you whether or not you have ever seen this gun before?"

"That is the gun that he gave me."

"Did he make any statement to you when he gave you the gun?"

"Yes. There had been some rather offensive telephone calls from a person who did not disclose his name and I was a little apprehensive."

"Now, was there any conversation specifically about the ownership of this gun which took place when it was handed to you?"

"Objected to as incompetent, irrelevant, and immaterial and as a self-serving declaration," Bailey said.

"I am simply asking for a conversation which was part of the *res gestae* of this particular transaction," Mason said. "It is a part of the transaction itself and it took place far in advance of this murder."

"That doesn't keep it from being a self-serving declaration, nor does it make it competent or relevant to the case at bar," Bailey said.

"I think I'll overrule the objection," Judge Alvarado said. "It is always my policy to give the defendant as much leeway as possible in cases of this sort. Answer the question."

"Yes," Desere Ellis said, "he said that it was his gun, one he had bought some time ago but had no use for."

"Did he show you anything about using it?"

"Yes, he took the shells out of it and taught me how to point it and pull the trigger."

"You knew then that it was a double-action revolver?"

"I beg your pardon, I don't understand."

"In other words, by pulling the trigger all the way back, you cock the hammer and then after the hammer has passed a certain point, it comes down on the firing pin so the shell is exploded and at that time the cylinder advances," Mason said. "The effect of this action is such that you can pull the trigger six times and fire six shots."

"Yes."

"What I am getting at," Mason said, "is that this gun he gave you was not an automatic; it was a revolver. In other words, the cylinder rotated."

"Yes."

"And what happened to this gun?" Mason asked.

"I kept it in a drawer in my bedroom, in a nightstand."

"When did you last see it?"

"I last saw it some two or three days before the twenty-first of September."

"Two or three days before the date of the murder?"

"Yes, sir."

"And when did you next look for the gun after that?"

"It was, I believe, either the twenty-third or the twenty-fourth of September."

"And how did you happen to look for it?"

"You asked me about it and I went to get it for you and then found it was gone."

"Cross-examine," Mason said.

Hamilton Burger, who seldom had an opportunity to cross-examine Mason's witnesses, inasmuch as Mason usually made a practice of winning his cases before the prosecution rested and by bringing out his defense from the prosecution's own witnesses, seized upon the opportunity with the eager avidity of a bird pouncing upon a hapless worm.

"What make was the gun that the defendant gave you?" he asked.

"What make?"

"Yes, who manufactured it? Was it a Colt, a Smith and Wesson, a Harrington and Richardson, a—"

She shook her head. "I don't know the brand, Mr. Burger."

"You don't know the manufacturer's name?"

"No, sir."

"You don't know the serial number?"

"No, sir."

"Yet when Perry Mason held this gun up in front of you and asked if you had seen this Smith and Wesson gun, number K524967 and you said it was the gun the defendant had given you, you were swearing to facts you didn't know. Is that right?"

"I relied upon Mr. Mason. It looked exactly like the gun Mr. Dutton had given me."

"Looked like it," Hamilton Burger sneered. "How many guns have you had in your possession?"

"Just the one."

"You never looked at the number on this gun?"

"No, sir."

"You don't even know where the number is located, do you?"

"No, sir."

"You say it looked like this gun," Hamilton Burger said, holding up the weapon. "People's Exhibit A-G?"

"Yes."

"Exactly like it?"

"As nearly as I can tell, exactly like it."

"Do you know how these weapons are made?"

"What do you mean?"

"You know that they are made by machinery and then assembled?"

"I assume as much."

"And do you know that there are hundreds—thousands—perhaps hundreds of thousands of guns of this exact make and model, guns which look exactly like this?"

"Well, I . . . I suppose so."

"You didn't notice any distinguishing marks on the gun which the defendant gave you, no scratches of any sort?"

"No, sir."

"So, for all you know, the defendant could have had half a dozen guns and simply handed you any one of these guns, told you that it was his and still been carrying another gun in his pocket?"

"Well, I . . . I can't identify this specific gun."

"Exactly," Burger said, "all you know is that the defendant gave you *a* gun. You don't know that he gave you *this* gun."

"I can't swear to it."

"Then you can't testify to it," Hamilton Burger said. "You're here to swear, not to guess."

The witness was at a loss for any answer.

Hamilton Burger tried a new attack.

"Prior to the disappearance of this gun, had the defendant called on you?"

"He had been at my apartment, yes."

"And while he was there, had he made some excuse to go to the place where you kept this gun? Think carefully now."

"He had a fight with Fred Hedley."

"Where did that fight take place?"

"In my apartment."

"I mean where in your apartment?"

"It wound up in my bedroom."

"In your *bedroom!*"

125

"Yes."

"That's where you kept this gun?"

"Yes, sir."

"And the defendant was in there?"

"Yes, sir."

"What was the date of this fight?"

"The twenty-first of September."

"The night of the murder?"

"Yes, sir."

"So on the night of the murder the defendant made an excuse to go to the room where you kept this gun, created a diversion there, then ran out and when next you looked in the bedroom for this gun, it was gone. Is that right?"

"Well, it wasn't—"

"Yes or no, please."

"Well . . . yes."

"That's all!" Burger announced.

Mason said, "One question on redirect. Who started the fight?"

"Fred Hedley."

"Who ran into the bedroom where you kept the gun?"

"He did."

"Fred Hedley?"

"Yes."

"That's all," Mason said, smiling, "and our next witness will be the defendant, Kerry Dutton."

Mason turned to Dutton. "It's up to you," he whispered. "If you can put it across, you're out, and if you can't, you're convicted."

"I'll put it across," Dutton promised, and strode to the place in front of the witness stand where he held up his hand; was sworn; took the witness chair and turned to face Perry Mason.

Mason led the witness along skillfully, showing his name, his occupation, his acquaintance with the father of Desere Ellis, the death of the father, the provisions of the will by which Dutton became trustee of a so-called spendthrift trust.

126

"What was the value of the various securities which you received under this trust at the time you received them?"

"Approximately one hundred thousand dollars."

"And the term of the trust under the will was how long?"

"Until the beneficiary, Desere Ellis, became twenty-seven years of age."

"And there was a provision in the will that the trust was created because her father believed she was at an impressionable age in life; that she was overly sympathetic, particularly to lost causes, and that he felt she needed to be protected from herself?"

"Yes, sir."

"And did you discuss with Miss Ellis the manner in which you proposed to administer the trust?"

"Yes, sir."

"The first conversation," Mason said, holding up the index finger of his left hand, "let's have the first conversation. What did you tell her?"

"I told her what the income from this money would be; that it wouldn't support her in the rather expensive style to which she had been accustomed; that she would undoubtedly be married prior to the termination of the trust, and that I proposed to give the money to her in such a way that she would have approximately equal monthly installments for four years. That this would enable her to have a good wardrobe, to travel, to keep herself in a position to meet the right sort of people."

"In other words," Mason said, "to exhibit herself favorably on the matrimonial market?"

Dutton frowned. "That wasn't what I said."

"How much have you given her on an average each year during the time the trust has been in effect?"

"Approximately twenty-four thousand dollars."

"What is the value of the money in the trust fund at the present time," Mason asked, "the market value of the securities and the cash on hand?"

"Approximately two hundred and fifty thousand dollars," Dutton said.

Judge Alvarado leaned forward sharply. "What was that figure?" he asked.

"Approximately two hundred and fifty thousand dollars."

"How does that happen?" Judge Alvarado asked. "You had a trust fund of one hundred thousand dollars. You dispersed ninety-six thousand dollars?"

"Yes, Your Honor, but under the provisions of the trust, I was empowered to make investments, to buy and sell securities and to keep the trust in a healthy condition."

"And you made that much profit?"

"After taxes," Dutton said.

"*Well*," Judge Alvarado remarked, "you certainly showed remarkable ability."

"Did you," Mason asked, "tell the beneficiary the extent of the trust funds?"

"No."

"Why not?"

"Objected to as incompetent, irrelevant and immaterial," Hamilton Burger said.

"I think I will sustain that objection," Judge Alvarado said. "The answer is that he didn't tell the beneficiary. To your knowledge, did she have any idea of the nature and the extent of the trust fund?"

"No."

"Now then," Mason said, "the trust fund was created so that you could protect her from herself."

"Yes."

"Did you feel that if she knew the exact amount of the trust, that it would tend to defeat the purposes of the trust; that she would extravagantly espouse some lost cause and—"

"Your Honor, Your Honor," Hamilton Burger literally shouted, "this question is viciously leading and suggestive. I object to it. It is incompetent, irrelevant and immaterial."

"Sustained," Judge Alvarado snapped. "Counsel will refrain from this sort of question."

However, the jurors, exchanging astonished glances, showed that the point had registered and made a deep impression on them.

"Now then," Mason said, "did you know and do you know a Fred Hedley?"

"Yes."

"What was his relationship to Desere Ellis?"

"He was described by her on occasion as her fiancé."

"Did you approve of him?"

"I did not."

"Why?"

"Objected to as incompetent, irrelevant and immaterial," Burger said.

Judge Alvarado hesitated. "I think," he said, "I am beginning to see a pattern in counsel's questions. A pattern which may well be pertinent to the defense. I am going to overrule the objection. The answer will be limited as to the state of mind of this witness. Further, it will be limited to the actions of the witness in connection with the trust fund."

"Answer the question," Mason said.

"I felt that he was a fortune hunter."

"And was it because of him that you refrained from telling Desere Ellis— Just a minute," Mason said, as he saw Hamilton Burger on his feet, "I'll reframe that question. Did that idea on your part have anything to do with your actions in connection with giving information of the amount of the trust fund? You can answer that yes or no."

"Objected to," Hamilton Burger said.

"Overruled," Judge Alvarado said.

"Yes, it did."

"In connection with the trust fund, did you have securities of a company known as the Steer Ridge Oil and Refining Company?"

"I did."

"Those had been part of the original securities transmitted to you as trustee under the terms of the will?"

"Yes."

"What did you do with those securities?"

"I sold them."

"Did you ever discuss that sale with the beneficiary?"

"No."

"What had she told you about the Steer Ridge stock?"

"She was very much interested in it. She became somewhat excited because they had sent her a brochure telling about the valuable oil properties they had under lease. She knew that her father had been enthusiastic about the stock."

"And did she make any request to you in connection with those securities?"

"She asked me to hang on to them."

"But you disregarded her request?"

"Yes."

"And then what?"

"Well, I sold the securities and . . . well, after a while I reinvested."

"In those same securities?"

"Yes, in a block of that same stock."

"Why?"

"I had a tip that— Well, I had reason to believe that there might be a proxy fight, and they might turn out to be a good investment if two different factions were going to fight for control of the company."

"How much did you buy?"

"Twenty thousand shares."

"In connection with those securities, did you have any contact with the decedent, Rodger Palmer?"

"I talked with him over the telephone, yes."

"And what was the nature of that conversation?"

"Palmer told me that he had been in touch with Desere Ellis; that he had been trying to get a proxy to vote her shares in the Steer Ridge Oil and Refining Company; that she had referred him to me; that if I would cooperate with him it would be possible for us to greatly enhance the value of the securities held by Miss Ellis or for her benefit."

"Just what did he want in that connection?"

"He said that it would be necessary for us to have a meeting in great secrecy."

"Did you arrange such a meeting?"

"After he told me that if I would see that he had the proxy for twenty thousand shares, and an unsecured loan of five thousand dollars, he would see that Fred Hedley would be placed in such a position that it would be impossible for him to marry Desere Ellis, I told him a meeting might be arranged."

"And what happened?"

"He told me that at a certain time on the evening of September twenty-first, I was to call a certain number; that that would be the number of a pay station; that the person who answered that number would give me another telephone number to call which would be the number of another pay station; that if I would call that number, I would be advised where to go in order to meet him."

"Did you make such a call as the first one?"

"Yes."

"And what were you told?"

"I was given the number of the other pay station, the number which I was to call."

"Was that the decedent, Rodger Palmer, with whom you were talking?"

"I don't know. The voice sounded disguised. It sounded like a man trying to talk in a high-pitched voice. It could even have been a woman. I thought at the time it was a man. Thinking back on it now I am not so sure."

"And you called the next number?"

"Yes."

"And what happened there?"

"A voice told me to go to the seventh tee at the Barclay Country Club, to be there just as soon as I could get there; that there had been some mix-up in time schedule; that the man I was to meet was going to be forced to leave in just a few minutes; that I was to get there at the earliest possible instant."

"Was anything said in any of these conversations about money?"

"Yes, I was to have five thousand dollars with me. If the information that was to be given me was as represented, I was to pay over the five thousand dollars."

"At the time of this telephone conversation, did you have occasion to notice the witness, Tom Fulton, who has previously testified?"

"Yes, sir, I saw him, but, of course, at that time, I had no idea he was taking any personal interest in me. I thought he was simply someone who was in a hurry to use the telephone. He came up to the telephone booth and made some sort of signs to me and I motioned him to go away."

"Subsequently, did you know that he was following you?"

"No, sir."

"You left the phone booth in a hurry and went through some red lights and a boulevard stop?"

"I'm afraid that I was in such a hurry that I violated several sections of the vehicle code."

"And went to the country club?"

"Yes."

"You are a member of that club?"

"Yes."

"Did you know that you had been followed to that club, or followed part of the way?"

"No, sir."

"What did you do?"

"I parked my car, used my key and went in. I looked around for the night watchman but didn't see him. I hurried out on the links."

"You were familiar with the location of the seventh tee?"

"Yes."

"What did you do?"

"I hurried out there and looked around; saw no one,

132

but finally noticed a dark object lying on the ground. I bent over that object and it was the body of this man, Rodger Palmer."

"You knew him at the time?"

"I had not seen him previously. I had talked with him over the telephone. That was all."

"How many times?"

"Several times. First, after he had requested Desere Ellis to give her proxy and she had referred him to me. He had called me and then I had had several conversations with him over the telephone concerning a suggestion that I pay him for this information which he offered to give me."

"What time was it when you got to the Barclay Country Club?"

"It was just a few minutes before ten."

"What did you do after you discovered the body?"

"I looked around— That is, I wanted to make sure he was dead."

"And when you did make sure, then what did you do?"

"I got to my feet. My right foot encountered a hard object. I bent over to find out what it was, and saw that it was a gun."

"And then what did you do?"

"I realized it was my own gun and suddenly became panic-stricken."

"And what did you do?"

"I left the country club. I drove down the road for a short distance, threw the gun under a culvert where I hoped it would never be discovered; went to Ensenada in Mexico and registered at the Siesta del Tarde Auto Court under the name Frank Kerry."

"Frank is one of your names?"

"Yes, my full name is Frank Kerry Dutton."

"You recognized the gun as your own?"

"I thought it was mine, yes."

"And you knew you had given that gun to Desere Ellis?"

"Yes."

"Were you trying to protect Desere Ellis in—"

"Objected to," Hamilton Burger said, "incompetent, irrelevant and immaterial, argumentative, leading and suggestive."

"Sustained," Judge Alvarado said.

"Cross-examine," Mason snapped.

Hamilton Burger, the district attorney, masked his true feelings behind a façade of extreme courtesy as he arose and approached the witness.

"I have a few questions," he said. "Simply for the purpose of clarifying your story in my own mind and for the jury, Mr. Dutton. I take it you have no objections?"

"Certainly not," Dutton said.

It was quite apparent that Hamilton Burger, having been warned by Mason, would make every effort to tear him to pieces. The defendant was agreeably surprised by this attitude on the part of the prosecutor.

"We'll start in with finding the body," Hamilton Burger said. "What time was it that you arrived at the seventh tee? I believe you said it was a minute or two after ten?"

"Yes, sir."

"Well, we should be able to clarify it a little better than that," Burger said. "You were in a hurry?"

"Yes."

"Is there, by any chance, a clock on the dashboard of your automobile?"

"There is."

"Was it accurate on the night in question?"

"I try to keep it accurate, yes, sir."

"Well, now," Burger said, smiling, "from the manner in which you make that statement, I gather that it is a habit of yours to be punctual and to know what time it is?"

"Yes, sir."

"So you keep your clock accurate at all times?"

"I try to, yes."

"Now, having made an appointment for that night

134

and being in a great hurry, you undoubtedly looked at your clock several times while you were driving from the telephone booth to the golf club—you must have."

"I'm quite sure I did," Dutton said, matching the district attorney's affable courtesy.

"Exactly," Hamilton Burger said, his voice low and well modulated, "so you must be able to tell the jury what you mean by a minute or two after ten?"

"I would say that it was one minute before ten when I entered the golf club. I think I arrived there and had parked the car at one minute after ten."

"I see," Hamilton Burger said, "and how long did it take you to get to the seventh tee?"

"I would say about three minutes."

"So you arrived at the seventh tee at exactly four minutes after ten?"

"We could give or take a few seconds, but for practical purposes, right around four minutes after ten."

"So it takes you about three minutes to go from the seventh tee to the clubhouse?"

"Yes."

"Now, you have heard the detective, Tom Fulton, testify that you left the golf club at ten-twenty-two?"

"Yes, sir."

"Did you, by any chance, look at the clock on your automobile when you left?"

"I was rather excited. I didn't look at the clock at that exact moment. No, I remember I did look at it when I stopped the car at the culvert."

"And what time was it then?"

Dutton smiled. "Frankly, I have forgotten, Mr. Burger. The time registered with me but it didn't seem to have any particular significance. I do remember, however, looking at the clock. I think it was right around ten-twenty-five or something like that. I am not sure."

"Why did you glance at the clock?"

"Just a mechanical reflex, I guess."

"I see," Hamilton Burger said. And then suddenly

added, "Oh, by the way, had you made up your mind to go to Ensenada at that time?"

"I was thinking of it, yes."

"So," Burger said casually, "you probably were checking the time to figure about how long it would take you to make the trip."

"I could have been, yes."

"Well, that sounds very reasonable," Burger said.

Dutton nodded.

"Now, let's see," Burger went on, "you got to the seventh tee at four minutes past ten. You were expecting to meet Rodger Palmer there, and, of course, expected him to be alive?"

"Yes, sir."

"There was a glow in the sky, that is, you could see the reflection of the lights of the city?"

"Yes, sir, quite a glow."

"Enough light for you to walk by and find your way?"

"Yes, sir."

"Not bright light, but a diffused light such as one would naturally expect on a golf course from the lights of the city reflected by the atmospheric impurities?"

"Yes, sir."

"And if Rodger Palmer had been standing up to meet you when you reached the seventh tee, he would have stood silhouetted against the skyline?"

"Yes, sir."

"Then you must have suspected something was wrong almost immediately on reaching the seventh tee and failing to see him?"

"I think I did. I think that's what started me looking around."

"Looking around?"

"Yes."

"What do you mean by looking around?"

"Well, taking a few steps; looking on the ground."

"Looking *on the ground?*" Hamilton Burger said, his voice suddenly changing. "So, you began looking for the man you were to meet on the ground?"

"Well, I was looking around. He wasn't standing up. He had to be someplace if he was there."

"I see," Hamilton Burger said, "so within a few seconds of the time you arrived at the seventh tee you began looking for him on the ground?"

"I didn't say within a few seconds."

"No, you didn't," Hamilton Burger said, "but it follows as a necessary inference. You expected him to meet you. You looked around; you didn't see him outlined against the lights of the horizon. So you started looking around. Now, it didn't take you over two or three seconds to ascertain that he wasn't standing up silhouetted against the horizon. Isn't that right?"

"Yes, sir."

"So then, right away, you began looking around—You'll pardon me, Mr. Dutton, I want to be fair with you. I want to see that the jury understands your story, that's all. It was within a few seconds, wasn't it?"

"Yes, I guess it was."

"So, you were then looking on the ground at least by five minutes after ten?"

"I guess I must have been, yes."

"And as soon as you looked on the ground, you discovered the body?"

"Well, not right away."

"But within a matter of seconds, eight or ten seconds?"

"I don't know that it was eight or ten seconds."

"Well, let's time it," Hamilton Burger said. "Just get up from the witness stand, if you will, and start walking around in a circle. I'll consult my watch and let you know when ten seconds are up."

The witness got up from the stand and started walking. He made a circle, then another circle.

"That's ten seconds," Hamilton Burger said. "Now then, considering your starting place as being at the seventh tee, would the body have been within that circle?"

"Well, perhaps a little wider circle."

"Then, perhaps it was twenty seconds after you started looking around that you found him?"

"I would say so. Perhaps even as much as thirty seconds."

"Thirty seconds would be the extreme limit?"

"I would say so, yes, sir."

"All right, then, within that circle that you made in thirty seconds, your foot struck against something?"

"Well, I saw something dark and prodded it with my foot."

"And found it was a body?"

"Yes, sir."

"And immediately dropped to your knees?"

"Yes, sir."

"Now then," Hamilton Burger said, "that was within thirty seconds. Let's say that you dropped to your knees—Oh, let's give you plenty of time, Mr. Dutton. Let's say that by six minutes past ten you had dropped to your knees by the side of the body."

"Yes, sir."

"That seems fair to you?"

"I think it is very fair."

"And you ascertained at once the man was dead?"

"Well, within a few seconds."

"Ten seconds again, Mr. Dutton?"

"I would say so, yes. Well within ten seconds."

"Now then," Hamilton Burger said, "you ascertained the man was dead and then what?"

"Well, I was just going to run and call the police when my foot struck against something heavy and I reached down and saw it was this gun."

"And then what did you do?"

"I recognized the gun as mine."

"You were sure it was yours?"

"I felt certain it was."

"So then what?"

"Then I suddenly realized I was in a peculiar position."

"One would certainly say so," Hamilton Burger said. "In fact, that's the understatement of the week. You *were* in a *most peculiar* position."

138

"Yes, sir."

"So you wanted to stop and take a while to think it over?"

"Yes, sir."

"Now, eventually you reached a decision and decided to leave the golf club without reporting the fact that you had found the body to the police?"

"Yes, sir."

"Once you reached that decision, you hurried from the seventh tee, out through the clubhouse, crossed to where your car was parked, jumped in and drove away?"

"Yes, sir."

"Now then, we have that time fixed," Hamilton Burger said. "That was ten-twenty-two. Now, by ten-o-six you had found the body and found the gun; that left you with an interval of over *fifteen minutes,* Mr. Dutton."

"Well, I didn't think it was that long."

"The indisputable evidence shows that it *was* that long, Mr. Dutton. An interval of fifteen minutes, during which time you were sitting by the corpse, holding that gun."

"It *couldn't* have been that long."

"What else were you doing?" Burger asked.

"I— Nothing else."

"Fifteen minutes," Hamilton Burger said. "A quarter of an hour. What were you trying to do, Mr. Dutton?"

"I was trying to clarify the situation."

"Were you, perhaps, concealing any evidence?"

"Certainly not. I wouldn't do that."

"But you knew the gun was evidence?"

"I assumed it was."

"And you concealed that."

"I took it with me."

"And concealed it in a culvert?"

"Yes, sir."

"So then you *did* conceal evidence?"

"Well, yes."

"Then there's no need in assuming a self-righteous attitude in front of this jury," Hamilton Burger said, "that

139

you wouldn't conceal evidence. So, I'm going to ask you again, what you were doing during those fifteen long minutes, during that quarter of an hour that you sat there in the dark by the corpse?"

"I don't know. I was trying to adjust myself."

"Now, you could see the sky. That was rather well lighted?"

"Yes, the horizon was lighted."

"But the ground was dark?"

"Well, not too dark."

"But dark enough so that you didn't see the body immediately?"

"I saw something dark."

"But you have just told us that it took from twenty to thirty seconds; in your own words, you were walking around for perhaps thirty seconds."

"Well, it wasn't that long. It was— I'll go back to my original statement that it was eight or ten seconds."

"Then you want to change your testimony that it was not thirty seconds?"

"I think the thirty seconds was an estimate of time that you placed on it. I said it was longer than ten seconds; that it might have been twenty seconds and you said you would give me thirty seconds to be sure and be fair."

"Yes, yes," Hamilton Burger said, "then your own estimate was twenty seconds?"

"Yes, sir."

"But *now* you say you think it was less than ten seconds."

"Well, after all, I didn't carry a stopwatch."

"That's right," Hamilton Burger said, "you didn't carry a stopwatch but you did testify to this jury under oath that you thought it was longer than ten seconds; that it might have been twenty seconds."

"Well, yes."

"Now you insist that it was under ten seconds."

"I think it could have been."

"Which was right?" Hamilton Burger asked, his voice taking on an edge, "ten seconds or twenty seconds?"

"I would say nearer ten seconds."

"Now, you picked up this gun?"

"Yes."

"And thought it was yours?"

"Yes."

"What made you think so?"

"Well, I saw it was a Smith and Wesson revolver of exactly the same type I had purchased."

"You *saw* it was a Smith and Wesson revolver?"

"Yes, sir."

"How could you do that if it was so dark you couldn't see the corpse for a matter of ten or twenty seconds? How in the world could you tell the make of the gun?"

"I had a small pocket flashlight."

"You *what?*" Hamilton Burger exclaimed, as though the defendant had just admitted to murder.

"I had a small pocket flashlight."

"Well, why in the world didn't you tell us about that?"

"Nobody asked me."

"Oh, you had a pocket flashlight with you and you didn't tell us about it because no one asked you."

"That's right."

"Do you have any other incriminating admissions to make that you have hitherto withheld because nobody has asked you?"

"I don't consider that an incriminating admission."

"You don't!" Hamilton Burger said. "You now admit you had a flashlight, why didn't you use that flashlight when you were looking around?"

"Well, it was in my pocket."

"And you were too lazy to take it out of your pocket?"

"Not too lazy. I saw no need for it."

"But you started searching the ground?"

"Yes."

"For an interval of at least ten seconds?"

"Perhaps that."

"And it never occurred to you to get out the flashlight?"

"Not then."

"Did you subsequently illuminate the body with your flashlight?"

"No."

"Why not?"

"I was only trying to ascertain whether he was dead."

"Well, well, well," Hamilton Burger said, "you had a flashlight and you weren't sufficiently interested to look at the man's features to see if you knew him?"

"I had never met Rodger Palmer. I had talked with him over the telephone."

"So you assumed the body was that of Rodger Palmer?"

"Yes."

"That was only an assumption on your part?"

"Yes."

"It could have been anyone else?"

"Well, it could have been."

"You weren't curious enough to look with a flashlight?"

"No."

"In other words, you *knew* the identity of the body, didn't you, Mr. Dutton?"

"No, sir. I tell you I didn't. I only assumed it."

"But as soon as you found the gun, you looked at *it* with a flashlight?"

"Yes."

"To make sure it was a Smith and Wesson revolver?"

"Yes."

"Did you check the numbers on the gun?"

"I believe I did."

"And noticed that one shell had been fired?"

"Yes."

"And you then realized that you had left fingerprints all over the gun?"

"Yes."

"What did you do about those?"

"I took my handkerchief and wiped the gun thoroughly."

"Oh!" Hamilton Burger said. "You took your handkerchief and wiped the gun thoroughly?"

"Yes, sir."

"Thereby wiping off, not only your own fingerprints, but those of anyone else?"

"Yes, sir, I suppose so."

"And yet you have just assured us that *you* wouldn't do anything to conceal evidence, oh, no, not *you!* Why in the world did you wipe the fingerprints of the murderer off that gun?"

"I wanted to remove my own fingerprints."

"Why?"

"I was afraid—I was afraid that it was my gun and I might be connected with the murder."

"So, you had a guilty feeling that you might have been connected with the murder at least as early as six or seven minutes after ten o'clock that night?"

"Well, how would you feel if your gun had been there?"

"How would I feel?" Hamilton Burger said, drawing himself up to his full height. "I would feel that I was a law-abiding citizen and wanted the protection of the police immediately. I would have taken every possible step to have preserved the fingerprints of the murderer on that gun. I would have dashed to the nearest telephone. I would have called the police. I would have said, 'I think this is my gun. I think my fingerprints are on it, but the fingerprints of the murderer should also be on it.' I certainly wouldn't have taken a handkerchief and scrubbed the murderer's fingerprints off the gun, nor would I have stopped at a culvert and thrown the gun under a culvert, nor would I have— But, come, come, I digress, Mr. Dutton, you asked me a question and I answered it. I shouldn't have. I should be the one asking you questions. Now, after you had rubbed the fingerprints off that gun, what did you do?"

"I hurried off the golf course and got in my car."

"No, you didn't," Hamilton Burger said. "Your testimony shows that you waited another fourteen minutes. What were you doing during that fourteen minutes?"

"Well, I was rubbing the gun for one thing."

"Polishing it like mad, I suppose?"

"I polished it vigorously."

"You breathed your breath on it so that the moisture in your breath would condense on the metal and help eliminate the prints?"

"I believe I did blow on it, yes."

"Well, well," Hamilton Burger said, "and all this from a man who wouldn't presume to conceal evidence!"

Hamilton Burger shook his head as though bewildered at such depravity on the part of any human being, turned and started back to his chair. Then, as though actuated by some afterthought, turned back to the witness. "Well, let's ask you a few questions about the trust, Mr. Dutton. You say there was some hundred thousand dollars in the trust when you received it, and, after paying out a hundred thousand, there is approximately two hundred and fifty thousand left?"

"Yes, sir."

"And the Steer Ridge Oil Company stock, you sold that?"

"Yes."

"But the reason you were meeting with this man, Rodger Palmer, was to discuss making a deal with him in connection with Steer Ridge Oil Company proxies?"

"Yes, sir."

"I don't understand," Hamilton Burger said. "You had sold the Steer Ridge Oil Company stock?"

"Well, I had some other stock."

"Other stock, Mr. Dutton?"

"Yes."

"Other Steer Ridge Oil Company stock?"

"Yes."

"Well, well, tell us about that, by all means," Burger said.

"I had some stock that I had purchased myself."

"When did you purchase that?"

"The first batch was several weeks earlier, then I in-

144

creased my holdings to the original amount only a few days before the strike."

"And had been holding this stock?"

"Yes."

"You sold the stock which the trust fund held in the Steer Ridge Oil Company?"

"Yes, sir. I sold that stock."

"Why?"

"Well, I thought it was highly speculative. I didn't think it was a good investment for the trust."

"But it wasn't too highly speculative to be an investment for you, yourself, as an individual?"

"I could afford to take a chance."

"I see," Burger said. "Now, with reference to the sale of the stock from the trust fund, did you sell yourself the stock from the trust fund?"

"I got my stock later and I paid the market price for it."

"But it has gone up in value?"

"Yes."

"How much has it gone up in value?"

"Quite a bit."

"What price did you credit the trust fund from the sale of that Steer Ridge stock?"

"Around ten thousand dollars."

"And what is that stock worth now?"

"Two hundred thousand."

"So you made a hundred and ninety thousand dollars' profit out of betraying the interests of the beneficiary?"

"I did nothing of the kind."

"You sold the stock from the trust fund and bought shares of that same stock yourself?"

"Yes—when I felt a proxy fight was on."

"And that stock is now worth many times what you paid for it?"

"Yes."

"And how did you justify that action as trustee, Mr. Dutton?"

"I felt the stock was highly speculative. I didn't buy it because I wanted it, but to protect the trust fund."

"And just how would you protect the trust fund by buying the stock in your own name?"

"I felt that I could give it back in the event the stock went up."

"Oh, I see," Hamilton Burger said, "you were buying the stock. If the stock went down you intended to absorb the loss. If the stock went up you intended to turn over the profit to the trust?"

"Well, something like that."

"Something like that!" Hamilton Burger repeated sarcastically. "Now, have you turned this stock back to the trust?"

"Yes."

"And it is because of turning this stock back to the trust that the trust now is worth two hundred and fifty thousand dollars?"

"That accounts for still further profits."

"Well, this certainly seems like financial jugglery to me," Hamilton Burger said. "Perhaps you can explain it a little better, because, after all, I'm not a financier. I believe you are a professional financial counselor, Mr. Dutton?"

"Yes, sir. I represent several clients."

"And with these other clients, do you surreptitiously sell the profitable stock to yourself?"

"These other clients are on a different basis."

"I see. They're on a basis where they ask, from time to time, for an accounting. By the way, how many accountings have you ever made to Miss Ellis?"

"I have made none."

"When did you tell her about selling the stock of the Steer Ridge Oil Company?"

"I didn't tell her."

"You didn't tell her?"

"No."

"I believe you said she asked you to hang on to that stock?"

146

"She wanted me to, yes."

"You didn't tell her that you had sold it?"

"No, sir."

"You didn't tell her that you had sold it to yourself?"

"No, sir."

"Nor that you were making a handsome profit on it?"

"No, sir, and the stock I purchased was not the trust stock."

"Now, you say you conveyed that stock back to the trust fund?"

"Yes."

"If this wasn't trust fund stock, why did you convey it back to the trust fund? Was it conscience money?"

"No, sir."

"Then, if it wasn't trust fund stock, why give it back? And if it *was* trust fund stock, why juggle it out of the trust and into your name?"

"I can't answer that question any better than I have."

"When did you transfer this stock to the trust fund with reference to the date of September twenty-first, about what time?"

"It was right around that time."

"Right around that time?" Hamilton Burger repeated. "How interesting! In other words, it was right around the time that this man, Rodger Palmer, started telephoning you that you transferred the stock back to the trust fund?"

"His telephone calls had nothing to do with my actions."

"Well, what else had happened at about that time?" Burger asked. "Had you, by any chance, consulted an attorney at about that time?"

The witness hesitated.

"Had you?" Hamilton Burger snapped. "Yes or no. Had you consulted an attorney at about that time?"

"Yes."

"And did you tell the attorney that you had embezzled the stock held by the trust fund?"

"I told him that I had sold certain stocks from the trust fund, stocks that I felt were going down in value."

"So you bought those same stocks?"

"The Steer Ridge shares, yes, sir."

"Are you accustomed to buying stocks that you think are going down in value?"

"I sometimes take a chance."

"You buy the stocks you think are going down in value?"

"I mean I sometimes buy speculative stocks."

"But when you buy a speculative stock, you think it is going *up* in value?"

"I hope so."

"So, when you bought this Steer Ridge stock you thought it was going *up* in value?"

"Well, I knew there was a possibility."

"Yet, as trustee, knowing that the stock was one which the beneficiary wanted you to hold; knowing that it stood a good chance of going up in value, you sold it from the trust?"

"I thought that was the best thing to do."

"The best thing for whom? For the beneficiary, or yourself?"

"For the beneficiary."

"So, later on you bought an equal amount yourself," Hamilton Burger said, musingly, "and you turned it back into the trust fund just a short time before the murder, on the advice of an attorney, and you never told the beneficiary anything about what you had done and you never made an accounting in the trust. Well, well, I'm glad I cross-examined you, Mr. Dutton, because otherwise these matters wouldn't have come out and I think the jury is interested in them. You didn't intend to tell the jurors about all this, did you?"

"I wasn't asked."

"You mean, on your direct examination, your attorney carefully avoided asking you these questions?"

"Objected to as argumentative," Perry Mason said.

"Sustained," Judge Alvarado promptly ruled.

Hamilton Burger grinned broadly at the jurors. "That concludes my cross-examination," he said, and walked back to the counsel table with the triumphant air of a man who has at last gratified a lifelong ambition.

19

■

"CALL MR. HOLBROOK," Mason said.

George Holbrook— -tall, gangling, his weather-beaten face and somewhat shambling gait claiming the attention of the jurors—took the oath and assumed his position on the witness stand.

"Do you have occasion to remember the evening of September twenty-first of this year?" Mason asked.

"I sure do."

"There was something that happened on that evening which made an impression upon you?"

"Yes, sir."

"What was it?"

"My wife's sister came to visit."

"What time did she arrive?"

"Eleven-ten was when she actually got there at the airport."

"Did you go to the airport to meet her?"

"We sure did."

"Now, calling your attention to that evening, did anything happen earlier in the evening which aroused your attention, anything at all that was out of the ordinary?"

"Yes, sir."

"What was it?"

"About nine o'clock, just right around a minute or two after nine, I heard the sound of a shot."

Hamilton Burger jumped to his feet. "I move to strike

out the latter part of that answer as calling for a conclusion of the witness."

"Oh, I think the expression is common enough so we'll let it go," Judge Alvarado said. "You may cross-examine him on that point."

"Could you determine the direction of that sound?" Mason asked.

"It came from the golf links."

"Now, where is your home with reference to the golf links of the Barclay Country Club?"

"We're along a street that parallels the golf club."

"Are you familiar with the location of tee number seven?"

"Yes, sir."

"In order that there may be no mistake about it," Mason said, "I show you this map which has been introduced in evidence and ask you to notice the cross street nearest your house and the location of tee number seven."

"Yes, sir, I see it."

"About how far are you located from tee number seven?"

"About a hundred and fifty yards."

"Cross-examine," Mason said.

Hamilton Burger, on his feet, managed to get an expression of puzzled perplexity on his face as he turned to the judge and said, "If the Court please, I move to strike out this entire evidence as being incompetent, irrelevant and immaterial."

Judge Alvarado turned to Mason. "Do you care to explain your reason for calling this witness, Mr. Mason?"

"I will be glad to," Mason said. "The autopsy surgeon has testified that death occurred between nine-thirty in the evening and two-thirty A.M. the following morning.

"On cross-examination, the autopsy surgeon admitted that a doctor couldn't fix the time of death as accurately as if one was standing by with a stopwatch. Death could conceivably have occurred at nine o'clock in the evening.

"The defendant has testified that Palmer was dead when the defendant arrived on the scene. Death could well have occurred an hour earlier."

Hamilton Burger laughed and then apparently tried to control himself with an effort. "All of this," he said, "is predicated upon the fact that somebody heard an automobile backfire or a distant sonic boom or a tire blowing out; and under the persuasive influence of counsel's suggestion has been led to believe that it was a shot. And now he wants this jury to believe not only that it was *a* shot, but that it was *the* fatal shot. I submit, Your Honor, that this evidence is far too nebulous and fantastic, far too conjectural to even be cluttering up the record, let alone influencing the jury."

Judge Alvarado shook his head. "I think your argument goes to the weight rather than the admissibility of the evidence, Mr. Prosecutor. The Court is going to allow the evidence to remain in. You may, of course, further amplify your point by cross-examination."

Hamilton Burger heaved a sigh, as much as to indicate to the jury the tribulations with which a district attorney had to contend, then turned to the witness. "How do you know it was nine o'clock?" he asked.

"I was out on the porch smoking and suddenly realized it was time for a favorite television program."

"What kind of a program?"

"A newscaster and analyst."

"You say it's a favorite of yours?"

"Yes."

"Do you listen every night?"

"Almost every night, yes."

"And is that the only program that you listen to?"

"Oh, no."

"You listen to others?"

"Certainly."

"What is the nature of these other programs you listen to?"

"Well, I have two or three favorite newscasters."

"Such as what?"

"Well, I have Carleton Kenny. I try to listen to him every night."

"Oh, yes," Hamilton Burger said, "he comes on at eleven o'clock?"

"Yes, sir."

"And what others?"

"Well, two or three others."

"What was the program you were listening to at nine o'clock when you heard this sound which you took to be a shot?"

"I was listening to Ralph Woodley."

"Woodley?" Hamilton Burger said.

"No, no," the witness corrected himself, "I meant George Tillman."

"Now, just a minute," Hamilton Burger said. "You said first it was Woodley you were listening to."

"Well, I thought it was. That is, I suddenly realized—"

Hamilton Burger said, "You suddenly realized that one program comes on at nine o'clock and the other program comes on at ten. You said that you were listening to Woodley. *He* comes on at ten, does he not?"

"Yes, sir."

"And when I asked you to give the program you were listening to, the name Woodley slipped out before you thought."

"It was an inadvertent slip of the tongue."

"But when I asked you, you said before you had any opportunity to think that you were listening to Woodley's program."

"Yes."

"Then the shot could have been at ten o'clock."

"No, sir, the shot I heard was at nine o'clock. It was just before I went in to tune in the nine o'clock program, the last thirteen minutes of it."

Hamilton Burger, his manner suddenly magnanimous, said, "Now, Mr. Holbrook, I don't want to take any unfair advantage of you. I want you to listen carefully. Suppose I should assure you, as I do now assure you, that two reputable citizens who lived even closer to the seventh tee than you do are prepared to swear that shortly after ten o'clock, just as the Woodley program was going on the air, they heard a single pistol shot, or a sound which they interpreted as being a pistol shot coming from the direction of tee number seven. Would that testimony change your recollection and would you then state that the sound you heard, which you took to be a shot, was at ten o'clock rather than nine o'clock?"

George Holbrook seemed for a moment completely baffled. Then he slowly shook his head. "I thought it was nine o'clock," he said.

"I know you did," Hamilton Burger said, his manner suddenly sympathetic, "but you *could* have been mistaken. There was a lot of excitement that night. You went to pick up your wife's sister?"

"Yes, sir."

"And how did it happen that you didn't report the matter to the police the next morning when you read of the murder?"

"I didn't read of the murder," Holbrook said. "We decided to take a trip and we threw some things together late that night, got three or four hours' sleep and took off at daylight the next morning."

"Oh, yes," Hamilton Burger said. "And how long were you gone, Mr. Holbrook?"

"Three weeks."

"And you didn't know anything about the murder all the time you were gone?"

"I knew about it but didn't know that it had taken place on the golf links right across from our front porch, so to speak."

"So you didn't realize the importance of this sound you had heard until some three weeks later?"

"Yes, sir—sometime later."

"And then you tried to reconstruct in your mind the exact date that you had heard this shot?"

"Yes, sir."

"And the time you had heard the shot?"

"Yes, sir."

"After an interval of three weeks?"

"Yes, sir."

"Three full weeks?"

"Yes, sir."

"And it could have been while you were listening to the Woodley program, just as you said when I first asked you?"

"Yes, I thought it was the— No, no, wait a minute. The Woodley program comes on at *ten* o'clock. This was at *nine* o'clock."

Hamilton Burger smiled indulgently. "If the other witnesses fix it as being when the Woodley program was on the air, would you change your testimony once more, Mr. Holbrook, and again say that it was at the time of the Woodley program?"

"Well, I . . . I thought it was at nine o'clock."

"You thought it was," Hamilton Burger said, his manner suddenly stern, and then leaning forward and fixing the witness with a direct gaze. "You can't swear to it, can you?"

George Holbrook thought for a long moment, then said, "No, I can't positively swear to it."

"Thank you," Hamilton Burger said. "That's all."

Hamilton Burger turned away from the witness, glanced at the jury and for a moment a swift grin came over his features. Then he masked his face as though desperately trying to keep his emotions concealed from the jury.

"Very well," he said, "that's all."

Judge Alvarado said, "I have a matter which has been on the calendar for some time set for this hour and it's a matter I have to take care of. I am going to continue this case until tomorrow morning at ten o'clock. During the recess of the Court, the jurors will remember the usual admonition of the Court not to form or express any opinion as to the guilt or innocence of the defendant, and to refrain from discussing the case among yourselves, and particularly not to let anyone discuss it with you. Court is recessed until ten o'clock tomorrow."

As the spectators started filing out, Dutton leaned toward Mason. "How did I do," he asked, "—on the stand?"

Mason, putting papers in his briefcase, said, "About the way I expected."

"You don't sound too enthusiastic."

Mason shook his head and said, "Go ahead and get a night's sleep and try to forget about the case. No one ever knows what a jury is going to do."

The lawyer nodded to the bailiff and to the officer who was coming forward to take Dutton into custody, managed a reassuring smile for Della Street, then walked out of the courtroom, his shoulders squared, his manner confident, his chin up, his stomach cold.

20

■

BACK IN his office, all of Mason's assurance vanished.

"Well?" Della Street asked.

"Get Paul Drake," Mason said. "We've got to do *something* or our man is going to be convicted of first-degree murder."

"What can you do?" Della Street asked.

"We've got to do something," Mason said. "We're going to have to think up something."

"You think it's that bad?"

"I know it's that bad. The idea of Dutton bucket-shopping the stocks in the trust fund and deliberately deceiving the beneficiary into believing the trust fund was being exhausted just didn't sit well with that jury."

Della said, "Paul Drake's on his way down here now."

155

A few moments later, Drake's code knock sounded on the door, and Della opened it to admit the detective.

Drake raised inquiring eyebrows and Della shook her head.

Mason, pacing the floor, was engrossed in thought.

Drake slipped across to the client's chair and seated himself.

Mason said, "We've got to pull a rabbit out of the hat, Paul."

Drake nodded.

Mason continued his pacing the floor. "Something dramatic. Something that will drive home our contention."

"How does it look?" Drake asked.

"You know how it looks," Mason said, without changing the tempo of his stride or even glancing at the detective. "Hamilton Burger has alienated any sympathy the jurors might have had for the defendant. He's mixed up the only witness we had who could give any evidence that would enable us to talk about reasonable doubt."

"You've licked him so many times in front of a jury," Paul Drake said, "that I think you're being unduly pessimistic this time."

Mason shook his head. "Usually Hamilton Burger doesn't have a chance to strut his stuff. I get the witness on cross-examination and uncover some point which enables me to prove that the prosecution's theory of the case is erroneous. Before he's ready to rest his case, he doesn't have any case left.

"This time I've had to go ahead and put witnesses on the stand. Burger has had a chance to cross-examine them. The roles have been reversed. He's ripped my witnesses to pieces."

"Do you think it's true that he has two witnesses who will swear it was at ten o'clock the shot was heard?"

"It has to be true," Mason said. "Of course, I'm going to have a chance to cross-examine those witnesses and, believe me, Paul, there's something queer about that."

"What do you mean?"

"If they had been as positive as he makes them sound,

he'd have put them on the witness stand as part of his case in chief. The fact that he's holding them for rebuttal indicates that he didn't intend to use them unless he had to."

"Do you think he'll just back away from the question now that he's got our witness confused?" Drake asked.

"I won't let him," Mason said. "I'm going to insist that he put those two witnesses on the stand and then I'm going to cross-examine them. I may get a break out of it, but I may not. I don't know. All I know is that the way the case looks at present, we've got a defendant who is headed for the gas chamber or for life imprisonment."

"Any suggestions?" Drake asked.

"I'm thinking of one right now."

"Such as what?"

Mason said, "Paul, start pulling wires. I want to get the latest and best metal detector that money can buy. I understand there are some new ones that are very sensitive."

"You mean mine detectors?" Drake asked.

"So-called," Mason said.

"And what do we do?"

"We go out to the Barclay Country Club and we start sweeping around the grass out in the vicinity of the seventh tee."

"Looking for what?"

"An expended cartridge."

Drake said, "Don't be silly, Perry! The murder was committed with a revolver. A revolver doesn't eject a fired cartridge."

"But a person who fires a revolver could eject a cartridge," Mason said.

"What do you mean?"

"If the murder was committed at nine o'clock, then someone who wanted a Patsy could have arranged to have Dutton out there at ten o'clock and then fired a shot the minute Dutton's car hove into sight at the golf club. Then he could have tossed the gun to the ground beside the corpse and sneaked back down through the low places where he wouldn't show against the silhouetted horizon and made his escape, leaving Dutton to hold the sack."

"And so?" Drake asked.

"And so," Mason said, "we go out on the golf course and start exploring with a mine detector."

"This is right during the busy time of the afternoon as far as that golf course is concerned," Drake said. "Court adjourned early and if we go out there now, we'll interfere with a lot of doctors and dentists, bankers and professional men playing their mid-week round of golf."

Mason nodded.

"They'd kick us out," Drake said.

"Well?" Mason asked.

Drake looked at him and grinned. "You mean you'd like to attract attention?"

"Why not?"

"It wouldn't prove anything," Drake said.

"But the fact that we were out there looking for an extra shell would show that *we* attached considerable importance to Holbrook's testimony."

Drake thought the matter over for a while, then grinned. "I suppose you wouldn't object if the newspaper reporters knew about it?"

"Not at all," Mason said. "In fact, anything that we do might become quite newsworthy."

"The judge has instructed the jury not to read the newspapers," Drake said.

Mason looked at him and grinned, then turned to Della Street. "This, Della," he said, "is business. Go to the most exclusive, most expensive place in the city where you can get a sport outfit which will attract the roving masculine eye. Get a golfing outfit. Money is no object, but it has to be a city editor's dream—one that will look so good in a photograph, and on you, it would make a page one placement."

Della Street jumped to her feet. "Watch me go through that door," she said.

■

21

A RATHER DIGNIFIED group of afternoon golfers watched Perry Mason, Paul Drake, Della Street, and one of Drake's operatives as they marched across the golf links toward the seventh tee carrying a portable metal detector.

Mason smiled affably at the group waiting at the tee. "Don't let me disturb your game, gentlemen. We'll wait until you drive."

"Until we drive?" one of the men asked.

Mason smiled and nodded toward Drake's operative who was carrying the metal detector.

"What's that?" the golfer asked.

"You knew, of course, about the murder that had been committed here," Mason said. "We're looking for evidence."

"What sort of evidence?"

"We think perhaps there's— Well, perhaps it isn't wise to disclose my hand in advance. There's perhaps something here that will have a bearing on the case."

The golfers crowded around, their game forgotten.

"You're Perry Mason," one of the men said, "the famous attorney."

Mason bowed and smiled. "Paul Drake, my private detective, one of his operatives, and—most important of all—Miss Street, my confidential secretary."

Della Street, attired in a form-fitting short skirt which the wind whipped about her knees, gave the men her most engaging smile.

Other golfers came up.

"Well," Mason said to the operative, "we may as well go to work."

The man plugged earphones in his ears, set the electrical dials so they were in proper balance, then started moving slowly along through the taller grass to the sides of the teeing-off place.

Within a matter of moments, fifty spectators had formed in a ring.

On the tee someone said, "It's your honor."

"To hell with the golf," the man said. "This is a lot more exciting. I'll concede every hole from here on in and pay off at that price. Let's see what's happening."

Word passed like wildfire around the links. Soon the manager of the club came hurrying out to find out what was going on.

At first he was frowningly uncompromising. Then as he saw the interest of the golfers, he became mollified and, after a few moments, hurried toward the clubhouse.

Drake said in an undertone to Perry Mason, "He's suddenly become publicity conscious, Perry. He's headed for a telephone to call the press."

"Well," Mason said in an equally low tone, "I'm certain nothing that *we* said could have prompted that idea."

"Moreover," Drake added, "he's about thirty minutes too late."

Mason gave the detective a searching look. "Your ethics are showing, Paul."

"It's all right," Drake said. "*If* my man should find anything, we'd have to tell the police about it, but there's nothing in the code of ethics which says I can't tell the press where I'm searching."

"As a lawyer," Mason said, "I couldn't use publicity in any way. It would be unethical."

Drake grinned. "I knew why you wanted *me* along on this one—at least, I thought I did."

The man with the metal detector moved slowly along, weaving the flat pan back and forth just over the surface of the grass back toward the green on the sixth hole, then down along the edge of a sand trap into the rough; back to the sand trap again, then down into the rough.

Suddenly he said, "Hey, I've got something!"

"Well, let's see what it is," Mason said.

The man held the pan of the device directly over the spot.

Drake, down on his hands and knees, felt with exploring fingertips in the grass. "I've got it," he said, and came up with an empty brass cartridge case.

Mason said jubilantly, "Drive a peg of some sort in the ground at the exact place where that was found, Paul. Let's mark it."

Drake took a small metal surveyor's stake from the place where he had been carrying it in his belt and pushed it into the ground, then tied a bright red ribbon in the loop.

"Camera?" Mason asked.

Della Street handed Mason a camera.

The lawyer circled the place, taking a dozen pictures from all different angles, showing the location with reference to all the fixed landmarks.

Then the lawyer carefully dropped the cartridge case into a pocket formed in a pocket handkerchief. Drake scratched the case. Mason examined it with a pocket magnifier.

The crowd of golfers, pushing closer, were almost breathing down the necks of the triumphant searchers.

"Just what does this mean?" one of the golfers asked.

Mason said, "It means that we now have corroboration— Well, I hadn't better discuss it here."

The lawyer looked up with a smile that was all but cherubic in its innocence. "I wouldn't want to be accused of trying to influence public thinking," he said. "You can look in the papers tomorrow and find much more than I am in a position to tell you now."

Drake touched Mason's arm. "Let's go where we can talk," he said.

Mason nodded, took Paul Drake's arm and smiled affably at the circle of golfers.

"If you'll pardon us just for a minute," he said, "we have a matter to discuss."

Mason led Drake through the circle which opened for them and over toward the rough.

"Well?" Mason asked.

Drake said, "Look, Perry, it's not up to me to tell you how to try a lawsuit, but you're going to get a terrific amount of publicity out of this."

"Well?" Mason asked.

"And it's going to backfire," Drake said. "If we had found a cartridge that had been taken from a revolver and thrown away, we'd have had something; but this is a shell that has been ejected from an automatic—a thirty-two-caliber automatic at that—and the murder gun is a thirty-eight-caliber snub-nosed Smith and Wesson revolver."

"And so?" Mason asked.

"So," Drake said, "no matter how you look at it, the thing can't be evidence."

"What do you mean it can't be evidence?" Mason said. "It was here. It's an expended cartridge."

"But there weren't *two* guns."

"How do you know there weren't?" Mason asked.

"Well, of course, we don't know, but we can surmise."

"Leave the surmising for the district attorney," Mason said. "You and I have just discovered a most important piece of evidence."

"Well, of course, it could be made to fit into your theory," Drake said, "but it would take a lot of high-pressure salesmanship to convince the jury that it meant anything."

"After all," Mason told him, "a lawyer is, or should be, an expert in the field of high-pressure salesmanship. Come on, let's get back to complete the search."

"What do you mean, complete the search?"

"Well," Mason said, "we wouldn't want to call it off when the search was incomplete."

"How much more do you intend to search?"

"Well, quite a bit," Mason said. "We want to be sure there's nothing else here."

"I get you," Drake said, wearily. "You're going to stall

along until the newspapers start covering what we're doing."

Mason's eyes became wide. "Why, Paul Drake, how you talk," he said. "We're doing nothing of the sort. We're simply completing the search."

Drake said suddenly, "Look here, Perry, did *you* drop that cartridge case so my man could find it?"

"Of course not."

"Did Della?"

"You'll have to ask her."

"The district attorney will claim you planted it either in advance or while we were searching."

"Can he prove it?" Mason asked.

"Good Lord, I hope not!"

"So do I," Mason said. "Come on, Paul, let's get back to work."

The circle of interested spectators opened for the lawyer and the detective. Mason said to the operative, "All right, I think we've found what we were looking for, but let's just make sure there's nothing else here. Let's complete the search."

Slowly, a step at a time, they moved around the golf course until Drake nudged Mason's arm.

The lawyer looked up to see a newspaper reporter and a photographer with a camera and flashgun hurrying toward them.

"Keep right on with your search," Mason told the operative with the metal detector, "although I think we've just about covered the ground here. I think we have everything we need."

The reporter hurried up, pushed his way through the circle of spectators, said to Mason, "What's going on here, Mr. Mason?"

Mason frowned as though the interruption were unwelcome. "We're looking for evidence," he said shortly.

"What sort of evidence?"

Mason thought for a long moment, then grudgingly admitted, "Well, as you can see for yourself, it's metallic evidence."

Someone in the crowd said, "They've already found one empty cartridge case."

"An empty cartridge case?" the reporter asked.

Mason nodded.

"May we see it?"

Mason said, "We're trying to preserve it as intact as possible."

He took a handkerchief from his pocket, carefully unfolded it and showed the reporter the cartridge case nesting in the cloth. "Don't touch it," he warned. "I doubt if anyone can find any fingerprints on it, but we certainly don't want the evidence contaminated."

The reporter pulled out some folded newsprint from his pocket, took a soft, 6-B pencil and started scribbling.

The photographer fed flashbulbs into the gun on his camera. He shot two closeup pictures of the cartridge, then backed away and took two pictures of the group, carefully including Della Street.

Mason very gently folded the handkerchief back over the cartridge case and put it in his pocket.

"Well," he said, "I think we have completed the search. I guess we found everything that was here."

He waited an appreciable moment, then added, "I may say that we've found everything that we thought was here."

"Just what caused you to think that cartridge was here, Mr. Mason?" the reporter asked.

Mason gave the question careful consideration. "There were," he said at length, "two shots. One at nine o'clock, one at approximately one hour later. Two shots mean two cartridges. There was only one empty cartridge in the gun which the police contend was the murder weapon."

"But that was a revolver," the reporter said. "This cartridge case that you have was ejected from an automatic."

"Exactly," Mason said, with an enigmatic smile, and then added, "I don't think I should be giving an interview at this time. Come on, folks, let's go."

22

JUDGE ALVARADO surveyed the crowded courtroom with something' of a frown. "The jurors seem to be all present, and the defendant is in court," he said. "I trust that the jurors have heeded the admonition of the Court and have neither listened to radio or television nor read papers concerning the case. I know that this imposes a hardship upon jurors, but the only alternative is to have jurors locked up for the duration of the trial and that is even more of a hardship.

"The jury will remember and heed the admonition of the Court. Gentlemen, you may proceed if you are ready."

"We are ready," Hamilton Burger said.

"We are ready, Your Honor," Mason rejoined.

"Then call your next witness."

Mason said, "Mr. Paul Drake, will you take the stand, please?"

Drake held up his hand, was sworn and took his position on the witness stand.

"What is your occupation?" Mason asked.

"I am a private detective."

"Are you familiar with the Barclay Country Club in this city?"

"I am."

"Are you familiar with the particular portion of the club which is in the vicinity of the seventh tee?"

"Yes, sir."

"When were you last there?"

"Yesterday afternoon at about three to four o'clock."

"What were you doing on the golf course at that hour?"

"I was participating in a search of the territory immediately adjacent to the seventh tee."

"Were you using your eyes or did you have some mechanical assistance?"

"We had a metal detector."

"And did you, at that time, discover anything?"

"Yes, sir."

"What?"

"We discovered a thirty-two-caliber empty, brass cartridge case."

"What did you do with that?"

"You took it into your possession."

Mason approached the witness and said, "I ask you if you made any identifying mark upon that cartridge case?"

"Yes, sir, a small scratch with the point of my knife."

"I show you an empty cartridge case and ask you if that is the cartridge case."

"Yes, sir, that is the one we found."

"If the Court please, we ask this be introduced in evidence as Defendant's Exhibit Number One," Mason said.

Hamilton Burger, on his feet, smiled at the court. "I believe, if the Court please, I have the right to examine the witness on *voir dire*."

"You certainly do," Judge Alvarado said. "Proceed."

"You state that you are a private detective, Mr. Drake?" Hamilton Burger asked, facing the witness.

"Yes, sir."

"You do a great deal of work for Mr. Perry Mason?"

"Yes, sir."

"Does his work account for all of your income?"

"No, sir, not all of it."

"A substantial part of it?"

"Yes, sir."

"As much as ninety per cent?"

"No, I would say perhaps as much as seventy-five per cent."

"I see," Hamilton Burger said. "Now, what are your regular rates of payment?"

"Fifty dollars a day and expenses."

"That is figured on an eight-hour day?"

"Theoretically, yes."

"That is something over six dollars an hour," Hamilton Burger said, "over ten cents a minute. Now, I take it that you are a good businessman and as such you strive to give Mr. Mason value received?"

"We try to keep our clients satisfied. Yes, sir."

"And you try to find what they want?"

"If we can do so, yes."

"You knew when you went out to the golf links that you were going to be searching for an empty cartridge case?"

"I so understood."

"And this cartridge case which you say that you found, there is nothing about it to show when it was fired?"

"No, sir."

"Nor is there anything about it to show when it was dropped on the ground."

"No, sir."

"It could have been dropped on the ground as much as a year ago?"

"I presume so."

"Or it could have been dropped to the ground within a matter of seconds before you so fortuitously found it."

Drake said, "There is nothing about the cartridge case, nor was there anything on the ground telling how long it had been on the ground."

"It could have been a matter of seconds?"

"I presume it *could* have been dropped at any time before we started searching."

"Or it might have been dropped during the search?" Burger asked with a sneer.

"I don't think so."

"You don't *think* so. Can you swear that it hadn't been?"

"I was watching."

"Were you watching every one of the people in your group all the time? Were you watching all of the assembled curiosity seekers who ceased playing golf to cluster around you?"

"It was physically impossible to watch everyone."

"So anyone in that group could have taken advantage of a time when your back was turned and tossed that empty cartridge case out into the grass?"

"I presume so, yes."

"That empty cartridge case has no commercial value?"

"No."

"But the value of your relationship with Mr. Mason is very great. In other words, his business represents an income of many thousands of dollars a year to you, does it not?"

"It has in the past."

"And you hope it will in the future?"

"Yes, sir."

"As long as you continue to serve him diligently."

"Yes, sir."

"And manage to *find* the articles that he wants you to find."

"I simply work to the best of my ability," Drake said.

"That is all," Hamilton Burger said, as he walked back to the counsel table with a manner that indicated that he was deliberately and contemptuously turning his back on the witness.

Mason, observing the gesture, whispered to Della Street, "The old so-and-so is certainly a past master of courtroom strategy."

"That concludes your *voir dire?*" Judge Alvarado asked Burger.

"Yes, sir."

"The defense has offered this in evidence. Do you have any objection?"

"I certainly do, Your Honor. I object on the ground it is incompetent, irrelevant and immaterial. It is a physical impossibility that this could have been fired from the murder weapon. Therefore, it has no significance standing by itself. The only possible significance could be in the place where it was found, or the time when it was found; and it has just been shown by the evidence of this witness who so fortuitously participated in *finding* this cartridge case, that it is impossible to vouch for the time when it was placed there."

"Nevertheless," Judge Alvarado said, "I think that, while your objection goes to the weight rather than to the admissibility of the evidence, the Court is going to allow this to be received in evidence. Counsel will have ample opportunity to argue to the jury as to what this means."

"In that case," Hamilton Burger said, "while I realize that this matter should be handled expeditiously, I would like to have a recess until tomorrow morning to try to find out more about this most fortuitous discovery."

Judge Alvarado frowned, started to shake his head.

Mason said, "We have no objections; if the prosecution wants this continuance, the defendant is willing to join in the motion, and since the jurors are not being confined, it should not work too great a hardship upon them."

"Very well," Judge Alvarado said, "on that understanding I will grant the motion, rather reluctantly, however."

Judge Alvarado turned to the jurors. "The jurors will understand that the Court is empowered to keep the jurors together during the trial of a case. This sometimes works an unnecessary hardship; and, if in the judgment of the Court it is not necessary, the Court is permitted to let the jurors return to their homes. The Court will admonish you, however, that the jurors will be violating their oath if they listen to any television discussion of this case, any comment about it on radio, or read anything in the newspapers. The jurors are again admonished not to form or express any opinion in regard to the merits of the case, not to discuss it among yourselves, and not to permit any person to discuss it in your presence.

"Under those circumstances, and in view of the fact that there has been a joint request for a continuance, the Court is somewhat reluctantly taking a recess until tomorrow morning at ten o'clock."

Judge Alvarado left the bench.

Paul Drake, his expression ominous, came over to stand by Mason while he glared across at the prosecution's table.

Hamilton Burger managed to avoid meeting the detective's eyes.

"Take it easy, Paul," Mason warned.

"Someday," Drake said, "I'm going to plant a punch right in the middle of his snout."

"He's only doing his duty," Mason said.

"Well, I don't like the way he does it."

"Neither do I," Mason agreed, "but there are some things about the way I conduct a case which he doesn't like."

"If he'll only look up here," Drake said, "I'll wish him a very good evening in a tone of voice which will be as sarcastic as his voice was when he said, 'That's all.'"

Mason got up, took Drake's arm and gently turned him around. "You'll do nothing of the sort," he said. "That isn't the sort of publicity we want at this particular stage of the game."

"You think the jurors are going to refrain from reading the newspapers?" Drake asked.

Mason smiled. "Come on, Paul, let's both quit being naïve."

Mason picked up his briefcase and smiled at Della Street.

∎

23

BACK IN his office, Della handed Mason the newspapers. "You take a good picture," she said.

"You're the one who takes a good picture," he told her. "Getting that outfit was a stroke of genius on which I pride myself.

"I think," he continued, "that the picture might not have been published if it hadn't been for the feminine angle."

"Angle?" she asked archly.

"Curve," Mason corrected.

She smiled.

Mason read the account in the paper.

"No wonder Hamilton Burger felt peeved," he said. "This makes quite a story."

Mason finished with the paper, started to put it aside; then a headline on an inside page caught his eye.

"Well," he said, "the decedent, Rodger Palmer, seems to have had his name cleared posthumously."

"How come?"

"Another one of those mysterious stocking murders in a cheap hotel.

"You remember that the report made by Drake's detective stated that at one time the police considered Palmer a suspect. He'd lived in two of the hotels where these stocking murders had been committed. He was in the hotel at the time of the crime. . . . That was just a little too much of a coincidence for the police.

"They, of course, took the names of every person residing in the hotel at the time of the crime and then checked those names with the guest lists of other hotels.

When they found Palmer's name on two lists, they descended on him like a ton of bricks."

"That certainly was a coincidence," Della Street said.

Mason nodded. "Those things happen in real life, and yet— Hang it, it *is* quite a coincidence. We'd have given it a lot of thought if it hadn't been that Palmer was very dead by the time we started investigating him.

"Get me that report from Drake's operative, Della. Let's study it again."

Della Street went to the file, returned with a report on the dead man.

Mason thumbed through the numerous typewritten sheets of flimsy. "The guy seems to have been pretty much of a lone wolf," he said, "never married, an oil worker, then down and out—sort of a sharpshooter.

"He may have been a professional blackmailer. He had something on the Steer Ridge Oil and Refining Company that was worth money to someone, or at least he thought it was. He was fighting for proxies . . . and he must have had something rather degrading on Fred Hedley—probably a prior marriage that had never been dissolved."

Mason slowly thumbed through the pages of the report; then went back and reread it.

Abruptly the lawyer straightened himself in the office chair, started to say something, checked himself, looked up at Della and back to the report.

"Something?" she asked.

"I don't know," Mason said thoughtfully.

The lawyer got up and started pacing the floor. Della, knowing his habits, sat very quietly so she would not interrupt his thinking. Later on, when the lawyer had clarified the situation in his own mind, she might ask him questions so that by answering those questions he could crystallize his thoughts, but right at the moment she knew he needed an opportunity for complete concentration.

Mason suddenly paused in his pacing.

"Della," he said, "I want an ad in the papers that will be in the night editions."

As she started to say something, Mason said, "I know that's impossible. I know those want ad pages are printed in advance, but I want this in a box somewhere in the newspapers, entitled, 'Too Late To Classify,' or something of that sort. Tell them that it's important to get it in. Money's no object."

"What's the copy?" she asked.

"Make it this way. Put the initials, capital P, capital M; then, 'The thing that was too hot for the grass on the golf course is now even more valuable than ever. Call this number at nine o'clock sharp and follow instructions.' "

"And the number?" Della Street asked.

Mason said, "Go to a service station in Hollywood. Find a telephone booth; get the number.

"Now then, you're going to have to work fast. You're going to have to get co-operation from the papers. Tell them it's a red-hot tip and if they'll put the ad in and say nothing about it to anyone, they may get a red-hot story later on.

"Then, while you're pulling wires, I'll get Paul Drake and we'll get an operative we can trust who will be at this number at exactly nine o'clock with instructions to act as decoy in case somebody bites on our little scheme."

"And in case no one bites?" Della Street asked.

"Then," Mason said, "Burger can show that Paul Drake got another fifty-dollar charge on his bill."

Della Street typed out the want ad, said, "I'm on my way."

Mason called Paul Drake. "Paul," he said, "I want an operative to be at a public pay station at nine o'clock sharp tonight, and if he is contacted there, to make an appointment to meet whoever calls at one of the most lonely, secluded spots your man will be able to pick out during the afternoon.

"That spot has to be wooded. It has to be within a reasonable distance of the highway. It has to be unlighted."

"Have a heart, Perry," Drake said. "About the only

place I know of would be a golf course, and we've had enough of golf courses in this case."

"Golf courses are out," Mason said. "Try a city dump."

"Suppose no one calls the operative when he's in the service station?"

"Then," Mason said, "we'll give him a call and give him further instructions.

"Get busy, Paul. This is of real importance. It may be the payoff."

"You have a live lead?" Drake asked.

"I'm playing a hunch," Mason said. "It's a wild hunch, but it may pay off."

Mason hung up; then picked up the other telephone and said to Gertie at the switchboard, "Get me Homicide at the police department, Gertie. I want to talk to Lieutenant Tragg."

"No one else, if he's out?"

"If he's out," Mason said, "I don't even want anyone to know who's calling."

24

PERRY MASON, Lt. Tragg, Della Street, Paul Drake and one of Drake's operatives huddled in the dark shadows of a group of stunted trees.

In their nostrils was the sour smell of a city dump.

"You certainly picked a sweet-smelling place," Lt. Tragg said.

Drake, speaking in a hushed voice, said, "It was the only one that we could find that gave us what we wanted."

Tragg said, "Now, let's have this definitely understood. There's to be no publicity."

"No publicity unless *you* give it publicity," Mason said.

"I don't publicize my wild goose chases," Tragg said.

"I don't want the D.A.'s office to know anything about this, and I'm risking my official neck just trying to play ball with you."

"I've put the cards on the table," Mason said.

"You certainly did, and I never saw such a collection of jokers in my life," Tragg grunted.

Paul Drake nervously reached for a cigarette, then checked himself as he remembered the admonition of no smoking.

Night insects shrilled in the distance. Somewhere a chorus of frogs started croaking, then lapsed into silence, then started croaking again.

"Suppose no one calls him?" Tragg asked.

"At five minutes past nine," Mason said, "one of Drake's operatives will call him. The phone will ring and the man in the booth will pick up the receiver just as though it were a bona fide call."

"And then?" Tragg asked.

"Then he'll start for here."

"And if anyone calls?"

"We'll know we're on the right track," Mason said.

"Well," Tragg told him, "that's the trouble with amateurs. You get crazy ideas. I'll bet ten to one no one calls him."

"We'll know pretty quick," Mason said, consulting his wrist watch and then raising the antenna on a walkie-talkie.

"He isn't carrying a walkie-talkie with him, is he?" Tragg asked.

"No," Mason said. "But he does have a citizen's band transceiver on his car, but I wanted to use a walkie-talkie for receiving because we don't want to have any loud noises."

Suddenly the walkie-talkie in the hands of Perry Mason made squawking noises, then a little pinched voice said, "Do you read me?"

"I read you. Come in," Mason said. "What's happened?"

"I'm on my way out."

"Call?"

"Only the decoy one we'd arranged."

"Okay," Mason said, his voice showing disappointment, "we'll follow plan number two. Over and off."

The lawyer snapped down the antenna on the walkie-talkie.

"Well," he said dejectedly, "it looks as if you win, Lieutenant."

Tragg snorted. "I would have bet you a hundred to one—a thousand to one."

"Well," Mason said, "the only chance now is that someone was watching and will follow him in a car."

"That's a good ten-thousand-to-one bet," Tragg said. "I'm holding you to your promise, Mason, that you'll never betray me on this."

"You have, my word," Mason told him. "Come on, let's deploy out into the shadows near the road. Drake's man is instructed to get out of the car and walk directly toward the dump for thirty-five paces, then stop, stand in the open for a few seconds, and then move into the shadows and drop to the ground."

Tragg said, "All right, we've stuck our necks out this far. Now we'll play along with your plan number two."

They moved slowly according to prearranged plan into the dense shadows near the roadway.

"How long will it take him to get here?" Tragg asked.

"We figured twelve minutes on a trial run this afternoon," Mason said.

"All right," Tragg said, "I've held the bag on your snipe hunting this far and I may as well throw twelve minutes down the rathole."

They waited until headlights appeared on the dirt road—headlights which danced up and down over the bumpy road, at times sending a beam up into the trees, at times pointing down as the car negotiated the bumps.

"That road is full of nails and tire hazards," Drake said. "I'll bet we have tire trouble with one of these cars."

"Don't be so pessimistic," Mason said. "Lieutenant Tragg has infected you with the gloom bug."

The car came to a stop. The headlights were switched off. A dark figure jumped from the car, walked rapidly for thirty-five steps, then stood for approximately thirty seconds, then moved into the shadows and dropped to the ground.

"Well," Tragg said, "the show's over. We may as well call it a night and go home."

"Wait a minute," Mason said. "We've got to give our quarry a chance."

"Your quarry!" Lt. Tragg snorted sarcastically.

"Silence!" Mason warned. "I think I heard the motor of a car."

They remained silent.

Drake said in a harsh whisper, "You're right. A car without headlights!"

The little group remained tense as the sound of a motor became plainly audible, a motor in a car which was being driven without headlights.

Abruptly the car came to a stop.

"If *this* thing works," Tragg muttered, "I'll be a monkey's uncle." And then after a moment, he added ruefully, "And if it doesn't work and this ever gets out, I'll be the monkey himself."

"Hush!" Mason whispered.

They held their positions, listening and watching. The dark shadows played tricks on their eyes. Once Della Street grasped Mason's arm, said, "Something moved."

No one else, however, had seen the movement.

They waited five minutes. Tragg sucked in his breath, starting to say something when, suddenly, they all saw a figure silhouetted against a patch of night sky.

Mason pressed the button of the powerful flashlight he was holding.

A figure interfused a forearm between eyes and flashlight. There was a glint of metal on blued-steel, then an orange spreading flash and the whistle of a bullet going past Mason's head.

The lawyer extinguished the flashlight. "Come on!" he said.

The group ran forward.

Twice more the reddish orange flame spurted into the night. Twice more they heard the whistle of bullets, then there were no more shots.

"We use plan three!" Mason shouted. "We don't want to kill unless we have to, and we don't want to move in and be sitting ducks."

They froze into immobility for what seemed an interminable period of silence, then, suddenly, they heard the roar of a car motor as it throbbed into life, and a second later headlights came on. The car, a hundred yards down the road, tried to make a U-turn, stalled, backed, crashed into a tree, then started forward.

The group ran to Lt. Tragg's police car which had been hidden in the brush. They climbed in hurriedly. Tragg throbbed the motor into life, switched on the red light, hit the siren, and at the same time called in on the radio asking the dispatcher to head off a car which was proceeding at high speed from the dirt road into the dump, asking that roadblocks be put up on the principal paved roads leading from the dirt road.

The car had traveled wildly, the taillights glowing like red rubies.

Tragg, driving the car with police competency, hustled over the road, gaining on the car ahead.

Abruptly the lights on the other car were switched off.

"Trying to find a side road to turn down," Tragg grunted, and switched on a powerful searchlight.

The searchlight not only held the car ahead in the beam of its illumination but the reflection in the windshield blinded the driver.

Again the lights of the car ahead were switched on, but during the period of dark driving the car had lost valuable ground.

The fleeing car made a screaming turn from the dirt road onto the pavement, and suddenly the blood-red brake lights flared into brilliance as the driver frantically depressed the brake pedal.

A police car was parked broadside in the road, and on each side of the police car were officers with drawn guns.

"I guess that does it," Tragg said.

"Let's hope she doesn't have enough presence of mind to throw the gun away," Mason said. "That's our best evidence."

The fugitive's car skidded to a stop. Mrs. Hedley's hate-distorted features were illuminated by the glaring lights as she slowly got out of her car with her hands up.

Tragg stopped his car immediately behind hers, and the party piled out.

Mrs. Hedley looked at them with venomous hatred.

Her eyes came to focus on Perry Mason's face. "How I wish I could have killed you!" she spat at him.

Tragg pushed past her, looked in the automobile and picked up an automatic from the seat.

"This your gun?" he asked.

"See my lawyer," she snapped.

"You won't need to ask any questions," Mason said. "Take that gun to ballistics. Check the empty cartridge case we found at the seventh tee for what the ballistics experts call the breech-block signature and you'll find the cartridge was fired from that gun."

Another car came driving up behind. Drake's operative got out and said, "Gosh, you folks get a man into all sorts of scrapes."

Perry Mason grinned at him. "When you get on the stand," he said, "tell Hamilton Burger that you were collecting the regular fee of fifty dollars a day and that you were shot at three times—all of which is only part of the day's work."

25

■

PAUL DRAKE, Della Street and Kerry Dutton were gathered in Mason's office the next afternoon. Dutton, still somewhat dazed from the rapid developments of the day, said, "Would you mind telling me how you did all this?"

Mason grinned. "I didn't," he said. "Lieutenant Tragg did. Lieutenant Tragg had to."

"Well, the papers certainly gave Tragg a wonderful spread of publicity. One would have thought he originated the whole idea."

"An officer has to take credit," Mason said. "It's part of the game. When Tragg consented to go with me, he knew I'd give him all the publicity if the scheme paid off—and keep him out of it if it didn't."

"But how did you know what had happened?"

"It was just simple reasoning," Mason said. "So simple that I almost overlooked it.

"Palmer was killed shortly after nine o'clock, but the murderess needed a Patsy, so the murderess picked on you. She decoyed you into going to the scene of the murder because she knew Palmer had been trying to put the bite on you. Just before you arrived, the murderess fired another shot so that if anyone happened to be listening, there would be the sound of a shot that would coincide with the time the murder was supposed to have taken place.

"Then, of course, you very stupidly played into the hands of the murderess just as she had expected you would, because she had planted Desere's gun by the body —a gun which she had taken from the bureau drawer in Desere's bedroom."

"And the reason?" Drake asked.

"Not the reason that any of us had thought of.

"Palmer had been in two hotels when these stocking strangulation murders had taken place. The police had, quite naturally, considered him as a suspect, but very foolishly they didn't consider him as a witness. They didn't ask him in detail about the people he had seen in the hotel although he probably wouldn't have told them if they had asked.

"We know now that he had seen Hedley in each of the hotels, and Hedley was the mysterious person who had registered under an assumed name and then vanished. The description fits him."

"And Mrs. Hedley knew what her son had done?"

"Her son has been a little bit off ever since he was a boy. She has a fierce protective instinct—an instinct which was strong enough to make her willing to kill if she had to in order to protect her boy.

"But the point is Palmer knew what Hedley had done, and Palmer desperately needed money to win his proxy fight in the Steer Ridge Oil Company. He felt that he could ultimately gain a million if he could only get operating capital.

"So Palmer put the bite on Mrs. Hedley. It was blackmail for the highest stakes possible. Either he got money or he put the police on the trail of her son on a series of murders.

"That's always a dangerous gambit. Palmer knew that, but he was playing for big stakes. He had to take the chance.

"And he lost his gamble."

"Hedley, himself, didn't—"

"Hedley, himself, didn't know anything about Palmer's murder," Mason went on. "It was his mother who was trying to protect him; his mother who killed the man who could have betrayed her son.

"When you stop to think of it, it had to be the mother. She could have had access to the bureau drawer in Desere's apartment. She was the only one who could have secured that gun, who had a sufficiently strong motive to commit murder if she had to.

"Hedley really gave himself away during that fight with you, Kerry. He ran into Desere's bedroom. He was looking for a nylon stocking. If he'd got his hands on one you'd have found him an expert garroter. He's had lots of practice.

"It was thinking about that rush to the bedroom and trying to find the reason for it that started me thinking along the right line."

Dutton shook his head. "I can still feel the arms of that metallic chair in the gas chamber."

"You certainly led with your chin," Mason told him, "trying to protect the girl you loved and trying to surprise her with an inheritance.

"Now then, make me a check for five thousand dollars covering my fee and Drake's expenses. Get out of here, hunt up Desere Ellis, tell her you love her and ask her to marry you."

"That last," Dutton said, "is probably the best advice I've *ever* had."

12/41

YOGA
FOR ALL AGES

Relax wound up nerves and muscles. Maintain youthful vitality and looks. And do it all in just a few minutes a day—with the world's fastest-growing way to physical well-being.

Fitness for the whole family

Now, **RACHEL CARR**, internationally famous Yoga teacher, has written a book that tailors this age-old science of health to the special needs of Americans of all ages. YOGA FOR ALL AGES shows you how to trim down or strengthen specific parts of your body...how to improve your ability to sleep...how to relax instantly...how to breathe for vitality and health.

Special features of this book:

—**Rachel Carr's Six-Week Yoga Course.** Acquire a basic mastery of physical yoga to help keep you fit for the rest of your life.
—**Yoga exercises you can do in a chair.** Ideal for office workers, old people, and the handicapped.
—**Yoga for children.** The Rooster, The Cobra, The Swan and other exercises which children find great fun.
—**Simple steps in relaxing.**
—**Concentration and Meditation.** An introduction to the mental and spiritual aspects of yoga.
—**Lavishly illustrated** with more than 250 step-by-step photographs and drawings.

At your bookstore or mail this NO RISK coupon

S 81/3

LOOK FOR THESE GREAT POCKET 🐇 BOOKS BESTSELLERS AT YOUR FAVORITE BOOKSTORE

THE PIRATE   Harold Robbins
HARLEQUIN   Morris West
THE SILVER BEARS   Paul E. Erdman
MURDER ON THE ORIENT EXPRESS Agatha Christie
SPY STORY   Len Deighton
THE JOY OF SEX   Alex Comfort
FORBIDDEN FLOWERS: MORE WOMEN'S SEXUAL FANTASIES Nancy Friday
MY SECRET GARDEN   Nancy Friday
AN AMERICAN LIFE   Jeb Magruder
JOURNEY TO IXTLAN   Carlos Castaneda
THE TEACHINGS OF DON JUAN Carlos Castaneda
A SEPARATE REALITY   Carlos Castaneda
ALONE   Rod McKuen
SHADOW OF EVIL   Frank G. Slaughter
BODY LANGUAGE   Julius Fast
TEN LITTLE INDIANS   Agatha Christie
RETURN JOURNEY   R.F. Delderfield
YOU AND ME, BABE   Chuck Barris
THE HAVERSHAM LEGACY   Daoma Winston
HOW TO IMPROVE YOUR MAN IN BED Lynn Barber
THE MERRIAM-WEBSTER DICTIONARY